C000039318

About t

A fifth generation Cali
lives in San Diego within
and knows with their help she can accomplish by
She takes particular joy and pride in her nieces and
nephews who are all bright, fit, shining stars of the
future. If she's not at a family event, you'll usually find
her at home reading or writing her next grand romance.

USA Today bestselling author **Catherine Mann** has
books in print in more than twenty countries with Mills
& Boon and other imprints. A six-time RITA® finalist,
she has won both a RITA® and Romantic Times
Reviewer's Choice Award. Mother of four, Catherine
lives in South Carolina where she enjoys kayaking,
hiking with her dog and volunteering in animal rescue.
FMI, visit: catherinemann.com

Elizabeth Bevarly is the award-winning, nationally
number one bestselling author of more than seventy
novels and novellas. Her books have been translated
into two dozen languages and published in three dozen
countries. An honours graduate of the University of
Louisville, she has called home places as diverse as
San Juan, Puerto Rico and Haddonfield, New Jersey,
but now resides back in her native Kentucky with her
husband, her son, and two neurotic cats (as if there
were any other kind).

Billionaire Boss

Billionaire Boss: Her Brooding Billionaire

TERESA CARPENTER

CATHERINE MANN

ELIZABETH BEVARLY

MILLS & BOON

First Published in Great Britain 2020
By Mills & Boon, an imprint of HarperCollins*Publishers*
1 London Bridge Street, London, SE1 9GF

www.harpercollins.co.uk

HarperCollins *Publishers*
1st Floor, Watermarque Building, Ringsend Road
Dublin 4, Ireland

BILLIONAIRE BOSS: HER BROODING BILLIONAIRE
© 2020 Harlequin Books S.A.

His Unforgettable Fiancée © 2015 Teresa Carpenter
Billionaire's Jet Set Babies © 2011 Catherine Mann
The Pregnancy Affair © 2017 Elizabeth Bevarly

ISBN: 978-0-263-29866-6

Printed and bound in Great Britain
by CPI Group (UK) Ltd, Croydon, CR0 4YY

HIS UNFORGETTABLE FIANCÉE

TERESA CARPENTER

This book is dedicated to Patty, Maria and the gang at the Grab & Go on 6th Street downtown San Diego. Much of my books are written during lunch. Thank you for your service and your patience. And for not throwing me out when I'm the last one there.

CHAPTER ONE

"G. DELANEY, YOU look beautiful tonight." Chet Crowder slurred the compliment.

Sheriff Grace Delaney glanced down at her khaki uniform, thought of her black cap of hair slicked back for convenience and her lack of makeup beyond a swipe of mascara and a touch of lip gloss, and figured if she needed any further evidence of Chet's intoxication she had proof of it in that comment.

"Is it midnight yet?" the eighty-year-old demanded. "I get a kiss at midnight." The words barely left his mouth when he bent over and puked all over the slick concrete floor.

"It's against procedures to kiss the prisoners." Grace cited policy as she nimbly avoided the deluge, stepping around the mess to escort him to the middle cell.

"But it's New Year's Eve," Chet protested with a burp. "You can make an ex-exception for New Year's Eve."

He didn't have to tell her it was New Year's Eve. Not even eleven o'clock and they already had three D and Ds— drunk and disorderly. Business as usual for the holiday. But not much longer for her. In a little over an hour she'd be handing over her gun and shield, her interim assignment as sheriff at an end.

"Rules are made for a reason," she stated. Her father's mantra, and thus the words she'd lived her life by. He'd been on her mind a lot tonight. "No exceptions."

"You're a beautiful woman, G. Delaney." Chet lumbered across the cell to the cot chained to the wall. "But no fun. That's why I didn't vote for you. Too serious, girl. Need to have a drink and lighten up some."

Grace's shoulders went up and back in instinctive defense against the criticism. It wasn't the first time she'd heard she needed to lighten up. She didn't understand it any more now than she had before. Being sheriff was serious business. Laws were meant to be upheld.

"Go to sleep, Chet. I'll release you in the morning." Well, someone would. She'd be on her way to San Francisco. With her term over and her dad gone she had nothing to stay here for—certainly not the pity job offered by her successor.

Moving to the mop bucket she'd had maintenance leave at the ready, she rolled it over and cleaned up Chet's mess. New Year's was one of two big festive events that got the residents drinking in Woodpark, California, entry to the Redwoods. The other was the annual fair and rodeo at the Fourth of July. She'd been told last year had been tame because of a heavy snowfall, but they'd still had eight citizens sharing cell space.

This year a crisp, clear night promised lots of revelry. Her successor set down the rules for the night. Depending on whether property damage was involved, D and Ds were allowed to sleep it off and be released in the morning. No need to book their guests.

Relaxing her standards made the muscles between her shoulder blades ache. She glanced at the clock. Only one more hour to endure.

She'd just tucked the rolling bucket back into the corner when patrol strolled in with a large man in blue jeans and a bloodstained white T-shirt.

The man's head hung forward, so his chestnut-brown

hair covered his features. He seemed tall, as even with his head and shoulders slumped he topped Mark's five-ten.

"What do we have here?" she asked.

"D and D. I found him walking on the road into town. He reeks of beer and has no identification on him. I brought him in to sleep it off. No hits on his prints. I ran them because he refused to give up his name. I figure we'll get his story in the morning."

"And the blood?"

"It was there when I picked him up. Must have been a brawl when he lost his wallet."

"Did you have medical look at him?"

"Yeah, he has a bump on the head, a small scratch. Nothing serious."

"Why is he in cuffs?"

"Didn't like my questions. Did a little resisting."

She nodded. With the man's size she wasn't surprised Mark had taken the precaution. She pushed the door open on the first cell so the patrol officer could walk the prisoner inside. "Right this way, sir."

"I shouldn't be here." The man's shoulders went back, his head lifted and he slowly turned to pin her with hard eyes. A dark scowl turned even features into a harsh mask. "I haven't done anything wrong."

"We frown on public intoxication in Woodpark." Now that she saw his face he looked vaguely familiar. She'd probably met him around town somewhere.

"I didn't have a drink." His expression shifted from displeasure to confusion and he repeated, "I didn't have a drink."

"What's your name, sir?"

Instead of answering he went to the cot and sat, letting his head fall forward once again.

"What's his blood alcohol level?" Grace asked Mark, leading the way into the open office space.

"I didn't run it. He was staggering and smelled of beer. It's already busy out there with the holiday and we're just letting the D and Ds sleep it off. I didn't think there was a need." He clipped his cuffs back in place. "Do you need me for anything else? I should get back in the field."

"No." Her shoulders tensed at the lack of procedure but it wasn't her department anymore. "You go ahead."

"Hey, if I don't see you again, good luck in San Francisco. You'll do better in the city. We're too low-tech here."

"Thank you." She appreciated the good wishes—she did—but she couldn't help noticing there were few expressions of regret that she was leaving. "Before you go, where are our mystery man's effects?"

"Property locker." He canted his head. "But there's not much—a jacket, chaps, a watch and a belt. If you're hoping to find a clue to his identity, you'll be disappointed."

"Probably." She'd check it out anyway. Not much to do besides monitor patrols and babysit the inmates. The town had less than five thousand citizens. At double duty there were six men on patrol. As a petty officer in the navy she'd been responsible for directing and training three times that many.

She missed the navy—the discipline, the control. She'd given it up to assist her father when he was diagnosed with prostate cancer. No regrets. Even though she'd lost him after seven months. She'd thought she was honoring him when she accepted the town's request to fulfill his remaining term as sheriff. Losing the recent election proved she'd failed to fill his shoes.

She'd lived with her father's exacting demands for thirty years. She didn't need to have him here to know he'd be disappointed.

Hopefully San Francisco would prove a better proposition for her. Or possibly Los Angeles or maybe San Diego. She knew she wanted someplace cosmopolitan. Thanks to the life insurance her father left her, she had half a million dollars to help her make her next life decision.

After hearing from her patrols and checking on her prisoners, she decided to look into the mystery man's property to see what she could find. She located the large plastic bag marked John Doe, the official designation for an unidentified individual, and brought it to her desk.

The strong scent of leather wafted into the room when she opened the bag. She pulled out a jacket, extra large, and chaps, extra long. Both were of fine quality, handstitched. In a smaller bag was a watch. Grace went through the pockets in the jacket, found nothing.

She pulled the chaps over, held them up in front of her and thought of the man in her cell, trying to picture him in this gear. Not difficult at all. Gave her a little thrill actually—a truth she'd keep between her and the mop bucket.

Something didn't measure up with John Doe. Broadshouldered with a lean, muscular frame, his downtrodden mien didn't fit with his physique. Or his protests of innocence, such as they were.

She ran her hands over the chaps, looking for hidden pockets, trying not to think of the leather framing JD's package. Of course she'd looked. She was trained to observe, after all. She found a matchbook from a tavern on the edge of town.

The watch was the real surprise. The heft and materials were quality all the way; the display of mechanics and the movement of gears gave the timepiece a sophisticated appearance. She looked closer—did that say Cartier? It did. And yes, she found similar watches on their website. Her eyes popped wide at the price: seventy thousand and up. Gah. Her next search was of robbery reports.

Nothing hit.

One thing was clear. JD had resources. Whether legitimate or not was another question. No hits on his prints only proved he'd never been caught. Yeah, call her a cynic. But why else wouldn't he want to give them his name? This guy wasn't adding up. He appeared familiar yet Mark hadn't known him.

The leatherwear shouted motorcycle, but where was the vehicle, his gloves and his helmet? Why was he walking along the side of the road?

The 101 ran right through the middle of town. Maybe someone ran him off the road and then robbed him? It fit the evidence. But why not tell them of the crime? Submissiveness didn't suit him, but he could be disoriented. He had a bump on the head. People often forgot events leading up to an accident. Maybe he was hurt more than the EMT was able to determine.

Time for a conversation with JD.

Thump. Thump. Pain pounded relentlessly through his head. Keeping his eyes closed helped marginally. Plus when he opened them there were only gray walls and cell bars to look at.

Man, he'd messed up big, to be laid out in a jail cell with a throbbing head.

Thump. Thump.

Problem was he couldn't remember what he'd done. The squat cop claimed he'd been drinking, but he had it wrong. He wouldn't feel as if he'd tangled with a semi if he had any alcohol in his system. His right shoulder and leg throbbed in time with his head.

At least he had the cell to himself.

Thump. Thump.

He wasn't even sure what map pin he inhabited. If only his head would clear, he was sure it would all come back. Then he'd get out of here and be on his way. Yep, as soon as his head got with the program, he'd explain things to the squat cop and then he'd be gone.

Thump. Thump.

The cell door clanked. He squeezed an eye open, spied the lady cop. He remembered her. The attitude. The uniform. The pretty blue eyes.

"How are you feeling?" she asked in a much friendlier voice than when he arrived.

"Like I was hit by a truck."

"Is that what happened?"

Thump! Thump! Suddenly his head hurt worse. Have mercy, he didn't think it possible. Couldn't people just leave him alone?

"I thought I was here because I was intoxicated."

"You denied drinking."

He had no answer for that. He'd jump on it if he thought she'd let him go, except he wasn't ready to move.

"You were walking when the officer came across you."

"It's not against the law to walk."

"No. But it's uncommon for tourists to arrive by foot."

He didn't respond. It hadn't been a question, after all. The low, husky timbre of her voice might be soothing if not for the interrogation.

"What do you drive?"

Drive? His brows drew together. Hadn't she just said he was walking?

"You were wearing a leather jacket and chaps. Where's your motorcycle?"

Thump! Thump!

He lifted his arm to lay it across his forehead. He gnashed his teeth at the show of weakness, but he had the desperate need to hold his head on, like if he didn't brace it in place it might explode.

"Are you okay?" Her voice hovered right above him and he smelled the freshness of peaches. She'd obviously moved closer.

"Can we do this another time? My head hurts."

"I'm going to check your wound," she warned him, the warm breath of her words blowing over his forearm. "It's possible you're hurt worse than we originally thought. This may hurt."

Her body heat warmed him as she loomed close. He shivered. With the pain racking him, he hadn't noticed how chilled he'd grown.

Thump! Thump! Sharp pain shot across his head.

"Ouch." He flinched away from her probing, all thoughts of the cold chased away.

"I'm sorry." She softly ran her fingers through his hair.

Yes. That felt good. He leaned toward the soothing touch.

"I need you to move your arm. I'm going to check your pupils." She suited action to words and he suffered the agony of a flashlight scorching his retinas.

"Irregular pupils. You have a concussion. I think we need to get you to the hospital," she declared.

"I'd be fine if you'd leave me alone." He dismissed her claim, waved off her hand. "I just need to rest here for a while."

"It's not up for discussion," she stated simply. "I'm obligated to see to your care. It's up to you whether we go in my cruiser or I call for an ambulance."

"I'm not riding in any cryptmobile."

"Then we need to get you on your feet."

"I think I'll just lay here for a while." Just for a bit, until he could breathe without pain and the room stopped spinning.

"I can't allow that. You have a concussion. You're disoriented. You need to be seen by a doctor. It's department policy."

"Well then." She wanted to disrupt him, ratchet up the pain, all to meet department policy? Right. He had fifty pounds on her. He wasn't going anywhere.

"How did you get hurt?"

Thump.

"Where's your motorcycle? Your wallet?"

Thump, thump.

"What's your name?"

Thump! Thump! Thump!

"Will you stop? Your talking hurts my head." So a few details were missing. It would come back once the pounding stopped.

"That doesn't really reassure me. Tell you what, if you stand up, look me in the eyes and tell me your first name, I'll consider leaving you alone."

"I don't want to stand up." Why wouldn't she just go away?

"Don't want to? Or can't?"

The taunt brought renewed pain as he frowned. He put his arm back on his head. Nice as her touch was, her insistence undid any good her soothing brought. Her goal, no doubt. It would take more than pride to drag him to his feet tonight. Possibly a crane would do it.

"Look, I'm not interested, okay? You're a beautiful woman, but I'm injured here."

"I'm not hitting on you." Outrage sent her voice up an octave. "I'm concerned."

"Are you sure? I've never had a cop run their fingers through my hair before."

"So you've been detained before?" She was quick to pick up on the inference.

He just stopped himself from shaking his head. "Just saying."

"That's it. I'm calling for an ambulance."

Everything in him rejected the option of being delivered to the hospital.

"Wait." He opened his eyes. She stood over him, hands on shapely hips, a scowl pinched between her stormy blue eyes. Clenching his teeth against the need to scream like a girl, he shifted to sit, and then pushed to his feet. Holding his shoulders back, he forced himself to meet her poppy blue eyes without flinching.

"Satisfied?"

She ran those cop eyes over him, assessing him from top to bottom. She nodded once as if satisfied by what she saw. It took all his strength not to sag in relief. But he wasn't out of hot water yet.

She cocked a trim black eyebrow. "And your first name?"

He was tempted to lie, to toss her any old name. But that felt wrong. Too easy. The falsehood didn't bother him—being predictable did. She expected him to blow her off. It was what he'd been doing since she'd entered the cell.

Forget that. Now he'd made the effort to get on his feet, he saw the value in getting a doctor's opinion. And some serious meds.

He met her stare-for-stare and confessed. "I can't remember."

"I can't remember." The words seemed to echo through the cell.

Grace blinked up at him. A rare enough occurrence—at five-nine she didn't often have to tip her head back to look a man in the face—but standing at his full height of six-three JD required her to do just that to assess his truthfulness.

Amnesia?

It seemed a stretch. Still, he had a sizable bump on his head and displayed signs of a concussion. It would explain his disorientation and his unwillingness to talk about himself.

Then again it was a tad convenient. Except why bother? He'd been told he'd be free to go in the morning.

"You don't remember your name?" She needed to determine the extent of his missing information.

"No."

"Do you know what year it is?"

He answered correctly.

"How about the President of the United States?"

Another correct response. He swayed on his feet, reminding her that, regardless of the state of his mind, his pain was all too real. She decided to let the doctor sort him out.

"Let's go." She led him to her desk, where she handed him his jacket. "I already made a call for Parker to come drive you. He should be here any minute."

"Oh, joy."

"At least he's familiar to you."

"I'm not dim-witted, you know." He sprawled in her desk chair with his jacket in his lap. "Just memory-challenged."

The corner of her mouth twitched at his show of humor. "All the more reason to stick with what you know until you've seen the doctor."

"I know you, and you smell better."

Now, why did that send a rush of heat to her cheeks? "I'd take you, but my duty is up in thirty minutes."

Probably a good thing. JD had managed to shake her up more than a little over the course of a mere hour.

"Check that." A deep voice announced. She recognized one of her other patrol officers. She stood to see him escorting a happy prisoner toward the back. "Brubaker, the new sheriff, has been monitoring the radio calls. Since I was bringing someone in, he told Parker to stay in the field. He wants you to take John Doe to see the doctor, and I'm to cover the rest of your duty here."

"Who will replace me at the hospital?"

The officer shrugged. "I'm sure Brubaker will send someone."

Right. She clenched her hands at having her control yanked away early. Brubaker had no authority to usurp her orders before midnight. But there was no use arguing.

"Okay," she said to JD. "Let's go." She'd already put her box of personal items in her SUV, so she grabbed her backpack and slipped into her hip-length leather coat.

The effort it took JD to gain his feet showed as it had in the cell, but he managed it and donned his jacket without uttering a sound. He stayed silent on their trip to her hybrid Escape.

In the vehicle he braced his head on a raised fist. "So I'm a John Doe."

"You're familiar with the term?"

"An unidentified person or body. I watch TV, the movies. I guess that means you didn't get a hit on my prints or you'd have a name for me."

"Right on both points." She stopped at a light on Main Street and three women in party hats, winter jackets and heels laughed and joked as they crossed in front of them. The light changed and she pulled forward.

"What happens if I don't get my memory back right away?" He slowly turned his head to pin her with a pain filled gaze. "How do you figure out who I am?"

CHAPTER TWO

How would they identify him? Good question. Woodpark was a small town with limited resources. They'd have to reach out to a larger city, or perhaps the feds. Grace didn't have the heart to remind him it wouldn't be up to her.

"Let's see what the doctor has to say before we worry about that."

A grunt was her answer.

A few minutes later she pulled into the hospital parking lot. Like the sheriff's office, the emergency center did a brisk business on New Year's Eve. Grace walked to the front of the line.

"Sheriff," the clerk acknowledged her and then glanced at JD. "We're very busy tonight."

"So I see. You're going to have to make room for one more. I have a prisoner with a head wound."

"Take a seat and I'll let the doctors know."

"Of course. Please let them know I'm quite concerned."

She found him a seat in the crowded waiting room. He looked about to protest at taking the last chair, but he sat instead. Whatever his background, he'd learned some manners. That he ignored them was testament to the extent of his injury.

"You sounded worried," he drawled.

"Head wounds are dangerous." She leaned against the wall next to him. "We already know of one complication."

"So it wasn't a ploy to advance our case?" He lifted his gaze to hers and arched a dark brow.

Under the bright lights she noticed his eyes were leaf green. And a hint of red played in his dark hair. She turned her attention back to the front desk. "Maybe a bit of a ploy."

"And calling me a prisoner?"

She allowed a small smile. "Oh, yeah, that was totally a ploy."

He laughed and then groaned and clutched his head.

She sobered. "It's also true. You are a prisoner until morning. No dying on my watch please. You can't imagine the paperwork involved."

"I might be touched if it didn't just pass midnight. You're officially off duty."

A glance at her watch confirmed his claim.

"Sheriff." The clerk had returned. "Dr. Honer will see you now."

Grace checked the door but no sign of her replacement magically appeared. JD walked past her and then stopped.

"Are you coming?" he asked. "I can handle this on my own if you prefer."

"You're in city custody. I'm coming."

She followed him to the back and stood in the hall while he changed into the paper hospital gown the nurse provided. It was a small room. She took heart in the fact he would look silly sitting there, decked out in the flimsy robe. Too bad he didn't use it. When she entered the room, she found he'd stripped down to gray knit boxer briefs.

OMG.

Cough. Cough. Good gracious, she nearly choked on her own tongue as drool flooded her mouth. Swallowing hard she made her way to the corner, trying hard not to stare at all the hard lines and muscular definition on full display.

"You were supposed to put on the gown."

"It tore. Don't worry about it. Turns out I'm not modest."

Of course not. Turned out she had a bit of a voyeur in her.

Confronted with the sight of all that flesh and muscle—toned, and tanned, and tantalizing—she missed at first glance that a wound marred his nice six-pack. Still pink and edged with staple marks, the slash ran about six inches long under his right rib cage.

"You've been stabbed."

He glanced down at himself. The action made him sway, so he quickly lifted his head. "Where?"

She moved closer to point. "It looks pretty ragged, which tells me it wasn't a switchblade. Maybe a serrated blade. Or a piece of glass, possibly a metal fragment. Any of that spark any memories?" If shock value had any power to activate his memory, learning he'd been stabbed should do the job.

Leaving her question unanswered, he used long fingers to explore the wound. He flinched a little, indicating the cut was still tender. Or perhaps it was just the thought of being stabbed.

"Does it hurt?" she asked, hoping to get him talking. He revealed so little she had a hard time reading him. Part of it had to do with his missing memories, but she had the sense his reticence went deeper than that, was actually a part of his personality.

"Sore, not painful." Emerald eyes met hers. "It's not from this accident?"

"No." She shook her head as she examined the wound from a safe distance. "I'd say it's a few weeks old. The doctor might be able to tell you more."

As if on cue, Dr. Honer, short and balding, opened the door. He addressed his patient first. "I'll be with you in a minute." Then he gestured to Grace. "Can I see you, Sheriff?"

She stepped into the hall and he pulled the door closed behind him.

"Sheriff Brubaker called." He informed her. "He's not authorizing any care for the prisoner. He's been released instead. An officer is going to drop off his property."

Just dandy. Brubaker, the mayor's brother-in-law—who until today had worked for his wife's insurance agency—obviously didn't care about the liability involved in releasing an injured prisoner. Or worse, didn't know.

One of Brubaker's campaign issues had been her overspending, because she'd insisted the town bring the department's technical capabilities up to the twenty-first century. It didn't surprise her that he refused to spend any funds on a D and D set to walk out the door in the morning. Much simpler and cheaper to cut the guy loose. Even if he was injured.

"Doctor, this man has a head injury, a concussion at the very least. And possible amnesia. He says he doesn't remember who he is. We haven't been able to identify him, as he was missing his wallet when he was picked up walking into town."

"Sounds like he's had a rough night. I'll examine him, of course, but if he has no means of payment and the sheriff's office refuses to pay, I'm limited in what I can do."

"Whatever you can do, Doctor, will be appreciated."

He nodded and pushed the door open. "That's why I voted for you, Grace. You may draw a hard line between black-and-white, but people matter to you. It's not all about the bottom line."

JD sat on the doctor's stool. At five-seven it was the only way Dr. Honer could see his patient. If JD laid on the exam gurney his head would be up against the wall, and if he sat up he'd be out of the doctor's reach unless he bent in half—something his equilibrium wouldn't allow for in his present condition.

After a thorough exam, Dr. Honer announced, "The good news is there doesn't appear to be any neck or spinal injuries. As for the head wound, I'm going to need an MRI."

Concerned by the need for a scan of his brain, she stayed with JD, following him down the hall and sitting with him while he waited to take the test. He sat staring at the wall.

"Are you okay?" the pretty cop asked, her voice low, careful.

"Apparently not, if the doctor wants to do tests."

"The tests could reveal good news," she suggested.

"Doubtful. It's never good news," he declared with a depth of feeling that belied his lack of memory.

What a fool, sitting here in the hall dressed in a freaking hospital gown—the nurse had found a cloth one big enough to fit—while the whole world paraded by. He glanced at his bare wrist and bit back a curse. Everything had been stripped from him. He couldn't even mark the time, except to note it was moving at a slug's pace.

"I hate hospitals. And you know the worst part?" He sent her a sidelong glance. "I don't even know why."

"It must be difficult."

"Frustrating, debilitating, terrifying. The not knowing goes on and on no matter how hard I try to remember."

"Maybe you should stop trying, give your brain a chance to heal."

"Easier said than done. There's just pain and a whole lot of nothingness." He leaned his head back against the wall, amazed at what he'd revealed to her. Who knew? Maybe he was a Chatty Cathy, but somehow he doubted it. More likely her soothing presence lulled him on a subliminal level. "Talk to me."

"Okay." A beat of silence follow as he watched her struggle to find a topic. "About what?" Right, exactly what did you discuss with a stranger who had no memory?

"Why are you still here? According to what I've heard, not only are you off duty, you're out of a job."

"That's right." She chirped cheerfully, the first false note he'd heard from her. "My term as sheriff is up. I'm footloose and fancy-free as of midnight."

"So answer the question. Why are you still here? I really can handle this alone, you know. I'm not stupid, I'm just—"

"Memory-challenged," she finished for him. "I know. But you shouldn't have to go through this alone, JD. You are the victim of an accident and possibly—probably—a crime in our town. It's the least I can do to help you until you can stand steady on your own two feet."

"Why?" She called him JD. He supposed it was better than John Doe, which reminded him of dead bodies.

She blinked at him, black brows drawn together. "Why what?"

"Why is it the least you can do? You don't owe me anything." And with a certainty he felt to his core he knew the generosity she offered wasn't as common as she made it sound. Not in his life. It made him itchy—both grateful and suspicious at the same time.

"For me law enforcement isn't a job, it's a calling." The simplicity of the statement did nothing to detract from her sincerity. "My instincts to protect and serve don't click on and off with the punch of a time card."

"Was that your campaign slogan? If so, I can't believe you lost."

"I didn't really run a campaign. I felt my work should stand for itself."

"So you're an idealist."

"No, I'm a realist."

"Wrong. In the real world a candidate's work should speak to whether they can do the job, but in reality the voters like to be courted. They want to think you care about their opinion, their vote."

"So you're a cynic."

"No, I'm a geek."

She sat up straight, her breasts pushing against her khaki uniform shirt. "That's a clue."

"What?" He dragged his gaze to her face, flushed with excitement.

"You said you were a geek. That's pretty specific. Your brain let that slip, it has to mean something."

"Like what? I belonged to the chess club?"

"I don't know. But no one would look at you and think geek."

"And we're back to me."

"Yes, but we have a clue. Actually we have several. The chaps and leather jacket tell me you were riding a motorcycle. The quality and the expensive watch tell me you have access to money. And now we know you're a geek. A picture is forming."

"Of a motorcycle-riding geek with a fetish for expensive watches? Maybe I don't want my memory back."

"Don't say that. So the clues don't appear to fit together. That's only because we don't have all the pieces yet. It's all part of a bigger picture."

He found himself staring at his bare wrist again. He rubbed his hand across it. "I wish I had my watch now. I hate waiting."

"I'd say we've found another clue, but I don't know anyone who likes to wait. Hang in there." She patted his knee. "The doctor said it wouldn't be long."

Oh, no, she didn't just treat him like a child to be pacified. Even half-dead he couldn't allow that to slide. There were consequences when a beautiful woman touched him, and she was about to learn what they were.

Shifting toward her, he reached for the hand that committed the offense and slowly drew it to his mouth. He turned her hand palm-up and pressed a kiss to the sensitive center, gazing into her eyes the whole time.

She looked a little shell-shocked, leading him to believe the men of this tiny burg were idiots.

Her eyes narrowed and she tugged at her hand, seeking freedom. He held on for another moment. "Thank you," he said, keeping his voice soft, intimate. Finally he released her.

Sparks flashed in her eyes and he braced to be read the riot act. "You could be married, you know."

Not exactly what he expected. And it made him stop and wonder if he had a woman in his life, and the wondering made his head hurt. He realized he was rubbing his hand over the wound below his rib cage.

"I'm not."

"You can't know that for certain."

"No," he agreed. Because she was right. No memories existed to support his claim. "Yet somehow I do."

He wished he knew where the certainty came from. Maybe then he could plumb the source for actual memories, for real recollections. But the more he fought for it, the worse his brain hurt.

Luckily a male tech strolled up. "We're ready for you. Please follow me."

"Wish me luck." He stood, hospital gown flapping around his knees, strangely reluctant to leave her.

"Good luck." She stood, too, tucked her thumbs in her back pockets. "You've got this. After all, you're a smart guy, just memory-challenged."

A smile tugged up the corner of his mouth. "Can you hang for a while longer?"

She nodded. "I'll be here."

More than a little flustered, Grace spent the next long, worry-fraught hour gathering her composure around herself. Memory failed her as to when a man last affected her so strongly. She had no reason to care, but she did.

When JD appeared, she hopped to her feet. He looked so drawn. Exhaustion and pain weighed heavily on him. Without a word she followed him back to the doctor's office and took up her position in the corner.

"Who is the President of the United States?" The doctor started in on the questions needed to determine the extent of JD's memory loss.

JD answered with a scowl, adding, "What is it with you two and your obsession with the president?"

"General questions are used to create a baseline," Dr. Honer said. "It helps to determine if you've forgotten learned elements, a chunk of time or personal memories."

"Well, I should know the president's name. I've met him three times."

Silence fell over the room.

"How do you know that?" she demanded.

JD carefully turned his head around to her. Confusion briefly flashed through his eyes before he blinked it away. "I don't know."

"Do you remember under what circumstances you met him?"

"No."

"Because we might be able to identify you from news reports if we can pinpoint the event."

"I can't recall. But I know I've met him, just as I know I didn't have a drink last night." He turned to the doctor. "How is that possible? To know something but not have the memory to support it?"

"The brain is a marvelous and complex thing," Dr. Honer responded. "We're still learning many of its capabilities. The results of injuries are as varied and unpredictable as the number of people who sustain them. Do you remember anything about your childhood? Where you grew up? Your parents' names?"

"No." JD pinched the bridge of his nose, clearly in pain, clearly exhausted.

"What is the prognosis, doctor?" Grace asked softly.

"As you suspected, Sheriff, he has a severe concussion and a less serious laceration. Though they are in the same general area I don't believe they are connected. Is it possible you were in a motorcycle accident?"

"I can't say, Doc."

"It's probable." Grace spoke up. "He was wearing leather chaps when Porter brought him in."

Dr. Honer nodded his balding head. "The surface bump and laceration aren't significant enough to cause the level of swelling revealed by the MRI or the symptoms you've described. They certainly shouldn't have caused a memory lapse. But if you were in a motorcycle accident, it would explain the additional trauma."

"How so?" JD wanted to know.

"The helmet protected your head, which probably saved your life, but you still connected with the ground with enough impact to shake your head up inside the helmet, causing the brain to ricochet against the skull. Probably knocked you out for a few seconds. An accident would account for the bruising on your hip, as well."

"And the laceration?" Grace asked.

"It had gravel in it, which tells me it most likely happened after he removed the helmet. He may have fallen on his walk into town. Or more likely someone knocked him down."

"More likely?" Grace mused in full sheriff mode. "What makes you say that?"

"There's faint bruising on his lower jaw and on the knuckles of his right hand inconsistent with his other injuries. Since you mentioned he didn't have a wallet on him, my guess is someone ran him off the road and attempted to rob him. He probably came to in the middle of it, fought back and took a right to the jaw. In his condition that's all it would take to put him on the ground, causing the bump and the cut. Double head trauma more than accounts for the possibility of memory loss."

"Does that mean I'll get my memories back once the bump goes away?"

The doctor scratched his cheek. "I'm more concerned with the swelling of the brain. It could be fatal if it reaches the point of critical mass."

"And what are the chances of that?" JD's calmness amazed Grace.

"I'm cautiously optimistic considering the time lapse since you were picked up. You need to remain under observation and have another MRI after a bit, to see if the swelling is increasing or diminishing. It's possible once the swelling goes down that you could regain some, if not all, of your memories."

"What are my options if the swelling reaches critical mass?"

"Some people respond to medication. Worst-case scenario—a hole may need to be drilled into your skull to relieve the pressure."

She shuddered. That sounded scary.

Dr. Honer directed his next comments to her. "I highly recommend he be moved to the city. We don't have the necessary equipment to handle a delicate procedure of that nature."

Great. No way Brubaker would authorize the cost of ambulance service to the city. He'd already released the prisoner. JD was on his own. And her duty ended over an hour and half ago.

She could have left at any time, but she kind of felt invested. She could only imagine what JD must be going through: in pain, dealing with strangers, unable to remember anything of his life, not even his own name. It must be frightening. Yet he handled it with stone-faced grace.

"Sheriff, if I can have another moment?"

"There's no need to leave, Doc." JD halted them, a grim note in his voice. "If it's about me, I have a right to hear it."

"You need another MRI and to be monitored throughout the night, if not the next few days. I've expended all the resources I can at this point."

"I'll drive him." The words were out before she fully considered them, but what the heck, she was leaving town anyway. This just moved her agenda up by a few hours. Her sense of duty didn't end with the removal of her title and paycheck. And it went against every instinct to leave an injured man to take care of himself.

Looking at JD, no one would doubt his ability to handle himself. Though injured, he radiated a quiet intelligence, his stoic endurance testament to an inner core of strength. Which said a lot. Between Dr. Honer's prognosis and JD's memory loss, his whole world was one big uncertainty.

"You can drive him. Good, that's good." Dr. Honer sighed in relief. "Take him to the free clinic on Main. I'll send a referral over, let them know to expect you."

"I can pay." JD stated with certainty.

She and Dr. Honer stared at him, neither wanting to question how he'd pay as it was clear this was one of those things he knew without knowing how he knew. Remembering the seventy-thousand-dollar watch, she tended to believe him. However, a hospital would be much less trusting.

A knock came at the door and the receptionist stuck her head into the room. "Sheriff's department dropped off this property bag for Sheriff Delaney."

"Thanks." Grace took the large, clear plastic bag, checked to make sure it still held all its contents and handed it to JD. "You've officially been released from custody."

CHAPTER THREE

JD ACCEPTED THE sealed bag. He'd been released. He supposed that was a good thing. But where did it leave him?

"Does that mean you won't be driving me to the hospital?" No big deal. He didn't really care for all this medical mumbo jumbo anyway. Especially the whole bit about drilling into his head. He'd take his chances on the swelling going down.

Once that happened, the doc said, his memories might come back. He could feel them out there, as if they were hidden behind a dark curtain in his head and all he had to do was find the lever that worked the curtain.

He'd miss Grace, though. She was the only constant he knew in this new world.

"I said I'd take you, and I will." She assured him. Her gruff tone made him wonder if she was insulted to have her word questioned or if she regretted making the offer in the first place.

She was an odd mixture of duty and concern, with a whole lot of pretty thrown in.

Funny thing, his bruised brain only managed to stay focused on two things: pulling back that curtain and the complex G. Delaney, ex-sheriff, misguided realist, delectable morsel. When he couldn't take the blankness for another second, he shifted his attention to the left and admired the fit of G. Delaney's uniform to her trim body and soft curves.

Her question about his marital status served as no deterrent. He wasn't married. The lack of guilt only supported his irrational certainty.

"I have to stop by my house first," she went on completely unaware of his imaginings. "To pick up the rest of my things."

"Keep an eye on him." Dr. Honer directed her. "You know what to watch for with a concussion. Wake him every few hours to check for nausea, pupil variation, incoherency."

"I will."

"I heard you were moving to San Francisco." The doctor went on. "Best of luck to you. And to you, young man. I hope you get your memory back real soon."

What if I don't, he wanted to ask, but he bit the words back. The doctor had done all he could. So JD simply said, "Thank you." He accepted the prescription for pain medicine and followed Grace's curvy butt from the room.

Grace made a last sweep through her small apartment, making sure she hadn't left anything behind. The one-bedroom apartment sat atop the garage of her father's house. She'd already packed her things, which didn't amount to much—a duffel bag and two boxes. She wouldn't be back unless it was to drive through on her way to somewhere else.

After she lost the election, she sold the house and rented back the apartment. Her lease ended tonight.

Her father had brought her here. With him gone she had no reason to stay. The citizens made that clear, casting an overwhelming vote. She got the message. She'd been too hard-core. They wanted someone who would let boys be boys on occasion. Someone connected, like Brubaker.

It baffled her why the town council even asked her to finish out her father's term if they didn't want her to carry on the regimen he'd put in place. He'd trained her, after all. Probably thought she'd have a softer touch, being a woman. But she couldn't be less than she was.

Disappointing, though. She'd thought she'd found the place she wanted to put down roots. Everyone had been so friendly, welcoming her into town when she came to help Dad. She'd mistakenly felt accepted when they asked her to finish his term. The experience made her wonder if she even wanted to continue in active law enforcement.

Finding nothing left behind, she locked up and skipped down the stairs one last time before sliding behind the wheel of her SUV. JD slept in the passenger seat. He'd dozed off on the way to her place and she hadn't bothered to wake him for this stop. He would have insisted on helping but was in no shape for it. Why put them both through that argument?

She believed rules were there for a reason and exceptions created chaos. In the case of the law, it also put people at risk. And if you gave one person an exception, everyone expected to get the same special treatment. Then why have laws?

Her father had been a stickler for discipline and order when she was growing up. Especially after her mother died when Grace was eight. Tightening the reins had been his way of coping. She understood that now. But to a grieving little girl, all the fun in life seemed to have died with her mother.

And that didn't change for a very long time. Still hadn't, if you talked to the townspeople. Grace Delaney didn't know how to have fun.

They were wrong. She liked to have fun as much as the next person. She just chose to do so in less gregarious ways. Hey, when you came off extended hours patrolling shore leave, a little peace and quiet was all the fun you could handle. And a good book or a fast video game was all the company you craved.

The activity of carrying her things down to the car served to revitalize her for the coming drive. Still, in order to help keep her alert, she pulled into the all-night diner and purchased a coffee to go. Though truthfully, JD's presence kept her on a low-level buzz.

He made her usually roomy SUV seem small. His broad shoulders and long limbs took up more than their share of space. The smell of man and antiseptic filled the air. And his heat warmed the car better than her heater.

Thinking of JD, she added a second cup to her order in case he woke up.

Grace carried the coffees to the SUV and headed the vehicle toward Santa Rosa. The clear night and full moon made the drive go fast.

JD stirred every once in a while but didn't wake up. She couldn't imagine what he must be going through. Bad enough to be robbed and left injured and abandoned on the outskirts of a strange town. How much more unnerving it must be to lose his memories, to lose all sense of self.

Except for that one moment of vulnerability before going in for the MRI, he took it in stride. She supposed it was all he could do to handle the pain of his physical ailments.

Not least of which was a stab wound. The doctor concurred with her time frame for the stabbing at less than a month. JD stated he had no memory of the incident. He'd sounded frustrated, an emotion she shared.

He had to be wondering about his life—the circumstances of the stabbing for one, the accident for another. He'd been alone when he met up with Porter, but he could well have a family out there wondering about him. A wife praying for his safe return.

A wife. Her shoulders twitched at the notion. Something

deep inside rebelled at the thought of him with another woman. Which was totally insane. There was nothing between the two of them.

For sugar's sake, they'd spent half their time together on separate sides of the law.

Not that it was an issue. He had no wife. Or so he said in that way of his that was so definite. How could he be so sure of some things, yet have no memory to support his conclusion?

Perhaps the amnesia was a hoax. One big fib to cover a crime.

So his prints didn't hit. There were plenty of criminals that never got caught.

He could have had a falling-out with his cohorts who ditched him and took his ride. Then he could have stumbled into town and unfortunately drawn the attention of a sheriff's deputy. Who would believe a motorcycle thug with a stab wound owned a seventy-thousand-dollar Cartier watch? No one. So he ditched his wallet and claimed to have lost his memory. All he had to do was sweat it out in the drunk tank for a few hours and he was home free.

Except for the do-good ex-sheriff who insisted on taking him to the hospital.

That version made more sense than the motorcycle-riding geek with an expensive taste in watches and a penchant for knowing things he couldn't back up with facts.

And yet she believed him.

The concussion was real. The pain was real. The frustration was real. The occasional flash of fear he tried to hide was very real. She'd been in law enforcement too long not to recognize those elements when she saw them. And there were medical tests to back it all up.

Not to mention the fact if he was a thug, she'd probably be lying on the side of the road back near Woodpark.

Well, he would have tried, anyway. She didn't go down so easy.

The lights of Santa Rosa came into view. She stole a sip of JD's coffee, wrinkling her nose at the lack of sugar. Surprisingly it still held a good heat. And the punch of caffeine she longed for.

No question about it, he was a puzzle, but a legit one.

Still, she'd be smart to take the things he was so sure of with a grain of salt. There was no sense, none at all, in fostering an attraction when neither of them was sure of their future. When neither of them was sure of themselves.

Because, yeah, losing the campaign had really shaken her. Not that she'd ever admit it out loud. She thought she'd been doing a good job, that the community liked her. But the votes hadn't been there. It had left her reeling. And feeling a little lost. She put her heart and soul into protecting and serving the citizens of Woodpark, and they chose a stuffed shirt who was more hot air than action.

Their loss, right? Except the experience threw her off stride, made her question her decisions and her vocation. Which was so not her. She always knew exactly what she wanted, and she went after it with a zealousness that earned her what she sought.

Not this time.

So, yeah, she had more empathy for JD than she might have had otherwise.

In a moment of connection and sympathy, she reached across the middle console and gripped his hand where it lay on his muscular thigh. His fingers immediately wrapped around hers, and her gaze shot to his face.

There was no change in his expression or posture, leaving her to wonder how long he'd been awake.

She pulled her hand free.

"We're about twenty minutes from Santa Rosa," she

told him. "I bought you a coffee. It has a little heat left if you want it. There is cream and sweeteners."

He straightened in his seat and scrubbed his hands over his face.

"How are you feeling?"

"Like I was in a cage fight with a motorcycle and lost."

"You need to choose your sparring partners more carefully."

He barked a laugh. "Yes, I do." He picked up the to-go cup and took a sip. "Black is fine." He stared over at her. "How are you doing?"

Wow. Tears burned at the back of her eyes. She couldn't remember the last time someone asked how she was doing. She blinked, clearing her vision, shoving aside the maudlin reaction to a simple question.

"Fine. The coffee has kept my body alert."

"Ah. And what's your mind been busy with?"

"Nothing. Everything."

"Well that narrows it down. Was wondering if I'm lying mixed in there somewhere?"

"Yes. I discounted it."

Silence met her response. And then in a hoarse voice, he asked, "Why?"

"The evidence supports your claim." She told him truthfully, and more hesitatingly, "And I trust my gut."

"I'm glad." He turned to stare out his window. "Because I'm trusting it, too."

She eyed his profile before focusing on the road again. "Then for both our sakes I hope it holds true."

"Do you have a job lined up in San Francisco?" Now she felt the weight of his gaze on her. "Is that why you're headed there?"

"I prefer the city." Amenity was easier in the city.

"Me, too."

"Another clue?"

"Yeah, let's call it that." He sipped his coffee, then dropped the empty cup into the holder. "Losing the election causing you to question your career choice?"

"My ego took a hit." She lifted one shoulder, let it drop. "I'll shake it off."

She hoped.

"Good. You're better than the lot of them."

"Really." His endorsement tickled her, bringing out a rusty smile. "And you base your accolades on what exactly?"

"On my observations. Everyone we talked to liked and respected you. It was a busy night, a holiday they were working, yet they thought enough of you to remember it was your last day and to wish you well in future endeavors. You would have won the election if you put a little effort into it. They'll be missing you soon enough."

Hmm. What he said made sense. And she liked it better than her version where they were all thinking good riddance. People did like to know their opinion mattered. Maybe she should have campaigned a little.

Too late now.

"Yes, well, on to the next adventure."

"And what will that be? Do you have a job offer?"

"I have options." Her future loomed ominously ahead of her like the fog creeping up on the west side as she took the off-ramp in Santa Rosa. "A town in the next county over offered me an undersheriff position." The city was bigger than Woodpark, but not by much. "And there are always patrol positions in San Francisco."

"You don't sound too excited by those options."

"The undersheriff is a higher rank, but San Francisco holds more appeal. It's a dilemma."

The truth? Neither of them appealed to her.

"The undersheriff position holds some appeal, except

for the location. I've seen too much of the world to be happy in a small town."

"Then why run for sheriff?"

Because she thought she'd found acceptance.

She explained how she got the job. "The people were decent for the most part and seemed to like me. For a while I felt like I belonged. But the election results don't lie. I wasn't one of them. The mayor's brother-in-law was one of them."

It was an old lesson, well learned. And yet she'd fallen for it again. The need to belong. As a child she'd suffered with every base change until she learned to Bubble Wrap her emotions. And as an adult she'd stayed in more than one relationship longer than she should have.

Her last boyfriend let her catch him cheating so she'd finally get the hint. Not one of her more stellar moments. Rather than fall into the pattern again, she'd stayed single for the past two years.

"A position in San Francisco holds a lot of appeal location-wise. It's a beautiful place with so much history and culture. The problem is it's an expensive city to live in and a beat cop doesn't make much."

"It would be a step backward for you."

There was that. "I don't mind working my way up, but I really wanted something more, something to challenge my mind."

And she wanted a home. Someplace permanent. She appreciated what she'd seen of the world, and had more countries she longed to visit. But more than anything she wanted a place to come back to, a place to call home.

"I'll figure it out." She pulled into the clinic parking lot. "We're here."

While JD had another MRI she found the cafeteria and got a cold soda. The idea of caffeine didn't bother her. When her head finally found a pillow, nothing would keep her awake.

Figuring she had a few minutes, she took a seat at a table, leaned her head against the wall and fell asleep.

It seemed only an instant later she opened her eyes. She yawned and blinked her watch into focus. An hour had elapsed.

Wondering when this night would end, she did a few stretches—oh, yeah, that felt good—gathered her soda and headed back to emergency. Clear down the hall she heard a ruckus going on and hurried toward the sound.

"You can't keep me here against my will," JD declared. He sat on the side of the gurney facing the doctor, a plump woman in a white lab coat with lovely mocha-colored skin and beaded black braids clipped atop her head.

He was refusing to be admitted at the doctor's request. Stubborn man.

"It's just for observation." The doctor spoke with re-signed patience.

"You said there was no additional swelling," JD pointed out.

"No. But you've sustained a severe concussion." The woman responded. "I highly recommend you be admitted for tonight and possibly tomorrow. Head wounds are unpredictable. It's for your own safety."

JD pushed to his feet. "I'm fine. I have the pain medicine the last doctor gave me. I can take care of myself."

"Sir, I really advise against leaving." She shifted her bulk to block his exit. "You need bed rest. Trauma of this magnitude requires time to heal. At this stage just being on your feet walking around could result in more damage."

The mulish look on JD's face revealed what he thought of her suggestion.

"JD," Grace interjected softly, "the night is almost over. Why don't you rest for a few hours and I'll come get you in the morning?" The stars knew it was what she longed to do. He could lie down and be out in a heartbeat. She still needed to find a hotel and check in before her head found a pillow.

His shoulders went back and he gave one slow shake of his head. "I hate hospitals. I've spent too much time in them already tonight. I'll rest better somewhere else. Anywhere else."

She sighed. He meant it. The tension in those wide shoulders, the clenched jaw, the faint flicker of panic in his emerald eyes told her his dislike went deeper than memories. He really intended to leave.

"You've done enough," he told her. "Thank you for all your help. I can take it from here."

It was the wrong thing to say. He tried sliding past the doctor, but she had her moves on, keeping him pinned while signaling to a nurse.

"Sir, we really can't release you without adult supervision. This level of traumatic brain injury results in disorientation and confusion. You represent a danger to yourself and others."

JD did not back down. "I need you to get out of my way."

"Get security." The doctor instructed the nurse.

Time to defuse the situation. "Doctor, we understand your concern. Of course he won't be alone. He's been lucid all night. You've confirmed the swelling hasn't gotten any worse. He's clearly determined to go. Won't causing him mental duress be worse than allowing him to leave?"

Faced with his stubborn determination, the doctor saw the sense in Grace's calm argument. "You'll be with him?"

JD opened his mouth. She shot him a don't-you-dare glare.

"Yes."

"And you'll bring him back in the morning?" The doctor pressed.

Green eyes narrowed. Grace agreed the physician was pushing it.

"I'll see he gets the care he needs."

The woman reluctantly agreed. She noted her concerns on the release form and reiterated her instructions and the symptoms to be concerned over.

"Mismatched pupils, vomiting, excessive sleepiness." Grace rattled off the last of the list. "Doctor, you've been very helpful. I think I should get him somewhere to lie down. Good night."

Taking JD's arm she led him away, not releasing him until they were out the door. "Don't look back." She warned him. "She might change her mind."

"They couldn't keep me against my will." He bit out.

"She's not wrong. With the concussion you're not thinking clearly."

"You told her I've been lucid all night."

"And you have. That doesn't mean you're making good decisions. You should have been admitted. At least for the rest of tonight."

Halfway across the driveway to the parking lot, Grace realized JD wasn't keeping pace with her. She swung around to find him hovering near the exit. She started toward him.

"Do you want me to pick you up?" Dang, she should have thought of that. She'd just been extolling his injuries but she kept forgetting how extensive they really were.

"No." He closed the gap between them. Surprised her when he bent to kiss her cheek. "Thanks for all you've done. I wouldn't have made it through the night without you." He shoved his hands into his jeans pockets. "But I can't take advantage of you any longer. It's time to say goodbye."

CHAPTER FOUR

"GOODBYE?" GRACE REPEATED. Then, more forcefully, "Goodbye?"

"Thank you for everything." He turned to walk away.

"Oh, no, you don't." She jumped into his path, pointed her finger toward her Escape. "You don't like hearing the truth so you're just going to walk away? Forget that noise. Get in the vehicle. Now."

He scowled. "You're no longer the sheriff and I'm not your prisoner. I appreciate your help. But I'll be fine. The test tech gave me the address for a local shelter. I can take it from here."

"No." She blocked his attempt to walk by her. "You can't. I just vouched for you in there, meaning I'm responsible for your butt. Like it or not, you are in my care. We'll be sticking together like sauce on spaghetti until I'm sure you've regained your faculties."

Which included the rest of the night at the very least. More likely twenty-four to forty-eight hours. At three-thirty in the morning exhaustion prevented her from thinking beyond that. The night nurse had recommended a nearby hotel. She planned to check in and immediately check out.

This delay was not making her a happy camper.

"I don't like it." He declared. He picked her up, set her aside and headed toward the street. "Good luck with the job search."

In a heartbeat she stood in his way, hand to his chest. "You don't want to mess with me, JD. Get in the car."

He struck out in a defensive move. She countered and they engaged in a brief tussle. He knew karate. And he was good. She was better. And she wasn't injured. In a few moves she had him on one knee. She released him.

"I'm sorry." He ran a hand over his neck. "I didn't mean to fight you. It was instinct."

"I get that. But stop battling me." Weariness dragged at her. "Neither of us has the energy for it. Listen, I can't let you wander off alone. If something happened to you or to someone because of you, I'd feel responsible. There's a hotel a few blocks away. Let's just go there for the rest of the night and see how you're doing tomorrow."

He walked by her toward the parking lot. "Let's go, then. I'm beginning to see why the citizens of Woodpark voted against you."

Grace flinched. Okay, that hurt more than it should have. She'd stood by his side all night and the first time she challenged him he struck out at her. She understood he was upset with the circumstances more than with her. Still, it felt personal.

Following after him, she clicked the locks open. They traveled the few blocks to the hotel in silence. Unfortunately, the hotel the nurse recommended looked small and shabby. Thankfully it had a sold-out sign in the window, taking the choice of staying there out of Grace's hands.

She was tired enough not to care where she laid her head tonight. Still, she preferred not to suffer regrets in the morning. A quick scan on her phone for local hotels brought up several national chains. She went with Pinnacle Express because they were known for their good service. She plugged the address into the GPS while JD called and made a reservation.

Given the need to monitor his health and his attempt

to walk away, she told him to make it one room with two beds. He lifted one brow but didn't question her.

When they reached the room, JD disappeared into the bathroom. She heard the shower turn on as she tossed her duffel bag on the nearest bed. Energy gone, she dropped into the only armchair to wait her turn. She had barely closed her eyes when she heard the door opening. Dragging heavy lids open, she watched him stroll across the room in gray knit boxer briefs.

He moved like poetry in motion. Graceful, muscles flowing with every step. So beautiful that for a moment she wondered if she was dreaming. The ugliness of his scar stripped the dream quality away. She sat up.

More alert, she noticed he moved carefully on his way to the bed. He didn't acknowledge her, simply sprawled out on his stomach and went to sleep. He didn't even cover up but lay with his tight, knit-clad butt facing her and went to sleep. Already soft snores filled the silence.

Shaking her head she set her phone alarm to wake him in a few hours to check him out. Yeah, that was going to be a joyous chore.

Let him sulk.

She wouldn't compromise her principles because he thought he was fine when medical science and personal experience told her his judgment was off right now. Better he be pouting than be dead.

She was reaching for the energy to get up and shower when she fell asleep.

An insistent beeping woke Grace. She opened her eyes to a strange room dimly lit by light from a bathroom. She stretched her neck, working out kinks.

It took a moment to remember where she was—a less than comfortable armchair in a hotel in Santa Rosa—and who she was with—a man she'd known less than six hours. A record for her. She was strictly a third-date-or-longer gal.

She shut off the annoying sound of the alarm and ran her fingers through her hair, taming spiked ends she could feel poking out at odd angles. After one last roll of her neck, she pushed to her feet. Half-asleep, she stumbled to his bedside.

Time to check JD's vitals, to torture him with more questions about his friend the president and what year it was. He was so out of it he hadn't heard the alarm going off.

"JD," she called his name. No movement. She called again, louder. Nothing.

She reached out to shake him then pulled her hand back. He still sprawled across the bed, naked except for the knit boxers that clung to his hard backside. Nowhere to touch besides smooth, bare skin. Fingers curled into her palm in instinctive self-preservation.

Already attracted, touching him seemed risky, almost a violation. But she was no longer a sheriff, just a Good Samaritan no longer bound by strict protocols. Which almost made touching him worse. Duty would drive her to see to his health.

And this was no different. Giving a mental tug at her big-girl panties, she placed her hand on his shoulder and shook. She was seeing to his health.

Uh-huh, so why did it feel as if she was stroking a lover? Snatching her hand back, she stood back and waited.

He didn't move. Dang it.

"JD." She shook him harder. He shifted, moving his head from one side to the other so he now faced her but he continued to sleep. Boy, he was out. Of course he'd had a long day.

Yeah, and hers was growing longer by the minute. Wait, why was she waking him? Oh, yeah, because of the concussion.

Half-asleep, she perched on the edge of the bed, and getting right down next to his ear, she said his name louder and gave him another shake. He shot up, rolling over and sitting up in one smooth motion. His eyes popped open, focused on her. The wanting in them sent a tingle down her spine.

They were face-to-face, eye to eye with nothing but knit boxer briefs and her suddenly inadequate clothes between them.

"Grace," he said.

Flustered and distracted at hearing him use her name for the first time, she was unprepared when he swept her into his arms and pulled her to him.

"Uh, JD." She wiggled and shifted. Trying to push away? If so, she failed. The way he held her, she only succeeded in rubbing her hip against him, causing his body to react. Not good. Her hands went to his chest, ready to push him away. The feel of his skin, the heat under her hands addled her senses.

"Oh."

"Grace," he whispered, and wrapping a hand around her head he pulled her to him as he lowered his head. He kissed her softly, slowly. A gentle caress, sexy but soothing at the same time. Then the contrary man slid his tongue into her mouth and, oh, he tasted good. She fought hard to throttle back her desire, to ease the growing passion. No easy task when all she wanted was to draw him to her for a long sensual snuggle.

He broke off the kiss, nibbled a path along her jaw and nuzzled a kiss behind her ear. She sighed and her body went limp in his arms.

"You're killing me here, JD."

He went still. And then pulled back, slowly disengaging his body from hers. He blinked once, twice. She knew immediately when confusion vanished and he became aware of where he was and what he was doing.

Her cheeks heated when he pushed away from her, not stopping until his back hit the headboard. Could he get far enough away?

"Uh, sorry." He apologized. "I don't usually grab women in my sleep." His dark brows pushed together. "At least I don't think I do."

She cleared her throat, reminded herself he was injured even though her body still reeled from the strength and warmth of his. "Don't worry about it. Concussions—"

He stopped her by blurting out the name of the president.

She frowned. "What?"

He stated the year, then took the phone she still gripped in her hand and flipped it open so the light shone between them. "Are my pupils even?"

Flinching away from the light, she narrowed her eyes to scrutinize him. "Yes."

"Good." He closed the phone and gave it back to her. "I'm all checked out." He slipped from the bed and moved to the other one. "Good night." He slid under the sheet and rolled so his back faced her.

"Good night." Ignoring a misguided pang of regret, she flopped down in the space he'd just left. The bedding smelled of him, held the heat of his body. For just an instant, she sank into a fantasy of what could never be. And moments later she followed him into slumber.

Grace woke to the smell of coffee and bacon. Groaning, she rolled over, slowly opened her eyes and stared into a leaf-green gaze.

"Good morning." JD greeted her with a tip of his mug.

She swung her feet around and sat up on the edge of the bed. The bed she thought he'd gone to sleep in the night before. Now he sat feet up leaning back against the headboard on the bed opposite her. Thankfully he'd covered the memorable gray knit boxers with his jeans. A white T-shirt and socks completed his apparel.

Exactly how had things gotten switched around? She had a vague niggling of something happening in the night, but she'd been so exhausted she couldn't pull it to mind. She could only pray it had nothing to do with the erotic dream he'd starred in.

"Morning," she mumbled.

"Actually, I got that wrong." His mouth rolled up at the corner. "It's after one."

"After one?" She was appalled. "Why didn't you wake me? Checkout was at noon. Now I'll have to pay for another night."

"Sorry. I haven't been up long myself. Just long enough to order breakfast."

Her stomach gave a loud growl at the mention of food. She covered it with her hand. "The coffee smells divine."

He gestured toward the desk. "I got one for you."

"Bless you." She headed for the desk.

"Bacon and eggs, too."

"Mmm," she hummed her approval and detoured to her overnight case for her toiletries. She longed for a shower, yet the growl in her stomach demanded she feed it first. A shower could wait, but she needed clean teeth to start her day.

"How's the head?" she asked on her way to the bathroom.

"Better than last night," he answered with a total lack of inflection.

She stopped and faced him, lifting an eyebrow. "But not by much?"

"The doctor said it would take time."

"Right." The woman had been sure to repeat it several times, making sure she included Grace so she would know the doctor held her accountable for his care. "So still no memory?"

"Not from my past, no."

Meaning what? He was making new memories? Like kissing her? There'd been kissing in her dream. She narrowed her gaze on his face. His expression gave nothing away. Dang it. How did she get in his bed anyway? Exhaustion really knocked her out last night. The last thing she remembered was admiring his tight bum in soft gray.

And then her alarm went off.

And OMG. He'd kissed her. It hadn't been a dream at all. He'd kissed her and then pushed her away.

Without looking at him, she ducked into the bathroom and closed the door. Amnesia looked pretty good right about now. She wouldn't mind losing a few minutes of memory. Actually just a few details.

She inhaled a deep breath, forcing herself to calm down. So he'd kissed her. No need to freak out. He'd come to his senses and apologized. No harm done.

Yep, that was her story and she was sticking to it.

Back in the room and sipping coffee between bites of bacon and eggs, Grace worried over what else might have happened during the night. The fact she still wore her clothes from yesterday was a big clue, and frankly a huge relief. At least nothing too compromising happened between them.

Well, if she discounted the kiss. And she did. Discount it. In fact, in her mind it never happened. A dream never to be discussed or brought to mind.

Yeah, right. Even after brushing her teeth she felt him on her lips.

"I meant to move on to San Francisco today, but since we slept in I think it'd be best to take it easy. Give you a day to recuperate. We'll go shopping, get you another set of clothes."

"Okay, this is not going to work for me." He set his paper mug aside and crossed his arms over his impressive chest.

"What's not working?" She hoped he wasn't going to be difficult again this morning. Afternoon.

"Having you call all the shots." He stood and went to the window, drawing back the drapes to let in the weak afternoon sun. "It was all right when I was near incapacitated. But I'm thinking better now. And I may not know who I am, but I can promise you I'm not the type to happily trail behind someone like a trained puppy dog."

"That's hardly been the case." Puppy dog? More like bulldog. He certainly hadn't been docile last night at the hospital. But given his attempt to leave, she should have expected another bid for independence. "I've only been trying to help."

"I know. I appreciate it. But I'm not a child that needs his hand held. I do, however, need to find out my identity. I called the local police department while I was waiting for breakfast to be delivered. Once the officer got past the idea I wasn't joking, he suggested I take my problem to San Francisco. A bigger police department or the FBI would have more sophisticated resources."

"Yes."

"And you're headed to San Francisco."

"Yes."

"So you've planned to take me with you?"

"Yes."

He nodded. "I want to hire you."

She froze with a piece of bacon halfway to her mouth. "What? Why?"

"I may have no control over my mind, but I insist on having control over my life. Putting a name to my face is only one step to getting my life back. You have resources, connections. You can help me to learn not just a name, but who I am. Where I belong. Tell me about the people in my life. I was stabbed. I need to know if it's safe for me to return to where I came from."

"You don't have to hire me to find that out. I've said I'll help you."

"No. You're used to being in charge. If you're just helping, you're going to feel you have a say in what I do. If I'm the boss, I have the say."

"JD, it's your life. You'll always have the final say."

"You think it's the concussion talking." He crossed his arms over his chest.

"I think you're trying to survive in a world that's suddenly foreign." Not so calm now. She set her fork down. "I'm not your enemy."

"I know." The intensity in his eyes didn't waiver. "We need to do this my way, Grace."

She could see they did. It was his way of making sense of what was happening to him. Of coping. She understood—probably more today than yesterday—the drive to control the areas of his life he could. And he wasn't wrong about her having an opinion. The thing was, him paying her wouldn't change that.

Of course, it would give him the sense of being in charge. Which was all that really mattered.

"I need a job for real."

"This is a real job."

"You know what I mean. The real job hunt needs to come first."

He frowned, but nodded. "Agreed."

"Well, if I agree, we'd need to set a time limit. Say two weeks, and then we reevaluate where things stand."

He hesitated but nodded again.

"Okay. How do you plan to pay me?" She gave in. No need to make things more difficult for the guy. And she knew how to present her case when necessary.

"With this." He walked to the night table between the beds, opened the drawer, and drew out his watch.

She shrank back in the chair. "I can't take your watch."

"Good, because I'm not giving it to you. But the thing is worth a small fortune. It can fund my search."

"You intend to pawn it?"

"Can you think of a better way to get fast cash? I can't continue to live off your charity."

"I can afford it." She assured him. She had a healthy savings account before leaving the navy. And now she had the life insurance money from her dad as well as the funds from the sale of his house. Once she found the right job, she planned to use the money to buy a house and put down some permanent roots.

But she had enough to help out a person in need.

"Save your money, Grace. You're unemployed. I'm not going to mooch off you."

"Well, pawning isn't the answer either. You won't get what the watch is worth. And you can't just sell it. A piece like that would require provenance. Plus, what if it has sentimental value?"

"I don't think so." He set the watch on the desk beside her plate. "Not many people can afford seventy thousand dollars' worth of sentiment. This is a flash piece, meant to intimidate and impress."

"You do know you're talking about yourself?"

"Maybe." He ran a finger over the glass front of the expensive piece. "I like the exposed gears."

"Well, you are a geek."

A small smile lifted the corner of his mouth. "So I am."

"We'll find a jeweler." She lifted the watch and examined the craftsmanship. It really was beautiful. "In San Francisco, not here. You'll get more for it in a bigger city. We'll get an estimate of the watch's value, and I'll buy it off you. When we get you home, you can buy it back if you want to, or I can sell it and get my money back."

With narrowed eyes and a clenched jaw, he looked as if he wanted to protest. Instead he nodded.

"I can live with that deal. Let's get going." He sat on the end of the bed and reached for his boots.

"No." She leaned back in her chair and took a fortifying sip of coffee to prepare for her first battle. "I know you're anxious to move forward, but I'm not ready to walk out the door. I have to shower and change. And today is a holiday. A lot of places are closed on New Year's Day. Plus we're going to have to pay for the hotel for another night anyway, so I suggest we do a little more recuperating today. Maybe shop for some clothes for you. We can put together a plan for when we get to San Francisco tomorrow."

He propped his hands at his sides. "You seem to have missed the part where I'm the boss now."

"Not when it comes to your health." She corrected. Best to be clear with him, because on this she wouldn't bend. "Let me clarify. As far as my services are involved, there's no compromising when it comes to your health. If I feel you're pushing it, I'll call a halt. I said that I'd be responsible for you and I take my duties seriously."

"So I've noticed." He tossed his boot down. "What happened to it's my life and the final decision is mine?"

"Still applies. Except when you're being bullheaded about your health. Today we rest. Tomorrow is up to you."

"You'll make some phone calls, set up some appointments in San Francisco?"

"Of course."

"Okay. We'll shop for clothes today. And put together a plan for tomorrow."

"And rest."

He scowled but nodded. "And rest."

"Good." One battle down. She pushed her plate aside and stood. "I'll shower and then we can go." Carrying her paper mug of coffee, she grabbed her duffel and disappeared into the bathroom.

JD listened to the shower come on and tried not to think of Grace with water streaming over her body. Yeah, not working. He easily envisioned being with her, raising soap bubbles by running his hands over her skin.

Nothing to feel guilty over. He knew he wasn't married or in a committed relationship. One of those odd things he was certain of. But Grace was now his employee.

Best if he kept his distance.

The situation had already created a faux intimacy between them that created a level of trust unusual in an acquaintanceship less than twenty-four hours old.

She didn't quite get the me-boss-you-employee relationship, but he'd work on her. Getting around her unrelenting sense of duty when it came to his health would be a bit of a problem. He was grateful to Grace, but she made rigid look loose when it came to her duty.

Still, as long as he kept his raging headache to himself, she should have no argument with his plans.

A good thing, because he needed to take control of his life. Being at the whim of fate felt wrong. Whoever he was, whatever he did, he hadn't been a follower. Deep in his gut he knew he'd been in charge. The Cartier watch sure seemed to indicate so.

He refused to sit around all day and brood over what he didn't know. But she was right, the holiday hampered them. And he could use a change of clothes.

Bottom line, this hotel room beat the heck out of the hospital. If he had to take another day to heal up, better here than in an antiseptic-scented hell.

He sat on the bed, leaned back against the headboard

and crossed his ankles. A pain pill went down easy with a swig of coffee.

She'd made no mention of the kiss they'd shared. Was that because she didn't remember, or because she preferred not to? Of the few memories he had, it rated right up there at the top. Waking to her bending over him last night had been a temptation he couldn't resist. Her nearness, the electric connection of her caring gaze broke through his defenses and he reached for her, claiming her soft lips in a sweet kiss. And oh, man. The tension they'd both tried to ignore throughout the night simmered over. Burned him up.

She'd been right there with him, her response explosive. He'd been ready to roll her under him and relieve their tension in the most basic way possible. He remembered the smell of her hair, the taste of the tender spot behind her ear.

When she'd moaned that he was killing her, it shocked him to his senses. Her surrender had him immediately backing off. He wanted her willing, not succumbing. If she was resistant at all, he had no business taking their relationship in a sensual direction. It would create unnecessary tension between him and the one person interested in helping him.

The water went off in the shower. And now he saw her running a towel over damp curves and that short cap of dark hair. He may have left her in her lonely bed last night, but the attraction remained alive within him.

He forced his mind away from the erotic imaginings. Instead he focused on the contacts she'd mentioned. He had to believe he'd soon have a name to replace the emptiness in his head.

It was the last thought he had before he drifted off.

Grace exited the bathroom to find JD napping on the bed closest to the window. She closed the drapes and wrote him a note telling she'd be back shortly. Grabbing her purse and phone, she went downstairs to the lobby to make a few phone calls.

The officer on duty in Woodpark stated a patrol had traveled the road JD had been walking on and there'd been no sign of his motorcycle or wallet.

"There was a report of an altercation at the Red Wolf Tavern including a man fitting JD's description. The bartender said he hadn't been drinking. He'd eaten, paid for the meal, apparently from a big wad of cash, and bumped shoulders with a guy on his way out the door. Got beer spilled on him. The other guy tried to get tough with him and the man fitting JD's description put the aggressor on his knees. The guy backed off and that was the end of it."

"Except for the part where the guy followed JD, ran him off the road and robbed him."

"That's a possible scenario."

Yeah. The probable scenario.

"That's all we've got."

And from his tone, all they were willing to do. JD had been released. Wasn't even in town. The new sheriff would see no reason to expend time or resources on finding JD's property or identity.

So no help there.

Next she called a friend from her boot camp days. Doug worked for the FBI, in the San Francisco office. She considered him their best bet for finding JD's identity because the government had face-recognition technology. The San Francisco Police Department may have it as well, but accessing it wouldn't be so easy. She didn't have any connections there, and it could take a while to get results.

She called Doug, but it turned out he and his wife were visiting her parents in Bend, Oregon, and he wouldn't be back in the office until Monday. Great. She could imagine JD's reaction to the delay. Good news, though. Doug was willing to help once he got back in town.

She sank back in the deep red chair, happy she'd gone with Pinnacle Express. She'd stayed at a few and never had complaints. So much better than the Shabby Inn. She enjoyed the muted grays, the push of red, the modern furnishings and artwork. And the large sleeping rooms, though sharing with a six-foot-plus man sure put large into perspective.

Sitting in the lobby watching families come and go, she felt safe, comfortable. Simple emotions most people in the United States took for granted, but she'd sat or patrolled in plenty of locations that didn't encourage such simple emotions.

Before her father's illness, she'd planned to finish her career in the navy. Now, she was glad to be home, looked forward to finding a place and making it her own.

But first she had to help JD find his home.

With him in mind, she stopped in the gift shop on her way back to the room and picked up a disposable razor, toothbrush, toothpaste, deodorant and a new T-shirt. It wasn't much and wouldn't last long, but it was a start. Shopping didn't strike her as an activity high on JD's list of favorite things to do. Hopefully he'd view a trip to obtain new clothes and a few personal items as forward momentum in his quest.

The selection consisted of shirts with towering redwoods, seascapes and big block letters spelling out CALIFORNIA. She decided on the redwoods, but, of course, there were none in his size.

The man was really running on a bad streak of luck—or she was. Grace hadn't decided which yet.

Given the size of JD's shoulders, his choice of shirt came down to a kelly green with seals frolicking on a beach or a bright red with California blazoned across the chest. She went for the red. The green might work well with his eyes, but he didn't strike her as a seal guy.

Which was only half the truth of why she chose the red. The truth had to do with the fact his green eyes were distracting enough without having them made more prominent by the color of his shirt. Her mind zigged right from thoughts of his gorgeous eyes to forbidden wonderings about his bone-melting kiss.

It started out so soft and grew into a searing melding of mouths, all while he cradled her to his hard body with a surety and strength that kindled a sense of passion and security. He pushed past her defenses until her body ignited, and then he eased off and apologized.

How mean was that?

She'd be a lot happier if she could relegate the incident to a dream rather than to a memory.

The last thing she remembered from the night before was her irritation at his prime body and sulky attitude. She'd been sitting in the chair, waiting for access to the bathroom, when he strolled out in nothing but his underwear and passed her as casually as if he was two and she his mother.

Not feeling motherly, uh-uh, not at all.

Which was why the kiss was so forbidden.

So yeah, the kiss would remain a memory. Because, oh, no, she was not talking to him about it.

He hadn't said anything. Hadn't given one hint they'd spent part of last night in each other's arms. Surely if it meant anything to him, he would have said something.

"Stop it," she said aloud.

"Ma'am?" a voice asked.

She turned to see she'd startled a man and his young son sharing the elevator with her.

She pulled on a smile. "Sorry. Internal argument."

The man nodded, but seemed relieved to get off on the next floor. The two of them gave her odd looks as they exited.

Grace groaned. She squeezed her eyes shut, then opened them and rehit the button for her floor. Regardless of the attraction she had for him, both subliminal and overt, she needed to shut it down. On every level—be it prisoner, victim or her boss—JD was off-limits.

And if the seventy-thousand-dollar watch was any indicator, he was out of her league, as well.

Her savings, the life insurance and what Dad left her put her in good shape financially. Enough so she didn't have to rush into a new job. She could take her time, really weigh her options and choose the right position for her. But she was nowhere near millionaire status.

How much money did you have to have to feel comfortable dropping nearly a hundred thousand on a watch? Lots. And lots.

More than a military brat was accustomed to.

She let herself into the room and found JD still sleeping in his bed. Or was it her bed?

Oh, no. She was *not* going down that tract again. Especially not with him stretched out right across the way.

She gave serious thought to waking him so they could go shopping, getting them both out of the room altogether. But he needed to heal, and the rest did him good in that regard.

Next came the idea of taking off and doing the shopping without him. He shouldn't care. Men rarely cared about missing a shopping spree. Except he would care. He wanted control of his life, which for JD, came down to picking out his own pair of jeans, and whatever else he decided he needed.

She wasn't so desperate to dodge her thoughts that she'd deny him his first steps of independence.

Feeling righteous, she stretched out on her bed and closed her eyes. But they didn't stay closed. She wasn't sleepy, and she wasn't usually the type to nap. Which meant she lay there, staring at the long lean length of JD sprawled in the bed across from her. And he looked good, causing her to have totally inappropriate, lascivious thoughts about her boss.

Unable to take it, she flipped over. Better to stare at the wall. Except she could still smell him. There was no escaping the yummy scent of soap and man.

Sheesh, she was in so much trouble.

Giving up, she swung her feet to the floor. Grabbing shorts and a T-shirt out of her duffel, she stepped into the bathroom and quickly changed. After updating her note, she headed out the door again.

Maybe she could pound him out of her head in the gym.

CHAPTER FIVE

"You were sleeping. I had calls to make and I didn't want to disturb you." She paused to look at a window display of boots. "I left you a note."

He'd seen it. A few words jotted on a hotel notepad stating she'd gone to the lobby, and then that had been crossed off and the word *gym* added. Envy caused his shoulders to tense for a moment. His restlessness told him he led a more physical life, if not manual labor, then he had the use of a gym. He would have joined her when he saw the note, except he had enough smarts to know his head couldn't take the physical exertion right now.

Not that he'd admit that out loud and give Grace any leverage.

Maybe that's what had him in a foul mood. He'd hired her, yet she was still calling the shots. Maybe his ego stung. Yet the explanation didn't fit. His ego may have taken a hit, but his intelligence recognized the reasoning. And accepted Grace had no control over the timing or the fact her friend was out of state.

It was the helplessness that grated on him. He hated it.

For a while after he woke up and read the note, he'd thought she'd abandoned him. That she wised up after his attack in the parking lot and finally left him. It didn't even matter that her duffel was still there. He'd been totally, irrationally freaked.

At least they were finally doing something. Even shopping beat sitting on his hands.

"Good. Because I would never hurt you." He felt compelled to reassure her. "It was an instinctive reaction when I struck out at you in the parking lot last night."

"I know." She met his gaze with confidence before turning those stunning blue eyes back to the boots. "Like any cop, a master-at-arms learns to read people. I wouldn't be here with you if I felt threatened in any way."

"Right." In jeans and a beige sweater all traces of Sheriff Delaney were gone. The loving cling of her sweater over the generous swell of her breasts knocked all thoughts of her uniform from his damaged mind. "As long as we're both clear on that point."

"We are." She pulled wistful eyes away from the tall, black leather boots in the window and moved on. She tossed him a teasing glance over her shoulder. "Are you afraid of me?"

Yes. The answer came without thought, without foundation. Why would he be afraid of her?

"I don't know. When you get your tough on, you're scary."

The corner of her mouth curled up in a pleased smirk. He had to smile. She enjoyed being a tough cookie.

"Of course, the rest of the time you're a marshmallow."

"I am not." Totally outraged she swung into his path. "Take that back."

"Marshmallow."

"Take it back, or I'll leave you here to do your shopping alone."

"Would never happen. You're too nice. You need to help. You can't help yourself."

"Don't test me, JD. I've been trained by the best to do what needs to be done."

He held up his hands in surrender. "You win. You're one

scary dude." He got the words out, but not with a straight face. His lips twitched a couple of times.

"Hmm." She surveyed him with narrowed eyes. "Believe it." She nodded her head to the left. "This shop should have what we need."

He followed her inside the menswear shop. The masculine feel and smell of the place immediately put him at ease. Much better than the hotel gift shop. He stepped in there for a few minutes and was grateful he wasn't wearing frolicking seals.

Grace wandered around, pulled a few things off the rack, but made no attempt to sway him. He saw a few things he liked, and then he saw the price tags.

No. He was not going to allow Grace to absorb any more costs for him. Frustration spiked the pounding in his head to a blinding level. Grabbing her hand, he pulled her from the store.

"Where are we going?" she demanded. "Didn't you see anything you liked?"

"We're finding a jewelry store. I want my own money." He stopped at a directory, scanned the specialty listing and turned back the way they came.

Resistance yanked at his hand as Grace dragged her feet. "We agreed you'd get a better estimate for the watch in San Francisco."

"I need money now." He didn't stop. And he didn't let go.

"You can pay me back." She caught up to him, worked at freeing her hand. He held on.

"No."

"JD."

"No."

"Can we at least talk about this?" She swerved toward the food court coming up on their right. "Let's get some lunch and discuss it."

He hauled her back to his side. "No. We can eat after."

"Okay." A touch of temper vibrated through the word. "You're going to want to stop yanking me around like a yo-yo."

"You'd be fine if you stopped fighting me." He spotted the jewelry store up ahead and quickened his step. "I'm the boss, remember?"

"Yeah, well. I don't usually hold hands with my employers."

"We're a small operation." He ran his thumb over the soft skin of her wrist just to mess with her. "I like to keep things intimate."

He felt the frost in her glare sting his skin but ignored it as they reached their destination. "We're here."

"Good afternoon and Happy New Year's." A tall, thin woman with black hair, a black dress and black pumps greeted them as soon as they stepped inside. "I bet I can guess what you're looking for." She clapped her hands. "And don't you make a lovely couple? Goodness, what beautiful babies the two of you will make together. Engagement rings are right over here."

She headed toward a glass case loaded with glittering diamonds.

JD followed.

Grace continued to yank at her hand.

"There must have been some enchantment in the air this New Year's." The woman rounded the case. "You're the third couple to come in today."

"Oh, no." Grace stated emphatically. She gave a mighty tug to free herself. He let go, and then had to catch her elbow to keep her from falling. Stepping away, she stood at attention. "We're not engaged."

"Oh." The woman—her name badge read Monique— looked back and forth between him and Grace. Finally she nodded and gave them a knowing smile. "Maybe for Valentine's Day?"

Grace's cheeks turned red. "No, not for Valentine's Day."

Monique smirked and held up her hands in surrender. "What can I do for you today?"

"I'd like to get this watch appraised." He unlatched the watch and set it on the glass counter. "It's a Cartier."

"Goodness, a Cartier." Monique picked up the time-piece and studied it. "I've never seen one outside of catalogs. Oh, my, it's gorgeous. Val will love this. He'll be the one to appraise it for you. He's out to lunch but should be back shortly. Do you have proof of purchase?"

"Not on me." He didn't hesitate, didn't look at Grace. "Do I need it to get an appraisal?"

"Not for an appraisal, no. If you wanted to sell it, you would. The owner requires it on high-price items like this."

"Your discretion is admirable."

Monique smiled as if he'd flattered her personally. "Thank you." She held up the watch. "Should I hold on to this for Val to look at?"

"No." JD took it from her. "We'll come back. Thank you for your help."

Placing a hand in the small of Grace's back, he ushered her from the store.

"Wait." This time it was her grabbing his hand. "I know you're frustrated, but it's for the best. I have a contact I trust looking into the resale value. I should hear from him soon. A jeweler could say anything and you wouldn't know any better."

She was right. And it annoyed him that he hadn't thought of the need for information before negotiation. It only made sense. It was a standard business practice and something he should have known.

Maybe the concussion did mess with his head.

"Okay." He agreed.

She nodded her approval and made for the food court.

He didn't budge and she jerked to a stop when she couldn't go any farther.

"What now?

"Not the food court. We're not spending any more money until I can buy."

"That's ridiculous. It's just lunch. And I'm hungry."

"Make it quick, then." He walked to a slated bench and sat. "Because we're doing this my way."

"You're being unreasonable." She sat next to him and drew out her phone and sent a text. "And stubborn. I think we've definitely found your first character trait."

"You say that like it's a bad thing." He let his head drop back and closed his eyes. Immediately the soft scent of her filled his senses. Orange blossoms and a hint of ginger, sweetness with a hint of depth. It suited her. And enticed him. Each breath helped to soothe the pain beating at his skull.

She laughed, not a pleasant sound. "Says the stubborn one."

"Sweet thing, you aren't in a position to toss stones." He opened his eyes to see her glance up from her phone.

"What's that mean?"

"It means you could teach stubborn lessons to a mule. Miss I-Won't-Compromise-On-My-Responsibilities."

Rolling her eyes, she went back to her watch search. "That's called having a sense of duty."

"Yeah, you keep telling yourself that." He propped his head on a closed fist.

"JD?"

A different quality in her voice and a soft hand on his arm drew him around to her. Blue eyes measured him. "Are you okay?" she demanded. "When was the last time you took your pain medicine?"

He stabbed her with a glare. "And I give you exhibit A."

"I'm serious."

"So am I."

She swiveled on her hips to face him. "I can see you're in pain."

Nice hips encased in blue denim. "I haven't been out of pain since I woke up on the side of the road."

"Which is no reason to be a martyr."

"I don't need it." Rather than look at her he turned his attention to the hat kiosk in front of him, to the rows of caps denoting NFL, NBA and other sports teams. He wondered if he had a team he supported.

"Listen, I know you're hot to find out who you are, but knowing your name won't mean a whole lot if you don't have your memories. When you push it, you may be delaying your recovery."

"I can't just sit around doing nothing." The pounding in his head escalated. He pulled his gaze away from the silver fangs on the football cap of the Las Vegas Strikers. Focused on the beige terrazzo flooring instead. "My mind doesn't shut off when I'm not moving around. It's constantly seeking information that's not there. That hurts more than staying occupied."

"Okay. I get that. But you need to rest, to heal, especially in these first few days." She leaned back on the bench and stared out at the post-holiday shoppers. "Obviously the money thing bothers you. I get that, too. You must feel helpless without funds of your own. Why don't I give you an advance until we get it appraised?"

"No." She was too generous, too trusting. How could she know he wasn't making this whole thing up to take advantage of her? As it was, he already owed her too much. Didn't like the fact she was lending him money at all. The watch meant nothing to him. He'd rather sell it and have his own resources.

"Yes." She countered. "It'll only be a few hundred dollars today, because that's my ATM limit."

Not waiting for a response from him, she got up and walked away. About a hundred feet up she stepped into an alcove. A few minutes later she was headed back to him.

The woman had no sense of self-preservation at all. Didn't she understand the risks she was taking with him? She'd been a law enforcement officer. She should know better.

When she held out the money, he folded his arms across his chest and refused to take it.

"Nothing is easy with you. I'm not giving you anything I'm not willing to lose. So far. We may have to work out incremental payments for the watch."

Okay, that made him feel slightly better. But he still didn't reach for the money. His resistance didn't deter her. She rolled the bills up, tucked them in the crook of his elbow and walked away.

"Whatever," she tossed over her shoulder. "I'm getting something to eat."

And she had the nerve to call him stubborn.

He was the one with the concussion, but she was the one not thinking right.

She had no reason to trust him. No reason to put her money at risk. Such generosity of spirit was foreign to him. Who knew who he'd be when he got his memory back? He could be a scumbag willing to prey on gullible fools.

Lord, he prayed he wasn't a scumbag. If that turned out to be the case, better he never regain his memory. Then he'd have a chance to start over. The question then was would his true character bleed through to his new identity?

It was too much to contemplate when his head felt ready to explode.

So yeah, he'd give in, but only on his terms.

He followed her into the food court. Bought a plate of

Chinese food—he had to admit it felt good to have money in his pocket—and joined her at a table in the communal dining area.

"Here." He held his watch out to her.

She just looked at him.

"You've lent me money using the watch as collateral. You need to hold on to the collateral."

She finished a bite of pasta. "That's not necessary."

"Yes, it is." He stared her down.

"All right." She took the watch and buckled it on. "If it'll make you happy." At its tightest point it dangled on her wrist like a bulky bracelet. He'd have to add another notch.

"It does make me happy." He felt it in the easing of the tension in his shoulders, which emphasized the throbbing in his head. Giving in to the pain, he pulled out his prescription bottle.

Grace watched in silence as he popped a pain pill with a sip of soda. At least she didn't gloat. Putting up with stubborn was bad enough.

"So you like Chinese?"

"Yeah. This is pretty good."

"And spicy. Risky, going with the kung pao chicken."

"I can handle it." He dug in, savoring the heat, the garlic, the nuttiness.

"How did you know you'd like it?" She wondered.

He shrugged. "One of those things I know without knowing how."

"So the real you *is* coming through. That has to be good, right?"

Another shrug. Who knew?

She cocked her head to the left. "There's a movie theater. You want to get out of your head? Let's go see a movie. Killing a couple of hours in a dark cinema should occupy you and still be restful."

"Yeah, we could do that." He stood and gathered their trash. "As long as it's not some chick flick."

"I like a good chick flick, but I was thinking something more shoot-'em-up."

"You like action-adventure?"

"I do. And sci-fi. But not horror."

In front of the theater, he surveyed the choices while she did the same.

They both chose the same one, her voice echoing his by a beat. He met her gaze, both brows lifted.

She grinned. And led the way inside, denim hips swaying.

A smile tugged at the corner of his mouth. He liked this idea better by the minute.

The mall shops were closed when they got out of the movie. So she took him to Walmart instead. The break seemed to settle him. And he was able to get everything he needed at prices that didn't make his head hurt, or so he said.

Afterward he wanted to take her to a nice steak dinner. They compromised on a decent dinner, and then she drove them back to their room, where they both fell asleep watching a *Breaking Bad* marathon.

Sunday morning he surprised her by joining her in church. She heard him saying The Lord's Prayer, so he'd been involved in religion at some point in his life.

They arrived in San Francisco midafternoon. Grace booked them into another Pinnacle Express, this time two rooms. JD looked out over the city and said it looked familiar. She refrained from asking how.

Her friend came through with a value for the watch of sixty to ninety thousand, depending on the condition of the watch. Rather than rush out to find a jewelry store, JD suggested another movie, followed by dinner in Chinatown.

Monday morning she knocked on JD's door. He let her

in. The drapes were open to a view of the bay and a slice of the Golden Gate Bridge. He wore his new jeans and a blue knit shirt that brought out the green of his eyes.

"How are you doing this morning?"

He ignored the question. "I told you the city felt familiar. I went downstairs and gathered up some brochures. Nothing stood out to me, except to confirm I know the city. For the last hour I've been scouring the *San Francisco Chronicle*, looking through back articles hoping something would click." He shook his head, indicating a lack of success. "I must wear glasses. It was hard to focus on the computer."

"It's the concussion." When he just shook his head, she moved on. "Are you ready to go?" They had a meeting with her friend Doug at the FBI. "We're a little early, but I don't know the area."

"Sounds good." He closed up the computer.

She considered taking a cab, because driving in San Francisco was insane. Parking was worse and required you have an offshore account. But she preferred to have her own vehicle.

Downstairs JD held the door for her and then walked around to slide in beside her. The roomy Escape felt cramped, with his big body taking up most of the space. His scent filled the air around them. To distract herself from the fact that only inches separated her from him, she watched as he took in the sights of the city.

"Anything look familiar?" she asked.

"All of it." He confirmed. "Just like with the brochures. I know the layout of the town. I can tell you where the theater district is. Where to get great seafood. But I don't know in what context I know it. Whether I lived here, worked here, traveled here. It's all a blank."

"Don't force it," she cautioned him. "The doctor said you should let the knowledge come to you."

"I'm trying." He leaned his head back, closed his eyes.

She glanced at the GPS and saw they were nearing their destination.

"Head for the Pinnacle Hotel," JD said. He opened his eyes and explained, "It's near Union Station, only a few blocks from Golden Gate Avenue, and there's a Sullivan's Jewels in the lobby. I want to see if they can give me a more exact appraisal."

"Okay." Grace checked the Cartier strapped to her wrist and decided they had time. At the hotel she pulled into valet parking, gathered her purse and jacket and exited, handing the attendant her keys before joining JD. He placed his hand on the small of her back and escorted her inside.

"Good afternoon, sir," the doorman greeted him. The Pinnacle Hotel was the five-star version of the Pinnacle Express. The liveried doorman held the door for them to enter.

Inside, a stunning water feature welcomed them. The lobby buzzed with activity as people came and went and stopped to conduct business or simply to chat.

JD didn't linger, escorting her directly into Sullivan's Jewels. The store had a traditional feel. Everything gleamed, from the dark woods and glass display cases, to the gold-and-crystal accessories. And inside the cases: sparkle, sparkle, sparkle.

"Good afternoon, sir." A personable young man in his twenties crossed the floor to greet them. "I'm Christopher. How can I help you today?"

"I'd like to get a watch appraised." JD held up the watch she'd given back to him on the trip across the lobby.

"Certainly, sir. May I ask, was there something wrong with the piece?"

"No. I'm thinking of selling it."

"Of course. We can handle that for you." The young

man assured him. "This way, please." He directed them to a private room furnished with leather chairs and a small table. "Please wait here. Can I get you some refreshments? Water? Coffee?"

"No, thanks. If we could make this quick, I'd appreciate it." JD slid into a leather chair. "We have to leave for an appointment in thirty minutes."

"Absolutely, sir. I'll get with the manager and be back in a few minutes."

"Well, you can't fault the service." Grace sank into her own chair. "He's eager, but I don't get a bad vibe off him."

"It's a reputable store. We'll get a fair appraisal here. Too bad they won't actually buy it. He didn't mention proof of purchase, but I don't see Sullivan's cutting corners."

"Me neither." She sighed, suffering from diamond envy. "We strolled by some gorgeous pieces."

"Huh." She felt his gaze like a touch as it ran over her. "You don't strike me as being big on bling."

"I'm not usually," she agreed. "But I don't generally spend so much time in jewelry stores. All this temptation coming my way, I might become a convert."

"If it turns out I'm rich, when this is over you can pick something out and I'll get it for you as a bonus."

"I'm not hinting, JD. You're already paying me when it's not necessary. I don't need a bonus on top of a wage."

"A bonus isn't about need." Elbow propped on the table, he massaged his temples with one hand. "It's about appreciation."

"Are you okay?"

"I'm fine. I think I've been to this hotel before. My head is throbbing and I've noticed a pattern. My head hurts more when my mind is struggling to assimilate something it recognizes but can't place."

"Wow, that could be helpful." And painful, though it

made sense in a way. "If you think you've been to the hotel, maybe someone at the front desk would remember you."

"Doubtful. Do you know how many people must go through here in a year?"

"You're probably right." But it might be worth a try if time allowed. In an investigation you followed up on every lead. She'd gotten results when the odds were worse. "Why don't you close your eyes while we wait?"

"Don't baby me, Grace."

She rolled her eyes. As if that was possible.

To keep from fussing at him, she texted Doug to let him know she and JD were in the area and would be on time for their appointment. Doug texted back to come on over, he could see them at any time.

"Doug is ready for us when we finish here," she passed on to JD. She snapped a picture of his profile and then requested he look at her. Once he complied, she snapped a facial shot and forwarded both to her friend.

"What are you doing?" JD demanded.

"I sent your pictures to Doug. Maybe he can get started without us."

"Good idea." The news perked him up. "We'll give it five more minutes and then leave. We can always come back."

Christopher returned a few moments later. "My manager is dealing with a delivery. He won't be able to examine the watch in the time you have. I can make an appointment for you, or I can give you a receipt and we'll have the appraisal ready for you when you pick up the watch."

JD showed no reaction as he held out his hand for the watch. "We'll try back after our appointment. I'm not sure how long we'll be."

"Of course. We're open until six."

JD escorted Grace from the store.

"Why didn't you leave it? It would only be for a short while. And we have to come back here for the car."

"This is all I have in the world." He handed her the watch. "I prefer to keep it with me." He made for the front doors. "It would be different if we weren't about to talk to the FBI. I'm hoping they can give me a name and I can learn about who I am without appearing a sick fool in public."

For the love of Pete, save her from the male ego. He didn't want to be at a disadvantage in front of the sales force. She should have guessed this was about control. Hopefully, this meeting would provide some answers.

Sighing, she gave in. They could always come back if the FBI failed to produce his identity.

She tucked her arm through his. "You're not sick, you're memory-challenged."

He grinned at her, the smile flashing a never before seen dimple. And her heart tilted just a little.

CHAPTER SIX

"Your name is Jackson Hawke," Doug Allen announced moments after escorting JD and Grace into an interview room. Of average height and weight, with average features and average brown hair in the expected FBI black suit, Doug waved for them to take seats.

JD let the name sink in, waited for it to trigger a flood of memories. All it brought was a sledgehammer beating in his head. An acknowledgment, of sorts, of its familiarity.

"Oh, my God." Grace breathed.

He glanced her way to find her staring at him wide-eyed.

"What?"

"Jackson Hawke. Oh, my gosh, JD. You're a billionaire." Her eyes narrowed as she ran her gaze over him. "You shaved off your goatee. And you're bigger in person. You're not missing." She turned that intense regard to Doug. "He's not a missing person, or I would have put it together."

Billionaire? Goatee? JD ran his fingers over his clean-shaven chin, still reeling from hearing his name. Nothing else seemed to compute.

"No." Doug confirmed. His alert gaze, which was anything but average, landed on JD. "There's no record of a missing-persons report. But he is part of an ongoing investigation in Las Vegas—an assault."

She sat up straighter at that news. "That must be when he was stabbed."

"That matches the report. I have some of the details here." Doug pushed a file across the table. "You doing okay, Mr. Hawke?"

JD clutched for Grace's hand under cover of the table, relaxed a little when her fingers curled around his. "I'm fine. It's a lot to take in."

"I'm sure it is. You're an important man, Mr. Hawke—"

"JD," he cut in. "Please call me JD."

"Of course, JD. I haven't broadcast this news yet, but the tech that helped with the face recognition probably has. I expect my bosses will appear soon. Let me just say now, the FBI is happy to lend any assistance we can. Are you under a medical doctor's care?"

"Better, I'm under Grace's care." He didn't feel like an important man. Didn't particularly want to deal with the FBI top brass. But he was grateful for their help, so he'd do what he had to.

"Those are pretty good hands to be in." Doug joked. "She always had the best scores in first aid."

"You did okay." Grace shot back. The friendship between the two was an easy camaraderie.

"I was better at putting holes in than plugging them up."

"Doug is a crack shot," Grace explained. She squeezed JD's hand, a sign her chitchat was intended to give him time to assimilate all he'd learned. At least that's how he took it. "The military tried to recruit him for sniper duty."

"Yeah, not my thing." Doug tucked his hands in his pockets. "I'm not afraid to use my weapon, but being a sniper is too premeditated for my taste. Your game 'Rogue Target' is pretty intense."

"My game?"

"You were right, JD," Grace answered. "You are a geek. A supergeek. You create digital video games. 'Pinnacle' was your first, some argue your best. It launched you into the big leagues against Sony and Nintendo. 'Unleashed' is currently the number one game in the world, and number two is 'Rogue Target,' which came out last Christmas."

"You own Pinnacle Enterprises," Doug informed him. "An entertainment conglomerate. As well as Pinnacle Games, you own TV and radio stations, Pinnacle Comics, Pinnacle Hotels and the Strikers football team in Las Vegas. Your net worth is in excess of ten billion."

"That's right." Grace tapped a finger off her forehead. "Pinnacle Enterprises. That's why the hotel looked so familiar today. You own it. And the others we've been staying in."

"You have a penthouse suite at the Pinnacle here in town. As well as in Las Vegas and New York. From what I've found, you have no residences outside the hotels. Your official address is your corporate address in Las Vegas."

He had no home. For some reason that rang true.

A knock sounded at the door and it opened to admit a tall man, rounding around the middle. He had sharp brown eyes and steel-gray hair.

"Doug," he said, his voice as deep as he was tall. "I hear we have a celebrity in the house today."

"Yes, sir. This is Jackson Hawke and my friend Grace Delaney. Mr. Hawke is experiencing a memory lapse. We were able to assist him by providing his identity. JD, Grace, this is Ken Case, Special Agent in Charge."

"I'm glad we could help. We've met a time or two at charity events around town."

"I'm sorry. I don't remember you."

"Not a problem." Ken drew out a chair and sat. "I'll be truthful. They were brief introductions. You probably wouldn't recall in any case. How did you come to lose your memory?"

Grace gave a brief rundown of events, managing to get the facts across without making him sound like a felon or a fool. Quite a talent she had there.

"The doctor is hopeful I'll get my memory back within a couple of weeks." JD added in the hopes of minimizing how lame he felt. He was a billionaire, and right this minute he couldn't hold two thoughts together at the same time.

"With the new information from the Woodpark sheriff's office yesterday, my theory is that after the altercation at the Red Wolf Tavern, the man who accosted JD followed him, ran him off the road and robbed him."

Ken nodded, his eyes speculative as they assessed Grace. "It's a likely scenario. Nice to meet you, Grace. Doug has mentioned you in passing. How did the election go?"

"I lost." Blunt and to the point, Grace didn't sugarcoat her response.

"Too bad. I have to think it's their loss." Ken appeared impressed with Grace, too. "Has Doug tried to recruit you to the wonderful world of the FBI?"

"He has." A tinge of red tinted Grace's cheeks. She wasn't immune to the attention of the head man. "And I'll admit I've been tempted. But I've lived my entire life moving at the whim of the navy, first as a military brat and then as an enlisted. For once I'd like to be able to choose where I live and what I do."

"Hard to argue with that." He stood. "If you change your mind, let me know. We'll talk."

"Thank you, I will."

"In the meantime she works for me." JD stood, as well. His head hurt and he was ready to go. "Can I take this report with me?"

"Of course." Doug moved to hold the door.

"Good luck." Ken offered his hand. "I hope you get your memory back soon. I want you to know you can count on the discretion of this office." After shaking hands, he took off.

With the exit in sight, JD subtly ushered Grace in that

direction. Doug walked with them. JD longed to escape, but he owed the man. "Thank you for your help. It's a huge relief to have a name to claim."

They stepped into the hall.

"You're seriously going to pass up a career in the FBI because you're tired of traveling?" Doug nudged Grace in the shoulder. "You were going to do your twenty."

"I know. It's different now I'm out. It's not even the traveling. There's still a large part of the world I want to see. But I want my own place. I want a sense of permanence."

"I know your dad left you some money. Buy a house somewhere, make it your base and come to work for the FBI. You'll have the continuity you want and a great career, as well."

She rolled her eyes at Doug's insistence. "I'll think about it. But don't get your hopes up. I really want a home."

"Sherry gives me that, wherever I am. She was hoping to get together, do some catching up."

JD tensed at the suggestion. Doug seemed like a nice guy, but JD wasn't up to socializing at the moment. Of course, he could let Grace go on her own. Except, no, the idea of being without her cinched the tension tighter.

Impossible. Jealousy was beneath him. He knew it to the soles of his feet. Grace would call it another clue. He just accepted that he didn't envy. He got his own, bigger and better than anyone else's.

Good thing he was a billionaire.

"I would love that, but I can't this trip. Maybe in a couple of weeks. I bet she's getting big. Only two months to go, Daddy."

Doug turned a little pale.

Was it petty of JD to feel a little satisfaction?

Grace laughed. "You'll be fine." She gave him a hug. "Thanks for your help."

"I'm glad I could be of assistance." He shook JD's hand, slapped him on the arm. "Nice to have met you."

"You've met a shell." JD pointed out.

"JD!" Grace exclaimed.

But the bitter comment didn't faze the other man.

"You're in there. And who knows, this may be the better man. Either way, Grace is a pretty good judge of character. If she's willing to put up with you, you must be worth knowing."

JD glanced at Grace. She stood with her hands braced on her hips eyeing the two of them. Finally he nodded. "I believe in Grace."

"So do I." Doug jutted his chin in acknowledgment before reaching for the door handle. "Take care of our girl."

And now he did feel petty.

"That was rude." Grace left him to call the elevator. "And after he went out of his way to help you."

"It was his job to help me." JD—Jackson—slapped the file folder against his leg.

"Maybe. But without his help you'd have had to go through a lot of red tape and waited a week or more for half the information you got." The elevator arrived and she stepped inside. "He didn't have to have the information ready when we walked in the door or give you a copy."

"So he's a good guy." He punched the button for the lobby. "I get it."

"Do you?"

"I said thank you."

"And then you disrespected everything he did with a dismissive comment."

She'd been hurt and embarrassed when he cut Doug off. It felt personal.

And why wouldn't it? Doug was her friend, doing a

favor for her. He'd provided JD with the information he'd been looking for only to take a hit.

JD—Jackson—said nothing.

She reached the glass doors of the building entrance and fisted her way through. JD followed, flinching from the light. He shifted to put the sun at his back.

She spied the frown lines at the corners of his eyes and the anger fizzled away. How could she forget that he was in pain? An hour ago he'd confessed it got worse when his brain tried to connect his past with the present. He must be in agony.

The way he interacted with others without giving away his condition amazed her.

He stood, shoulders back, chin up, braced to take on the world. While speaking with the FBI, he'd handled himself with such quiet confidence she doubted Doug or Special Agent Case noticed he suffered from a massive head injury. Well, until the end when he got surly.

"Come on." She strolled to the quick mart on the corner.

He kept pace. The fact he didn't bother to ask where they were going confirmed her suspicion. It was all he could do to deal with the pain.

In the small market she found a pair of sunglasses with extra dark lenses and carried them to the counter. She started to pay, but JD drew out his new wallet. She'd given him more cash this morning. The clerk removed the tags and JD wore the glasses out of the store.

"Thank you. These help."

"I'm sorry," she said.

"For what?" He started off for the Pinnacle where they'd left the SUV. "You were right. I was rude."

"You were hurting." She caught up to him, and wrapped her arm through his. He stiffened, but she didn't let go. "And, I imagine, a bit disappointed. It would be hard not to hope your memories would come back once you learned your name."

He shrugged. But she saw his jaw tighten.

"You don't have to pretend with me, JD."

He stopped and swung to face her. "What am I going to do, Grace?" His face revealed his distress. "I can't step into the shoes of a billionaire and confess I lost my memory. The whole world would pity me. And that's just the beginning of the problems. I can't run a multibillion-dollar company. Not only would I not know what I was doing, I don't even know who my employees are. Can you imagine the damage I'd do to my own company?"

"The first thing is not to panic." She tugged on his arm, got him walking again. "You don't have to rush into anything. First we'll read through the file, get a feel for who you are. Then we'll go from there. Research your people so you know them when you meet them. It's going to be fine."

A billionaire. Grace kept her gaze facing forward. She would never have guessed. Of course, the hugely expensive watch had been a clue. One she hadn't ignored. She'd done a search for millionaires under forty and went through six months of Forbes magazine.

The problem was he had a reputation for keeping a low profile and protecting his privacy. So there weren't that many photos of him out there to find, except for the odd photo snagged by the paparazzi at social events.

She'd probably looked right at a picture of him while doing her research and not recognized JD.

In all the pictures that came to mind he'd had long hair and a goatee. And his well-toned body must be one of the nation's best-kept secrets, because she'd had no idea he was such a hottie.

Though now that she thought about it, his name had been linked with beautiful actresses and models.

Lucky for her he had no memory of them. Because,

seriously, how did an average girl like her compete with actresses and models? Not that she was actually competing. She was helping him, that was all. They weren't dating or anything.

Good thing. Because he was way out of her league.

He stopped again. Faced her again. "You're going to stay with me?"

"You hired me, remember? I promised you two weeks."

"What about the job with the FBI?"

"I'm not taking a job with the FBI."

"You should. You'd be good at it. Doug wants you to. Case liked you. He'd help you. The job is there if you want it."

"I don't want it."

"Doug had a sound suggestion," he argued, "buy a place, make it your base. It would give you the sense of permanence you crave, yet you'd be free to pursue a career where you can really make a difference."

His insistence gave her pause. Maybe he was trying to give her an out. "So you're releasing me from my promise to help you?"

"No." The denial had no maybe attached to it. He took her hand and began walking again. "But the offer will be there when we're done. You should think about it."

"Maybe I will." How could she not? But it didn't feel right. She craved permanence and to her that meant having a place of her own to go home to each night.

At the hotel he walked right past the valet station. Surprised, she hurried to catch up.

"Where are you going?"

"Supposedly I have a room here. I want to check it out."

"Without any identification?"

"I'm betting they know me. You suggested it yourself earlier."

The law enforcement officer in her cringed at the notion of the hotel letting just anyone into JD's—Jackson's—suite. But then he wasn't just anyone. He was Jackson Hawke. His identity hadn't completely sunk in. She'd taken a billionaire to Walmart. Now that was cringe-worthy.

She matched her stride to his as they crossed the marble floor of the huge lobby. The furnishings were modern, the art abstract. As they drew closer to registration, she noted there was a line to check in both for regular guests and for VIPs. She glanced at JD's profile, wondering what he would do. Would the owner of the hotel stand in line?

"Good afternoon, Mr. Hawke. It's good to see you again." Ah. Saved by the bell. In this case, the bell captain. "May I assist you with luggage today?"

"No, thank you, Watkins." JD replied smoothly. "I prefer to go directly to my rooms."

"Of course. Let me get your key for you." Watkins stepped around the registration desk and quickly returned with a keycard he presented to JD. "We were not advised you'd be staying with us. Your suite is ready as always, but there are no refreshments. I'll take care of that immediately."

"Thank you, Watkins." JD shoved the key into his pocket. "Perhaps you'll join us first. You can tell my companion, Ms. Delaney, of all the hotel's features on the way to our room."

"Certainly, sir." Chest puffed out with pride, he ushered her and JD to the elevators where he inserted a keycard before pushing the button for the top floor. "As with all Pinnacle Hotels, the building is modeled after the silver sphere in 'Unleashed,' Mr. Hawke's first game. It has thirty floors representing the thirty levels of the game. Each floor is smaller than the floor below it, creating the rising pinnacle. We have a shopping mall, a salon and spa, a gym complete with sauna, a pool and some of the best restaurants in the city."

"Everything a girl could want," Grace mumbled, over-whelmed by what JD owned.

"Including diamonds," Watkins agreed. "Sullivan's Jew-els has a store in the lobby."

"We noticed." She smiled thinly, her shoulders going back. Was he inferring she was with JD because he could buy her diamonds?

"Watkins," JD said softly from beside her, "You aren't insulting my guest, are you?"

The chill in his voice sent a shiver down her spine.

"No, sir." The man paled. "Never. I cherish my job. Ev-eryone at the Pinnacle does. I would never disrespect you or your guest." He turned to her. "I apologize if I offended. I just know my wife drools over Sullivan's displays when-ever she comes by."

"They do have lovely items." She conjured a smile, em-barrassed she'd overreacted. "No harm done."

JD lifted one dark brow.

Watkins cleared his throat. "I bought my wife a neck-lace from one of Rett Sullivan's collections for our twenty-fifth wedding anniversary. She wears it every chance she gets."

"A wise choice, I'm sure," JD stated, letting the poor guy off the hook.

The elevator doors opened feeding them into a large foyer. In the middle of the room, a glass pedestal table housed a towering flower arrangement in various shades of blue. Three archways led deeper into the suite. Wat-kins pressed a button on a remote, and royal blue drapes opened to display a glass wall highlighting the San Fran-cisco skyline.

"I'll see that refreshments are sent up." Watkins re-placed the remote and returned to the elevator. "May I make reservations at the steak house for you both? Or per-haps you prefer sushi tonight?"

"The steak house," JD decided. "At eight."

"Very good, sir. Please call me if you need anything." The elevator doors closed and he was gone.

"I'm sorry if he upset you." JD took her hand.

"It was a foolish reaction." She pulled away, moving toward the skyline. "I guess all this glamour—" she swept an arm out to indicate the posh suite "—is throwing me a bit. I'm not used to penthouse suites."

The slick, modern feel of the furnishings downstairs were repeated here, but where the blue was an accent color downstairs, it dominated here. The chairs and sofa were large, white and built for comfort, despite the sharp lines of their design. A low glass coffee table seemed to float atop a blue rug swirled through with silver and black.

Across the way stood a dining table that looked as if it came from the captain's mess of the *U.S.S. Enterprise* and was large enough to seat half the crew. Beyond was a chef's dream. The gourmet kitchen gleamed with copper and stainless steel.

And all of it opened onto the world.

"This is spectacular, JD. I don't know how to take it all in."

She felt his heat behind her and then he was turning her to face him. He lifted her chin on the edge of his hand until her gaze met his.

"How do you think I feel? I own all this. It blows my mind." He released her chin to run his hand through his hair. "Almost literally. My head feels like it's about to explode."

"I'm sorry. I'm making this about me and that's just wrong." How could she forget this was about him? So she experienced a little discomfort. It was nothing to what he suffered. She cupped his face, stared into his eyes, automatically checking his pupils. They were even but pain lurked there. "We should go back to our hotel, let you rest before we move in here."

Annoyance flooded the green irises. "I told you not to baby me." He retreated to the dining table with his folder from the FBI.

"Then stop making me the bad guy." She gritted her teeth at his obstinacy, swept over and grabbed the folder. "You have a head trauma. Even without the loss of memory, it's going to take days to recuperate. You've learned enough until some of the pain has subsided. With the concussion you probably can't read it anyway. And, no, you probably *don't* wear glasses. I know you don't want to keep hearing it, but a concussion isn't something you can dismiss. It can mess with your vision."

Tucking the folder under her arm, she strolled to the kitchen. She set her purse on the open counter separating the kitchen and dining room and opened the full-size refrigerator. No water, but Watkins had warned them there were no refreshments stocked. In fact, the refrigerator was off, so she turned it on and then moved to the cupboards, where she found a square glass made of fine crystal and ran water into it.

"Drink." She set the glass on the counter. "You need to stay hydrated. I find when I'm taking pain medicine it helps to drink lots of water."

He stalked up to the counter, pushed the water aside and held out his hand. "Give me the folder."

"No."

"I'm the boss."

"Except when it affects your health. Then I have veto power. Veto."

"Grace."

"JD." Shoot, shoot. She really needed to remember to use his name. Now she'd lost her edge. Pretending she hadn't, she lifted her chin and countered. "Jackson."

He pressed his lips together. "You can call me JD."

"No, we both need to get used to Jackson."

He couldn't argue with that, so he didn't. But his hand still demanded the folder. Stubborn.

"Okay." She took a page from the folder, glanced at it and set it in front of him. "Read me the last paragraph."

He picked up the paper, looked at it, moved it forward, moved it back. "It's referencing the Las Vegas property."

"Yes. Now read the address."

He scowled at the paper, then tossed it down. "Maybe I do need glasses."

"No glasses, no contacts. Not according to your California driver's license." She tucked the page back in the folder. "It's the concussion, Jackson. It's not a weakness, it's just something you have to get through. I know it chafes, but right now resting is the best thing you can do to help yourself."

His eyes narrowed and focused intently upon her. Gaze locked on her, he prowled around the end of the counter, the action so predatory she forced her feet not to retreat.

When he got within a foot and kept coming, she planted a hand on his chest. It didn't stop him. He clasped her hand, drew it down to the side and invaded her space.

"What are you doing?" She reared back.

"This." He lowered his head and took her mouth with his.

She stiffened. This was not a good idea. But he stood back, claiming her with his mouth only. He lulled her by taking it slow, keeping it easy. He tilted his head to the perfect angle. His lips were moist, soft, mobile, exerting the right amount of pressure. He lingered, seducing her slowly, until she deepened the kiss by stepping into him.

His arms came around her pulling her against him and his tongue swept over her bottom lip seeking entrance. Closing her eyes, she sank into sensation. Her surrender motivated him to heighten the caress to the next level, building heat and passion until she strained against him, wanting to be closer, needing more.

She forgot to breathe and didn't care. His touch mattered, his taste. A silly thing like air could wait.

He eased back. Chest heaving, he kissed her on the temple. Then released her.

She blinked at him. Was he stopping? Now? Uh-uh. She stepped into him again. This time he caught her hands to keep her from touching him. He shook his head, moved away.

"What the heck, JD?"

He reached for the glass of water and drained it. "You'll have to forgive me. I didn't mean for it to go so far. After days of lacking memories and feeling like an invalid, I needed to do something that made me feel good and that I'm good at."

She went still. "You used me?"

CHAPTER SEVEN

"YOU USED ME?" The stricken expression on Grace's face ricocheted through JD.

"It wasn't like that." He tried to dismiss his blunder. "Come on, let's see what the rest of this place has to offer."

He reached for her arm, but she yanked it away.

"I'm sorry, Grace." He shifted closer and she shifted away. He had to make this right. "I didn't mean to use you."

"We talked about keeping our relationship professional."

"Yes." He cleared his throat. "I know."

"So how did you mean it?" She cocked her head, blue eyes icy cold. "Is this one of my duties? Am I to make myself available for the occasional kiss whenever you feel the need to show your prowess? Because, oh, yeah, you are accomplished. I got hot, I got bothered."

"Grace, you can stop. I feel bad, okay?"

"I just need to know what my job duties entail. Am I supposed to moan, to give you audible cues?"

Anger flared. She didn't need to make such a big deal out of a little kiss. So frustration got the best of him and he lashed out, trying to grab a moment of joy at something he was good at. After the kiss in the bed that first night, he knew they were compatible.

He should have known she'd blow it out of proportion. The women he knew would just go with it. Hell, they'd make the most of the moment. But not by-the-rules Grace.

She needed to talk it to death, set parameters, probably write up procedures.

He wanted to order her to forget it, but the heft of that lead balloon wouldn't fly. He had enough brains not to let his defensiveness get the better of him.

"Can't we just put this behind us?" He tried for a charming smile. "I probably have a game console here somewhere. We can play a bit, relax. All very restful stuff."

She simply stared at him. "You know, JD, I've given you a lot of leeway. Let things go because I know you're hurting and that the loss of memory and concussion can make things confusing. But I draw the line at being used as a sensual punching bag. If that's a condition of helping you, I'm going to have to retract my offer of assistance."

"Sensual punching bag?" he repeated, offended by her attitude. "You said it was good."

"I said I got hot and bothered," she corrected, easing some of the burn only to ratchet it back up by demanding, "Is that the point?"

"No. Look." He held his hands up in surrender. "Hands-off. It won't happen again."

"I'm not sure I can trust you. Because it happened before, didn't it? In bed that first night."

He rubbed a finger over his throbbing temple. "It just happened."

"It just happened?" she repeated incredulously. "How? Tell me, JD, how does a kiss just happen?"

"Right. I can see you're not going to be happy until I spill the whole humiliating story."

Arms crossed over her chest, she lifted one dark eyebrow urging him to get to it already.

"I guess you deserve an apology for that, as well." To delay the inevitable he walked around the counter and stood facing her with his hands braced on the marble. "I woke up and you were sitting next to me in the bed. You probably meant to test my vitals, check on the current state of the presidency and so on. Anyway, I was half-asleep and you were there and it happened."

"That's your story? You woke up and it happened?"

"Yeah," he pushed back. His actions had been instinctive. "I was half-asleep and you looked sexy with your hair all mussed up. I reached for you without thinking about it."

With blue eyes narrowed, she studied him as she contemplated his story.

Really? As if he'd make up being a lecherous fool.

"And what happened next?"

Geez, he knew five-year-olds who asked fewer questions. Okay, maybe not, but he wished she'd bury the bone already. How was he supposed to defend himself properly when it hurt to think?

"Once I came to my senses, I broke it off. You checked my vitals and I moved to the other bed." He glanced away, and straightened the folder on the counter. "That was the end of it."

"That's everything?"

"I apologized."

"An apology isn't always enough. You can't be doing this, JD."

"I've said I'm sorry, and I am. I don't want you to quit. I know ours is a professional relationship. And I respect that. But I'll tell you this, having you around calms me. You ground me in a world out of control. Ever since I realized my memory was gone, it's all about getting it back, finding my identity. Everything is focused out.

"Kissing you is something I did for me. It brought me peace. It brought me joy. It took me out of myself and into you. And I am sorry if it hurts you, but it just may have saved my sanity. So do I regret it? No."

"I don't know what to say to that. Because a kiss involves two people, JD. It can't just be about you."

Oh, no, she didn't. He leaned halfway over the counter. "Don't pretend you weren't right there with me."

Flames flared in her eyes, confirmation she couldn't deny her full participation. She picked up her purse, and swung the strap over her shoulder. "I think we need a break from each other. I'm going back to the other hotel. I'll stay there tonight and bring our stuff over in the morning."

She swung around and headed toward the arch leading to the foyer.

No. This wasn't what he wanted at all.

"Grace," he called out. "You don't have to go."

"I really do."

But she stopped and came back. His spirits lifted. She wasn't leaving him, after all.

She grabbed the folder. "I'm taking this with me." Without waiting for a response she headed out again. "Enjoy your steak dinner."

A moment later the door closed with a distinct thud.

He wasn't feeling any joy now.

Wait, the women he knew? That was strange. Not that the women in his past had little in common with Grace— he was getting used to the certainty without foundation. But he'd experienced no pain with the thought.

If Grace was here, she'd probably claim it was a sign of his mind healing.

Testing, he tried focusing on his last girlfriend; he opened his mind and tried to picture her here. Pain shattered through his head. Nausea curled in his stomach. Dots danced before his eyes. He dropped onto a dining room chair and lowered his head between his knees.

Sweet merciful dog biscuits. As the ringing in his ears began to fade, he conceded. Maybe he did need to rest.

* * *

Grace let herself into the Pinnacle Express hotel room and tossed her purse on the bed. She needed this time alone. JD had her so off-kilter she didn't know how to act.

Her mind buzzed, refusing to settle on a single thought. She was flustered. And a master-at-arms never got flustered.

She hadn't signed up for this. She'd agreed to a professional relationship.

Kissing did not belong in a professional relationship.

She dropped into the armchair and looked out on the pool. It was empty, the cool weather chasing most guests away. But in the far corner a small family enjoyed the bubbling spa.

Her bubbling emotions were much less fun.

The memory of their first kiss rolled on the screen in her head. The temptation of him sprawled nearly naked on the bed, the surprise of him reaching for her, the tenderness in his touch, the sensual feel of his mouth on hers. And him pushing her away.

Except she wasn't one for self-deception. And she didn't miss the fact he was the one to pull away in both encounters. She obviously had no restraint when it came to him. And, just as obviously, he did. So she'd given in to her instincts to flee, to put time and distance between them. If she was smart, she'd keep going.

Yet she'd committed to helping him.

And she had. He now knew his name. Jackson Hawke, billionaire. The truth was he didn't need her anymore. Sure, he felt vulnerable, but he had grit and fortitude. He'd be fine. His people could give him the support he needed to find his way in the corporate world. In fact, they'd be better qualified than her by far.

But she took pride in keeping her promises. And she

understood the desire to prep before putting yourself in an unknown situation.

She liked helping him. Being honest, she admitted he'd helped her, too. In the beginning the challenge of his situation gave her something to focus on at a time when she was at a loss.

The problem was he kept breaking the rules.

The kiss changed things. Her response changed everything.

She'd worked with men too long not to know they pushed the limits at every opportunity. She'd been kissed on the job before, but she'd managed to correct the misguided fool's perception of their relationship and still work effectively with him.

Not with JD. No chance of pretending he hadn't melted her insides. He'd called her on that bit of self-deception.

Best to end their connection now. The obvious chemistry between them would only complicate their working relationship. Because unlike the other instances of men crossing the line with her, she actually liked kissing JD. A lot.

She pushed to her feet and began gathering JD's things into the bag he'd bought. Cheap things he'd probably never use. Another reason to end things between them. They were from different worlds. He was high finance, glitz and glamour at its peak. She was a military brat, a law enforcement officer with an uncertain future.

And she hadn't missed the fact he had no residence beyond hotel suites. They really had nothing in common.

So why did she miss him so much?

JD missed Grace as soon as she walked through the door. She was the only constant in the short memory of this life.

Jackson Hawke, billionaire. How freaky was that?

He wandered the suite, taking in the luxurious accommodations. There were three bedrooms and five bathrooms, including a master bath as big as the sleeping rooms he and Grace had stayed in the past few nights.

It all felt so foreign.

More familiar was the computer room, which looked like a James Bond command center. And the media/game room, furnished theater-style in dark gold, deep brown and comfortable leather. Sliding into the center seat, he ran his hand over the console. Oh, yeah, he felt right at home.

Too bad he had no one to share the moment with.

Missing Grace, he continued to wander. He found a closet with a full wardrobe of clothes. Everything from jeans to a tuxedo. All in his size. Poking around, he pulled open a drawer and found a safe. He pressed the switch at the bottom and a palm plate lit up.

He stared down at it.

"Here goes nothing." He placed his palm on the plate. Tumblers clicked and the plate beneath his hand lifted.

Guess that settled the doubts percolating in the back of his head that the FBI had made a mistake. Something eased in him at the confirmation. Flipping the lid, his eyebrows popped up to his hairline. Cash, lots of it, filled half the box, which was about the size of a large laptop computer but about eight inches deep. A few pieces of masculine jewelry were tossed in the other half, including another watch—expensive, but not as nice as the Cartier. Under the jewelry were some papers, but he didn't bother looking at them.

He wouldn't be able to read them anyway.

Ah, score. No need to be able to read to recognize the passport he plucked from a plastic sleeve at the back. His brows rocketed again when he opened it to find it nearly full with stamps from foreign lands. It appeared he was well traveled.

He looked around to share it with Grace—actually

walked into the next room looking for her before he recalled she'd left. So he reached into his pocket for a phone. Only he didn't have one. Damn concussion, messing with his head. It wasn't the first time he'd blipped on something so obvious. This one, like the others, he'd keep to himself.

Missing Grace, and grumpy over the fact he couldn't contact her, he returned to the closet, did a quick count of the cash—three hundred thousand dollars—snagged a bundle worth five thousand and then closed and reset the safe.

A knock came at the door. He answered to find housekeeping had arrived to stock the suite. He left them to it and headed downstairs. At the concierge desk Watkins came to attention.

"Mr. Hawke, how can I help you?"

"I have a few things I need. I'm hoping you can help me."

"Of course."

JD laid out his requests and received the same compliant response. Yeah, he could get used to this. When he finished, he gave Watkins a few bills to cover the costs and another for a tip.

Then he strolled across the lobby to Sullivan's Jewels. Maybe he could find something that would help Grace accept his apology. But he'd have to be thoughtful about it. He didn't want to upset her and end up owing her another apology.

Grace's cell phone rang startling her from a light doze as she watched TV. "Hello."

"Hi, Grace." A deep male voice came down the line.

"JD?" Her heartbeat quickened. A reaction she dismissed as surprise. She didn't think he had her number.

"Yeah. I had Watkins pick up a phone for me."

Of course he did. "Did you need something?"

"Yes. I was wondering if you had a chance to read through the file."

Her gaze went to the file open on the bed next to her. "I flipped through it. Doug gave you the highlights. I'll do a search for your key personnel tonight and we can go over the information tomorrow."

"How about tonight? Come back, join me for dinner."

She hesitated, tempted to do just that. The very fact she wanted to explained why she couldn't. "I think it's best if we take this time apart."

"So you said." He sounded disappointed. Or was that wishful thinking? "Let me know if you change your mind."

Grace stormed into Jackson's suite. She powered right through the foyer into the living area. The fact he wasn't there blasted her ire further up the scale.

"Jackson Hawke, show yourself." The sharp demand rolled through the rooms.

"You're back." He appeared in the arched doorway.

"You have some nerve." She tossed her purse on the white couch. "How dare you have me evicted from my room at the Pinnacle Express hotel?"

"Did they upset you?" A frown drew his reddish brown eyebrows together. "I expressly requested they not upset you."

"Oh, the manager was very nice." She paced in front of the window. "As he threw me out of my room. How can that be anything but upsetting? I was so embarrassed."

"They were instructed that you were being upgraded to this hotel. Why would that be embarrassing?"

"Oh, I don't know," she mocked. "Maybe because they now think we're romantically involved and that I'm available at the click of your fingers." Seeking calm she drew in a deep breath, let it out slow. "What's the deal, Jackson?"

"I wanted you here. I owe you a nice steak dinner."

"It was a gross misuse of your authority. I was coming back in the morning. There was no need to go to such drastic measures."

He drew closer until he invaded her space. He stopped short of touching her, though his fingers twitched as if he wanted to. "Why are you calling me Jackson?"

"It's your name." And her way of calling to mind the differences between them. Her chin lifted. No need for him to know that.

"I didn't want you spending your money over there when there's plenty of room here. The place has three bedrooms. We can be apart in separate rooms."

"It's not the same."

"I know. I know. That's the other reason I did it." Giving her a sad smile, he gazed into her eyes and confessed, "I was lonely without you."

Her anger deflated like a pinpricked balloon.

"You were out of line," she declared, unwilling to let him charm her so easily.

"I won't do it again." His fingers feathered over her hand, before he pulled back. "Not without warning you first."

She narrowed her eyes, reproaching him.

He shrugged. "It's the best I can do. And seriously, I couldn't enjoy my steak dinner without you."

"You could have changed the reservation to tomorrow."

"I considered it. But I wanted you here." He held his hand out toward the doorway. "Come, let me show you the rest of the suite."

Her eye landed on his new phone. She picked it up. "You need to be careful what you do. The hotel may let you slide on the bill, but you're still going to need money until you can get new identification and new credit cards. I leave you alone for a few minutes—"

His finger on her lips shushed her. "How about this—

you don't treat me like a child, and I won't treat you like a sensual punching bag. Fair trade?"

An argument sprang to her lips. She bit them together, holding it back.

"Fair trade."

"Good." He smiled and, wrapping his fingers around hers, led her out of the room. "Now, let me show you what I've found."

She tried to work her hand free, but it was a halfhearted attempt, and he ignored her as he moved through the suite showing her bedrooms, an office that rivaled British Command, a media room with a full-size billiard table and finally a master suite to die for.

"OMG." The bathroom took her breath away. The walls were made of glass, thick bricks on the bottom to obscure visibility and preserve privacy, but the top part was clear, blue-tinted glass. The huge walk-in shower was made of quartz rocks and lush, overhead greenery. Multiple showerheads promised a luxurious drenching. When you took a shower, you'd feel as if you were at the top of a waterfall looking down on the world. "Dibs on the shower."

He laughed. "I've already used it. It's quite spectacular."

She poked her head in a sauna. "Is this what you wanted to show me?"

"No. I saved the best for last." He disappeared back into the bedroom. She slowly followed, her feet reluctant to leave the bathroom oasis.

Inside the bedroom he'd disappeared altogether. "Jackson?"

"In here." His head popped out of a closet.

She joined him, stopping on the threshold to blink and take it in. Okay, maybe owning a house was overrated. Maybe she didn't need to own the ground under her feet to consider the space she occupied as home. Because, seriously, she could live in this room.

"Wow. Just wow." Forget sleek and slick in here. Warm wood and creamy marble welcomed her inside. Suits lined one side split by a three-way mirror, while shoes filled the opposite side and down the center ran a marble-topped island with a sink at one end and drawers on all sides. Three chandeliers lit the room and a chaise lounge provided a spot to sit. "I think I'm in love."

"And I think that's the most girlish thing I've heard you say."

"I'm a girl," she defended her reaction.

"Mostly you're a cop."

"Seriously? You're going to go there after the whole kissing incident?"

His expression was total innocence. "I didn't say you weren't pretty."

She scowled, as mad at herself for the surge of pleasure as she was at him for the asinine comment. Shaking a finger at him, she advised, "You may want to stop while you're ahead."

"I'm ahead?" He grinned, flashing his dimple.

"Better watch it," she cautioned. "You didn't care for the consequences the last time you provoked me."

Jackson sobered. "You don't strike me as the type to run from your problems."

"I'm not. But I'm not a martyr either, so I do believe in stepping back to cool off. An occurrence that shouldn't be necessary in a professional relationship. At least not often."

"Okay, okay." He raised his hands in surrender. "Message received. We'll keep it professional. Now, look."

He grabbed her hand and drew her next to him where he stood over an open drawer in the island. She shook her head. The man needed a pamphlet on respecting people's boundaries.

She glanced in the drawer. Oh. "It's a safe." With a palm plate lock. She looked up at him. "Did you try to open it?"

"I did. Watch." He placed his hand on the lock.

She held her breath.

It clicked open.

She grinned around a rush of air. How horrible would it be if he'd only been a Jackson Hawke look-alike? Yeah, it might have been rough explaining their presence in a billionaire's personal suite to the San Francisco Police Department.

And then he opened the safe and all thought left her head. She stared at a stack of cash easily equal to a quarter of a million dollars.

"Good gracious," she breathed clasping her hands behind her back to keep from touching. "Jackpot for you."

"And the cash isn't all that's in here." He pulled out a passport. "This will work for ID right?"

"Yes, it will."

"Good. I had Watkins contact my people in Las Vegas to let them know I lost my wallet. He reported I'd have replacement cards in the morning."

"Sounds like you're all set." She was right, he had done just fine without her. And she wasn't sure how she felt about that.

CHAPTER EIGHT

"Do NOT EVEN think of dodging out on me," he whispered in her ear. "I know that's what you're thinking."

"It's something to consider," she countered, for her benefit as well as his. "You did all this on your own. And you have people now that can help you."

"Which is why I need you now more than ever." He reached for something deep in the vault. "No need to sell my watch." He glanced down at her. "It does have sentimental value now. And I'm keeping the provenance papers on my person, just in case."

"Hopefully nothing like this will happen to you again."

"Hopefully. But I have the stab wound, too. So obviously stuff happens."

"I guess. But you can't live your life based on fear."

"I don't intend to, but there's such a thing as precaution. I'll carry the papers for a while. And I got this for you." He handed her a four-inch square jeweler's box with the name Sullivan's scrawled across the top. "For all your help."

Again her hands went behind her back. "I can't take that."

"Of course you can. I can afford it. I'm getting the sense that being rich comes naturally to me."

She sent him a droll stare. "Being rich and being a jerk are not the same thing."

"Ouch. I probably deserve that."

"No probably about it."

He ignored her. Instead he ran his hand down her arm and pulled her hand around to place the box in her palm. "I want to do this for you. You don't really understand what your help has meant to me. I'm bad at verbalizing it, and yeah, I've messed up a couple of times. I'm nobody to you, a stranger, yet without hesitation you stepped up to help me. Paying my way when you didn't have a job yourself and there were no apparent means of me being able to pay you back."

"There was the watch," she reminded him. "I didn't do anything anyone else wouldn't do." She set the box on the counter and edged away from Jackson until she stood across from him. "And you are paying me."

"You don't even understand how special you are. Let's be clear, I'm paying you for your knowledge and your connections. There's no way to fully pay you for your compassion, your patience, your faith in me. This," he said, pushing the box toward her, "is a mere token of what you deserve. My hope is you'll know my gratitude whenever you wear it. And because it seemed right, it's Cartier."

"Jackson." She stared at him helplessly. A Cartier? It was too much. Of course it was too much. She couldn't take it. Could she?

"It'll go to waste if you don't take it. I'll put it back in the safe and it'll stay there forever."

"No." Her hand moved protectively toward the package before her mind engaged and she curled her fingers closed. But the thought of his gift languishing, forever unopened, seemed wrong. "That would be a waste. You should return it or give it to someone else."

"It isn't meant for someone else. It wouldn't have the same value. It's for you, or no one."

"Oh, give it to me already." She held her hand out palm up.

His eyes lit up. Knowing better than to say anything, he grandly placed the package in her grasp.

"You are never to tell me how much this cost."

"Rest assured it was below ninety thousand."

Her gaze flew to his face. "It better be well, well below."

"You said not to tell you."

"Oh, my gosh. You are evil." Opening the box, she peaked inside and forgot to breathe. "Oh, my. Oh, JD." She lifted out a thin rope of diamonds set in white gold. "It's beautiful."

"Let me." He took it from her, wrapped it around her right wrist and connected the clasp. "It looks good on you."

"It would look good on a cat." She moved her arm, admiring the flash of the diamonds in the light. It really was too much.

"No going back." Again he seemed to read her mind. "And it'll go really good with the little black dress I got you to wear to dinner."

"What? Oh, no, nothing more." She was talking to his back. "I'm not taking anything else from you."

"Not even the shower?" he said over his shoulder. "Everything is laid out in your room."

"Everything? No. No. No." She dogged his heels. "Jackson, I'm serious. No more."

"I'll be in the game room when you're ready." He stopped and gave her a wink. "Our reservation is at eight." He turned into the game room leaving the door open behind him.

Grace dug in her heels determined not to chase after him any farther. She was an intelligent, competent woman, not a witless fool. He had no power over her. She'd wear an outfit of her own choosing.

Don't look, she warned herself as she entered her room and headed straight for the bathroom. *Pay no attention to the clothes on the bed.*

She might have made it, except the room itself stopped her. Done in white, gold and silver, the decor took her breath away. Decked out all in white, the bed appeared to float. Above it, large gold discs drew your attention up. A silver geometric design in the white carpet was repeated on the ceiling trim. In front of the window a modern sofa and chair in a soft silvery-gold invited her to come sit and relax.

No way was that possible with the clothes strewn across the bed.

Of course she looked.

And her feet betrayed her by taking her closer. Oh, my. He'd gone with the classic little black dress. It lay stretched across the white down-filled duvet. And he nailed her taste to a T. The dress had a boatneck with three horizontal strips of sheer mesh between the neckline and bustline and then again at the bottom of the slightly flared skirt ending with the mesh a few inches above the knee. The dress managed to be both sexy and conservative at the same time.

A pair of peep-toe heels sat on the floor, and a tiny black patent-leather purse rested next to the dress on the bed, along with a box and a bag from Victoria's Secret. For a woman who'd spent a good part of her life in uniform, the ensemble was irresistible.

Still, her resolve may have held except she kept remembering the exotic waterfall shower in Jackson's bathroom. The devious man had connected the two, making her feel she had to wear the dress to have use of his facilities. Heights had never bothered her, and oh, how she longed for a top-of-the-world experience.

And by gosh, she meant to claim it.

If that meant wearing the dress, she'd wear the dress and wear it well. Her legs were one of her best features.

Shouldering her duffel, she left the lovely room and headed straight for Jackson's bathroom. She closed and locked the door. Using the control panel on the outside of the shower she keyed in the number of shower panels—all—and temperature—hot—she wanted. Then she checked out the contents of the Victoria's Secret bag. Shampoo and conditioner and body wash and lotion, all in her favorite orange-blossom scent. Nodding, she stripped and stepped inside.

Water washed over her from all sides.

Heaven.

Well worth a small slice of her pride. For which he'd pay. Oh, yeah, she'd make him sweat for forcing the issue, for stealing kisses and ignoring the rules. And get dessert, as well. Sweet.

The shower grotto ran about seven feet long and five feet deep. About four feet of it was glass bricks topped by clear glass. The other three feet was a stone wall made up of smooth multisize rocks that curved around to create the side of the grotto. A stone bench followed the curve.

Water rained down on her, hot and steamy. She stood on smooth rocks while green fronds draped over the top and sides of the glass partition. The glass bricks came to her bust, safeguarding her modesty. Moving up to the glass, she looked down. The magnificent city spread out before her. In the distance the ocean reflected the clear blue sky and rippled with whitecaps. To her left the Golden Gate Bridge spanned the water to Oakland.

The intoxicating scent of the luxury soaps and shampoos only added to the experience. And made her hair and skin so soft. She never wanted to leave.

The only thing missing was a man to share it with.

Immediately a picture of Jackson sprang to mind. Even in their bare feet he'd tower over her. His broad shoulders would shield her from the brunt of the spray as he kissed her neck.

She turned so the water pulsed against her neck.

And lower. She imagined his hands smoothing away bubbles and his mouth on her body.

When her blood heated to the temperature of the water, he moved them away from the glass to the wide bench and his mouth and hands slid lower yet.

A knock at the door interrupted her fantasy. "Let me know if you need anything." Jackson called out. "The control panel inside the shower includes a phone feature. I plugged my new cell number in for you."

Her eyes popped open.

"I'm fine," she nearly snarled.

Resting on the edge of fulfillment, she glared at the door. What lousy timing. But apropos. She had no business fantasizing about him. Especially after the hands-off speech she gave him.

In retaliation for her traitorous imaginings, she flipped the hot water off first. An icy blast of water hit her heated body. She shivered and quickly keyed off the cold.

"Brr." Outside the grotto she reached for a towel from the stack on a nearby shelf. The thick terry cloth was warm to the touch and the size of a small blanket. She sighed as the warmth enveloped her.

Using a smaller towel—also warmed on the heating rack—she dried her hair and recalled Jackson's comment about being accustomed to wealth. Hmm. More likely it was too easy to give in to the seduction of luxury.

It was okay for him to immerse himself in this world. He belonged here, after all.

She, on the other hand, needed to take care she didn't succumb to the temptation of what couldn't be.

Jackson shot a tiger and swung across the ravine on a tree vine that dropped him short of the opposite side so he fell into a raging river. He caught a ride on a floating log and made it to the other side, but he had a strenuous climb ahead of him.

"I'm ready," Grace announced from the back of the room.

"Me, too. Ah, cagey croc." A crocodile morphed from a log to attack him. "Just one minute," he muttered to Grace as his avatar went after the croc.

"Take your time."

He caught sight of her as she rounded the front of the seats. That brief glance he got of her legs demanded a full-blown perusal. He sat back, ran his gaze from the pink-tipped toes peeking out of her black pumps, up smooth, shapely legs. The dress clung in all the right places, and yes, one of the sheer mesh strips perfectly framed a nice view of her cleavage. A pretty sheen highlighted her lips and eyes. And sweet merciful peaches, she'd mussed her black hair so she looked as if she'd just made love.

"Smokin'."

Amusement lit up her blue eyes. "Me? Or the game?"

"Kak." The game sounded, then announced, "Raptor, you have lost your first life."

"What?" Shifting back to the monitor he saw the croc had eaten him. "Pisser."

"Oh, did you die? Hate when that happens."

"Humph." He might be annoyed with her, except damn, smug never looked so good. "Do you play?"

"Sure. You want to go a round?"

"I'll take you on." The game allowed for a player to play individually or against one or more players. He nodded to the seat next to him, as he reached for the control pad. "Fair warning, I created the game."

"Not now, Jackson." Her hands went to her shapely hips. "We have reservations, remember? Plus, I'm hungry."

"Right. Right." He surged to his feet. "May I say how stunning you look?"

"No, you may not." She turned on her heels and headed out. "That would only be bragging. You coming?"

Following after her, Jackson slowly shook his head. For someone who looked so soft, the woman had no give in her.

The steak-house restaurant went against the futuristic theme of the hotel, going instead with rich, dark woods, marble counters and fine crystal. They offered their clients privacy and range-fed beef. He saw Grace seated and ordered them each a nice glass of wine.

She sipped the wine, savored it on her tongue, then set the glass down.

"Shall I order for you?" He offered.

"I'm a big girl. I can order for myself." She opened the menu and began to scan the choices.

His menu remained on the table. While killing time earlier, he'd checked out the menu online. Better to struggle over the words in his suite than at the restaurant. He hadn't used the top-of-the-line unit in the office. It was password protected, and his head wasn't spitting out any clues to what it might be.

He could not wait until his memory returned.

He'd bought a new tablet at one of the stores in the attached shopping mall. He applauded his decision to make the mall part of the hotel. Travelers often had unexpected needs. He'd certainly found it handy.

He'd enjoyed shopping for Grace. Enjoyed seeing her in the things he'd bought.

The lighting was muted to heighten the sense of privacy, yet as she moved her head to read the menu, light flickered from one spiked tress to the next. She bit her lip in indecision, and he sucked in a breath. White teeth dented plump flesh. It was all he could do to stay in his seat.

More as a distraction than out of need, he opened the menu.

He wouldn't act on his desire. He respected her too much.

Needed her too much, come to that. No matter what she believed.

The waiter appeared. Grace surprised Jackson by ordering the rib eye. He would have pegged her as a salad girl. She kept surprising him. He liked that.

When they were alone again, he sought for a topic of conversation. Easy. "Tell me what you found in my file."

She sat back on her bench seat, and clasped her hands on the table in front of her.

"You were a foster child. Mother died when you were five. Your father was unknown. There was a note in the file that a friend may have knowledge of who he was, but they were unable to locate the friend so no investigation was lodged."

"So I just went into the system?"

"Yes. From what I read, you were passed around to several homes, longest stay was two years. You were quiet and smart, kept to yourself for the most part, but suffered some bullying. A few incidents of cyber retaliation—quite creative, I must say—got you expelled. So you went to three different high schools."

"How many homes overall?"

"Nine."

"Over thirteen years?" It was a lot. He waited for emotions to come—loss, anger, resentment—but he felt nothing. Only the pounding in his head.

"Obviously you had a tough childhood. I can relate, to a degree. Being a military brat, I know how it feels to be uprooted and moved to a new home every few years. How hard it is to start over again and again. You learn to protect yourself."

"I don't remember any of it," he confessed.

She laid her hand over his. "That may be a good thing. With this background, if you lost your memory but remembered your childhood, you would have found it difficult to accept help, however honestly offered."

The food arrived, saving him from the need to reply. He'd also gone with the rib-eye steak and paired it with shrimp. His mouth watered at the aroma coming off the plate. He cut into the steak and found a warm, pink center. The meat melted in his mouth. Across the way he watched Grace savor her first bite and bit back a groan at the ecstatic expression on her face.

She caught him staring and a rush of red rose in her cheeks. She gave a sheepish smile. "It's good."

While they ate, she shared more of what she read in the file. He'd done a stint in juvenile detention for hacking into a school to change grades. Not just his own, apparently, but every student who took English with Mrs. Manning, who he stated was a frigid old crow who got her jollies putting down students to make herself feel superior.

"It sounds like I was doing the world a service. The report seems quite detailed."

"The FBI is thorough."

"So it appears. Can we move past my school years? At least skip to college."

"What makes you think you went to college?"

The question drew his attention away from the peekaboo view of her cleavage. "I didn't go to college?"

"You tell me," she prompted. "Do you remember anything about college?"

He gave it a beat, two. Nothing. "Quit playing with me, Grace."

"Okay. I'm just testing your memory. Despite the hacking incident, you earned a scholarship to Berkeley. You attended for two years. You created your first game there. And it was all uphill from there. As Doug said, you made your first million by the age of twenty-two and your first billion when you were twenty-seven. You own companies and/or properties in fifteen countries. Your net worth is in excess of ten billion. You were *Look* magazine's Man of the Year and *People*'s Sexiest Man Alive the year you made your first billion."

"Very thorough. No wife?"

"No wife. No kids. You were right about that. You're a bit of a player. You've been connected with actresses, models, high-powered executives. Mostly short-term. You have a couple of long-term relationships." She arched one black eyebrow. "If you consider a year long-term."

He lifted one shoulder in a half shrug. "Sounds like I have commitment issues. With my childhood and bankroll, can you blame me?"

"We all have to grow up sometime. And love has to do with trust not your bank account."

"Says the woman who's never been married. How many long-term relationships have you had?" His life was an open book, or more precisely an open file, to her. Turnabout was fair play.

Her pretty lips pursed as she contemplated him. "Three," she finally answered. "If you consider a year long-term."

He laughed. "Gotcha."

"We're talking about you, not me."

"I'm sounding like a sad character. Properties all over the world but no home. Replaceable women. I hope I have good friends."

"I don't know about that, but I did an internet search, and you have a lot of influential acquaintances."

"That's reassuring." The sarcastic comment slipped out. He tried hard not to whine. But the whole situation tore at his patience.

"Sorry."

He shrugged. "Not your fault. Anything about the people I work with?"

"You have four people in your top echelon. Your legal counsel, Ryan Green. Financial advisor, Jethro Calder. And security executive, Clay Hoffman. The three of them go back to your foster days with you. Your associate Sierra Ross is a Harvard attorney. I've just started looking into them. I'll have more tomorrow."

"Good." He finished his wine and asked, "What about the stabbing? You haven't mentioned that."

"Are you sure you want to hear this tonight? We can go over it tomorrow, when you're more rested."

"I want to hear it now."

"Okay. Well, according to the report, you stated a woman you were dating went wacko when you refused to let her spend the night. Her name is Vanessa Miller. She began by throwing things at you, and when you tried to restrain her, she stabbed you with a piece of broken metal frame. Sometime during the altercation, you were able to activate a panic button. She slipped away while security was seeing to you."

"A real winner. I guess I can really pick them." Every word she spoke drilled a nail into his skull.

"Don't judge yourself too harshly." She gave him an out, sympathy strong in her voice. "Dating is a difficult prospect these days. I imagine it's even more so for a man in your position."

He imagined so, too. Truly, how could he know for certain if his date was into him or his money?

"Have the police apprehended her?"

"No. They suggested you beef up your security. Instead, you decided to take a vacation. You took your Harley and went off the grid. That was three weeks ago. Does any of this strike a chord with you?"

Pain streaked down his neck when he shook his head. "It's like hearing a story that happened to someone else.

But if the throbbing in my head is anything to go by, it's dead-on."

"Are you okay?" She leaned forward to study his eyes. "Do you want to head back to the room?"

A glare sent her back into her seat.

"I'm just saying I'm ready when you are."

"You need dessert," he insisted. He wouldn't be the reason her meal was cut short. She deserved this treat for all she'd done for him.

"I don't want dessert."

"All women want dessert. Order some anyway."

Blue eyes narrowed on him. "First of all, I'm not all women. Second, I couldn't even finish my steak. We can leave now."

"I'm fine. And I saw you drooling over the chocolate mousse cake when you were looking at the menu. You know you want some."

As if summoned, the waiter appeared. "May I get you anything else tonight?"

"The lady would like dessert." Jackson answered before Grace could send the man away.

Her eyes flashed with annoyance but she smiled at the waiter. "I'll take a piece of the chocolate mousse cake." She turned her saccharine sweet smile on Jackson. "To go, please."

Leave it to her to find a way around him. Fine with him. He'd been staying for her anyway. The waiter quickly returned with the boxed dessert and the bill. Jackson charged it to his room.

In the elevator on the way to the suite Grace dropped a bomb. "Here's something you need to know. A few years ago you started a foundation for displaced teenagers. They're having a big fund-raiser three days from now. You're scheduled to be there, and from all accounts it's something that's pretty important to you."

"I guess that starts our clock ticking then, doesn't it?" Hearing about his childhood, he was proud of the fact he'd also created a way to help. Which meant facing the world whether he had his memory back or not.

"I'll make sure you're ready," she promised.

He keyed them into the suite. Inside, a handful of pink message slips had been placed on the foyer table. He picked them up and waved them for her to see. "I hope you're right, because ready or not, the world has found us."

CHAPTER NINE

SHE TOOK THE pink message slips from him and returned them to the table. "These can wait until tomorrow. I'm ready for our game. Prepare to go down."

Over the past hour she'd seen how rehashing his past had aged him before her eyes. Pain etched lines around his eyes and a clenched jaw drew tendons tight in his neck. The world may be knocking on the door, but it could wait until tomorrow. Tonight he needed to relax. Whether he liked to admit it or not, he was still healing.

"Now, that's just crazy talk." The tension visibly drained from his shoulders. "Nobody beats the master." Without glancing at the messages he headed for the game room.

"I don't know." She trailed behind him, pretending she didn't notice the nice fit of his dress pants over his firm posterior. "The master is broken. I think I've got a shot."

He stopped suddenly and swung around. Her reflexes were excellent and she stopped short of running into him, but they were still nose to chin. The predatory light in his eyes rooted her to her spot. She could show no weakness.

"Your trash talk won't get to me. I'm not broken, I'm memory-challenged."

She groaned.

"Hey, my instincts and reflexes are as sharp as ever. I've got this."

"Yeah, you keep telling yourself that," she tossed back. He seemed to thrive on the competition. "Just know there will be no mercy when you start whining that you have a concussion." She slid past him, deliberately knocking his shoulder with hers. "I'm going to change. I want to be comfortable when I kick your butt."

"Hmm," he mused, "probably for the best. You'd only distract me in that getup."

"Nice try." She exaggerated the sway of her hips, smiled when she heard him groan. "Five minutes, Hawke. Don't go to sleep on me."

"Babe, I'll be warming up your seat."

In her room she wasted no time kicking off her heels and trading out the dress for jeans and a comfortable sweater. After pulling on a pair of soft socks, she strolled down the hall to claim her seat.

"You're a hoot, Hawke." With her hands on her hips, she stared down at the deep candleholder with three flames flickering merrily about. "This is how it's going to be?"

"I promised you a warm seat." He slouched in his seat, his hands on the control.

"Very funny." She moved the candleholder to the credenza where the reflection of the flames danced on the wall and then dropped down beside him. Scrolling through the avatars, she chose her favorite, a shaggy-haired redhead with more muscles than curves who went by Ruby.

The big screen was split into two separate viewing areas. In "Unleashed," the characters have been dropped in a remote part of the Amazon to be hunted as live prey. The player can save himself if he reaches civilization in the form of the Amazonia Resort and Conservation Range near the origination of the Amazon River in Peru. Many routes ended in dead ends or insurmountable dangers. If the hunters didn't get you, the environment probably would.

She and Jackson would be playing the same game but running their own course. They could well run into each other in a kill-or-be-killed scenario. They each started with three lives and two weapons of their choice. She went with a nine millimeter and a machete. Jackson had a fishing knife and a crossbow. She noticed both were silent weapons.

"Okay, here are the rules, we'll play nine levels."

"Nine." He muttered a curse under his breath. "That's a tease."

"We're not going for a marathon here. I just explained I have work yet to do tonight. So, whoever has the most points at each level wins that level. Whoever wins the most levels wins the game."

"No way. Speed is an element of the game. I don't want to be twiddling my thumbs while you wander about collecting points. Whoever finishes level nine first is the winner."

"Okay, you're on. First to finish nine wins." It wouldn't change how she played. Rushing is what lost the game for most players. "Man up, Hawke, we're wasting time. I have searches running on your entourage. I want to do an initial read-through tonight."

"I have my choice." He flicked his thumb and a tall wiry kid, who looked a lot like Where's Waldo? minus the hat, emerged from the shadows.

"Slippery Syd? You're kidding me. I thought for sure you'd choose one of the muscle-bound behemoths."

"A common mistake many players make. This guy is tough, smart and versatile."

She eyed his profile as he set up the game. "So you do remember how to play."

He sent her a sidelong glance. "I was born knowing."

"Bragging does not equal skill." Squirming in her seat she got set for the go. "I can promise I'll make you work for it."

"Babe," he said, as the game started, "I won't break a sweat."

"Honey, you're going to crash and burn."

At least she hoped so. He kept discounting his concussion, but she counted on it, both to slow down his reflexes and his cunning. She had skills—a girl had to do something to fill the long nights—but he was Jackson Hawke. Her bravado was all bluff.

This may not meet the definition of rest his doctor would recommend, but in her opinion it was better than letting him brood on what was missing in his head or on what he faced in returning to his life without his memories. Playing may require him to use his brain, but it wasn't the part that caused pain every time he had a thought that challenged the block in his head.

Playing relaxed and energized him. Winning would give him confidence to face his friends and associates. Not that she'd let him win. Her avatar slid past a coiled snake, snagged the knapsack that would garner her fifty points and hopefully some ammo and rappelled out of the pit.

She'd disciplined herself to use his real name earlier, for her benefit, but also for his. He needed to get used to hearing and reacting to the name. That's also why she'd switched to his last name to razz him about the game.

Out of the corner of her eyes she saw Slippery Syd taking on an anaconda in level three. Good luck, pal.

If she could get past the sleeping jaguar to get the first aid box on the other side of him, she'd have enough points to advance to level three, as well. One wrong move and she'd be back at the start of level two. She went up and then, by hopping from rock to rock, made it past the napping cat to snag her prize and move up in the game.

While the game reset her at level three, she shook her hands and flexed her fingers.

"Congratulations," Hawke taunted, "you're only half a level behind."

"A quarter level," she corrected. "And that can change in a heartbeat."

As she spoke, he missed his footing on a jump and landed in the river. Piranhas were on him in an instant and he lost his first life.

"Poor Slippery Syd. Now we're even again." Her level three started and she had a plan. There was antivenom on this level she may need later. She'd make for that before Hawke could get there and then advance straight to level four.

As the game went on, they continued to jab good-naturedly at each other. He combined quick wit and easy flirting to make her laugh. She kept striking at his ego, but it had little effect. Her barbs bounced off his thick hide.

No doubt she could distract him by responding to his flirtation. But uh-uh. They'd already been down that road, and she wasn't encouraging him. Her sanity and ability to do her job depended on her restraint.

But, oh, how he tempted her.

He was funny and quick. And he smelled good. Such a distraction.

He reached the ninth level right ahead of her and they were both down to their last lives. She decided to forgo any attempt at points or resources to go straight for the finish line.

She chanced a quick look at his screen and determined he'd made the same decision. Dang, he must have muscle memory for this game because he seemed to know right where to go.

Don't rush, she cautioned herself. *Sure and steady will win this game.*

Stealth was needed on this level as the hunters were close. At one point she saw Slippery Syd ahead of her on the path to the waterfall. If he continued straight, he'd get to the top faster than her, but he'd be exposed. She chose to go farther down the river, under cover of the foliage. The ascent was less severe but longer.

She had to hope he made a mistake.

Because she was watching him reach the waterfall summit, she walked right into a hunter. He had his sights on Slippery Syd, but when she stumbled into the clearing, he immediately turned his gun on her. Ruby dove to the ground expecting the kill shot. Instead there was a thump. She slowly lifted her head to see a bow bolt had taken out the hunter. Slippery Syd had saved her.

And he'd also won. Except a shot rang out, echoing on both screens. And Slippery Syd fell, his last life taken by a hunter. Because he'd revealed his position to save her.

Next to her, Hawke cursed.

No fair. He'd had the win. She made a mad dash and wild jump, windmilling her arms and legs in an attempt to reach a ledge on the rock face of the waterfall. Ruby missed and fell, suffering the same fate as Slippery Syd.

"You didn't have to do that." Jackson admonished her.

"I kind of did." She assured him. "The win is yours."

"You had more points."

"And you reached more levels faster."

"I'm not claiming a game I didn't win."

"Fine, we'll call it a draw." She tucked her control pad into the sleeve on the front of her seat. "I look forward to the rematch." His insistence said a lot about his sense of fair play. One more thing to admire about the man, when there were already so many.

"I'm ready if you are." His slumberous gaze rolled over her, suggesting he was ready for more than a friendly game.

She licked her lips, suddenly wishing he was just JD, someone in her sphere she might actually have a chance at having a relationship with, someone who might stick around and build a home with her. From the number of stamps in his passport, Jackson was a jet-setter. Out of her reach and out of her league.

"Oh, no." She rose and backed away. "Shall we say tomorrow night, same time, same place? Ah… I…uh, have some reading to do. I'll see you at breakfast."

Whipping around, she fled temptation.

Grace jerked awake. Something had broken her sleep, but what? She'd left her door ajar an inch or two in case Jackson called out. Was that what woke her? Was he in distress? She sat up.

Then she heard it, a hoarse call sounded from down the hall.

Jackson!

She pushed the covers aside and, not worrying over the fact she wore only an oversize white T-shirt and Tweety pajama shorts, she raced down the hall.

Another shout.

She reached his door and found it slightly open, but by less than an inch. Knocking, she called out, "Jackson? Are you okay?" She waited a beat and then repeated, "Jackson?"

A low moan leaked through the crack in the door. Waiting no longer, she knocked again and pushed into the room. A three-inch swath of light from the bathroom illuminated the room.

"Jackson." He sat up in bed, bare to the waist where the covers pooled around him. He slumped forward, head cradled in his hands. She sat on the edge of the bed and placed her hand on his blanket-covered thigh. She realized he was shaking. "What is it? Do you need a pain pill? Or a doctor?"

"No." And more emphatically, "No." But he didn't release his head. He cursed. "I'm fine. You can go back to bed."

"I don't think so. Tell me what's going on."

"Nothing. Stupid nightmare." He groaned through gritted teeth. "Maybe I will take a pain pill." He reached for a bottle on the nightstand.

"I'll get you some water." She went to the bathroom and returned with a glass of water. He took the pill and she placed the bottle and glass on the bedside table. "Tell me about the dream."

He rolled one bare shoulder. "It's gone. Go to bed. I'm sorry I woke you."

Ignoring him, she reclaimed her spot on the bed, curling one leg up under her. Men were such babies when it came to being in pain, physical or mental. And dealing with them was much the same as dealing with an infant. You knew something was wrong, but it was up to you to figure out what.

"I've heard it's good to talk about a nightmare right after. It's supposed to help release its grip on you."

He laid his hand on top of hers on his leg. Only then did she realize she'd been petting him. "Fair warning, if you don't leave my room, I'm going to get a grip on you."

Knowing he meant the sexual threat to chase her away, she dismissed the warning. The medicine would help, but he was in no shape to make love. "I'm not worried. I'm pretty sure I could knock you down with a feather."

"Babe," he drawled, his voice low and sleep-roughened, "it would be a mistake to equate down with out."

Okay. A shiver of awareness rolled down her spine.

"When you say gone, do you mean the dream is over and done or you don't remember the dream?"

"Does it matter?"

"No," she acknowledged, watching him closely. At least the shaking had eased under the hand he held to his thigh. Evidence the pain pill was working. Good. "I imagine it would be disconcerting either way."

"All I remember is being stabbed and then waking up to crushing pain in my head."

"Interesting. Perhaps it wasn't a dream, but a memory. Maybe that's why your head hurts. You said that happens when a memory tries to come through."

"Maybe."

Seriously? Could he be more stubborn? "Did you get a sense of the woman at all? I'd really like to have more than a driver's license picture to go on as we get ready to head to Las Vegas."

"I'm with you on that." He ran his thumb over the back of her hand. "One of the first things I want to do is go in and talk to the detectives, get an update on where things stand."

"Good idea." He'd already mentioned his desire for more information. But the heat in his eyes told her his mind had shifted away from the conversation to more basic functions. Maybe he wasn't as debilitated as she thought. Time to go.

"Ah, you look like you could sleep now." She tried to ease her hand away from him. "I'll just go."

His hand tightened on hers and she tensed. Then he released her and she thought for a moment she was free. But in one quick move he circled her waist in his big hands, pulled her up and over him and then turned so she was under him. In the space of a few seconds she went from sitting on the edge of the bed to blinking up at a man with wicked intentions on his mind.

"So, Delaney, where is this feather you were talking about?"

His molten gaze rolled over her curves, touching on the skin where her shirt had ridden up at the waist, lingered on the dark shadow of nipple under white cloth and traced the flow of shoulder into neck exposed by the stretch of her collar.

"Huh?" She dragged in a much-needed breath. Sweet potatoes and pecan pie, she was in so much trouble. If just the feel of his eyes set her on fire, what would happen when he actually used his hands on her?

She couldn't risk finding out.

"Okay," she said, wincing because it was more of an aroused croak, "I get the message." She wiggled to the right, gained a few inches of space. "I'll see you in the morning."

"Uh-uh." He dragged her back and hooked a leg over hers to keep her from squirming away. "I gave you your chance to get away." He buried his nose in her hair, and moaned softly. She almost echoed the sound. He smelled so good, of citrus and spice and a touch of woodiness that made her mouth water. "You didn't take it, which tells me you are right where you want to be."

"We really shouldn't do this." His hand landed on her stomach right where the shirt left her bare. Pure instinct had her arching into his touch. Still, she fought for reason. "I'm listening now. I'll go."

"Too late." The heat of his breath on her throat sent a shiver racing through her. "I take my threats seriously. Unlike you, since there is no feather to knock me away with. Ah, the things I could do to you with that feather."

To demonstrate he trailed his fingers, featherlight on the cotton of her shirt, up her torso, along the side of her breast, over her collarbone, where skin met skin and she lost her battle to contain a moan. When he reached her neck, he flipped his hand to use the back of his fingers to lift her chin to the perfect angle to receive his kiss.

Oh, so soft, his mouth settled on hers. She opened for him instantly. His tongue met hers in a dance of wonder. Not a passionate tango, but a slow waltz of turns and holds and the occasional lunge. She sighed and went boneless beneath him.

"Stop," she pleaded. No matter how good this felt, she worked for him. "You have to stop."

"Careful." He nipped her chin with his teeth. "Or I will."

"Oh, you're evil."

"Because I insist you admit you want me as much as I want you?" He fondled the lobe of her ear with his tongue. Her entire lower body tightened. "Or because I don't agree we need to keep business and personal separated? Yes, I'm a bad, bad man."

His hand went to the bottom of her T-shirt, and bunching it, he pushed the fabric upward. Looking her in the eye, he demanded, "Yes or no?"

She knew what she should say, what her dad had taught her, what her career and all her training warranted. Yet never had she yearned for a man more. His strength tempered by his vulnerability got to her on a visceral level. Arching into him as he drew her closer, her eyes fell shut on a sigh.

"Yes. Oh, please, yes."

She expected her clothes to disappear, for him to jump on her offer. And her. Which, oh yeah, she was more than ready for. Instead, he leaned down and soft lips opened over hers. His tongue sought hers and now they tangoed. He led with authority, a true aficionado who seduced with desire and demand. Senses dazzled, she followed every synchronized twist and slow, passionate pivot, sinking into the bedding and drawing him to her.

Her clothes did disappear somewhere along the line, and she reveled in his touch on her flesh. She fought past blankets to reach him, to rid him of whatever he wore, only to find smooth, unencumbered skin. Oh, my. Long and lean, he was beautiful, marred only by the nearly healed wound on his abdomen. Her fingers went to the scar.

"Learning the details of what happened probably sparked your nightmare. Won't you talk to me?"

He was silent for a beat then he sighed. "I can't recall much, mostly emotions—confusion, anger, shock. It gives me a massive headache to think about it," he stated dismissively. His fingers closed over hers, pulling her hand away from the scar. "Does it offend you?"

Surprised by the question, she blinked up at him. In the shifting of his gaze she saw the geek lurking behind the stud. "No." She squeezed his hand and then freed herself to caress the scar with her thumb. "I was a master-at-arms in the navy. I've seen much worse. But that doesn't mean it's not still raw. It won't hurt you to make love?"

He grinned, confidence fully restored. "Babe, my head bothers me more than that little cut. Fortunately, you gave me a pain pill. I'm primed and ready to go, and I can't think of a better way than in your arms. Such a sweet armful. I may have no memory, but I know spectacular when I'm curled up next to her in bed."

Ah, so smooth and yet her heart still melted.

"Still wishing I had a feather, though."

"Would you forget the feather?"

"Not going to happen," he assured her. "I'll just have to improvise some more." He continued to tease her, drawing a single finger between the valley of her breasts and then to a peak, where the light touch tormented her into arching into his touch, demanding more.

Instead he shifted his attention, moving his imaginary feather lower.

"Stop," she said around a giggle, grabbing his hand at her waist. "Well, we've learned you aren't inhibited."

"I'd say not, as I consider feather play to be quite tame."

Have mercy. It made the mind boggle at what he would find to be kinky.

He nuzzled her neck, using his tongue to dampen her skin, and then blew gently in a new form of sensual teasing. The shift from the heat of his mouth to the cool of his breath brought goose bumps to her skin and the desire to get closer. She bowed her neck, giving him better access.

"And you are quite skilled."

She felt him grin against her skin. "So happy you're pleased."

"Oh, I am. But I have to wonder." She moved her hands around from his back and trailed her thumbs slowly, oh, so slow, down his sides. "Are you ticklish?"

"Let's not find out." He bucked up, grabbed her hands in both of his, anchored them to the bed and took her mouth again, slowly lowering himself onto her, linking them in the ultimate dance. Where thought surrendered to sensation and bodies communicated without words.

No longer teasing, he twirled her between moments of utter tenderness, when she felt cherished and special, to sweeps of passionate intensity that drew the wanton out of her. Oh, yeah, she liked that, liked demanding he please her, liked hearing his groans when she pleased him.

Touch for touch, kiss for kiss, her heart raced to the beat of his as pleasure spiraled past excitement and joy to euphoria. And she clung to him as they both plunged into bliss.

Grace curled up in Jackson's arms. Her life had changed forever. She loved him. Crazy, of course. She was a former public servant and he was a billionaire. She wanted to put down roots and he lived in hotels. She craved order and he created games that thrived on chaos.

There was no future for them. She accepted that, but she could have now. She could have his back and make sure he got the rest he needed to heal. And grab every moment possible with him before he got his memory back and didn't need her anymore.

She had her head on straight when she met Jackson in the first-floor restaurant for breakfast. She admired the

French-bistro vibe as she ordered fresh fruit and a crois-
sant. Between bites of strawberries and buttery, flaky
bread she filled him in on his senior staff.

"They're quite an impressive bunch." He flipped
through the reports she'd given him. He still couldn't read
well, but there were pictures so he could put faces to names.

"You're pretty impressive, too." She handed him her
last packet, a file on him he could read when his vision
improved. "You have to remember you're not working at
your normal speed. When I had a concussion, it took me
four weeks to feel right again. I know people where it
took months."

"So you keep saying."

"Because you're expecting too much from yourself too
soon."

He pushed his plate of unfinished eggs aside. "I don't
have a choice, do I? Two days from now I have to be back
in Las Vegas to face a room full of people as a man I have
no idea how to portray."

"Actually, sooner than that." She faced the front of the
restaurant and over his shoulder she saw two men ap-
proaching. "Bogies at six o'clock. Jethro Calder and Clay
Hoffman are headed this way. That's your financial advisor and your head of security."

Both men were tall, dark and handsome. Not exactly a
cliché she could rattle off to Jackson. The executives were
about the same height—easily six feet, maybe an inch
or two over—and wore expensive business suits. Jethro
Calder wore navy blue with a pin-striped tie. He had short
black hair and his picture failed to show the depth of his
blue eyes. Clay Hoffman carried more weight, in the form
of muscle mass, and wore black on black with no tie. His
hair and eyes were dark chocolate-brown.

Both were larger-than-life characters, confident, asser-
tive, intimidating. And Jackson put them both to shame.

"Maybe we should have responded to those message slips, after all."

"And said what? Jackson can't come to the phone right now because he doesn't remember who you are?" He chugged a sip of coffee as if it was a bracing shot of fine whiskey. "I'll handle this."

"Jackson," Jethro Calder greeted him as the two men arrived at the table. "You're a hard man to get a hold of." He felt comfortable enough with the boss to pull out a chair and join them at the table for four.

Clay was more direct as he took his seat. "What the hell, Hawke? You can't go off the grid without letting me know. I've had men looking for you for the past two days." His dark gaze narrowed in on Jackson's jaw. "Is that a bruise?"

"I knew this trip was a bad idea," Jethro tossed in. He grasped Jackson's chin to turn his head for a better view of the bruise. "What happened to you?"

Jackson pulled away and held up a staying hand. "First of all, Grace, these Neanderthals work for me. Jethro Calder and Clay Hoffman, this is Grace Delaney."

Two assessing gazes landed on her.

"Ma'am." Clay nodded at her, his dark eyes already having cataloged everything about her, from her shoe size to her short crop of hair. "How long have you and Jackson been friends?"

"Not long," she assured him. She'd only brought her wallet downstairs. She pulled out an old business card, flipped it over and wrote her social security number on it before calmly handing it to him.

"You don't have to do that, Grace," Jackson's protest had a bite to it. He nailed his men with an intent stare. "She's with me. That's all you need to know."

"I have nothing to hide," she soothed him. "He'll check me out anyway. This just makes it easier for everyone."

"Sheriff of Woodpark?" Clay mused.

"Ex-sheriff, actually. My term ended on the thirty-first."

"Hmm." He tucked her card into his pocket as he turned back to Jackson. "Tell us about the bruise."

Jackson simply lifted one dark eyebrow.

The security exec didn't back down. He rolled his impressive shoulders and pinned Jackson to his chair with an intense stare. "Protecting you is my job. I can't do that when you take off on your own. I need to know what happened to determine if you need additional medical care."

"He does," Grace said.

"I don't." Jackson sent her an admonishing glare.

The two men looked back and forth between them.

"Which is it?" Jethro asked.

"He has a severe concussion. And he left the hospital against the doctor's recommendation." Her gaze never left Jackson's during her revelation so she saw the flash of hurt quickly replaced by irritation.

"You're supposed to be on my side."

"Always." She made it a promise. "Which is why your health comes first. He's handling himself." She flicked her gaze to Clay. "But he should definitely see his physician when he returns to Las Vegas."

"Maybe you need to start from the beginning." Clay directed the comment to his boss.

Jackson sighed. Showing his aggravation, he crossed his arms over his chest. "As she said, I have a concussion. Our best bet is someone ran me off the road and stole my wallet and my motorcycle. I don't remember much about the incident."

Grace hid her surprise. She hadn't expected him to be so forthcoming.

"An officer took me to the sheriff's office, where I met Grace. She's been an angel."

He ran a finger over the back of her hand on the table. Dang the man. The deliberate gesture was obviously meant to solidify the impression they were a couple. She narrowed her eyes in a what-the-heck look and he moved his head in a sideways just-go-with-it gesture. She didn't like where this was going, but she left her hand where it was.

"She went with me to the hospital and then drove me to Santa Rosa for more tests. And, no, I didn't want to stay overnight for a pounding head. You know how I am about hospitals."

"Concussions can be dangerous."

Uh-huh. Grace applauded Clay's warning. Vindicated at last. Perhaps his associate could actually get Jackson back to the doctor. She'd caught on to his game. He was giving them just enough truth to placate them without revealing the true extent of his injuries.

"Believe me, Grace isn't letting me overexert myself."

"Does the sheriff's department have any leads on your motorcycle?" Jethro asked.

"Not as of yesterday." Graced fielded the question. "It would be helpful if someone could forward the license and vehicle identification numbers to the sheriff's office. Jackson was a little slim on details."

"A concussion can mess with short-term memory." Clay played right into Jackson's version of events.

"What brings you two here?" Jackson changed the subject. "Any fires I need to know about?"

"No. We have things covered," Jethro assured him. "Development is eager to have your input on the new game, but mostly we were concerned at not hearing from you for nearly a week. Especially after recent events."

"So they haven't apprehended Vanessa yet?"

Jethro glanced at Grace before answering. "No."

Jackson gave a grim nod. "Sorry to give you a scare. I guess with this head thing I forgot it had been so long since I checked in."

"Yeah." Clay leaned back in his chair. "I can see you've

been distracted. We have the corporate jet. Do you want to catch a ride with us back to Las Vegas?"

"No."

"Jackson." Both men spoke at the same time.

He shrugged. "I want another day with Grace."

"I think we should go," Grace inserted. Jackson scowled, but she nodded subtly. "Your people need you. It's time for us to join the real world. It had to happen sometime." Grr. She turned her hand over and threaded their fingers together. "We'll still be together."

His fingers tightened on hers. "You heard the lady. I guess we're headed home to Las Vegas."

CHAPTER TEN

GRACE HIGHLY RECOMMENDED flying by private luxury jet. The one they traveled on had a seating area—better than the normal first class—a living room area, with a big-screen TV and wet bar, and a bedroom area. Both bathrooms had small showers. The appointments were luxurious, the seating comfortable.

The flight took less than two hours. And then she and the three men were in a limousine headed for the Las Vegas Pinnacle Hotel, the showpiece of the Pinnacle properties.

Her jaw dropped as she walked hand in hand through the lobby with Jackson. Just like San Francisco the hotel followed the theme of the game, but to a much larger degree. She felt as if she'd walked into a city wrestled from the desolation of the apocalypse and jazzed up as only Vegas could do.

"This is too cool." Jackson leaned down to whisper in her ear. "I want to shake these guys and explore."

Jethro and Clay walked ahead of them, leading them to the elevators.

"I want to shake these guys and talk." She held up their joined hands and nodded to them significantly. They hadn't been alone since breakfast. His executives joined them in the suite while they packed up and then they'd been on the road.

"We will," he assured her.

Clay walked past the bank of hotel elevators, turned

right and pushed through a door marked Private. Down a short hall was a bank of service elevators. He stopped in front of the first one and used a keycard to activate the call button.

"I called ahead and requested a new set of keys for you. Since you lost your wallet, we recoded all the locks just to be on the safe side. Sierra will have yours upstairs." The elevator arrived and he used the keycard again to access the penthouse level.

"So Jackson has a secret elevator?" Grace asked. "How covert."

Clay looked down his nose at her. "It's a matter of security."

"Because of the woman who stabbed him?"

He lifted a dark eyebrow, showing his surprise that Jackson had confided in her about the attack. "She's a good example of why precautions are necessary."

"Ms. Delaney," Jethro cut in. "Once we reach the penthouse, Jackson's associate will escort you to your room. We have to catch him up on business matters."

"She'll be staying with me," Jackson declared.

Shock rolled across Jethro's face. He sent a questioning glance Clay's way. Trained to show no emotion, Clay masked his reaction. Their surprise was quite telling. Obviously Jackson didn't normally allow his companions to stay with him in his suite. He really did hold himself apart.

No wonder the two men didn't know what to make of her. She didn't fit in his world and he wasn't acting himself. Tension tightened through her shoulders. All her arguments against putting on a false romantic front just took a hit. If they wanted to avoid suspicion, Jackson's pretense of a relationship was their best bet.

People did crazy things when they were in love. His uncharacteristic behavior would make his staff all the more suspicious of her, which gave them the added bonus of switching their focus from Jackson to her.

Uh-huh. Just because it was a brilliant strategy didn't mean she'd let him get away with launching it without talking to her first.

The hotel suite matched the owner's suite in San Francisco. She imagined in everyday life the familiarity gave Jackson a false sense of homecoming. In these unusual circumstances, it helped with his charade.

She led the way into the living room and a spectacular view of the Las Vegas strip opened up before her. The hotel rooms resembled each other, but the views were singular. No pretending you were in the same place when the view was on display.

Then again, a push of a button could fix that problem.

A slim blonde in a chic navy dress and an older gentleman, round in the middle and bald on top, waited in the living room. Jethro took care of introductions.

"Grace, this is Sierra Ross, Jackson's personal assistant. And Dr. Wilcox, his personal physician. Sierra, Doctor, this is Jackson's new friend, Grace Delaney."

"Hello." To cover Jackson's sudden tension, Grace broke away to shake hands. "Dr. Wilcox, I'm glad to see you, though I'm sure you know Jackson isn't."

The man laughed and patted her hand before releasing it. "Oh, I'm aware I'm not his favorite person. A necessary evil at best. But he sends me a stellar bottle of brandy for Christmas every year, so it's a trade-off."

"Don't be upset, Jackson." Sierra brought her brooding boss into the conversation. "Clay mentioned you had a concussion and that Grace recommended you see Dr. Wilcox. I thought it best to bring him here."

"It's fine." Jackson strolled forward and held out his hand. "Thank you for coming, Doc. Do you mind if we get this over with?"

"No problem." The doctor patted his arm after shaking hands. "Shall we go to your room?"

"That works." Jackson came to her. "You'll be all right on your own?" He kissed her on the temple. Up close his displeasure seared her. He whispered, "When I'm done, we need to talk."

"Yes, we do." She lovingly ran her hand down his chest while talking through gritted teeth. "Do yourself a favor, be frank with the doctor. You might be surprised at how he can help you."

"Do you want to come with me?"

"No. You're a big boy. And I agree with your first instinct. These guys would find it odd if I joined you. It's obvious you don't let women get too close."

"Yeah, well, the last one I dated stabbed me. And come to think of it, you're probably armed."

She didn't respond and his eyes went wide.

"You are armed, aren't you?"

"Shh. Not at this moment. But yes, I own a gun. If your man hasn't confiscated it."

"I should have known." Anxiety clouded his gaze. "I'm supposed to be a genius, and it doesn't occur to me that a woman who is ex-military, ex-sheriff would carry a gun."

"It's the concussion." She brushed the hair from his eyes, watched heat push back the anxiety. "Talk to the doctor. Let him help you."

He sighed. "Okay. But it's going to cost you." And he kissed her. In front of everyone. His mouth covered hers in a soft claiming. It lasted only a moment. A hot, sensual moment that stole her breath and had her hooking an arm around his neck to get closer, to extend the caress that ended way too soon.

No, the kiss didn't last long, but the power of it reached all the way to her tingling toes. She slowly opened her eyes to find him smiling down at her.

"These guys are smart. It has to look real to fool them."

Grace sank back on her heels. "Oh, your strategy is working. All too well." Best she remember it was all for show. "Go away now."

He left with the doctor and she found herself alone with his cohorts. Pretending a confidence she only half felt, she chose a chair and sat.

"Would you care for some coffee?" Sierra rose from the futuristic sofa as she made her way to the bar where a carafe and cups were situated. "I must say I've never seen Jackson so attentive."

Before Grace could respond to the leading comment, the suite door opened and a man walked in. Sweet merciful angels, he was gorgeous. Of mixed heritage, he had light brown skin and dreamy gold eyes. He wore his black hair skull close.

"Sorry I'm late." He stopped in front of her. "You must be Grace."

His eyes weren't so dreamy now. They raked over her, assessing every little detail. Jackson's chief counsel made no secret he questioned her presence here.

"And you must be Ryan. Nice to meet you."

"Really? Has Jackson told you a lot about me?" He spread his arms wide, asking, "About us? We can't say the same about you."

"Oh. Well, our relationship is still very new." She gave a half shrug. "Don't blame him. He's not totally himself at the moment."

"Exactly." Jethro jumped on her response. "So you can understand our concern that he's taken up with a stranger."

"I would think you'd be happy he had someone to help him in a moment of dire need. Or is your concern only of a professional nature? Is Jackson simply your boss, or do any of you look on him as a friend?"

The room bristled with hostility.

Clay surged to his feet. "We've been a team for ten years. You have no right to question our loyalty to him."

She relaxed as the others nodded, confirming his impassioned declaration. "Good. Then we all have Jackson's best interests at heart."

"Do we?"

"Ryan, gentlemen, why don't you all have a seat?" Sierra suggested as she poured two cups of coffee—one black, one with two sugars. "And Grace can tell us more about herself."

The men sat, all of them perching on the edge of their chosen seat. All focused their attention on her.

Great. She'd always longed to have the undivided attention of three of the most powerful men in corporate America.

Not.

Yet here she was. Nothing for her to do but bluster her way through it.

"You mean in addition to what you've all read in the report Clay had done before we ever touched ground in Las Vegas?" She met each person's gaze straight on. She had nothing to hide. The secrets were Jackson's, not hers. "I think you all have a fair idea of who I am."

Sierra joined them in the living area. She handed one cup of coffee to Ryan and kept the other.

"You grew up a navy brat. Speak four foreign languages—French, German, Italian and Japanese."

"Are they really foreign if you live there?" she asked rhetorically.

"Joined the navy at the age of seventeen with your father's permission. Your military record is clean. You received several commendations and were accelerating well through the ranks until you quit to care for your ailing father, a retired Senior Chief Petty Officer." Jethro ran through her history as if reading a list. Probably because he had. "Finished your father's term as sheriff in Wood-park when he passed. Ran for sheriff yourself but lost."

"Why is that, Grace?" Clay demanded. "What did you do to upset the good citizens of Woodpark?"

Being it was a question she'd asked herself more than once, the query threw Grace as her confidence took a hit. He knew right where to strike to make her question her-self. But she quickly regrouped. She'd done her best for the people of Woodpark. It wasn't her skills that had been in question.

Now she inhaled a deep breath, fought back her inse-curities and projected a calm she didn't feel to attempt to put them at ease.

"I did my job." The point wasn't to sell herself to them, but to let them know she wasn't a threat to Jackson. She crossed her legs. "But that's not what you really care about is it? What you really want to know is what my intentions are regarding your boss. The answer is I have none."

"None." Ryan infused the word with skepticism.

"None," she confirmed. She ran a finger down the crease in her jeans. "Look, we met under unusual cir-cumstances, which caused us to bond quickly. At first I didn't know who he really was. He needed help and I was happy to put Woodpark in my rearview mirror. Bottom line, we all agree he's not his usual self. I don't expect our relationship to last past his full recovery. But it's not every day a girl gets romanced by a billionaire. I'm just enjoy-ing the time we have together."

She knew immediately it was the right note to strike. The men looked at each other and relaxed back in their seats.

"He has a lot of money." Jethro stated the obvious.

"He does." She left it at that. She had no designs on Jackson's money, but the more she tried to convince this group of that fact, the less credible she'd sound.

"A lot of women lose sight of the man for the money." Clay observed.

"I knew the man first, his money doesn't interest me. But the trappings are fun. I've never flown in a private jet before."

"So we all agree this will be a short-lived affair."

"No." A deep voice stated from the archway near the foyer. Jackson stood there. "We are not in agreement. My relationship with Grace is none of your business. I'll thank you all to stay out of it."

"Jackson," Sierra sought to appease him, saying, "we're only looking out for you."

By the jut of his chin she'd failed. "I don't need you to look out for me. Grace is the last person I, or you, need to worry about. My money is safe from her. Grace." He held out his hand to her, a demand to join him.

She made her way to his side, took his hand. "Don't overreact," she warned him.

"I won't let them intimidate you."

"I can handle myself. These are the people you rely on daily, who will be here for you long after I'm gone from your life."

"You're the one I know. The one who is here for me now. I won't let them hurt you."

"They haven't." Only he had the power to do that.

But that was her problem.

The fact she loved him changed nothing. Yes, having him take her side reinforced that feeling, but as far as this group was concerned their relationship didn't go beyond a fun time. Couldn't go beyond that. She *was* enjoying their time together, and that was all there could ever be between them.

"Hmm." His gaze flicked to his associates, skepticism clear in the green depths. Had he heard more than she thought? A hand in the small of her back urged her through the archway. "Let's go."

"Jackson," Ryan hailed him. "Are you leaving? I wanted to get with you."

"Later. I need to take my lady shopping."

Shopping? Grace hid an inner grimace. She just got this crew on her side and he probably wiped all her hard work out with that one statement. Not to mention, shopping for what?

"I'm not letting you buy me another thing," she muttered for his ears only.

On the other side of him Ryan said, "I thought you'd want to catch up on what we've done while you've been gone."

"Jethro indicated everything was under control." Jackson threaded his fingers through hers. "After what I overheard, I need to spend the next few hours showing Grace I want her here." Jackson released Grace to walk over and hand Sierra his phone. "I lost my old phone in the accident. Can you update all my contacts and then send me the itinerary for the foundation gala?"

"Uh, sure." Sierra looked shell-shocked. As did the men, to a lesser degree.

Jackson came back and reclaimed her hand. As he led her through the archway, he tossed a final comment over his shoulder. "Grace's number is in there. If anyone needs me they can call her number."

Fury fueled Jackson's pace into the elevator and then to the front desk.

"Good afternoon, sir." A young man dressed in the dark blue-and-black hotel colors greeted him.

"Do you know who I am?" Jackson demanded.

The young man's eyes widened as if he'd been presented

with a sudden pop quiz. He cleared his throat. "Of course, Mr. Hawke. It's good to have you back with us."

Jackson nodded. "I'd like two keys to the penthouse suite." He drew Grace forward. "This is my guest, Grace Delaney. She is to be treated with respect. Anything she asks for is to be charged to me."

"Of course. Welcome, Ms. Delaney."

"Thank you." Next to Jackson, Grace tensed. She twisted her hand in his seeking freedom.

He held on. He always held on.

"You need to calm down," she murmured softly when the clerk looked away to deal with the keys.

"I'm fine." He seethed with indignation on her behalf. She'd done nothing but help him and those self-satisfied blowhards upstairs treated her like a money-grubbing groupie.

"No, I'm fine," she argued. "*You* are overreacting."

"Don't tell me how to feel." Pain spiked as the high emotions sent the blood pounding through his head. He didn't care. Bring on the hurt. He wouldn't allow Grace to be disrespected. His so-called entourage better get behind the notion real quick or they'd be looking for new jobs real soon.

"Here you go, Mr. Hawke. Is there anything more I can help you with?"

"Thank you, no." With keys in one hand, her hand in the other, he headed back to the elevator and the shops down below but changed his mind halfway there and went for the front door instead. He'd had enough of this fishbowl.

A valet immediately appeared. "Hello, do you have a ticket?"

"No." But Jackson automatically patted his pocket, which reminded him he held the keys. He dropped one in his pocket and handed the other to Grace. "Just bring something around," he said.

"Excuse me, sir," The valet, a man in his late twenties with sideburns and a goatee, protested. "You need a ticket. Or would you like a taxi?"

Great. Just when he counted on his identity to work for him, he gets the one valet who doesn't know who he is.

"Mr. Hawke." The concierge bustled up. His name tag read R. Schultz. "I have this, Pete. What can we do for you, sir?"

Finally. "I have vehicles here, right?"

"Yes, sir." The robust man took the question in stride. "You have six vehicles housed here in a private section of the garage."

Six? Jackson figured he had something besides a motorcycle, but six? What did he do with six vehicles? Never mind, he didn't even want to think about that.

He nodded for the concierge's benefit. "Have something brought around, would you?"

"No preference, sir? Perhaps the Ferrari or the Hummer?"

"Something simple, please," Grace spoke up. "Mr. Hawke isn't feeling himself this afternoon."

Jackson's neck twitched. He dropped Grace's hand. He didn't care to have his condition advertised to the world. Something he'd let her know once they were alone.

"Of course." Schultz waved Pete over and passed on the request. "Your car will be right here. I hope you feel better soon, sir."

"Thank you." Jackson gave him a generous tip. And when Pete pulled up in a sporty BMW, Jackson tipped him well and prepared to slide behind the wheel.

"Jackson."

Hearing his name, he paused to see Jethro striding toward him. His associate extended a slim leather wallet toward him. "If you're shopping, you'll need these. Sierra had your cards replaced."

Jackson accepted the wallet, nodded and slipped into the driver's seat. He wasted no time putting the car in gear and pulling away from the hotel.

"There was no need to mention my health." He gritted out between clenched teeth as he pulled out on Las Vegas Boulevard known the world over as The Strip.

"I wouldn't have had to if you hadn't looked like you were about to explode." She adjusted the seat belt over her middle. She stared straight out the windshield, her profile perfectly capturing her mood with the proud jut of her chin.

"Someone needs to be upset over how you were being treated. I won't have them disrespecting you."

That brought her head around along with the full force of her ire. "I told you I can handle myself. It may not have looked like it back there, but I won that skirmish, and you wiped it all out with your stupid comment about going shopping."

"Don't call me stupid. I'm a genius, after all." Being a billionaire was hard work, so many elements to juggle. The money was good, but sometimes he wished he could go back to being JD.

"I didn't call you stupid. I said your comment was stupid. There's a difference."

"Not from where I'm sitting." He inched the car along, overshadowed by the marble columns of Caesar's Palace on one side and the Eiffel Tower on the other. "I heard them all but call you a gold digger." He gave her a brief glance. "You're important to me. They're not."

"Yes, they are," she said with exquisite gentleness. "You just don't remember them right now. And yes, they want to protect you. Were they out of line? A little. Was I insulted? No." She waved her hand at him saying, "Billionaire," and then at herself continuing, "Peon. What are they supposed to think?"

"That I can take care of myself. That I have the intelligence to choose a companion I can trust."

There was a beat of silence as she did him the courtesy of not mentioning the woman who stabbed him.

"Okay," he conceded, "so they may have a small reason for concern."

She laughed, a soft chuckle that invited him to join in the fun. "See, you are a smart man. Please tell me we aren't really going shopping."

"Yes, we are. Unless you have a ball gown tucked away in that duffel bag of yours."

"Uh, no." He felt her studying his profile. "Why would I need a ball gown? Because of the gala? I'm okay. I have the black dress you bought."

"You can't go in the black dress."

"Why not? It's a beautiful dress."

"And you looked beautiful in it. But didn't you see the posters at the hotel? They showed everyone dressed up in monkey suits and long gowns. You might ordinarily get away with wearing the black dress, but you'll be my date so you'll have to wear something spectacular."

"Humph." She settled back in her seat. "The things I do for you. Well, you're not buying it."

"Actually, I am." She could argue all she liked, he was firm on this.

She huffed. "We're not going through this again."

"Nope. Because as you said, you're doing this for me. That means I pay."

"I can afford my own clothes."

"I can afford it more." He sent her a quick, emphatic glance. "Resign yourself, Grace. I'm not letting you pay for anything more while you're helping me. At the very least I can cover your costs."

She stared out her window, tapping on her armrest. "I could point out your friends would then be right about me."

"Come on, Grace, don't do that." He rolled his neck, working on the tension building there.

"Instead I'll ask, why is it so important to you?"

He spotted a billboard advertising a mall in Caesar's and maneuvered a U-turn while he considered how to answer her. Instinctively he sought to protect himself, then he remembered she'd been his advocate before he knew he needed help. She was his one constant since losing his memory.

Bottom line, he trusted her.

He waited to answer until after he left the car with the valet and led her inside the mall.

"I have so little control over anything right now. My memory is shot. I'm supposed to be a genius, yet I feel as though it takes forever to process anything."

She looked ready to protest but he'd heard her argument enough times to know what she'd say. So he shook his head and cut her off. "I know it's the concussion, but it's still my reality."

"I know it's tough." She stopped, forcing him to come to a halt, forcing him to face her. The compassion in her blue eyes almost undid him. "Time will help. It's really only been a few days."

"On top of everything else, I'm a billionaire and I live in a hotel. There's nowhere I can go, nothing I can do where I'm not recognized. And if that's not enough, I have an entourage standing by to critique my every move."

Invading his space, she cupped his face in her hands and read him. He stood still under her intense regard, but it took an effort. Finally she nodded and surprised him by brushing her soft lips across his cheek. He almost missed what she said next. "You need to give yourself a break."

She stepped back and swiped at his cheek where her lips had rested. "I'm sorry. I shouldn't have done that."

Suddenly he fought a minor battle between pulling his

head away to keep her from brushing the kiss away and the desire to lean into her touch. "You can put your lips on me anytime you want. The professional standard is yours, not mine."

"And it's a good standard." With her hands on her hips, she seemed to waver, then set her chin. "Back to my point. You need to relax, not take everything so seriously. Remember, you chose not to tell anyone about your memory loss. If you want to change your mind, you can. People would understand."

"No." Because she'd opened the door to it, he leaned down and kissed her silky cheek, inhaling her clean, orange-blossom scent. The tension coiled deep in him eased a little more, allowing him to breathe freely. He linked his fingers with hers and started walking again. "The only thing worse than being stared at would be being stared at with pity."

"Compassion and empathy are not pity."

"Yes, they are."

"You could tell your royal guard. Much of their protective posturing was because they care about you."

"Maybe," he conceded. "They seem decent enough. But I'm still peeved at them for their treatment of you." He spied a boutique with evening wear in the window and veered in that direction. "I'd have to know them better first."

"You really don't need to worry over every little move, every little detail. Letting your staff believe we're involved was a brilliant move. What they don't attribute to your concussion, they'll attribute to your infatuation."

"Ah, about that—"

"Don't pretend you came up with the idea on the spur of the moment. You had it planned out before Clay and Jethro ever showed up."

He shrugged. He should have known she'd figure it out.

"A romance allows us easy access to each other without anyone questioning it."

"You could have discussed it with me. Whoa." Grace caught sight of their destination, of bold colors and daring necklines of the dresses in the window and dug in her heels. "Not this place. It looks expensive. Let's try one of the department stores."

He tugged her forward. "I like this place. I can afford expensive."

"But I probably won't have occasion to wear the dress again. Just because you can afford expensive doesn't mean you should waste your money."

"Nothing spent on you is wasted." He pointed to a dress in the window. "The red would look stunning on you."

She bit her bottom lip as she studied the gown, her gaze slowly turning wistful.

"Let's see if they have your size." He drew her inside.

The place smelled nice, like a beautiful woman. It was well lit and spacious. Most of the merchandise was modeled by mannequins for a full three-dimensional effect. An older woman in a black suit came forward to greet them. She displayed no sign of recognizing him and he relaxed.

"Hello, I'm Eileen. What type of occasion are you shopping for?" she asked.

"We'll be attending the Hawke Foundation Gala for Displaced Youth," Grace responded.

"Oh, yes." Eileen nodded. "We've sold several gowns to people attending. It sounds like it'll be a lovely event. And for such a worthwhile cause. Wait, that's tomorrow." Her eyes went wide, but she smiled. "That just means we work harder."

"We want to see the red dress in the window." Jackson got down to business.

"I don't know, Jackson," Grace vacillated, "it's so extravagant. I don't think I could pull it off."

"My dear," Eileen enthused, "the dress would be striking with your dark hair and light skin. It just came in today, and I know it won't last long."

"Try it on," he urged Grace. The longing in her eyes told him what she wanted better than her mouth did.

There she went, chewing her lip again, but she gave in. "Okay, but let me look around. Maybe try on a few simpler dresses, too."

"Go ahead. I'll wait here." He dropped into a chair in a seating area set up in the middle of the store. Let her have some fun. If he had his way, they'd be leaving with the red dress. "Oh, Eileen, she's not to know the cost of anything."

CHAPTER ELEVEN

"I WANT TO APOLOGIZE for the third degree we put you through yesterday." Sierra said as she sipped her second cup of coffee. Behind her the Las Vegas strip dazzled the senses.

"I understand." Grace responded.

The two of them sat at the dining room table. The counter between the kitchen and dining room held a full breakfast buffet. The men had just left for a morning meeting and had taken Jackson with them.

He'd brushed them off completely yesterday. Mostly her fault. After they finished shopping, she decided he could use a break, so she directed him east to Hoover Dam. He relaxed on the drive. As she hoped, being in control of something— even a vehicle—bolstered his floundering confidence. When she suggested they take the tour, he jumped on the chance. He'd been as excited as a child, and as inquisitive. He'd loved it. He'd been in a much better place when he got home last night.

"It isn't personal." Sierra assured her.

"It's very personal," Grace corrected her. "But I get it. He's been away and the last gal he was seeing hurt him."

"She did, more than he knows."

"What do you mean?" Grace pushed her plate away and reached for the last of her coffee.

Sierra studied her for a moment obviously calculating how much she should share. "I don't know what to make of you." She confessed. "You're nothing like the women Jackson usually chooses. He likes tall, beautiful and dim."

"Really?" Surprise sent Grace's eyebrows rising. "I would think he'd get bored with dim rather quickly."

"Oh, he does," Sierra assured her. "But he says he wants to be able to relax when he's with a woman, not talk."

"Hmm." Grace decided she preferred her version of Jackson.

"Right?" Sierra demanded as if she'd been awaiting validation of her opinion. "Okay, dim is probably overstating it. And in all fairness, next to him most people fall short on the IQ range."

"Perhaps it's a form of self-defense for him. Maybe dim—for lack of a better word—equates with lack of calculation. So he feels he can trust their emotions more."

Sierra stared at her for a moment. "I never considered that, but you may well be right. Not that he gives his trust. He's the most guarded man I know. And the other three aren't far behind. I understand the foster care shuffle will do that to you."

"The four of them are lucky they found each other," Grace stated.

"Yes, they were all in the same house late in their teens. A good home run by an older couple known for taking on tough cases. They became a family. I met them in college, except Clay, who joined the marines. He joined them in the business later, after it was more established."

"I was a military brat," Grace told her. "So I know how hard it is to pack up and leave the familiar for the unknown. You learn not to expose yourself to the hurt of leaving friends behind by putting up guards."

"Yes. It's created a bond between them that won't be easily broken. But the wealth they've accumulated hasn't made relationships easy, especially for Jackson. Being a billionaire always raises the question of whether the woman is with him for the man or the money. His reticence is as much self-preservation as it is habit."

"But Vanessa got to him."

"Yes, and by hurting him physically she messed with his mind. Any emotional advancement he'd made in the past few years was shot to heck. He went off by himself while the police investigated and we didn't see him for weeks. We've been worried."

"It must have been traumatic. Some alone time is probably just what he needed."

"Obviously. He seems happy. I've never seen him be with anyone like he is with you. I really don't know what to make of it."

"And how is that?"

"Open. Accessible. He doesn't generally allow his companions in the penthouse. He has a suite on a lower floor he uses when he's keeping company."

Did he? Interesting. No wonder his inner circle was so freaked-out.

"I wouldn't make too much of it." Grace downplayed the importance for Sierra's sake. "We've been through a lot together the past few days. When the novelty wears off, I'll be on my way and things will get back to normal."

Sierra wagged a finger at Grace. "That would make the guys happy. But I'm not so sure it would be for the best. I think you're good for Jackson."

"Hmm. And what about you? Who's the guy?"

"What do you mean?"

"You wouldn't be telling me all this if you didn't have romance on the mind. Who are you on the fence about?"

Flustered, Sierra tried to wave Grace off. "I'm not seeing anyone right now."

"But you want to." Grace prompted her. "Who is he, a coworker, friend of a friend? No, then they could champion him. Someone you met at an event?" Grace continued to guess. "Or through work?" Ah, a blush. "That's it. Not a coworker then, but maybe a vendor?"

"Okay, you got me." Sierra tried to hide a smile. Oh, yeah, she was in serious crush mode. "He works for the city. He's in charge of juvenile activities. We've been working together on the foundation gala. We've had coffee a couple of times. He seems really nice."

"And you're wondering if he's interested in you, your money or your connections?"

Eyes wistful Sierra nodded. "It's so hard to know when your emotions are engaged whether you're being played or not."

"So check him out," Grace suggested. "You have the resources. As I know from experience."

"I couldn't." Sierra got fidgety. "The reports we draw are pretty inclusive, because we deal in large amounts of money on business deals, and this is a highly competitive field so we want to be sure of who we're hiring. But this is personal. I don't want to violate his privacy in that way."

"So don't run a report. Do a social search." Grace got up to get her computer from the living room. She set it on the table and pulled up the biggest social media platform on the internet. "What's his name?"

"Oh, we can't do this." Sierra moved her chair closer. "We shouldn't do this, should we?"

"We should. A woman needs to be careful in this day and age. A man, too, as Jackson's experience shows."

Sierra gave the name Nick Collins. Grace typed it in.

"This takes patience," Grace explained as she clicked through pages, cut and pasted information.

Sierra leaned forward to read better. A few minutes later, Grace handed her a report that held public details of his career, community involvements and relationships. "It's by no means a comprehensive report, but you'll have a good sense of who he is."

"Obviously he has some issues." Disappointment filled Sierra's voice. "This was very helpful, Grace. You're easy to talk to." Sierra set her coffee cup aside. "No wonder Jackson and Ryan like you so much."

More than surprised by that, Grace had to smile. "Ryan likes me?"

"Oh, yes. You stood up to him. Presented your arguments as if you didn't care if he accepted them or not, and got Jackson to agree to Dr. Wilcox's examination without putting up a fight. Ryan was quite impressed."

"Really?" Surprising, but Grace would take it. If Ryan liked her, all the better for Jackson. This whole situation was hard enough on him. He deserved any break he could get.

"Really. And that's not easy to do. Well, I've wasted enough time on this." Sierra stood and gathered her dirty dishes. "I have to get to work. Thanks for the help. If you're interested, I have friends who would pay for the same info."

"Sure. I'm happy to help."

Sierra nodded. "Let me know if you need anything."

"I will, thanks."

Sierra carried her dishes to the kitchen. "Don't worry about the cleanup," she advised. "I'll let housekeeping know we're done." With a final wave, she departed.

With time to kill, Grace decided to do another search. She went to her room and grabbed the file on Jackson. Doing the search for Sierra had given her some ideas for finding his father. Social services hadn't been able to find his mother's friend twenty-nine years ago. But times had changed. She typed in the friend's name and hit Enter.

Grace's phone rang. She pulled the cell phone out of her pocket but didn't recognize the number. She began to hit

Ignore, but remembered she had job feelers out. This time with Jackson was only temporary.

"This is Grace Delaney."

"Hello, Grace Delaney, should I be congratulating you?"

"Doug!" Happy to hear her friend's voice, she sank down on the sofa and looked out over the Strip. "Why would you congratulate me? Did I get a job I don't know about?"

"Not unless you're ready to join the FBI," he responded.

"I've actually been giving it some thought. I've really enjoyed the profiling and background work I've been doing for Jackson. I might be interested in an analyst position with the FBI."

"We always need good analysts. I'll pass the word. But what I'm talking about is your upcoming wedding. The tabloids have announced you're engaged to Hawke."

"Seriously?" she asked, her heart clenched at the news. How she wished she could dismiss his revelation as sheer craziness. She and Jackson had known each other for only a week. But the truth was she'd fallen, and fallen hard. "Well, I can promise you any rumors of an engagement are greatly exaggerated."

"I'm glad to hear it," Doug said. "So how come I don't believe you?"

Because he knew her too well. "Maybe because I wished it was true?"

"You've fallen for him."

She nodded, though he couldn't see her. "Foolishly, I have."

"Why foolish? You'll make a great billionaire's wife."

Her heart squeezed even tighter. "Ah, that would require the billionaire to have feelings for me."

"So what's the problem? The man I saw clearly held you in high regard."

Hope bloomed, but she blocked it. She needed to be

realistic. "I think you're confusing desperation for a connection. I was the only person he knew in a world gone crazy."

"I don't know. He was jealous of me. That points to a connection if you ask me."

"Jealous?" She forced a laugh. "You're imagining things."

"There must be something there, or the tabloids wouldn't have the two of you getting married."

"There's…chemistry."

"Ah." Silence beat down the line. "If you love him, you have to fight for him."

"Fight for who?" she demanded, raw emotion tearing through her. "Jackson has his name thanks to you, but his memories are still defunct. When he gets them back, I'll just be another memory."

"It's not like you to be a defeatist."

"No, I'm a realist." And an emotional mess. "He lives in hotels, Doug. And you heard me the other day. The only thing I'm certain of is a need for a home, for permanence."

"So get him to buy you a house. He's a bachelor, Grace. And travels a lot for business. Just because he doesn't have a home doesn't mean he doesn't long for one." A call sounded in the background. "Listen, Sherry needs me. Stay strong. The next time we talk, I hope I'll be offering congratulations for real."

"Give Sherry hugs from me. I'll think about what you said," she promised.

"I hope so, because you deserve to be happy. And I'm talking to Ken Case about that analyst position."

The line disconnected and Grace dropped her phone on the couch, staring unseeing out the picture window. Doug made it sound so simple. Fight for Jackson, get him to buy the home they both longed for. So perfect.

Yet so far out of reach.

* * *

Jackson sat at the head of the conference table, listening to the conversation flowing around him. He'd admitted to Grace to being nervous about reporting to work, but diving back into his life was both exhilarating and challenging. He found it fascinating, and luckily much of the knowledge was there, even if the details and people were still blanks.

Again and again he looked around for Grace, wanting to share something with her, but dragging his girlfriend into a meeting would be pushing it.

Other than that, the plan was going great. Her preparations, sourced onto his new cell phone, put all the pertinent info he needed at his fingertips. Names of department heads along with pictures, descriptions of his games, a list of ventures and properties he owned. No one questioned him looking at his phone.

It worried him sometimes that he'd become so dependent on her. Everything he'd learned since arriving in Las Vegas pointed to self-reliance. More, it was clear he kept women at a distance.

He couldn't imagine relegating Grace to her own suite. The best part of his day was waking with her in his arms. But would he feel the same way when his old life caught up to his new one?

His past, losing his mother so young and being in nine foster homes before finding a home with Mama Harman, was a memory bomb waiting to explode. How could he know how he'd feel once those memories returned?

He couldn't. But he knew he wanted Grace by his side when that time came. She'd helped him through every mishap so far. He trusted her instincts, trusted her to put him first. Getting his memories back wasn't going to change that. No matter what those memories held.

The meeting wrapped up and Jackson met Grace in the lobby.

"Hi. Oh. Where are we going?" she demanded when he simply wrapped an arm around her waist and swept her along. "I thought we were going to go over the game plan for the gala tonight. I have the profiles for the invited VIPs. I also asked Sierra for a list of the coordinators and their assistants and did brief profiles on them. And I included the roster of your executives, with the pictures attached."

"Excellent. I can look at them in the car." A large black SUV pulled up as he urged Grace through the door.

"It's going to take you a while to go through that." She slid in when he held the door open for her but stopped him from closing her in. "There are more than forty profiles for the VIPs alone."

"I'm good with facts and faces." He shut the door and rounded the vehicle. Inside the partition was up between them and the driver. "I will admit things seem to take forever to absorb. Took me nearly an hour to get through the file the FBI did on me when I was finally able to read it."

"An hour?" Her pretty blue eyes widened with amazement. "It took me all afternoon."

"I've found I'm a fast reader." He flipped through the file on the tablet she'd handed him, squinting, as his vision still blurred occasionally. That had been the only problem in the meeting earlier. It helped that she used a large font. These profiles included both personal and business details. "I'm amazed you were able to put this together so quickly."

"Yeah, well, I'm good with facts and faces, too." She gave him a rundown of her report. As the gala was a fundraiser, she'd sorted the VIP profiles based on net worth. While he read, she fell silent as the wonders of the Strip caught her attention. Once they left the excitement behind, she turned to him. "Where did you say we're going?"

"To police headquarters. I made an appointment with the detective investigating my case."

"Are you sure you want to do this today? With the gala

tonight? You're bound to see or hear something that makes your head hurt."

"Knowledge is worth the pain. We're here. And I want to get through this." He hopped out of the SUV. She was waiting on the other side. He took her hand and led the way inside to the information desk. "We're here to see Detective Hunt in Special Investigations," he told the clerk.

The woman directed them to the third floor and Jackson led Grace to the elevators.

She turned concerned eyes on him. "I'm just worried it'll ruin your mood for the gala tonight."

"And it may help me to remember." He pushed the up button. "You're always talking about my mind providing clues. Well, this is what my mind is prompting me to do."

"Okay." She squeezed his hand once they were inside the elevator. "But don't expect too much. They probably won't be able to tell you much more than was in the report."

Her concern touched him. He bent and kissed her softly. "I'm glad I have you with me."

A bright sheen came into her eyes and for a heartbeat he thought she might cry. The very notion of his stalwart Grace in tears made his heart twist. But she smiled and the moment disappeared.

She started to say something when the elevator doors opened onto the second floor and a woman who looked to be in her fifties stepped on.

"Good morning," she greeted them with a smile and pushed Five.

From a distance he heard Grace respond. The woman's scent, an Oriental perfume with touches of citrus and rose, hit him the minute the doors opened. His head spun and pain exploded behind his eyes. He knew that perfume. From a long time ago. It belonged to someone important. Someone who represented warmth and comfort. He had the strongest desire to grab the woman and hold her close.

"Jackson." Grace pulled on his hand.

He didn't budge. The woman smiled kindly.

"Jackson!"

He blinked at Grace. "What?"

"We're here." She drew him off the elevator. "Are you okay? You look like you just saw a ghost."

The doors closed behind him. He swung around but the woman was gone.

"Jackson, you're scaring me."

"I'm fine." He spotted a bench against the wall down the way and made his way to it. "Do you have one of my pain pills with you?"

"Yes." She sat next to him and dug in her purse. "Here." She presented him with a tiny white pill and a bottle of water. "What happened back there?"

"I did see a ghost. Or, more accurately, smelled one." Head reeling, he chased the pill with a sip of water and watched her brow furrow in confusion. "That woman's perfume struck a chord. I think my mother wore the same scent."

"Oh, Jackson." Her hand covered his knee. "What makes you associate it with your mother? Did you have an actual memory?"

"No. It was more like emotions that seemed to be from a long time ago. Sensations of love and warmth and happiness. But there was no memory, no face to go with the feelings."

His frustration with the lingering amnesia echoed between them.

"I think that's enough for today," she suggested again.

"No. Don't you get it? I need knowledge. If my brain won't provide me with the facts of my life, I'll get them any way I can." He surged to his feet. "Come on, we have an appointment."

He started down the hall but soon realized she wasn't

with him. Turning around, he spotted her right where he left her. Arms crossed over her chest, she stood with her head cocked watching him. Damn it. He wanted her with him.

He retraced his steps. "Aren't you coming?"

Those watchful blue eyes never shifted from his face. "You've already had a traumatic event. I'll go with you, but only if I get to call a halt if it looks like it's getting to be too much for you."

"Yeah, all right." He grabbed her hand, determined not to leave her behind again.

Her hand moved but her feet didn't. When he came to a stop, he turned to glare at her down the length of their two arms. Her expression hadn't changed. "Promise me."

He gritted his teeth, disliking having limitations placed on him. But the one true thing he knew was Grace cared about him. It was the foundation of his world. "I promise."

She nodded. "Okay then, lead the way."

A few minutes later Detective Hunt stood to greet them. "Mr. Hawke, welcome back. And this must be Ms. Delaney."

"Please call me Grace. Thank you for seeing us on such short notice. I'm sure you can understand Mr. Hawke is anxious to get an update on the investigation. Do you have anything new on the assailant?"

"Not much." Hunt gestured behind them with the file in his hand. "Why don't we take this to a conference room?" A few feet down the hall, he opened a door and ushered them inside. "My partner is on a call regarding another case. She'll join us if she can."

Jackson nodded and sank into one of the cushioned seats. He reached for Grace's hand before giving Hunt his full attention. "What more have you learned about Vanessa? Tell me you are close to apprehending her."

Hunt opened the file, flipped through the pages. "Vanessa Miller's family has money. She gets a monthly allowance and all her household expenses are paid. She has no close friends. Interviews with her neighbors revealed she has a bad temper and sometimes gets violent. We got a search warrant for her home and found a prescription for an antianxiety medication. After talking to her doctor, we determined she has a psychotic explosive disorder."

"That doesn't sound good," Grace spoke up.

"No. People suffering from the disorder can be fine for long periods of time, and then something will set them off and they become verbally and physically abusive. It means she's capable of overreacting to the point of violence over any little thing. The medication is supposed to help, but she's known to go off it, which of course increases the chances of episodes. Your company has security on her residence 24/7, with instructions to contact us if she's spotted, but she hasn't returned to her home."

"You stated she has no friends or employers. What other avenues are you pursuing?" Jackson asked.

"We've interviewed the guests at the party where you met. Nobody particularly remembers her and nobody admits to inviting her. We talked to her neighbors. She's been involved in several disputes so we went out and spoke to the responding officers. Seems she is well-known for blowing up and then being very contrite. Always pays bigger and better for any repairs needed. Still, people are afraid of her and tend to give her a wide berth. She put her maid in the hospital for trying on a pair of shoes, but again she was really sorry, and the family paid the woman off, so no charges were ever filed."

The more Jackson heard, the angrier he got. "If she's such a menace, why hasn't she ever been charged or put in a care facility?"

"Unfortunately, it's not that easy," Grace said. "Unless she actually breaks a law there's nothing the police can do but take a report. Sometimes accumulative reports will build a history supporting action or adding to charges if any are ever brought."

Hunt nodded. "The family should do something, but they've set her up in the house and pretty much washed their hands of the situation."

"I am pressing charges," Jackson declared. "Someone who can lose their temper and stab a guy needs to be put away."

"I'm glad to hear it." Hunt shuffled the papers back together, and a picture slid out. Jackson automatically reached for it as he listened to Hunt. "A lot of men are too embarrassed to admit a woman hurt them."

Forget that. "I think my reputation can survive it."

"Good, good. Have you remembered anything more you think can help us?"

Jackson exchanged glances with Grace. She gave a subtle nod that he took to mean she thought he should reveal his condition to the detective. He responded with a negative shake of his head. He couldn't see where confessing his vulnerability helped the situation.

"No, nothing new." He casually looked down at the picture. It wasn't the driver's license shot, which was what he'd seen before. This was a candid picture of a woman at a party. She had lighter hair, animated features and was dressed in a minidress sipping a martini.

Seeing her in the context in which they met triggered something in his mind.

He dropped the photo to grab his head as pain streaked from temple to temple and thunder pounded behind his eyes. He knew her. Vanessa, pretty, fun, crazy. Images, thoughts, memories began to crowd his mind, of her, of his past, his friends, his company. Everything.

It was too much. Too fast.

"Jackson?" Grace's voice sounded as if she was shouting in a tunnel.

"Mr. Hawke?" Hunt sounded the same.

"I'm okay." Jackson tried to say but it came out as a croak.

He wanted out of there. To be home. And alone until he sorted everything out.

Tension radiated off Jackson. That and the fact his grip nearly crushed her knuckles told Grace something was wrong. She hid her anxiety behind a polite smile.

"It's the concussion," she explained to Hunt. "He was in an accident a few days ago. Is it possible for us to have the room for a few minutes?"

"Of course, take your time. A last word of caution, Mr. Hawke. Vanessa knows she's done wrong. If she follows her pattern, she could be waiting for you to resurface in order to apologize. But she's clearly unstable. Do not engage with her. And your security people should notify us immediately if they see her."

"Thank you, Detective." Grace pulled her hand free to move to the door, a gesture meant to hurry the detective along. "We'll take every precaution. And I'll personally pass your message on to security."

"Tonight's gala is a public event. We're concerned she may take the opportunity to get close to Hawke."

"I'll have Sierra add you and your partner to the guest list."

"Thanks. Let me know if you folks need anything more, otherwise I'll see you tonight." Hunt gathered up his folder and left the room.

Grace closed the door behind him then rushed back to Jackson's side.

"Jackson, what is it? What's wrong?"

She got a groan in response. So not good.

She dug in her purse for another pain pill and the water bottle. The doctor had said Jackson could take two pills if necessary. He'd refused to take more than one and she'd practically had to force-feed the few he'd taken. But he gave her no argument about taking a second pill. He shoved it in his mouth and swallowed on a gulp of water.

Wanting to do something more, she began massaging his temples. He stiffened but didn't ask her to stop. After a bit she shifted her fingers to the top and then the back of his head, working down until she used her thumbs along the chords at the base of his head leading to his neck. He moaned and the tension lessened through his shoulders.

"You remembered something," she guessed. It's the only thing she could think of that could incapacitate him like this.

"I remembered everything." His voice was rough as if squeezed through a vise.

Everything?

"Congratulations." Joy for him washed through her along with a pinch of dread, but now wasn't the time for celebrating or anticipating the end. The surge of intel had obviously overloaded his senses. She needed to get him home so he could rest. His brain needed to shut down for a while in order to absorb everything. "Do you think you can move?"

"Yes. Just give me another minute." He reached for the bottle and drank it dry.

She used the time to call his driver and instruct him to meet them at the front doors.

Jackson pushed to his feet. He gave her a small smile as he reached for her hand. "If I fall, don't let them take me to the hospital."

"Someday you're going to have to tell me what that's about." Grace opened the door and they started down the hall. When he swayed, she wrapped her arm around his waist. His arm automatically went around her shoulders. "Lean on me. I'll get you out of here."

CHAPTER TWELVE

JACKSON LOOKED LIKE a billion dollars. The cut of his tux, the straight line of his posture, the jut of his chin, all spoke of confidence and determination, both elements Grace saw every time she looked at him. But there was more tonight. There was a surety of self that had been missing until now.

He was in his element, among his people. And he was thriving.

Still, she kept an eye on him, watching for any sign of distress or fatigue.

She'd tried to talk him out of attending the gala. He'd crashed this morning when they returned from meeting with the detective. Slept for hours. She woke him around four and suggested skipping the event or merely putting in a brief appearance.

He refused to hear of it. Said he was fine and proved it by pulling her with him into the grotto shower for a lovely interval. She'd been forced to agree he was fine indeed.

The memory brought a touch of heat to her cheeks.

Hard to believe making love with Jackson could get better. It had. The man knew his way around a woman's body. She had no doubt he'd made a thorough study of it at some point in the past.

He laughed at something said in the group he was speaking with and then wished them well and broke away. Several people had joined the group after he did, and she'd ended up standing somewhat behind him. Now she watched as he moved off without her toward the next group.

She slowly followed in his wake. He'd been solicitous all evening, keeping her within hands' reach. Until now. Maybe she should have been the one to beg off the event.

He stopped suddenly and swung around. A frown drew his dark brows together until he spotted her. The approval in his eyes as he walked back to her almost made up for his leaving her behind.

"There you are. I missed you."

She shook her finger at him. "You forgot me."

"A momentary blip. I'm told that can happen when you have a concussion."

"Oh, now it's convenient to have a concussion. I can't believe you're using it as an excuse to me."

"Hmm. Have I told you how beautiful you look tonight?"

Oh, how sly. Of course she knew he meant to distract her. And he knew just how to get to her. The dress was strapless in a deep true red, the fitted, drop-waist bodice hugged her curves to the hips, and the full ballroom skirt, completely covered in ribbon roses, flowed around her when she moved.

She'd never felt more like a woman, or more beautiful. Except in his arms.

Because she wasn't mad, just a little sad to see the end creeping up on her, she let him off the hook.

"You did." She swished the skirt back and forth and smiled up at him, enjoying the spark in his eyes as they lingered on her. "Thank you. For the dress and for insisting it was the right one. I'll never forget this night. I feel like Cinderella at the ball."

"Good grief, does that make me Prince Charming? I don't think I can live that one down."

"Not so." She straightened his already perfect bow tie.

"JD may have stumbled a bit here, but Jackson is in his element. These people are lining up to eat out of your hand. You are every bit the prince of all you survey."

He glanced around at the crowd surrounding them. And there was just a little surprise in the gaze he turned back to her. "I suppose you're right." He wrapped an arm around her waist and pulled her to him. "I guess I'm just used to them versus me."

"I'm sure that's true in some cases." She leaned against him. "But not always. Tonight they're all backing you. This is a good thing you're doing here. And you don't need me hampering your progress. Why don't I find a quiet corner while you work the room for a while?"

Concern flashed into his green eyes. "Are you not feeling well?"

"I'm fine." It warmed her that his focus went to her first. "I just think you can move around easier without me tagging along."

"Absolutely not." He planted a soft kiss on her upraised mouth. "You saved my butt by interpreting Japanese for Mr. Watanabe. We were struggling without his interpreter."

"You were doing fine."

"I wasn't kidding when I said I missed you. My head is a mishmash of old and new. You help to ground me between the two. I can be myself with you."

It meant a lot that he felt that way. Love welled up causing her throat to tighten. She blinked back tears. Oh, yeah, the end was zinging at her with the speed of a bullet. But she could have this last night.

She cleared her throat and lifted onto her toes to kiss his cheek. "Okay, but if Cinderella's feet start to hurt, Prince Charming is going to carry her shoes."

"It's a deal." He kissed her again, lingering over the caress long enough to make her toes curl. Then he released her but kept hold of her hand as he headed toward another group of people.

He'd gone only a few steps when Clay intercepted them. "Jackson, I'll be shadowing you for a while."

"You've been shadowing me all night, Clay. What's changed?"

"A bit of a disturbance in the tunnel from the casino."

"What kind of disturbance?"

"Someone trying to break in. My men are handling it, and Hunt and his partner are headed over to check it out. It's probably nothing. But it means I'll be shadowing you from a foot away rather than ten."

"Do they think it's Vanessa?" Grace asked.

"Wouldn't that make the night a true success?" Clay fell into step with Jackson. "We should know soon."

"I can help if you need an extra hand," she offered.

"You're not going to need an extra hand, are you, Clay?" Jackson made it clear her assistance would not be tolerated.

"You do know I'm trained to handle situations like this."

"Yeah, I do. And I appreciate your willingness to help. But I won't risk you."

"That's just ridiculous." She tugged at her hand, wanting free of the bullheaded man.

"Don't care." He held on tight.

She threw up her free hand in frustration and looked to Clay for help.

He shrugged. "Works for me. I'm counting on you as a last line of defense."

"Ha." She smirked at Jackson.

He glared at Clay. "What the hell?"

Clay remained stoned-faced. "You're my number one concern. I'll use what tools I have to ensure your safety."

Jackson stepped right into her space and cupped her face, forcing her gaze to his. "How much would I have to pay you to get out of law enforcement?"

She blinked at him. What was he talking about? "It's what I do, who I am."

"You could learn something new with what I'm willing to pay. The thought of you getting hurt flays me."

The intensity in his expression shouted the truth of his words.

"I'm good at what I do," she reassured him. "And you were the one encouraging me to join the FBI."

"I was wrong. You should teach kindergarten or become a florist."

"A florist?" she repeated confused with where this was going. Seriously, she killed off cacti, something he didn't know about her, but still. She brushed the hair back at his temple. "Is your head hurting? Maybe we should take a break."

A pleading look toward the other man had him stepping forward.

"Jackson—"

"I don't need a break." Jackson ignored Clay. "I need for you to be safe."

"I am safe, right here by your side. You know as well as I do Clay isn't letting anyone get past him."

"And what about next week or a month from now? I have a scar to remind me things happen you never expect. Working in law enforcement comes with an expectation of being harmed in the line of duty."

"True. But I'm not taking money from you to change careers, so can we get back to enjoying the night?"

"Okay."

Yeah. He'd taken the hint in her tone and backed off.

"But the subject is not closed."

Or maybe not.

"I have confirmation," Clay broke in. "They just apprehended Vanessa."

* * *

Early the next morning, Grace woke to Jackson leaning over her. His lips caressed her cheek. "Sleep in. I have things to catch up on."

And then he was gone.

But there was no going back to sleep. Too much had happened yesterday for her mind to settle back into slumber. Not when she knew a difficult decision loomed ahead of her.

She was so happy for Jackson that Vanessa had been found and incarcerated. And still dread lay lead-heavy in her stomach.

His concern over her welfare touched her, but it also worried her. It would be different if they were a real couple, but her time with Jackson was more fantasy than reality. Their relationship was temporary at best.

She'd be a fool to let a fleeting lover influence her next career choice. Yet it would be too easy to do, considering she loved him. She'd known as soon as he regained his memory that her time with Jackson was limited, but with Vanessa still at large she'd figured she had a little extra time. Now that excuse was gone. She should make the break sooner rather than later.

Being a kept woman wasn't her style.

No, the fantasy only worked as long as she had something to bring to the relationship. Jackson no longer needed her, so it was time to go.

Just forming the thought in her head broke her heart. But it was for the best. She loved Jackson but not his transient lifestyle. She'd compromised in that regard for too long. She may be undecided with what she wanted to do for employment, but finding a place to put down roots was the one constant her soul never wavered on.

And for all his professions of missing her and his bargaining to find her a safer career, the longer the evening wore on, the more distant he became. Sure, he shackled her to his side, but he drew her into the conversation less and less. And for the past hour he sat her on a bar stool and completely ignored her while he talked to a group of old cronies several feet away.

It gave her a chance to observe him. He laughed, he talked, he listened, but always he maintained his distance. His stance, the angle of his head and the extra inches between him and those he conversed with shouted a need for space. And people gave it to him, happy just to have his attention.

His attention had been full-on when he made love to her last night, but his early disappearing act just confirmed he was reverting to his old ways. With each passing hour, the Jackson she knew morphed into the Jackson he used to be, which by all accounts meant a lack of emotional commitment.

What she'd learned from reading his file and talking with Sierra revealed a man shut off from the world. He lived in hotel suites, kept women and the world at a distance, and 90 percent of the work he did was in his head. His associates were his family, the company his home.

She couldn't live that way.

The man she knew wasn't quite so closed off, but with his memory back she had no doubt he'd soon revert to his former self. Too bad. The signs were there that he longed for more. He'd created the facsimile of a home by having all the penthouse suites designed the same. And his work with the foundation showed he had a heart.

He just wasn't willing to risk it by letting anyone too close.

So sad, because the man she knew was warm and generous, intelligent and funny. He'd make a great dad.

Good gracious, now she was thinking of children? That

settled it. She threw back the covers and made her way to the bathroom for one last shower in her own personal grotto.

She needed to leave, and she needed to leave today. Before she completely lost her mind.

As Grace zipped up her duffel bag, a text sounded on her phone. Jackson, letting her know he was wrapping up a meeting and would be up in the next few minutes.

She blew out a breath. Showtime.

Carrying her bags into the living area, she set them down near the archway. Being a bright guy, Jackson was sure to get the meaning and start the conversation for her.

A few minutes stretched into twenty and then thirty. More to occupy her hands and mind than because she was hungry, she worked in the kitchen, putting together a snack tray of veggies, fruit and cheese. After a while, she heard Jackson come in.

"I'm in here," she called out.

"Sorry, that took longer than I anticipated. This looks good." A kiss landed on her cheek as he snagged a broccoli floret before opening the refrigerator for a bottle of water. "I've been thinking this morning. I've come up with the answer to your career decision."

A sinking feeling settled on top of the dread she already sported.

"I'm not going to work for you."

"Way to undermine a guy." His Adam's apple bobbed as he drank. "Why not? It's the perfect solution."

So not perfect. Silly her, she longed for a proposal, not a job offer.

To give herself a moment, she carried the tray to the living room and set it on the glass coffee table. Jackson followed on her heels.

"You can work with Clay on our internet security team.

Electronic games are a highly competitive field. Espionage is rampant, but there's little chance of being physically hurt."

"Cyber security isn't really where my talents lie."

"You're being modest. I've seen your work, remember. The reports you've done for me, the profiles you put together for the gala have all been efficient and thorough. Top-notch." He reached for a piece of apple and spotted her luggage. His brows narrowed into a frown. "What's this?"

"I commandeered the suitcase you bought in Santa Rosa to hold the dresses you gave me. I didn't have the heart to squash them into the duffel bag."

"What are you doing, Grace? This sounds like good-bye."

"It is. You're home, Jackson. You have your memory back. You don't need me anymore." She thanked her years in the navy for managing to deliver the message in a strong voice.

A scowl drew his dark brows closer together. "That's not true. I have my memory back, but I'm still having headaches from the concussion."

"Dr. Wilcox can help you with those. And your friends will keep you from doing too much."

"Vanessa—"

"Has been apprehended. She's no longer a threat."

He cupped her cheek in his hand, ran his thumb over her chin, his touch nearly reverent. His eyes entreated her to stay. "I'm not ready to let you go."

Just for a moment she leaned into his hand, savoring the comfort of his touch, knowing this was the last connection they'd have.

"I don't want to go." The words squeezed past the lump in her throat. "Which is why I have to go now."

"That doesn't make sense."

"But it's the way it has to be."

"No," he argued, "there's another way. Come work for me."

Her head began shaking before he finished the sentence. "That's not a good idea."

"It's a great idea," he corrected, his voice going husky with his enthusiasm. "You're already working for me. You can just continue to do so. It's perfect."

"Except I don't want to work where a job has to be created for me. I want to be useful." Could he truly not see how he cut her each time he made the offer?

"You are useful. I couldn't have made it through the last week without you."

"But these were special circumstances. You don't need me to stand over your shoulder to do your business."

"Maybe I do." He broke away to pace. "Your notes saved me at my meeting yesterday. I've been vulnerable, not myself."

"Wrong." She wouldn't let him use his vulnerability against her, because he was so much stronger than his ailments. He'd proven that again and again. "You have been yourself. Pride, stubbornness, intelligence, determination, confidence—all those elements are you. The difference is your shields were down for a while. You've been more open to the world around you, allowed people to get closer. Experienced things like a regular man again."

"I'm not a regular man," he proclaimed with conviction. "I can't allow myself to be vulnerable."

That he believed that made her sad.

"Yes, you can. It takes a strong man to be open to being hurt. If nothing else, this experience has more than proven how strong you are. I hope that now you've regained your memory you'll take the lessons you learned this last week and apply them to your life going forward. Not all women are like Vanessa. They're not going to stab you. Give yourself a chance to be happy."

"Having you work for me will make me happy."

"Stop, Jackson." She couldn't take any more of this. His persistence chipped away at her determination. "Why are you doing this?"

"I told you, I'm not ready for you to go."

"Why not?" Her breath held in the back of her throat as she waited for his answer.

He struggled for words. And when he found them, they shattered her world. "Because I owe you."

She closed her eyes against the pain, then immediately opened them. Nothing to do about the fact they were overly bright. Forcing a smile, she began backing away, suddenly in full retreat.

"Wrong answer. Ah...huh." She cleared her throat. "But it's all good. An honest answer is never really wrong, is it?"

"Wait." He grabbed her hands and held on. "It is if it makes you leave. What did I do wrong?"

"For a smart man you can get some silly ideas. You don't owe me anything. I helped you because I wanted to, not for what I could get out of the experience."

"No." Shock rolled over his face. "I didn't mean that. You know I don't believe that. I want you to stay. We're good together."

"Oh, Jackson. We are good together, but we're nothing alike. I want roots, you want room service. I'm boots and jeans and you're a tuxedo and Italian leather. I need goals, schedules and order. You're spontaneous, creative and thrive in chaos. We are good together, too good. Which is why I can't stay. You think a few weeks together will allow you to work this attraction out of your system. But a few weeks together will only make it harder for me to go. Because it's more than chemistry for me. I love you."

He stopped his pursuit of her so suddenly he rocked on his heels. "Huh?" Wide-eyed, he stared at her, apparently stunned stupid.

Now there was the reaction a girl wanted when she revealed her love. Proof she was right to leave. Never again would she settle for less than love. And she wanted more than the emotion, she wanted the words and dedication that proclaimed she was valued above all else.

"Don't worry about it." She squeezed the words past the constriction in her throat, the pain in her heart. "My problem, not yours." Time to go. Her purse, she began a frantic search with her eyes. She needed her purse. "Listen, I want to thank you. This wasn't all one-sided. I learned a lot in the time we spent together." About herself, about a world she had no place in. "I met some really great people." She met his gaze straight on, because she wasn't a coward. "And a wonderful man."

She crossed to where he was still stuck in the middle of the room. "I've loved my time with you. I'll cherish it forever. Best it ends before it turns into something we both regret." She kissed him softly on the mouth. "Have a happy life."

"Sir," Jethro's assistant interrupted his meeting with Ryan, Clay and Sierra. "The manager of the hotel just called to say security has been dispatched to the owner's suite. There are sounds of destruction and breaking glass."

Clay's phone beeped as they all pushed to their feet. He met Jethro's gaze as they went through the door together. "Where's Hawke? He's alone? Are you sure? Where's Ms. Delaney?" The group stepped onto the executive elevator. "Okay, I'm on my way. Knock. If he doesn't answer, go in. If he's unhurt, I want you to pull back and wait for me."

"What's going on?" Jethro demanded. "Sounds like Jackson is trashing his suite."

"Where's Grace?" Sierra asked.

"She took a taxi to the airport twenty minutes ago."

"Okay, guys, that's not a coincidence."

"Come on, Sierra." Ryan shook his head. "It's not like Jackson to freak out over a woman."

"His relationship with Grace has been un-Jackson-like from the beginning."

"True," Jethro acknowledged as the elevator doors opened on the hallway outside Jackson's suite. Four security officers stood at the ready guarding the open door.

"Mr. Hawke is alone, sir," the head officer reported. "The room is trashed but he appears unharmed."

Clay nodded. "The four of you can go."

A crash came from inside the suite, followed by a foul curse.

"It's best if I go in alone," Jethro stated. The others nodded and he braved the threshold.

In the living room Jackson stood with hands on hips silhouetted against the Las Vegas skyline. Slices of fruits and vegetables were scattered at his feet amid shattered glass. Behind him the room looked as if a tornado had swept through—the coffee table was upended, furnishings were askew and the bar reeked of alcohol from broken bottles.

"You've made quite a mess here, buddy." Jethro joined Jackson at the window and, like him, stared out over the city. "Feel better?"

"No."

"Want to tell me what happened?"

"Grace left." Two words, devastating impact.

"I heard."

"I asked her to stay, to be with me."

"You proposed?"

Jackson heard the shock in Jethro's voice. Right. Why would he even go there? "No. I offered her a job."

"Oh."

"She said she loved me." The truth of that still rocked him.

"Ah."

He turned to stare at his friend's profile. "What does that mean?"

"Nothing. What did you say?"

Nothing. He'd frozen. Too surprised and confused by the declaration to act. Ever since he'd regained his memories, he felt out of sync, as if he was a round peg trying to fit in a square hole. He cherished what he had with Grace, but it was so far from who he was he didn't know how to reconcile JD with Jackson. Except to know he wasn't ready to let her go.

"She left. Why do the people I care about always leave?"

"At least you've known love, Jackson. My mom threw me in a dumpster."

That shocked Jackson from his fugue to focus on his friend. "Good Lord, Jethro, I never knew."

"Yeah, I don't share the fact my mom considered me trash very often. But for you I feel the need." He turned to face Jackson. "Not everyone leaves. Clay, Ryan and I are still here. You're my family, our family. We'll always have your back. The women in your life haven't left voluntarily. Your mom and Mama Harman died. And you knew when you started with Lilly how it would turn out. She was a year older than you, and there's no give in the foster world. Eighteen and you're out."

Jackson wanted to argue it hurt just the same, but his mother had loved him. He remembered her hugs, her laughter, how she had listened to him and read to him. Somehow he'd allowed the sadness of losing her to overshadow the love. The same with Mama Harman and Lilly.

But when placed against the stark knowledge of Jethro's experience he got some perspective. Maybe his recent experience allowed him to be more open to the truth. Grace's influence softened him, allowing him to trust again. He had been lucky to have love in his life. Still, the pattern was too entrenched in him to be easily shifted.

"Dude, you know I look on you as a brother. And you might be right about the rest, but Grace left." The admission cut deep.

"Did she?"

"She's not here, is she?"

"Jackson, Grace didn't leave you. She turned down a job offer."

"She knew I wanted her to stay."

"But did you give her a reason to stay? I've never seen you with anyone like you are with Grace. You've been different since you've been back. Happier. She's been good for you."

No denying that. From the moment he'd opened his eyes in a jail cell, alone and unknowing, to the long, duty-bound night of the gala when she'd stood by his side supporting and encouraging him. Her determination, intelligence and loyalty grounded him during a difficult time. Without her he'd have been lost.

Without her he would be lost.

"You're saying don't mess this up."

"That's what I'm saying."

"I'm going to need a plant."

The two-hour flight to San Francisco gave Grace plenty of time to suffer a few regrets. Pride sent her running, but had she flown from the only man she'd ever love? Shouldn't she have grabbed what time she could with him? He may not love her, but she knew he cared.

And that was the problem. Too often she'd accepted an inequitable relationship, even with her own father. This time she couldn't do it. She loved him too much to compromise. Respected herself too much to trade her pride for a few months' charade.

Doug had suggested Jackson might long for a home as

much as she did, but the way he froze when she said she loved him shouted just the opposite.

No, she'd been smart to end it before her heart got more engaged.

Or so she thought until she walked into the garage at the San Francisco Pinnacle to find Jackson leaning against her SUV. Her traitorous heart rejoiced at the sight of him.

"What are you doing here?"

"I live in a tuxedo world, but I like jeans, too. If you remember, that's what I was wearing when we met."

She blinked at him. "Seriously? That's what you want to say to me?"

"Yes. I run a billion-dollar organization." He blocked her when she tried to walk around him. "Believe me, I value organization as much as I do creativity."

"Jackson, this is futile."

"I'm not going to apologize for the room service. I'm sure you'll come to appreciate it."

"Doubtful, since we won't be together." She tried again to get around him, shutting her ears to his sensible arguments. She'd made up her mind. Again he blocked her.

"I'm not giving up on you, Grace."

"I'm sure there are any number of people able to play cyber cop for you."

He flinched. "I deserve that. But give a guy a break. I've had a lot to assimilate the last couple of days, and I'm told a concussion can cause confusion and disorientation."

"You keep throwing my words back at me." Why did he persist in doing this? She didn't know if she had the strength to say no a second time.

"What can I say? You're a smart woman."

"You're not making any points here."

The elevator dinged and a couple stepped out. They whispered to each other and laughed as they passed. It was a vivid reminder of everything Grace wanted. And Jackson didn't.

"I'm tired, Jackson. I really don't want to do this again." She deserved to be loved. Unless he had three little words to say, she didn't want to hear it.

"I could also point out that I don't trust easily, yet I invited you into my inner sanctum. I haven't done that in ten years."

She blinked again, the impact of his statement catching her unawares. She'd been so upset by the offer she hadn't seen it from his side, hadn't acknowledged the import of it. Still, nothing had changed. He'd offered her a job when she longed for so much more.

"Jackson—"

He placed a finger over her lips. "We agree we're good together. We can work out any differences, explore them, exploit them, rejoice in them."

"You're going to a lot of trouble to recruit a new employee."

"Forget the job." He leaned down and kissed her softly. "It's yours if you want it, but I'm talking a lifetime commitment. I need you in my life. The job was my way of keeping you with me. But I have a better way." Reaching behind him, he grabbed something off the hood of the SUV and presented it to her.

She stared at the plant, a charming little houseplant, some kind of ivy if she wasn't mistaken. "What's this?"

"The first plant for our new home." There was just the slightest shake to his voice. "I want to put down roots with you, Grace Delaney." No shake now. "In Las Vegas, or San Francisco if you want to pursue the position with the FBI. Wherever you want, as long as we're together."

"I think I'm going to start my own business as a private security consultant specializing in profiles and some private investigations. Including you, I've already had four clients. And I found your father."

"My father?" He looked perplexed, then laughed. "That's wonderful." He framed her face. "You're wonderful. Will you marry me?"

This time she blinked back tears. The words were right, the gesture perfect. Dare she hope? For so long she'd believed home was associated with a person. It was how she grew up moving from base to base with her father. But as an adult that never proved true, so she thought she could find home in a place. With his words she realized home followed the heart, and she hadn't found it because she hadn't found the right man. Until Jackson.

But it would only work if he felt the same.

"Why?" she whispered, too afraid to hope.

"Oh, baby." He took the plant and set it aside before pulling her into his arms. He tilted her chin until their gazes met. "Because I was happier staying with you in an economy hotel and having no money than I've ever been as a billionaire. Because you get me. Because I trust you. But most of all, because I love you."

Joy burst through her. She threw her arms around his neck and kissed him with all the love in her heart. He immediately deepened the kiss with an urgency and passion that echoed her emotions. When he lifted his head, she grinned up at him.

"Right answer."

"Does that mean yes?"

"That means yes."

* * * * *

BILLIONAIRE'S
JET SET BABIES

CATHERINE MANN

To Amelia Richard: a treasured reader, reviewer and friend. Thank you for all you've done to help spread the word about my stories.
You're awesome!

One

Alexa Randall had accumulated an eclectic boxful of lost and found items since opening her own cleaning company for charter jets. There were the standard smart phones, portfolios, tablets, even a Patek Philippe watch. She'd returned each to its owner.

Then there were the stray panties and men's boxers, even the occasional sex toys from Mile High Club members. All of those items, she'd picked up with latex gloves and tossed in the trash.

But today marked a first find ever in the history of A-1 Aircraft Cleaning Services. Never before had she found a baby left on board—actually, *two* babies.

Her bucket of supplies dropped to the industrial blue carpet with a heavy thud that startled the sleeping pair. Yep, two infants, apparently twins with similar blond curly hair and cherub cheeks. About one year old, perhaps? A boy and a girl, it seemed, gauging from their pink and blue smocked outfits and gender-matched car seats.

Tasked to clean the jet alone, Alexa had no one to share her shock with. She flipped on another table lamp in the main compartment of the sleek private jet, the lighting in the hangar sketchy at best even at three in the afternoon.

Both kids were strapped into car seats resting on the leather sofa along the side of the plane, which was Seth Jansen's personal aircraft. As in *the* Seth Jansen of Jansen Jets. The self-made billionaire who'd raked in a fortune inventing some must-have security device for airports to help combat possible terrorist attacks on planes during takeoffs and landings. She admired the man's entrepreneurial spirit.

Landing his account would be her company's big break. She needed this first cleaning of his aircraft to go off without a hitch.

Tiny fists waved for a second, slowing, lowering, until both babies began to settle back to sleep. Another huffy sigh shuddered through the girl before her breaths evened out. Her little arm landed on a piece of paper safety-pinned to the girl's hem.

Narrowing her eyes, Alexa leaned forward and read:

Seth,
You always say you want more time with the twins, so here's your chance. Sorry for the short notice, but a friend surprised me with a two-week spa retreat. Enjoy your "daddy time" with Olivia and Owen!
XOXO,
Pippa

Pippa?

Alexa straightened again, horrified. Really? Really!

Pippa Jansen, as in the *ex*-Mrs. Jansen, had dumped off her infants on their father's jet. Unreal. Alexa stuffed her fists into the pockets of her navy chinos, standard uniform for A-1 cleaning staff along with a blue polo shirt bearing the company's logo.

And who signed a note to their obviously estranged baby daddy with kisses and hugs? Alexa sank down into a fat chair across from the pint-size passengers. Bigger question of the day, who left babies unattended on an airplane?

A crappy parent, that's who.

The rich and spoiled rotten, who played by their own rules, a sad reality she knew only too well from growing up in that world. People had told her how lucky she was as a kid—lucky to have a dedicated nanny that she spent more time with than she did with either of her parents.

The best thing that had ever happened to her? Her father bankrupted the family's sportswear chain—once worth billions, now worth zip. That left Alexa the recipient of a trust fund from Grandma containing a couple of thousand dollars.

She'd used the money to buy a partnership in a cleaning service about to go under because the aging owner could no longer carry the workload on her own. Bethany—her new partner—had been grateful for Alexa's energy and the second chance for A-1 Aircraft Cleaning Services to stay afloat. Using Alexa's contacts from her family's world of luxury and extravagance she had revitalized the struggling business. Alexa's ex-husband, Travis, had been appalled by her new occupation and offered to help out financially so she wouldn't have to work.

She would rather scrub toilets.

And the toilet on this particular Gulfstream III jet was very important to her. She had to land the Jansen Jet contract and hopefully this one-time stint would impress him enough to cinch the deal. Her business needed this account to survive, especially in today's tough economy. If she failed, she could lose everything and A-1 might well face Chapter 11 bankruptcy. She'd hardly believed her luck when she'd been asked by another cleaning company to subcontract out on one of the Jansen Jets—this jet.

Now that she'd found these two babies, she was screwed. She swept particles of sand from the seat into her hand, eyed the fingerprints on the windows, could almost feel the grit rising from the carpet fiber. But she couldn't just clean up, restock the Evian water and pretend these kids weren't here. She needed to contact airport security, which was going to land Jansen's ex-wife in hot water, possibly him as well. That would piss off Jansen. And the jet still wouldn't be serviced. And then he would never consider her for the contract.

Frustration and a hefty dose of anger stung stronger than a bucket full of ammonia. Scratch cleaning detail for now, scratch cinching this deal that would finally take her company out of the red. She had to locate the twins' father ASAP.

Alexa unclipped the cell phone from her waist and thumbed her directory to find the number for Jansen Jets, which she happened to have since she'd been trying to get through to the guy for a month. She'd never made it further than his secretary, who'd agreed to pass along Alexa's business prospectus.

She eyed the sleeping babies. Maybe some good could come from this mess after all.

Today, she would finally have the chance to talk to the boss, just not how she'd planned and not in a way that would put him in a receptive mood…

The phone stopped ringing as someone picked up.

"Jansen Jets, please hold." As quickly as the thick female Southern drawl answered, the line clicked and Muzak filled the air waves with soulless contemporary tunes.

A squawk from one of the car seats drew her attention. She looked up fast to see Olivia wriggling in her seat, kicking free a Winnie the Pooh blanket. The little girl spit out her Piglet pacifier and whimpered, getting louder until her brother scrunched up his face, blinking awake and none too happy. His Eeyore pacifier dangled from a clip attached to his blue sailor outfit.

Two pairs of periwinkle-blue eyes stared at her, button noses crinkled. Owen's eyes filled with tears. Olivia's bottom lip thrust outward again.

Tucking the Muzak-humming phone under her chin, Alexa hefted the iconic Burberry plaid diaper bag off the floor.

"Hey there, little ones," she said in what she hoped was a conciliatory tone. She'd spent so little time around babies she could only hope she pegged it right. "I know, I know, sweetie, I'm a stranger, but I'm all you've got right now."

And how crummy was that? She stifled another spurt of anger at the faceless Pippa who'd dropped her children off like luggage. When had the spa-hopping mama expected their father to locate them?

"I'm assuming you're Olivia." Alexa tickled the bare foot of the girl wearing a pink smocked dress.

Olivia giggled, and Alexa pulled the pink lace bootie from the baby's mouth. Olivia thrust out her bottom lip—until Alexa unhooked a teething ring from the diaper bag and passed it over to the chubby-cheeked girl.

"And you must be Owen." She tweaked his blue tennis shoe—still on his foot as opposed to his sister who was ditching her other booty across the aisle with the arm of a major league pitcher. "Any idea where your daddy is? Or how much longer he'll be?"

She'd been told by security she had about a half hour to service the inside of the jet in order to be out before Mr. Jansen arrived. As much as she would have liked to meet him, it was considered poor form for the cleaning staff to still be on hand. She'd expected her work and a business card left on the silver drink tray to speak for itself.

So much for her well laid plans.

She scooped up a baby blanket from the floor, folded it neatly and placed it on the couch. She smoothed back Owen's sweaty curls. Going quiet, he stared back at her just as the on hold Muzak cued up "Sweet Caroline"— the fourth song so far. Apparently she'd been relegated to call waiting purgatory.

How long until the kids got hungry? She peeked into the diaper bag for supplies. Maybe she would luck out and find more contact info along the way. Sippy cups of juice, powdered formula, jars of food and diapers, diapers, diapers…

The clank of feet on the stairway outside yanked her upright. She dropped the diaper bag and spun around fast, just as a man filled the open hatch. A tall and broad-shouldered man.

He stood with the sun backlighting him, casting his face in mysterious shadows.

Alexa stepped in front of the babies instinctively, protectively. "Good afternoon. What can I do for you?"

Silently he stepped deeper into the craft until overhead lights splashed over his face and she recognized him from her internet searches. Seth Jansen, founder and CEO of Jansen Jets.

Relief made her knees wobbly. She'd been saved from a tough decision by Jansen's early arrival. And, wow, did the guy ever know how to make an entrance.

From press shots she'd seen he was good-looking, with a kind of matured Abercrombie & Fitch beach hunk appeal. But no amount of Google Images could capture the impact of this tremendously attractive self-made billionaire in person.

Six foot three or four, he filled the charter jet with raw muscled *man*. He wasn't some pale pencil pusher. He was more the size of a keen-eyed lumberjack, in a suit. An expensive, tailored suit.

The previously spacious cabin now felt tight. Intimate.

His sandy-colored hair—thick without being shaggy—sported sun-kissed streaks of lighter blond, the kind that came naturally from being outside rather than sitting in a salon chair. His tan and toned body gave further testimony to that. No raccoon rings around the eyes from tanning bed glasses. The scent of crisp air clung to him, so different from the boardroom aftershaves of her father and her ex. She scrunched her nose at even the memory of cloying cologne and cigars.

Even his eyes spoke of the outdoors. They were the same vibrant green she'd once seen in the waters off the Caribbean coast of St. Maarten, the sort of sparkling green that made you want to dive right into their cool depths. She turned shivery all over just thinking about taking a swim in those pristine waters.

She seriously needed to lighten up on the cleaning supply fumes. How unprofessional to stand here and gawk like a sex-starved divorcée—which she was.

"Good afternoon, Mr. Jansen. I'm Alexa Randall with A-1 Aircraft Cleaning Services."

He shrugged out of his suit jacket, gray pinstripe and almost certainly an Ermenegildo Zegna, a brand known for its no-nonsense look. Expensive. Not surprising.

His open shirt collar, with his burgundy tie loosened did surprise her, however. Overall, she got the impression of an Olympic swimmer confined in an Italian suit.

"Right." He checked his watch—the only non-*GQ* item on him. He wore what appeared to be a top-of-the-line diver's timepiece. "I'm early, I know, but I need to leave right away so if you could speed this up, I would appreciate it."

Jansen charged by, not even hesitating as he passed the two tykes. *His* tykes.

She cleared her throat. "You have a welcoming crew waiting for you."

"I'm sure you're mistaken." He stowed his briefcase, his words clipped. "I'm flying solo today."

She held up Pippa's letter. "It appears, Mr. Jansen, your flight plans have changed."

Seth Jansen stopped dead in his tracks. He looked back over his shoulder at Alexa Randall, the owner of a new, small company that had been trying to get his attention for at least a month. Yeah, he knew who the drop-dead gorgeous blonde was. But he didn't have time to listen to her make a pitch he already knew would be rejected.

While he appreciated persistence as a business professional himself, he did not like gimmicks. "Let's move along to the point, please."

He had less than twenty minutes to get his Gulfstream III into the air and on its way from Charleston, South Carolina, to St. Augustine, Florida. He had a business meeting he'd been working his ass off to land for six months—dinner with the head of security for the Medinas, a deposed royal family that lived in exile in the United States.

Big-time account.

Once in a lifetime opportunity.

And the freedom to devote more of his energies to the philanthropic branch of this company. Freedom. It had a different meaning these days than when he'd flown crop dusters to make his rent back, in North Dakota.

"This—" she waved a piece of floral paper in front of him "—is the point."

As she passed over the slip of paper, she stepped aside and revealed—holy crap—his kids. He looked down at the letter fast.

Two lines into the note, his temple throbbed. What the hell was Pippa thinking, leaving the twins this way?

How long had they been in here? And why had she left him a damn note, for Pete's sake?

He pulled out his cell phone to call his ex. Her voice mail picked up immediately. She was avoiding him, no doubt.

A text from Pippa popped up in his in-box. He opened the message and it simply read, Want 2 make sure you know. Twins r waiting for you at plane. Sorry 4 short notice. XOXO.

"What the h—?" He stopped himself short before he cursed in front of his toddlers who were just beginning to form words. He tucked his phone away and faced Alexa Randall. "I'm sorry my ex added babysitter duties to your job today. Of course I'll pay you extra. Did you happen to notice which way Pippa headed out?"

Because he had some choice words for her when he found her.

"Your ex-wife wasn't here when I arrived." Alexa held up her own cell phone, her thumb swiping away a print. "I tried to contact your office, but your assistant wouldn't let me get a word out before shifting me over to Muzak. It's looped twice while I waited. Much longer and I would have had to call security, which would have brought in child services—"

He held up a hand, sick to his gut already. "Thanks. I get the picture. I owe you for cleaning up after my ex-wife's recklessness as well."

His blood pressure spiked higher until he saw red. Pippa had left the children unattended in an airplane at his privately owned airport? What had his security people been thinking, letting Pippa just wander around the aircraft that way? These were supposed to be the days of increased precautions and safety measures, and yet they must have assumed because she was his ex-wife that garnered her a free pass around the facility. Not so.

Heads were going to roll hard and fast over this. No one put the safety of his children at risk.

No one.

He crumpled the note in his fist and pitched it aside. Forcing his face to smooth so he wouldn't scare the babies, he unstrapped the buckle on his daughter's car seat.

"Hey there, princess." He held Olivia up high and thought about how she'd squealed with delight over the baby swing on the sprawling oak in his backyard. "Did you have fruit for lunch?"

She grinned, and he saw a new front tooth had come in on top. She smelled like peaches and baby shampoo and there weren't enough hours in the day to take in all the changes happening too quickly.

He loved his kids more than anything, had since the second he'd seen their fists waving in an ultrasound. He'd been damn lucky Pippa let him be there when they were born, considering she'd already started divorce proceedings at that point. He hated not being with them every day, hated missing even one milestone. But the timing for this visit couldn't be worse.

Seth tucked Olivia against his chest and reached to ruffle his son's hair. "Hey, buddy. Missed you this week."

Owen stuck out his tongue and offered up his best raspberry.

The petite blonde dressed in trim, pressed chinos popped a pacifier into Owen's mouth then knelt to pick up the crumpled note and pitch it into her cleaning bucket. "I assume today isn't your scheduled visitation."

She would be right on that. Although why the disdain in her voice? Nobody—single parent or not—would appreciate having their kids dumped off in their workplace. Not to mention he was mad as hell at Pippa for just dropping them off unannounced.

What if someone else had boarded this plane?

Thank God, this woman—Alexa—had been the one to find them. He knew who she was, but Pippa hadn't known jack when she'd unloaded his children.

Of all the reckless, irresponsible…

Deep breath. He unbuckled Owen as well and scooped him up, too, with an ease he'd learned from walking the floors with them when they were infants. Just as he'd needed calm then, he forced it through his veins now.

Getting pissed off wouldn't accomplish anything. He had to figure out what to do with his children when he was scheduled to fly out for a meeting with multimillion dollar possibilities.

When he'd first moved to South Carolina, he'd been a dumb ass, led by glitz. That's how he'd ended up married to his ex. He'd grown up with more spartan, farm values that he'd somehow lost in his quest for beaches and billions.

Now, he itched inside his high-priced starched shirt and longed for the solitude of those flights. But he had long ago learned if he wanted to do business with certain people, he had to dress the part and endure the stuffy business meetings. And he very much wanted to do business with the Medina family based out of Florida. He glanced at his watch and flinched. Damn it. He needed to be in the air already, on his way to St. Augustine. At the moment, he didn't have time for a sandwich, much less to find a qualified babysitter.

He would just have to make time. "Could you hold Owen for a second while I make some calls?"

"Sure, no problem." Alexa stopped straightening his jacket on the hanger and extended her arms.

As he passed his son over, Seth's hand grazed her breast. Her very soft, tempting breast. Just that fast touch pumped pure lust through his overworked body. It was more than just "nice, a female" kind of notice. His body was going on alert, saying "I will make it my mission in life to undress you."

She gasped lightly, not in outrage but more like someone who'd been zapped with some static. For him, it was more like a jolt from a light socket.

Olivia rested her head on his shoulder with a sleepy sigh, bringing him back to reality. He was a father with responsibilities.

Still, he was a man. Why hadn't he noticed the power of the pull to this woman when he'd walked onto the plane? Had he grown so accustomed to wealth that he'd stopped noticing "the help"? That notion didn't sit well with him at all.

But it also didn't keep him from looking at Alexa more closely.

Her pale blond hair was pulled back in a simple silver clasp. Navy chino pants and a light blue shirt— the company uniform—matched her eyes. It also fit her loosely, but not so much that it hid her curves.

Before the kids, before Pippa, he would have asked Alexa for her number, made plans to take her out on a riverboat dinner cruise where he would kiss her senseless under a starry sky. But these days he didn't have time for dating. He worked and when he wasn't on the job he saw his kids.

With a stab of regret, his gaze raked back over her T-shirt with the A-1 Aircraft Cleaning logo. He'd seen that same emblem in the cover letter she'd sent with her prospectus.

He also recalled why he hadn't gotten any further than the cover letter and the fledgling business's flyer—where he'd seen her headshot.

Following his eyes, she looked down at her shirt and met his gaze dead-on. "Yes, I have a proposal on your desk." Alexa cocked one eyebrow. "I assume that's why you were looking at my shirt?"

"Of course, why else?" he answered dryly. "You should have received an answer from my secretary."

"I did, and when you're not in a hurry—" she smoothed back her already immaculate hair "—I would appreciate the opportunity to explore your reasons for rejecting my initial bid."

"I'll save us both some time. I'm not interested in the lowest bidder or taking a risk on such a small company."

Her sky-blue eyes narrowed perceptively. "You didn't read my proposal all the way through, did you?"

"I read until my gut told me to stop." He didn't have time to waste on page after page of something he already knew wasn't going to work.

"And you're saying that your gut spoke up quickly."

"Afraid so," he said shortly, hoping to end an awkward situation with his best boardroom bite. A suspicion niggled. "Why is it you're here cleaning today instead of someone from my regular company?"

"They subcontracted A-1 when they overbooked.

Obviously I wasn't going to turn down the opportunity to impress you." She stood tall and undaunted in spite of his rejection.

Spunky and hot. Dangerous combo.

He fished his phone from his suit coat again. "I really do need to start making some calls."

"Don't let me keep you." She dipped her hand into the diaper bag and pulled out two rice cakes. She passed one to Owen and the other to Olivia. All the while Owen tugged at her hair, watching the way the white-blond strands glittered in the light. "That should keep them quiet while you talk."

Interesting that Alexa never once winced, even when Owen's fingers tangled and tugged. Not that he could blame his son in the least.

Seth thumbed the numbers on his phone and started with placing a call to his ex-wife—that again went straight to voice mail. Damn it. He then moved on to dialing family members.

Five frustrating conversations later, he'd come up empty on all counts. Either his kids were hellions and no one wanted to watch them, or he was having a serious run of bad luck.

Although their excuses were rock solid. His cousin Paige was on lockdown since her two daughters had strep throat. His cousin Vic had announced his wife was in labor with child number three—which meant *her* sisters were watching her other two kids, in addition to their own. But damn it, he'd needed to take off five minutes ago.

Brooding, he watched Alexa jostle Owen on her shapely hip. She was obviously a natural with kids. She wasn't easily intimidated, important when dealing with his strong-willed offspring. She'd protected the kids when she found them alone on the plane. He'd seen proof of her determination and work ethic. An idea formed in his head, and as much as he questioned the wisdom of it, the notion still took root.

In spite of what he'd told her, he had read more of her proposal than the cover letter, enough to know something about her. He was interested in her entrepreneurial spirit—she'd done a solid job revitalizing a company that had virtually been on financial life support. Still, his gut told him he couldn't afford to take a risk on this part of his business, especially not now. Now that he was expanding, he needed to hire a larger, more established cleaning chain, even if it cost him extra.

But he needed a nanny and she'd passed the high-level background check needed to work in an airport. Her life had been investigated more thoroughly than anyone he would get from a babysitting service. Not to mention a babysitting service would send over a total stranger that his kids might hate. At least he'd met this woman, had access to her life story. Most importantly, he saw her natural rapport with the twins. He would be nearby in the hotel at all times—even during meetings—if she had questions about their routine.

She was actually a godsend.

Decision made, he forged ahead. "While I don't think your company's the right one to service Jansen Jets, *I* have a proposal for *you*."

"I'm not sure I understand?"

"You fly with me and the kids to St. Augustine, be Owen and Olivia's nanny for the next twenty-four hours and I'll let you verbally pitch your agency's proposal to me again, in detail." The more he spelled it out, the better the idea sounded. "I'll give you a few pointers about why my gut spoke up so quickly in case you want to make adjustments for future proposals to other companies. I'll even pass along your name to possible contacts, damn good contacts. And of course you'll be paid, a week's worth of wages for one day's work."

Was he taking advantage here? He didn't think so. He was offering her a business "in" she wouldn't have otherwise. If her verbal proposal held together, he would mention her business to some of his connections. And yes, give her those tips to help cinch a deal elsewhere. She would land jobs, just not his.

She eyed him suspiciously. "Twenty-four hours of Mary Poppins duty in exchange for a critique and some new contacts?"

"That should be long enough for me to make alternative arrangements." There'd been a time when twenty-four hours with a woman would be more than enough time to seduce her as well. His eyes roved over Alexa's curves once more, regretting that he wouldn't be able to brush up on those skills during this trip.

"And you trust me, a stranger, with your children?" Disdain dripped from her voice.

"Do you think this is the right time to call me a crummy father?" Though he had to appreciate her protective instincts when it came to his children.

"You could just ring up a nanny service."

"Already thought of that. They wouldn't get here in time and my kids might not like the person they send. Olivia and Owen have taken to you." Unable to resist, he tapped the logo just above her breast. Lightly. Briefly. His finger damn near shot out a flame like a Bic lighter. "And I do know who you are. I read enough of your proposal to learn you've passed your security check for airport work."

"Well, tomorrow is usually my day off…" She dusted the logo on her shirt, as if his touch lingered. "You'll really listen to my pitch and give me tips, mention my company to others?"

"Scout's honor." He smiled for the first time all day, seeing victory in sight.

"I want you to know I'm not giving up on persuading you to sign me up for Jansen Jets as well."

"Fair enough. You're welcome to try."

She eyed both the children then looked back to him. He knew when he'd presented an irresistible proposition. Now he just needed to wait for her to see this was a win-win situation.

Although he needed for her to realize that quickly. "I have about two minutes left here," he pressed. "If your answer's no, get to it so I can make use of the rest of my time to secure alternative arrangements." Although God only knew what those might be.

"Okay." She nodded in agreement although her furrowed brow broadcast a hefty dose of reservation. "You have yourself a deal. I'll call my partner to let her know so she can cover—"

"Great," he interrupted. "But do it while you buckle up the kids and yourself. We're out of here." He settled Olivia back into her car seat with a quick kiss on her forehead.

Alexa looked up quickly from fastening Owen into his safety seat. "Where's the pilot?"

He stared into her pale blue eyes and imagined them shifting colors as he made her as hot for him as he was for her. God, it would be damn tough to have this jaw-dropping female working beside him for the next twenty-four hours. But his children were his top priority.

So he simply smiled—and, yes, took a hefty dose of pleasure in seeing her pupils widen with awareness. "The pilot? That would be me."

Two

Her stomach dropped and she prayed the Gulf-stream III wouldn't do the same in Seth Jansen's hands.

Turning off her cell after deleting four missed calls from her mother and leaving a message for her partner, Bethany, Alexa double-checked the safety belts for both children and buckled her own. Watching Seth slide into the pilot's seat, she reminded herself he owned a charter jet company so of course it made sense he could pilot a plane himself. She'd flown on private aircraft during her entire childhood, trusting plenty of aviators she'd never even met to get her safely from point A to point B. So why was she so nervous with this guy at the helm?

Because he'd thrown her off balance.

Boarding the plane earlier, she'd had such optimism, a solid approach in place and control of her world. In the span of less than ten minutes, Seth Jansen had seized control of not just the plane, but her carefully made plan.

The kind of bargain he'd proposed was so unexpected, outrageous even. But too good an opportunity to pass up. She needed to take a deep breath, relax and focus on learning everything she could about him, to give her an edge in negotiations.

Even knowing he must have his pilot's license, she wouldn't have expected someone as wealthy as him willing to fly himself. She'd thought he would have someone else "chauffeuring" while he banged back a few drinks or took a nap. Like her dad would have done during their annual family vacation, a one-week trip that was supposed to make up for all the time they never spent together during the year.

Not that she saw much of either of her parents even then. While on vacation, the nanny had taken her to amusement parks or sightseeing or to the slopes while her father attended to "emergency" business and her mother went to the spa.

Simmering over old memories, Alexa polished the metal seatbelt buckle absently with the hem of her shirt as she watched Seth Jansen complete his preflight routine.

The door to the cockpit had been left open. Seth adjusted the mic on the headset, his mouth moving, although she couldn't hear him as the engines hummed to life. Smooth as silk, the plane left the hangar, past a row of parked smaller aircraft until he taxied to the end of the runway and stopped.

Nerves pattered up from her stomach to the roots of her hair. The jet engines roared louder, louder still, and yet she could swear she heard Seth's deep voice calmly blending with the aerial symphony.

Words drifted back…

"Charleston tower… Gulfstream alpha, two, one, prepared… Roger… Ready for takeoff…"

The luxury craft eased forward again, Seth's hands steady on the yoke and power. Confidence radiated from his every move, so much so she found herself relaxing into the butter-soft leather sofa. Her hands fell to rest on the handle of each car seat, claiming her charges. Her babies, for the next twenty-four hours.

Her heart squeezed with old regrets. Her marriage to Travis had been an unquestionable failure. While part of her was relieved there hadn't been children hurt by their breakup, another part of her grieved for the babies that might have been.

The nose of the plane lifted as the aircraft swooped upward. Olivia and Owen squirmed in their seats. Alexa reached for the diaper bag, panic stirring. Did they want a bottle? A toy? And if they needed a diaper change there wasn't a thing she could do about that for a while. Just when the panic started to squeeze her chest, the noise of the engines and the pacifiers she'd used to help their ears soothed them back into their unfinished nap.

The diaper bag slid from her grip, thudding on the floor. Relaxing, she stared across the aisle out the window as they left Charleston behind. She also left behind an empty apartment and a silent phone since her married friends had dropped away after her divorce.

Church steeples and spires dotted the ocean-locked landscape. So many, the historic town had earned nicknames of the Holy City and the City by the Sea. After their financial meltdown, her parents had relocated to a condo in Boca Raton to start over—away from the gossip.

How ironic that her parents' initial reservations about Travis had been so very far off base. They'd begged him to sign a prenuptial agreement. She'd told them to take their prenup and go to hell. Travis had insisted he didn't care and signed the papers anyway. She thought she'd found her dream man, finally someone who would love her for herself.

Not that the contract had mattered in the end since her father had blown through the whole fortune anyway. By the time they'd broken up, her ex hadn't wanted anything to do with her, her messy family dysfunction, or what he called her germaphobic ways.

The way Travis had simply fallen out of love with her had kicked the hell out of her self-esteem there for a while. She couldn't even blame the breakup on another woman. No way in hell was she going to let a man have control of her heart or her life ever again.

All the more reason she had to make a go of her cleaning business and establish her independence. She had no other marketable skills, apart from a host of bills and a life to rebuild in her beloved hometown.

So here she was, on a plane bound for St. Augustine with a stranger and two heart-tuggingly adorable babies. The coastline looked miniscule now outside the window as they reached their cruising altitude.

"Hey, Alexa?"

Seth's voice pulled her attention away from the view. He stood in the archway between the cockpit and the seating area.

Her stomach jolted again. "Shouldn't you be flying the plane?"

"It's on autopilot for the moment. Since the kids are sleeping, I want you to come up front. The flight isn't long, but it will give us the chance to talk through some specifics about your time with the twins."

She saw the flinty edge of calculation in his jewel-toned eyes. He may have offered her a deal back at the airport, but now he intended to interview her further before he turned over his children to her. A flicker of admiration lit through the disdain she had felt for him earlier.

Giving each baby another quick check and finding them snoozing away, binkies half in, half out of their slack mouths, she unbuckled, reassured she could safely leave them for a few minutes. She walked the short distance to Seth and stopped in the archway, waiting for him to move back to the pilot's seat.

Still, he stood immobile and aloof, other than those glinting green eyes that swept over her face. The crisp scent of him rode the recycled air to tempt her nose, swirling deeper inside her with each breath. Her breasts tingled with awareness, her body overcome with the urge to lean into him, press the aching fullness of her chest against the hard wall of manly muscles.

She shivered. He smiled arrogantly as if completely cognizant of just how much he affected her on a physical level. Seth stepped back brusquely, returning to the pilot's spot on the left and waving her into the copilot's seat on the right.

Strapping in, she stared at the gauges around her, the yoke moving automatically in front of her. Seth tapped buttons along the control panel and resumed flying the plane. Still, the steering in front of her mirrored his movements until she felt connected to him in some mystical manner.

She resented the way he sent her hormones into overdrive with just the sound of his husky voice or the intensity of his sharp gaze. She was here to do a job, damn it, not bring a man into her already too complicated life.

Twisting her fingers together in her lap, she forced her thoughts back to their jobs. "What's so important about this particular meeting that it can't be rescheduled?"

"I have small mouths to feed. Responsibilities." He stayed steadily busy as he talked, his eyes roving the gauges, his hands adjusting the yoke. "Surely you understand that, and if not, then I don't even need to read your proposal." He winked.

"Thank you for the Business 101 lecture, Mr. Jansen." She brushed specks of dust from a gauge. "I was really just trying to make conversation, but if you're more comfortable hanging out here alone, I'll be glad to return to the back."

"Sorry... And call me Seth," he said with what sounded like genuine contrition. "Long day. Too many surprises."

She glanced back at the sleeping babies, suddenly realizing they had miniature versions of his strong chin. "I can see that. What do you do to relax?"

"Fly."

He stared out at the expanse of blue sky and puffy clouds, and she couldn't miss the buzz radiating from him. Jansen Jets wasn't just a company to him. He'd turned his hobby, his true love, into a financial success. Not many could accomplish such a feat. Maybe she could learn something about business from him after all.

"You were looking forward to this time in the air, weren't you? What should have been your relaxing hour for the day has become a stressor."

"I've gotta ask…" He looked over at her quickly, brow furrowed. "Is the psychoanalysis included in the cleanup fee?"

She winced as his words hit a little too close to a truth of her own. Travis used to complain about that same trait. Well, she did have plenty of practice in what a shrink would say after all the time she'd spent in analysis as a teenager. The whole point had been to internalize those healthier ways of thinking. She'd needed the help, no question, but she'd also needed her parents. When they hadn't heard her, she'd started crying out for their attention in other ways, ways that had almost cost her life.

Her thoughts were definitely getting too deep and dark, and therefore too distracting. Something about this man and his children made her visit places in her mind she normally kept closed off. "Like I said, just making small talk. I thought you wanted me to come up here for conversation, to dig a little deeper into the background of your new, temporary nanny. If you don't want to chat, simply say so."

"You're right. I do. And the first thing I've learned is that you don't back down, which is a very good thing. It takes a strong person to stand up to the twins when they're in a bad mood." He shuddered melodramatically, his complaint totally undercut by the pride in his voice. Mr. Button-Up Businessman loosened up a little when he spoke of his kids. "What made you trade in your white gloves at tea for white glove cleaning?"

So he knew a little about her privileged upbringing as well. "You did more than just read my cover letter."

"I recognized your name—or rather your return to your maiden name. Your father was once a client of a competing company. Your husband chartered one of my planes."

"My ex-husband," she snapped.

He nodded, his fingers whitening as his grip tightened on the yoke. "So, back to my original question. What made you reach for the vacuum cleaner?"

"Comes with the business."

"Why choose this particular line of work?"

Because she didn't have a super cool hobby like he did? She'd suffered a rude awakening after her divorce was finalized a year ago, and she realized she had no money and no marketable skills.

Her one negligible talent? Being a neat-freak with a need to control her environment. Pair that with insights into the lifestyles of the rich and spoiled and she'd fashioned a career. But that answer sounded too half-baked and not particularly professional.

"Because I understand the needs of the customer, beyond just a clean space, I know the unique services that make the job stand out." True enough, and since he seemed to be listening, she continued, "Keeping records of allergies, favored scents, personal preferences for the drink bar can make the difference between a successful flight and a disaster. Flying in a charter jet isn't simply an air taxi service. It's a luxury experience and should be treated as such."

"You understand the world since you lived in it."

Lived. Past tense. "I want to be successful on my own merits rather than mooch off the family coffers."

Or at least she liked to think she would have felt that way if there had been any lucre left in the Randall portfolio.

"Why work in this particular realm, the aircraft world?" He gestured around the jet with a broad hand.

Her eyes snagged on the sprinkling of fair hair along his forearm. Tanned skin contrasted with the white cuffs of his rolled up sleeves and wow did her fingertips ever itch to touch him. To see if his bronzed-god flesh still carried the warmth of the sun.

It had been so long since she'd felt these urges. Her divorce had left her emotionally gutted. She'd tried dating a couple of times, but the chemistry hadn't been there. Her new business venture consumed her. Or rather, it had until right now, when it mattered most.

"I'm missing your point." No surprise since she was staring at his arm like an idiot.

"You're a…what…history major?"

"Art history, and being that close means you read my bio. You do know a lot more about me than you let on at first."

"Of course I do or I never would have asked you to watch my children. They're far more precious to me than any plane." His eyes went hard, leaving no room for doubt. Any mistakes with his son and daughter would not be tolerated. Then he looked back at the sky, mellow Seth returning. "Why not manage a gallery if you need to fill your hours?"

Because she would be lucky if working in a gallery would cover rent on an apartment or a lease on an economy car, much less food and economic stability. Because she wanted to prove she didn't need a man to be successful. And most importantly, *because* she didn't ever again want the freaked out feeling of being less than six hundred dollars away from bankruptcy.

Okay, sort of melodramatic since she'd still owned jewelry she could hock. But still scary as hell when she'd sold off her house and car only to find it barely covered the existing loans.

"I do not expect anyone to support me, and given the current economy, jobs in the arts aren't exactly filling up the want ad sections. Bethany has experience in the business, while I bring new contacts to the table. We're a good team. Besides, I really do enjoy this work, strange as that may seem. While A-1 has employees who handle cleaning most of the time, I pitch in if someone's out sick or we get the call for a special job. I enjoy the break from office work."

"Okay, I believe you. So you used to like art history, and now you enjoy feeding people's Evian habits and their need for clean armrests."

The deepening sarcasm in his voice had her spine starching with irritation. "Are you making fun of me for the hell of it or is there a purpose behind this line of questioning?"

"I always have a purpose," he said as smoothly as he flew the plane. "Will your whim of the week pass, once you realize people take these services for granted and your work is not appreciated? What happens to my aircraft then? I'll be stuck wading through that stack of proposals all over again."

He really saw her as a flighty, spoiled individual and that stung. It wasn't particularly fair, either. "Do you keep flying even when people don't appreciate a smooth or on-time flight, when they only gripe about the late or bumpy rides?"

"I'm not following your point here. I like to fly. Are you saying you like to clean?"

"I like to restore order," she answered simply, truthfully.

The shrinks she'd seen as a teen had helped her rechannel the need for perfection her mother had drilled into Alexa from birth. She'd stopped starving herself, eased off searching the art world for flawless beauty and now took comfort from order, from peace.

"Ah—" a smile spread over his face "—you like control. Now that I understand."

"Who doesn't like control?" And how many therapy sessions had she spent on *that* topic?

He looked over at her with an emerald-eyed sexy stare. The air crackled as if a lightning bolt had zipped between them. "Would you like to take over flying the plane?"

"Are you kidding?" She slid her hands under her thighs even though she couldn't deny to herself just how tempting the offer sounded.

Who wouldn't want to take a stab at soaring through the air, just her and the wide-open blue rolling out in front of the plane? It would be like driving a car alone for the first time. Pushing an exotic Arabian racehorse to gallop. Happier memories from another lifetime called to her.

"Just take the yoke."

God, how she wanted to, but there was something in his voice that gave her pause. She couldn't quite figure out his game. She wasn't in the position to risk her livelihood or her newfound independence on some guy's whims.

"Your children are on board." She knew she sounded prim, but then hey, she was a nanny for the day.

"If it appears you're about to send us into a nosedive, I'll take over."

"Maybe another time." She leaped up from the seat, not about to get sucked into a false sense of control that wouldn't last. "I think I hear Olivia."

His low chuckle followed her all the way back to both peacefully sleeping children.

Alexa could hear his husky laugh echoing in her ears two hours later as they settled into their luxurious hotel room in St. Augustine, Florida.

She had seen the best of the best lodgings and the Casa Monica—one of the oldest hotels in the United States—was gorgeous by any standards, designed to resemble a castle. The city of St. Augustine itself was rich with history and ornate Spanish architecture, the Casa Monica being a jewel. The hotel had been built in the 1800s, named for St. Monica, the mother of St. Augustine, the city's namesake.

And here she was with Seth and his babies. She could use a little motherly advice from a patron saint's mom right now.

She also needed to find some time to touch base with Bethany at work. Even though she was sure Bethany could manage—it had been her company at one time— she really did need to speak with her partner and give Bethany her contact information.

Seth had checked them into one of the penthouse suites, with a walk-out to a turret with views of the city. The suite had two bedrooms connected by a sitting area. The mammoth bath with a circular tub called to her muscles, which ached from working all day then lugging one of the baby carriers around. Then her thoughts went to images of sharing the tub with a man...not just any man...

She turned back to the room, decorated in blue velvet upholstery and heavy brocade curtains. Seth had claimed the spare bedroom, leaving her the larger master with two cribs inside. She trailed her fingers over the handle to Olivia's car seat on the floor beside the mission style sofa in the sitting room. Olivia's brother rested in his car seat next to hers.

"Your twins sleep well. They're making this job too easy, you know."

"Pippa doesn't believe in bedtimes. They usually nap hard their first day with me." Seth strode into the spare bedroom. "Expect mayhem soon enough when they wake up recharged. Owen's a charmer, so much so it's easy to miss the mischief he's plotting. He's always looking for the best way to stack furniture and climb his way out. You can see where he's already had stitches through his left eyebrow. As for Olivia, well, keep a close eye on her hands. She loves to collect small things to shove up her nose, in her ears, in her mouth..."

Affection swelled from each word as he detailed his children's personalities. The man definitely loosened up when around his kids or when he was talking about them. He seemed to know his offspring well. Not what she would have expected from a distant dad. Intrigued, she moved closer.

Through the open door, she could see him drape his suit coat on the foot of the bed. He loosened his tie further and unbuttoned his collar, then worked the buttons free down his shirt.

Alexa backed toward her own room. "Um, what are you doing?"

Seth slipped his still-knotted tie over his head and untucked the shirt. "Owen kicked his shoes against me when I picked him up after we landed." He pointed to smudges down the left side. "I need to change fast before my meeting."

His all-important meeting. Right. Seth had told her he was having dinner with a bigwig contact downstairs and she could order whatever she wanted from room service. He would be back in two to three hours. If she could get the kids settled in the tub, she could sit on the side and make some work calls while watching them. Check voice mail and email on her iPhone, deal with the standard million missed calls from her mom before moving on to deal with work. Her staff wasn't large, just four other employees, including Bethany. Her partner was slowing down, but could hold down the fort. In the event an emergency arose, Bethany would make sure things didn't reach a boiling point. So she was in the free and clear to spend the night here. With the kids.

And Seth.

She thumbed a smudge from the base of the brass lamp. "Can't have shoe prints all over you at the big meeting. That's for sure."

"Could you look in the hang-up bag and get me another shirt?"

"Right, okay." She spun away before he undressed further. She charged over to the black suitcase resting on top of a mahogany luggage rack.

Alexa tugged the zipper around and…oh my. The scent of him wafted up from his clothes, which should be impossible since they were clean clothes. But no question about it, the suitcase had captured the essence of him and it was intoxicating.

Her fingers moved along the hangers until she found a plain white shirt mixed in with a surprising amount of colorful others. Mr. Buttoned-up Businessman had a wild side. An unwelcome tingle played along her skin and in her imagination. She slapped the case closed.

Shirt in hand, she turned back to Seth who was now wearing only his pants and a T-shirt. His shoulders stretched the fabric to the limit. Her fingers curled into the shirt in her hands, her fingertips registering Sea Island Cotton, high-end, breathable, known for keeping the wearer's body cool throughout the day.

Maybe she could use some Sea Island Cotton herself because she was heating up.

Alexa thrust the shirt toward him. "Will this do?"

"Great, thanks." His knuckles brushed hers as she passed over his clothes as if they were intimately sharing a space.

And more.

Awareness chased up her wrist, her arm, higher still as the intimacy of the moment engulfed her. She was in a gorgeous hotel room, with a hot man and his beautiful children, helping him get dressed. The scene was too wonderful. Too close to what she'd once dreamed of having with her ex.

She jerked back fast. "Any last minute things to tell me about the kids when I order up supper?"

"Owen is allergic to strawberries, but Olivia loves them and if she can get her hands on them, she tries to share them with her brother. So watch that—hotels do the strawberry garnish thing on meals."

"Anything else?" She tried to pull her eyes away

from the nimble glide of his fingers up the buttons on his shirt.

"If you have an emergency, you can contact me at this number." He grabbed a hotel pen and jotted a string of numbers on the back of a business card. "That's my private cell line I use only for the kids."

"Got it." She tucked it in the corner of the gold gilded mirror. She could handle a couple of babies for a few hours.

Right?

"Don't lose it. And don't let Owen find it or he will eat it." He unbuckled his belt.

Her jaw dropped.

He tucked in his shirttails—and caught her staring. Her face heating, she turned away. Again.

Looking out the window seemed like a safe idea even though she'd been to St. Augustine about a dozen times. She could see Flagler College across the way, a place she'd once considered attending. Except her parents refused to pay if she left Charleston. Students at the Flagler castlelike fortress must feel as if they were attending Hogwarts. In fact, the whole city had a removed-from-reality feel, a step out of time. Much like this entire trip.

A Cinderella carriage pulled by a horse creaked slowly by as a Mercedes convertible whipped around and past it.

As Charleston had the French Huguenot influence, buildings here sported a Spanish Renaissance flair, and if Seth didn't get dressed soon, she would run out of things to look at. He was too much of a threat to her world for her to risk a tempting peek.

Her body hummed with awareness even when she

didn't see him. What a hell of a time for her hormones to stoke to life again.

"You can turn around now." Seth's voice stroked along her ragged nerves.

She chewed her lip, spinning back to face him, a man too handsome for his own good—or hers. "I've taken care of babies before."

Not often, but for friends in hopes she could prepare herself for the day it was her turn. A day that had never come around.

"Twins are different." He tugged the tie back over his head.

If he was so worried, he should cancel his meeting. She wanted to snap at him, but knew her irritability for what it was. Her perfect plan for the day had gone way off course, complicated even more by how damn attracted she was to the man she wanted to woo for a contract, not as a bed partner.

Memories of rustling sheets and sweat-slicked bodies smoked through her mind. She'd had a healthy sex life with her ex, so much so that she hadn't considered something could be wrong until everything fell apart. She definitely couldn't trust her body to judge the situation.

"Seth," she said his first name so easily she almost gasped, but forced herself to continue, "the twins and I will manage. We'll eat applesauce and fries and chicken nuggets then skyrocket your pay-per-view bill with cartoon movies until our brains are mush. I'll watch Olivia with small objects, and Owen's charm won't distract me from his climbing or strawberry snitching. They'll be fine. Go to your meeting."

He actually hesitated before grabbing his jacket from

the edge of the bed. "I'll be downstairs in the bar if you need me."

Oh, her body needed him all right. Too much for her own good. She was better off using her brains.

Seth stepped from the elevator into the lobby full of arches that led to the bar and restaurant. He scanned the chairs and sofas of rich dark woods with red-striped fabrics. Looking further, he searched past the heavy beams and thick curtains pulled back at each archway.

Thank God, somehow he'd managed to make it here ahead of his dinner partner. He strode past an iron fountain with Moorish tiles toward the bar where he was supposed to meet Javier Cortez, a cousin to royalty.

Literally. Cortez was related to the Medina family, a European monarchy that had ended in a violent coup. The Medinas and relatives had relocated to the United States, living in anonymity until a media scoop exposed their royal roots last year.

Cortez had served as head of security to one of the princes prior to the newsbreak and now oversaw safety measures for the entire family. Landing the Medinas as clients would be a huge coup.

Seth hitched up onto a stool at the bar, waving to the bartender for a seltzer water. Nothing stronger tonight.

Jansen Jets was still a small company, relatively speaking, but thanks to an in, he'd landed this meeting. One of those "Human Web" six degrees of separation moments—his cousin's wife's sister married into the Landis family, and a Landis brother married the illegitimate Medina princess.

Okay, that was more like ten degrees of separation. Thankfully, enough to bring him to this meeting. From this point on he had to rest on his own merits. Much like he'd told Alexa. *Alexa...*

Damn it all, did every thought have to circle back around to her?

Sure he'd noticed her on a physical level when he'd first stepped on the plane, and he'd managed the attraction well enough until he'd caught her eyes sliding over his body as he'd undone his pants. The ensuing heat wave sure hadn't been a welcome condition right before a meeting.

But he needed her help, so he would damn well wrestle the attraction into submission. His kids were his number one priority. He'd tried calling his ex multiple times since landing in St. Augustine, but only got her voice mail. Life had been a hell of a lot less complicated when he was flying those routes solo in North Dakota.

There didn't seem to be a damn thing more he could do about his mess of a personal life. Hopefully he could at least make headway in the business world.

Starting now.

The elevator dinged, doors swished open and Javier Cortez stepped out. Predictably the bar patrons buzzed. The newness of having royalty around hadn't worn off for people. The forty-year-old royal cousin strode out confidently, his Castilian heritage fitting right into the hotel's decor.

The guy's regal lineage didn't matter to Seth. He just appreciated the guy's hard-nosed efficiency. This deal would be sewn up quickly, one way or another.

"Sorry I'm late." Cortez thrust out his hand. "Javier Cortez."

"Seth Jansen." He stood to shake Javier's hand and then resettled onto a barstool beside the other guy.

The bartender placed an amber drink in front of Javier before he even placed an order. "I appreciate your flying down to meet with me here." He rattled the ice and looked around with assessing eyes. "My wife loves this place."

"I can see why. Lots of historic appeal."

It was also a good locale to conduct business, near the Medinas' private island off the coast of Florida. Although Seth hadn't been invited into that inner sanctum yet. Security measures were tight. No one knew the exact location and few had seen the island fortress. The Medinas owned a couple of private jets, but were looking to increase their transport options to and from the island as their family expanded with marriages and new children.

Cortez tasted his drink and set it on the cocktail napkin. "Since my wife and I are still technically finishing up our honeymoon, I promised her a longer stay, the chance to shop, laze around by the pool, soak up some Florida sun before we head back to Boston."

What the hell was he supposed to say to that? "Congratulations."

"Thanks, thanks. I hear you have your kids and their sitter with you."

Of course he'd heard, even though Seth had only been in town for about an hour. The guy was a security whiz and obviously didn't walk into a meeting unprepared. "I like to work in time with them whenever I can, so I brought the kids and Mary Poppins along."

"Excellent. Then you won't mind if we postpone the rest of this discussion."

Crap. Just what he didn't need.

The stay here extended. Less taken care of tonight, more tomorrow and even the next day. "Of course."

Cortez stood, taking his drink with him as he started back toward the elevator. Seth abandoned his seltzer water.

They stepped into the elevator together, and Cortez swiped his card for the penthouse level. "My wife and I would enjoy having you and your kids meet us for breakfast in the morning, your sitter, too. Around nine? Great," he said without waiting for an answer. "See you there."

Holy hell. Breakfast in a restaurant with a one-year-old was tough enough. But with two of them?

He stepped out onto the top floor, Javier going right as he went left.

The closer he came to the suite's door, the louder the muffled sounds grew. Squealing babies. Damn. Was one of them hurt? He double-timed toward his room, whipped the key card through just as the door opened.

Alexa carried a baby on each hip—two freshly bathed and wet naked babies. Her cheeks were flushed, her smile wide. "I just caught them. Holy cow, they've got some speed for toddlers."

He snagged a towel from the arm of the sofa and held it open. "Pass me one."

She handed Owen over and Seth saw...

Her shirt was soaking wet, clinging to every perfect curve. Who would have thought Mary Poppins could rock the hell out of a wet T-shirt contest?

Three

Alexa plucked at her wet company shirt, conscious of the way it clung to her breasts. She didn't need the heat in Seth's eyes. She didn't need the answering fire it stirred in her. They both had different goals for what remained of their twenty-four-hour deal. They were best served focusing on the children and work.

Turning away, she hitched Olivia up on her hip and snagged the other towel from where she'd dropped it on the sofa to chase the racing duo around the suite. "You're back early from your dinner meeting."

"You need some clothes." The sound of his confident footsteps sounded softly behind her on plush carpet.

"Dry ones, for sure." She glanced through to the bathroom. Towels were draped on the floor around the circular tub, soaking up all the splashes. "I let the babies use the Jacuzzi like a kiddie pool. A few plastic cups and they were happy to play. Supper should be arriving soon. I thought you were room service when I heard you at the door."

"They'll need cleaning up again after supper." He tugged out two diapers and two T-shirts from the diaper bag.

"Then I'll just order more towels." She plucked the tiny pink T-shirt from his hand and busied herself with dressing Olivia to keep from noticing how at ease he was handling his squirming son.

"Fair enough." He pressed the diaper tapes in place, his large masculine hands surprisingly nimble.

"Did your meeting go well?" She wrestled a tiny waving arm through the sleeve.

"We didn't get through more than half a drink. He had to postpone until the morning." A quick tug later, he had Owen's powder-blue shirt in place. He hoisted his son in the air and buzzed his belly before setting him on his feet. "I'll just call room service and add my order to the rest."

He wasn't going back to work? They would be spending the rest of the evening here. Together with the children, of course. And after the toddlers drifted off? He'd mentioned Pippa kept them up late. With luck the pint-size chaperones would burn the midnight oil.

"Too bad your dinner companion couldn't have told you about the delay before you left Charleston. You would have had time to make other arrangements for the children." And she would have been at home in her lonely apartment eating ice cream while thinking about encountering Seth on his plane. Because without question, he was a memorable man.

"I'm glad to have the time with them. I assume you can arrange to stay longer?"

"I'll call my partner back as soon as the kids are asleep. She and I will make it work."

"Excellent. Now we just need to arrange extra clothes and toiletries for you." He reached for the room phone as Olivia and Owen chased each other in circles around their father. "When I order my supper I'll also have the concierge pick up something for you to change int—"

"Really, no need." She held up a hand, an unsettling tingle tripping up her spine at the thought of wearing things purchased by him. "I'll wear the hotel robe tonight and we can have the hotel wash my clothes. The kids and I will kill time tomorrow browsing around downtown, shopping while you finish your meeting. You do have a double stroller, don't you?"

"Already arranged. But you are going to need a change of clothing sooner than that." The furrows in his brow warned her a second before he said, "My business prospect wants to have breakfast with the kids and there's not a chance in hell I can carry that off on my own. It's my fault you're here without a change of clothes."

A business breakfast? With two toddlers? Whose genius idea was that? But she held her silence and conceded to the need for something appropriate to wear.

She stifled a twinge of nerves at discussing her clothing size. She was past those days of stepping on the scales every morning for her mom to check—what a hell of a way to spend "mother-daughter" time. And thank God, she was past the days of starving herself into a size zero.

Size zero. There'd been an irony in that, as if she could somehow fade away…

Blinking the past back, she said, "Okay then, tell them to buy smalls or eights, and my shoes are size seven."

His green eyes glimmered wickedly. "And underwear measurements?"

She poked him in the chest with one finger. "Not on your life am I answering that one." God, his chest was solid. She stepped away. "Make sure to keep a tally of how much everything costs. I insist on reimbursing you."

"Unnecessarily prideful, but as you wish," he said it so arrogantly she wanted to thump him on the back of his head.

Not a wise business move, though, touching him again. One little tap had nearly seared her fingertip and her mind. "I pay my own way now."

"At least let me loan you a T-shirt to sleep in tonight rather than that stifling hotel robe."

His clothes against her naked flesh?

Whoa.

Shaking off the goose bumps, she followed the toddling twins into the master bedroom. The rumble of his voice followed her as Seth ordered his meal, her clothing and some other toiletries…

Olivia and Owen sprinted to check out the matching portable cribs that had been set up on the far side of the king-size bed, each neatly made. Everything had been provided to accommodate a family. A real family. Except she would crawl under her own covers all alone wearing a hot guy's T-shirt.

Alexa wrapped her arms around her stomach, reminded

of the life she'd been denied with the implosion of her marriage. A life she purposefully hadn't thought about in a year since she'd craved a real family more than her next breath. Being thrust into this situation with Seth stirred longings she'd ignored for too long. Damn it, she'd taken this gamble for her company, her employees, her future.

But in doing so, she hadn't realized how deeply playing at this family game could cut into her heart.

Playing pretend family was kicking his ass.

Seth forked up the last bite of his Chilean sea bass while Alexa started her warm peach bread pudding with lavender cream. They'd opted to feed the babies first and put them to bed so the adults could actually dine in peace out on the turret balcony. Their supper had been set up by the wrought-iron table for two, complete with a lone rose in the middle of the table. Historical sconces on either side of the open doors cast a candlelit glow over the table.

Classical music drifted softly from inside. Okay, so it was actually something called "The Mozart Effect— Music for Babies," and he used it to help soothe Olivia and Owen to sleep. But it still qualified as mood-setting music for grown-ups.

And holy crap, did Alexa ever qualify as a smoking hot adult.

She'd changed into one of his T-shirts with the fluffy hotel robe over it. She looked as if she'd just rolled out of his bed. An ocean breeze lifted her whispery blond hair as late evening street noises echoed softly from the street below. Tonight had been the closest he'd come to experiencing family life with his children.

He hadn't dated much since his divorce and when he had, he'd been careful to keep that world separate from his kids. Working side by side with Alexa had more than cut the tasks in half tonight. That made him angry all over again that he'd screwed up so badly in his own marriage. He and Pippa had known it was a long shot going in, but they'd both wanted to give it a chance, for the babies. Or at least that's what he'd thought, until he'd discovered Pippa wasn't even sure if he was the biological father.

His gut twisted.

Damn it all, Olivia and Owen were *his* children. *His* name was on their birth certificate. And he refused to let anyone take them from him. Pippa vowed she wasn't going to challenge the custody agreement, but she'd lied to him before, and in such a major way, he had trouble trusting her.

He studied the woman across from him, wishing he could read her thoughts better, but she held herself in such tight control at all times. Sure, he knew he couldn't judge all females by how things had shaken down between him and Pippa. But it definitely made him wary. Fool him once, shame on her. Fool him twice. Shame on him.

Alexa Randall was here for one reason only. To use him to jump-start her business. She wasn't in St. Augustine to play house. She didn't know, much less love, his kids. She was doing a job. Everybody in this world had an agenda. As long as he kept that knowledge forefront in his mind, they would be fine.

He reached for his seltzer water. "You're good with kids."

"Thanks," she said tightly, stabbing at her pudding.

"Seriously. You'll make a good mother someday."

She shook her head and shoved away her half-eaten dessert. "I prefer to have a husband for that and my only attempt at marriage didn't end well."

The bitterness in her voice hung between them.

He tipped back his crystal glass, eyeing her over the rim. "I'm really sorry to hear that."

Sighing, she dipped her finger in the water and traced the rim of her glass until the crystal sang. "I married a guy who seemed perfect. He didn't even care about my family's money. In fact, he sided with my dad about signing a prenup to prove it." Faster and faster her finger moved, the pitch growing higher. "After always having to second-guess friendships while growing up, that felt so good—thinking he loved me for myself, unconditionally."

"That's how it's supposed to work."

"Supposed to. But then, I'm sure you understand what it's like to have to question everyone's motives."

"Not always. I grew up in a regular farming family in North Dakota. Everyone around me had working class values. I spent my spare time camping, fishing or flying."

"Most of my friends in private school wanted the perks of hanging out with me—shopping trips in New York. For my sixteenth, my mother flew me and my friends to the Bahamas." She tapped the glass once with a short fingernail. "The ones with parents who could afford the same kind of perks were every bit as spoiled as I was. No wonder I didn't have any true friends."

Having to question people's motives as an adult was tough enough. But worrying as a kid? That could mark a person long-term. He thought of his children asleep in the next room and wondered how he would keep their lives even-keeled.

"So your ex seems like a dream guy with the prenup... and...?"

"His only condition was that I not take any money from my family." Her eyes took on a faraway, jaded look that bothered him more than it should have for someone he'd just met. "My money could go into trust for our kids someday, but we would live our lives on what we made. Sounded good, honorable."

"What happened?" He lifted his glass.

"I was allergic to his sperm."

He choked on his water. "Uh, could you run that by me again?"

"You heard me. Allergic to his swimmers. We can both have kids, just not with each other." She folded her arms on the edge of the table, leaning closer. "I was sad when the doctor told me, but I figured, hey, this was our call to adopt. Apparently Travis—my ex—didn't get the same message."

"Let me get this straight." Seth placed his glass on the table carefully to keep from snapping the stemware in two with his growing anger. "Your ex-husband left you because the two of you couldn't have biological children together?"

"Bingo," she said with a tight smile that didn't come close to reaching her haunted blue eyes.

"He sounds like a shallow jerk." A jerk Seth had an urge to punch for putting such deep shadows in this woman's eyes. "I would be happy to kick his ass for you. I may be a desk jockey these days, but I've still got enough North Dakota farm boy in me to take him down."

A smile played at her lips. "No worries. I kick butts on my own these days."

"Good for you." He admired her resilience, her spunk. She'd rebuilt her life after two nearly simultaneous blows from life that would have debilitated most people.

"I try not to beat myself up about it." Sagging back in the wrought-iron patio chair, she clutched the robe closed with her fists. "I didn't have much practice in making smart choices about the people I invited into my life. So it stands to reason I would screw that one up, too."

"Well, I'm a damn good judge of character and it's obvious to me that *he* screwed up." Seth reached across the table and touched her elbow lightly where the sleeve fell back to reveal the vulnerable crook. "Not you."

Her eyes opened wider with surprise, with awareness, but she didn't pull away. "Thanks for the vote of confidence, but I know there had to be fault on both sides."

"Still, that's not always easy to see or say." His hand fell away.

"What about *your* ex?" She straightened the extra fork she hadn't needed for her dinner. In fact, she hadn't eaten much of her fire-grilled sea scallops at all and only half of her bread pudding. Maybe the cuisine here didn't suit her. "Does she make it a regular practice to run off and leave the kids?"

"Actually, no." Pippa was usually diligent when it came to their care. In fact, she usually cried buckets anytime she left them.

Alexa tapped the top of his hand with a whisper-soft touch. "Come on now. I unloaded about my sucky marriage story. What's yours?"

Normally he preferred not to talk about his failures. But the moonlight, good food—for him at least—and even better company made him want to extend the evening. If that meant spilling a few public knowledge facts about his personal life, then so be it.

"There's no great drama to share—" And yeah, he was lying, but he preferred to keep it low-key. He was used to glossing over the truth in front of his kids, who were too young to understand paternity questions. "We had a fling that resulted in a surprise pregnancy—" Pippa had just failed to mention the other fling she'd had around the same time. "So we got married for the children, gave it an honest try and figured out it wasn't going to work. We already had divorce papers in motion by the time the babies were due."

"If you don't mind my asking—" she paused until he waved her on "—why did you get married at all then?"

He'd asked himself the same question more than once, late at night when he was alone and missing the twins. "Old-fashioned, I guess. I wanted to be around my kids all the time. I wanted it to work." Wanted the babies to be his. "It just…didn't."

"You're so calm about it," she said with more of those shadows chasing around in her eyes.

Calm? He was a holy mess inside, but letting that anger, the betrayal, fly wouldn't accomplish anything. "I have the twins. Pippa and I are trying to be good parents. At least I thought we were."

Her hand covered his completely, steadily. "By all appearances you're doing a great job. They're beautiful, sweet babies."

The touch of her soft skin sent a bolt of lust straight through his veins, pumping pulsing blood south. He wrestled his thoughts back to the conversation, back to the care of his offspring. "They're hell on wheels, but I would do anything for them. Anything."

So there was no need for him to stress over the fact that Alexa turned him on so hard his teeth hurt. He'd been too long without sex, only a couple of encounters in the year since his divorce. That had to be the reason for his instantaneous, out of control reaction to this woman.

Gauging by the pure blue flame in her eyes, she was feeling it, too.

He was realizing they had a lot more than just a hefty dose of attraction in common. They were both reeling from crappy marriages and completely focused on their careers. Neither of them was looking for anything permanent that would involve more messy emotions.

So why not hook up? If he wanted to act on their attraction and she was cool with the fact that being together had no effect on his business decisions, this could be the best damn thing to happen to him in months. *She* could be the best thing to happen to him in months.

Yeah, this could work.

Simple, uncomplicated sex.

They had an empty second bedroom waiting for them. He always carried condoms these days. One surprise pregnancy was enough. They had moonlight, atmosphere. She was even already half-undressed. There was nothing stopping him from seeing if she was amenable.

Decision made, Seth pulled the rose from the vase and stroked it lightly down her nose. Her eyes blinked wide with surprise, but she didn't say a word, didn't so much as move. Hell, yeah.

Emboldened, he traced her lips with the bud before he leaned across the table and kissed her.

Four

The warm press of Seth's mouth against hers surprised Alexa into stillness—for all of three heartbeats. Then her pulse double-timed. Surprise became desire. The attraction she'd been feeling since first laying eyes on him, since he'd taken off his tie, since she'd felt the steamy glide of his gaze over her damp clothing now ramped into hyperdrive.

He stood without breaking contact, and she rose with him as they stepped around the small table into each other's arms. She gripped his shoulders, her fingers sinking into the warm cotton of the shirt she'd chosen for him earlier. Her defenses were low, without a doubt. The romantic meal, moonlit turret and alluring dinner companion had lulled her. Even the soft classical music stroked over her tensed and frazzled nerves. It had been so long since she'd relaxed, too busy charging ahead with rebuilding her life. Even opening up about her divorce had felt—if not good—at least cathartic.

It had also left her bare and defenseless.

The man might be brusque in the way he spoke sometimes, but, wow, did he ever take his time with a kiss. She slid one hand from his shoulder up to the back of his neck, her fingers toying with the coarse texture of his hair. Her body fit against his, her softness giving way to the hard planes of his chest. The sensitive pads of her fingers savored the rasp of his late day beard as she traced his strong jaw, brushed across his cheekbones and back into his thick hair.

His mouth moved over hers firmly, surely, enticing her to open for him. Her breasts pressed more firmly against him as she breathed faster and faster with arousal. The scent of aftershave mingled with the salty sea air. The taste of lime water and spices from his dinner flavored their kiss, tempting her senses all the more to throw reason away. The bold sweep of his tongue made her hunger for more of this. More of *him*.

How easy it would be to follow him into his bedroom and toss away all the stress and worries of the past years as quickly as discarded clothes. Except, too soon, morning would come and with it would come all those concerns, multiplied because of their lack of self-control.

God, this was so reckless and unwise and impulsive in a way she couldn't afford any longer. Scavenging for a shred of self-control, she pushed at his shoulders since she couldn't seem to bring herself to tear her mouth away from his.

Thank goodness he took the hint.

He pulled back, but not far, only a whisper away.

Each breath she took drew in the crisp scent of him. The starlight reflected in his green eyes staring at her with a keen perception of how very much she ached to take this kiss further.

Her chest pumped for air even though she knew full well the dizziness had nothing to do with oxygen and everything to do with Seth's appeal. Slowly he guided her back to her chair—good thing since her legs were wobbly—and he returned to his as well, his eyes still holding her captive. He lifted his crystal glass, sipping the sparkling water while watching her over the rim.

She forced a laugh that came out half strangled. "That was unexpected."

"Really?" He placed his glass on the table again. The pulse visibly throbbing in his neck offered the only sign he was as shaken as she was by what they'd just shared. "I've wanted to kiss you since I first saw you on board my plane. At that moment, I thought that attraction was mutual. Now, I *know* it is."

His cool arrogance smoked across the table.

A chilling thought iced the heat just as quickly as he'd stoked it. "Is that why you asked me to watch your children? Because you wanted a chance to hit on me?" She sat straighter in her chair and wished she wore something more businesslike than a borrowed terry-cloth robe and his shirt. "I thought we had a business arrangement. Mixing business and personal lives is never a good idea."

"Then why did you kiss me back?" He turned the glass on the tablecloth.

"Impulse."

His eyes narrowed. "So you admit you're attracted to me."

Duh. Denying the mutual draw would be pointless. "You know that I am, but it doesn't mean I've been making plans to act on the feeling. I think Brad Pitt's hot as hell, but I wouldn't jump him even if given the opportunity."

"You think I'm Brad Pitt-hot?"

Damn the return of his arrogant grin.

"I was just making a point," she snapped.

"But you think I'm hot."

"Not relevant." She flattened her hands on the table. "I'm not acting on the impulse any further tonight or ever. If that means you renege on your offer to read my proposal and refer me to others in the business, then so be it. I will not sleep my way into a deal."

She pushed to her feet.

"Whoa, hold on." Standing, he circled the table to face her, stroking her upper arm soothingly. "I didn't mean to imply anything of the sort. First, I don't believe you're the kind of person to get ahead in the world that way. And second, I have never paid for sex, and I never intend to."

She froze, his touch sending fresh skitters of awareness up her arm. The darkness and distant night sounds isolated them with too much intimacy.

Alexa eased back a step toward their suite and the soft serenade of Mozart on the breeze. "Have you looked into finding someone else to take care of your children?"

Still, he didn't move. He didn't have to. His presence called to her as he simply stood a couple of steps away, his broad shoulders backlit by the moon, starlight playing across his blond hair, giving him a Greek godlike air.

"Why would I need to do that?" he asked. "You're here for them."

"Our agreement only lasts for twenty-four hours," she reminded him, holding onto the door frame to bolster her wavering resolve.

"I thought we established the time frame had expanded because my meeting with Javier Cortez fell through tonight." He stepped closer, stopping just shy of touching her again. "You even rearranged things at your work to accommodate our business agreement."

He was right, and she'd allowed him to scramble her thoughts once more. She locked onto his last three words and pushed ahead. "Our *business* agreement."

"You're angry."

"Not…angry exactly. Just frustrated and disappointed in both of us."

His eyes flared with something indefinable. "Disappointed?"

"Oh—" she suddenly understood his expression "—not disappointed in the kiss. It was… Hell, you were here, too. There's no denying the chemistry between us."

Another arrogant grin spread across his face. "I agree one hundred percent."

"But back to the Brad Pitt principle." She stiffened her spine and her resolve. "Just because there's an attraction doesn't mean it's wise to act on it. I'm disappointed that we did something so reckless, so unprofessional. My business has to be my primary focus, just as you've said your children are your main concern."

"Having my priorities in order doesn't cancel out my attraction to you. I can separate business from pleasure." He held her with his laser hot gaze. "I'm very good at multitasking."

Anger did build inside her now alongside the frustration. "You're not hearing me! This thing between us is too much, too soon. We barely know each other and we both have high stakes riding on this trip." She jabbed him in the chest with one finger. "So, listen closely. No. More. Kissing."

She launched through the door and into the suite before he could shake her resolve again. But as she raced across the luxurious sitting area into her bedroom, his voice echoed in her ears and through her hungry senses.

"Damn shame."

She completely agreed. Sleep tonight would be difficult to come by as regrets piled on top of frustrated desire.

Staring off over the city skyline, Seth leaned back in his chair, staying on the turret balcony long after Alexa left. The heat of their kiss still sizzling through him, he finished his seltzer water, waiting for the light in her room to turn off.

He'd only met her today, and he couldn't recall wanting any woman this much. The strength of the attraction had been strong enough on its own. But now that he'd actually tasted her? He pushed the glass aside, his deeper thirst not even close to quenched.

Now he had to decide what to do about that feeling. She was right in saying that giving in to an affair wasn't wise. They both had important reasons to keep their acquaintance all business.

His life was complicated enough. He needed to keep

his life stable for his kids. No parade of women through the door, confusing them.

He eyed his smartphone on the table where it had been resting since his four attempts to contact Pippa. She still wasn't returning his messages, and his temper was starting to simmer. What if there had been something wrong with one of the kids and he needed to contact her? She should at least pick up to find out why he was trying to reach her.

His phone vibrated with an incoming call. He slammed his chair back on all four legs and scooped up his cell fast. The LED screen showed a stored name... his cousin Paige back in Charleston.

Not Pippa.

Damn it.

Even his extended family kept in better contact with him than the mother of his kids. His cousins Paige and Vic had both moved from North Dakota, each starting their families in the Charleston area. With no other family left out west, Seth had followed and started his own business.

He picked up without hesitation. "Paige? Everything okay?"

"We're fine." His cousin's voice was soft as if lowered to keep from waking her children. Classical guitar music played softly in the background. "The girls are both finally asleep. I've been worried about you all afternoon. How are you and the twins? I feel so bad that I couldn't help you out."

"No need to call and apologize. We prefer to steer clear of strep throat."

"Actually I'm calling about Vic and Claire..."

Oh. Hell. In the chaos with the twins, he'd actually

forgotten that his cousin Vic's wife had gone into labor today. "How's she doing?"

"She delivered a healthy baby boy just before midnight. Nine pounds thirteen ounces, which explains the C-section. But Mom and baby are doing great. His big sister and big brother can't wait to meet him in the morning." Two boys and a girl. A family.

Seth scratched the kink in his neck. "Send my congratulations when you see them. I'll swing by for a visit when I get back in town."

"I'll let them know." The reception crackled as it sounded like she moved her phone to the other ear. More guitar music filled the airwaves… Bach, perhaps? "Actually, I called for a different reason. Now that Claire's had the baby and Vic has picked up their kids, her sister Starr says she can watch the twins. They know her two kids. They'll have a blast. You could fly Olivia and Owen up early in the morning before your first meeting."

"That's a generous offer…"

"My girls won't be contagious in another day or two once the antibiotics kick in, so I can relieve her then. No worries."

Her plan sounded workable. And yet, he hesitated, his gaze drawn back to the suite where Alexa slept. "You're all busy with your own families, and I have a plan in place here."

"You're family," Paige insisted sincerely. "We want to help."

"I appreciate that." Except he genuinely wanted his kids near him—and he wanted to keep Alexa near him, too.

The thought of cutting his time with Alexa short—it just wasn't happening. Crazy, really, since he could contact her later, after this deal was cinched. If she was even still speaking to him once she realized he never intended to give her the Jansen Jets contract.

No. His time to get to know Alexa was now. He needed to figure out this unrelenting draw between them and work through it. She was here, and he intended to keep it that way. "Thanks, Paige, but I meant it when I said I'm set. I have help."

"Hmm…" Her voice rose with interest. "You have a new nanny?"

His family chipped in most of the time, but he didn't want to take advantage so he hired a couple of part-time nannies on occasion, all of which Paige would already know about. "Not a nanny. More of a sitter, a, uh, friend actually."

"A female friend?" she pressed, tenacious as ever.

"She's a female, yes." *Definitely* female.

"That's it?" Paige laughed. "That's all you're going to tell me, eh?"

"There's not much to tell." Yet. His eyes drifted back to the suite as he envisioned Alexa curled up asleep, wearing his shirt.

"Ah," she said smugly, "so you're still in the early stages, but not too early, right, or she wouldn't be there with your children. Because, as best as I can remember, you haven't dated much and none of those women ever got anywhere near the twins."

His cousin was too insightful. The way she homed in on the intensity of his draw to Alexa so quickly made him uncomfortable.

He shot up from his seat. "That's enough hypothesizing about my personal life for one night. I need to go."

"I'm not giving up. I'll want details when you return,"

Paige insisted, getting louder and louder by the second. "And I want to meet her. I know you guard your privacy, but I'm family and I love you."

"Love you too, cuz."

"So you'll talk to me? Let me know what's going on in your world rather than hole up the way you did after Pippa—"

"I hear a kid," he cut her short. "Gotta go. Bye." He thumbed the off button and flipped the phone in his palm, over and over.

Guilt kicked around in his gut for shutting down Paige and for taking advantage of Alexa's help. He should send Alexa back to Charleston and then impose on the sister of a cousin-in-law because his ex-wife had dumped his kids off without warning...

Hell, his life was screwed up, and he needed to start taking charge. He'd meant it when he said he could separate the personal from the professional. But he also heard Alexa when she said this was moving too fast for her. She needed more time, time they wouldn't have if she went back to Charleston while he stayed here. He suspected once she went home, she would erect mile-high walls between them, especially once she learned he'd never planned to sign her cleaning company.

He needed longer with her *now*.

His mind filled with a vision of Alexa chasing his kids around, all wet from the tub. Warm memories pulled him in with a reminder of the family life he should be having right now and wasn't because of his workload. Having Alexa here felt so right.

It *was* right.

And so, he wasn't sending her back in the morning. In fact, he had to find a way to extend their window of time together. He not only needed her help with the children, but he also wanted her to stay for more *personal* reasons. The explosive chemistry they'd just discovered didn't come around often. Hell, he couldn't remember when he'd ever burned to have a particular woman this much. So much the craving filled his mind as well as his body.

The extension of their trip presented the perfect opportunity to follow that attraction to its ultimate destination.

Landing her directly into his bed.

Sunlight streamed through the window over the array of clothes laid out on the bed. So many clothes. Far more than she needed for a day or two.

Although as Alexa looked closer, she noticed the variety. It was as if whoever had shopped for her had planned for any contingency. Tan capris with a shabby chic blouse. A simple red cocktail dress. A sexy black bathing suit that looked far from nannylike and made her wonder who'd placed the order. At least there was a crocheted cover-up. And for this morning's breakfast…

She wore a silky sundress, floral with coral-tinted tulips in a watercolor print. Strappy gold sandals wrapped up and around her ankles. She scraped her hair back with a matching scarf that trailed down her back.

There was a whole other shopping bag that a quick peek told her held more clothes, underwear, a nightgown and a fabric cosmetics bag full of toiletries. Once upon a time, she'd taken these kinds of luxuries for granted, barely noticing when they appeared in her room or at a hotel.

These days she had a firm grasp on how hard she would have to work to pay for even one of these designer items. What a difference a year could make in a person's life. Yet, here she was again, dancing on the periphery of a world that had almost swallowed her whole.

Steeling her resolve to keep her values firmly in place, she strode from the bedroom into the sitting area where Seth was strapping the twins into the new, top-of–the-line double stroller.

He looked up and smiled. The power of his vibrant green eyes and dimples reached across the room, wrapping around her, enticing her to move closer into the circle of that happiness. A dangerous move. She had to step away, for her own peace of mind. She wasn't wired to leap into intimacy with a stranger.

A stranger who became more intriguing by the second.

Surely a billionaire who knew how to work a stroller couldn't be totally disconnected from everyday reality. That insight buoyed her, and inspired her. Actively learning more about him would help her on many levels. Knowing more about him was wise for her work.

For work, damn it, not because of this insane attraction.

"Are you ready?" he asked.

"Yes, I believe I am." She could do this. She could keep her professional face in place, while discovering if Seth Jansen harbored any more surprises in that hulking hot body of his.

"Glad the clothes fit. Although for breakfast with the twins, we might be better off draping ourselves in rain ponchos."

Before she could laugh or reply, his phone rang and

he held up a hand. "Hold on, I've got to take this. Work call coming in."

He started talking into his cell and grabbed his briefcase off the sofa. Opening the door, he gestured her ahead. She wheeled the stroller forward, out into the hall and toward the elevator.

The fabric slid sensuously against her skin with each step as she pushed the stroller into the elevator while Seth spoke on his phone to his partner…Rick… briefcase in his other hand. Each glide of the silky dress against her skin reminded her how vibrantly in tune her senses were this morning, and, as much as she wanted to credit the sunshine, she knew it was last night's kiss that had awakened something inside her.

Something that made professional goals tougher to keep in focus.

Two floors down, the doors slid open to admit an older couple dressed casually in sightseeing clothes that still shouted Armani and Prada. They fit right in with the rest of the clientele here. Except the woman carried a simple canvas bag with little handprints painted on it and signed in childlike handwriting. Stenciled along the top of the bag were the words Grandma's Angels. Alexa swallowed a lump of emotion as she counted at least eleven different scrawled signatures.

The husband leaned closer to his wife, whispering, pointing and smiling nostalgically. The wife knelt to pick up a tiny tennis shoe and passed it to Alexa. "You have a beautiful family."

Before Alexa could correct them, they reached the lobby and the couple exited. She glanced sheepishly toward Seth and found him staring at her with assessing eyes as he tucked away his phone. Her mouth went dry.

She grabbed the stroller, grateful for the support as the now increasingly predictable wobbly knees syndrome set in.

Ever aware of his gaze following her, she wheeled the twins from the elevator. She needed to get her thoughts in order ASAP. She was seconds away from meeting royalty for breakfast, pretty heady stuff even given her own upbringing. Seth was certainly coming through on his promise to introduce her to prestigious connections. Knowing the Medina family could be a serious boon to her fledgling business.

Although she was confused by a person who invited twin toddlers to a business breakfast at a restaurant with silk, antiques and a ceiling hand-painted with twenty-four karat gold.

The clink of silverware echoing from the room full of patrons, she didn't have to wonder for even a second which pair of diners to approach. A dark-haired, aristocratic man stood from a table set for six, nodding in their direction. A blonde woman sat beside him, a flower tucked behind her ear.

The wheels of the stroller glided smoothly along the tile floor as they passed a waiter carrying plates of crepes on his tray. Alexa stopped by their table.

Seth shook the man's hand. "Javier, I'd like you to meet—"

The man took her hand. "Alexa Randall. A pleasure to meet you," Javier said with only a hint of an accent. He motioned to the elegant woman beside him. "This is my wife, Victoria."

"Lovely to meet you." Victoria smiled welcomingly, while tucking her fingers into the crook of her husband's arm. He covered her hand automatically with a possessive and affectionate air.

Good God, this place was chock full of couples swimming in marital bliss. First the elderly couple in the elevator. Now her dining companions for breakfast. She didn't even dare look at the couple feeding each other bits of melon at the table next to them.

The numbers of fawning couples here defied national divorce statistics. Although, now that she thought about it, she and Seth had enough breakups to even out the scales.

Leaning into the stroller, Victoria grinned at the twins and spun a rattle attached to the tray. "Would you mind if I held one of these sweethearts?"

Seth pulled back the stroller canopy. "Sure, this is Owen—" he picked up his son "—and this is Olivia."

As Victoria reached down, the little girl stretched her arms up toward Alexa instead. Alexa's heart squeezed in response. So much so, it scared her a little. These babies were quickly working their way into her affection. Victoria eased back gracefully and left Alexa to settle the baby girl into her high chair beside her brother's. The adults took their seats and placed their orders, so far, with no mishaps.

As the waitress placed each person's dish on the table, Victoria spread her linen napkin across her lap. "I told Javier he really put you on the spot insisting you bring along babies, but the twins are total dolls." She tickled Olivia's chin. "Hopefully you'll warm up to me, sweetie, so I can entertain you while Alexa eats her breakfast, too."

"I think I can manage, but thank you." She reached past her smoked salmon bagel for her goblet of juice.

How well did this woman and her husband already know Seth? What kind of information might she learn during this breakfast about Seth and his possible contacts?

While Javier detailed the must-see sights in St. Augustine, Olivia and Owen fed themselves fruit—which scared Alexa to her last frazzled nerve as she watched to be sure strawberries stayed on Olivia's tray but not Owen's.

Seth shoveled in steak and eggs, spooning oatmeal into the twins' mouths, while holding a conversation. She was in awe.

And a little intimidated.

She'd almost flooded the floor last night during their bath. If he hadn't shown up early, she wasn't sure how she would have wrestled them both into clothes. Whenever she thought she'd moved everything dangerous out of their reach...

Oh, God...

She lunged for Olivia just as Seth smoothly pulled the salt shaker from her grasp. Her pulse rate doubled at the near miss with catastrophe. So much for using this breakfast to learn more about Seth from the Cortez couple. She would be lucky to make it through the meal with her sanity intact.

Victoria rested her knife at the top of her plate of half-eaten eggs Benedict. "I hope he's treating you to some vacation fun after all these stodgy business meetings are over."

"Pardon?" Alexa struggled to keep track of the twins and the conversation in the middle of a business meeting and a dining room full of tourists.

Glasses and silverware clinked and clattered. Waiters

angled past with loaded trays as people fueled up for the day ahead.

Victoria swiped her mouth with the linen napkin. "You deserve some pampering for watching the kids solo here at the hotel during the day."

"I'm helping out with temporary nanny detail."

Leaning closer, Victoria whispered, "It's obvious he doesn't look at you like a nanny."

She couldn't exactly deny that since she was likely searing him with her own glances, too. "Honestly we don't know each other that well."

Victoria waved away her comment, her wedding rings refracting light from the chandelier. "The length of time doesn't always matter when it comes to the heart. I knew right away Javier was the one." She smiled affectionately at her new husband, who was deep in conversation with Seth. "It took us a while to find our way to each other, but if I'd listened to my heart right off, we could have been saved so many months of grief."

"It's a business arrangement," she said simply, hoping if she repeated it enough she could maintain her objectivity. "Only business."

"Of course," Victoria conceded, but her smile didn't dim. "I'm sorry. I didn't mean to be nosy. It's just that given what I understand from Javier, Seth has been a workaholic since his divorce. He hasn't had time for relationships."

"There's nothing to apologize for." Alexa knew full well she and Seth were sending out mixed signals. As much as she'd been determined to keep things professional with Seth the businessman, she found herself drawn to Seth the father. A man so tender with his children. At ease with a baby stroller. As adept at flying a spoonful of oatmeal into a child's mouth as he was at piloting a plane through the sky.

These surprise insights proved a potent attraction, especially after living with her own distant father and then the way her ex had checked out on her.

Victoria's voice pulled Alexa out of her musings.

"Honestly, my thoughts may be selfish. I was thinking ahead that if Javier and Seth settle on a contract, then I was hoping we would get to see more of each other. As much as I adore my husband, his world is narrow and he's suspicious of expanding the circle. I'm always grateful for some girl time."

"That would be lovely, thank you." Alexa understood perfectly about lonely inner circles, too much so. She felt a twinge of guilt over her thoughts about using the Cortezes for contacts.

All her life she'd been warned about gold diggers. She'd always known the chances of someone seeing through the money to love her for herself was slim. And still she'd made a royal mess. She didn't want to let the Cortez money and their Medina connections blind her to who they really were.

"I mean it. And regardless of how much time we spend visiting, let's enjoy the day…let's have fun."

Fun? She should be home, at work. She took a deep breath. This situation would help her at work. Or she hoped so.

She couldn't ignore the fact that her wish to stay right here was increasing by the second. "I appreciate how helpful you've been here at breakfast. The twins are my responsibility. We're going sightseeing with the stroller, maybe do a little shopping."

"Perfect," Victoria declared. "I'm at loose ends. I

love a good walk and shopping. And after that, we can wear them out at the pool."

Alexa did have a swimsuit and she had absolutely no reason not to take Victoria up on her generous offer. No reason other than a deep-seated fear of allowing herself to be tempted back into a world she'd been determined to leave behind. A way of life embraced by Seth and his precious children. Her eyes were drawn back to the twins.

Just as Owen wrapped his fist around one of his sister's strawberries—a food he was allergic to.

Panic gripped Alexa as she saw the baby's lightning fast intent to gobble the forbidden fruit. "No! Owen, don't eat that."

Lurching toward him, she grabbed his chubby wrist just before his hand reached his mouth. His face scrunched into utter dejection as his tiny world crumbled over the lost treat. Alexa winced a second ahead of his piercing scream. Seth leaned in to soothe the temper tantrum. Before Alexa could even form the words of warning…

Olivia flipped the bowl of oatmeal straight into Javier Cortez's lap.

Five

The cosmos must have been holding a serious grudge against him because the sight of Alexa in a bathing suit sucker-punched him clean through.

Seth stopped short by the poolside bar outside the hotel and allowed himself a moment to soak in the sunlit view, a welcome pleasure after a tense work day that had started with his kid dumping oatmeal in a prospective customer's lap. Thank goodness Javier Cortez had insisted it didn't matter.

And Alexa had acted fast by scooping up both twins and taking them away for the day.

Now, she looked anything but maternal as she rubbed sunscreen down her arms, laughing at something Victoria said. The twins slept in a playpen under the shade of a small open cabana. Only a half dozen others had stayed this late in the day—a young couple drinking wine in the hot tub and a family playing with a beach ball in the shallow end.

His attention stayed fully focused on the goddess in black Lycra.

He should be celebrating the success of his day's meeting. Javier wanted him to tour the landing strip at the king's private island off the coast of St. Augustine. Their time here was done. The king's island even came equipped with a top-notch nanny for the twins, a nanny the king kept on staff for his grandchildren's visits.

And yet, Seth was all the more determined than ever to keep Alexa with him, to win her over, to seduce her into his bed again and again until he worked this tenacious attraction out of their systems. He hadn't yet attained that goal but was determined to keep her around until he succeeded.

The black bathing suit was more modest than the strings other women wore that barely held in the essentials. Still, there was no denying her sensuality. Halter neckline, plunging deeply until the top of her belly button ring showed.

A simple gold hoop.

His hands itched to grasp her hips and slide his fingers along the edges, slipping inside to feel the satiny slickness he knew waited right there. For him.

Splashing from the deep end snapped him back to reality. Damn, he seriously needed to rein in those kinds of thoughts out here in public. Even when they were alone. He needed to be patient. He didn't want to spook her into bailing on this time they had together.

He thought back to how fast she'd retreated after their kiss. She'd been undeniably as turned on as he was and yet, she'd avoided him that morning as they'd prepared for the day. Although he thought he sensed a bit of softening in her stance as the day wore on. At breakfast he'd thought he caught her eyes lingering on him more than once. He could see the memory of their kiss written in her eyes as she stared at him with a mixture of confusion and attraction.

Shoving away from the bar, Seth strode alongside the pool toward Alexa. "Good afternoon, ladies."

Jolted, she looked over at him. Her eyes widened and he could have sworn goose bumps of awareness rose along her arms. She yanked her crocheted cover-up off the glass-topped table and shrugged into it almost fast enough to hide her breasts beading with arousal. His own body throbbed in response, his hands aching to cradle each creamy globe in his palms.

"Seth, I didn't expect you back this early."

Out of the corner of his eyes, he saw Victoria gather her beach bag. "Since you're done for the day, I take it my husband's free, so if you'll both excuse me…"

The woman made a smooth—and timely—exit.

Seth sank down into her vacated lounger beside Alexa as a teenager cannonballed into the deep end. "Did you and the babies have a good afternoon?"

"No problems or I would have called you. I wrote down everything the children ate and when they went to sleep. The pool time wore them out." She toyed with the tie on her cover up—right between her breasts.

He forced his gaze to stay on her face. "I want you to extend your time with us for a couple more days."

Her jaw went slack with surprise before she swallowed hard. "You want me to stay with you and the children?"

"Precisely."

"My business is a small operation—"

"What about your partner?"

"I can't dump everything on her indefinitely and still meet our obligations."

His point exactly as for why hers wasn't the company for Jansen Jets—hers wasn't large enough and didn't have adequate backup resources. He leaned forward, elbows resting on his knees. "I thought you were cleaning my plane to meet with me."

"That certainly was my intent—and to impress you with A-1's work." She hugged her legs. "But I do clean other aircraft in addition to my obligations to office work."

"That doesn't leave much time for a private life." Late day sun beating down on his head, he shrugged out of his suit jacket and draped it over the back of the lounger. He loosened his tie. God, he hated the constraining things.

"I'm investing in my future."

"I understand completely." His eyes gravitated toward his children, still sleeping peacefully in the playpen—Olivia on her tummy with her diapered butt up in the air, Owen on his back with his arms flung wide.

"You've achieved your goals. That's admirable. I'm working on my dream now." Determination coated each word as fully as the sunscreen covered her bared skin.

He *really* didn't need to be thinking about her exposed body right now.

Already, he was on the edge of a new deal with Javier Cortez to supply charter jets for the royal Medinas. That huge boon would take his company to the next level and free him up to set up an entire volunteer, nonprofit foundation devoted to search and rescue operations. His first love, what had drawn him into flying in the first place. That love of flying had helped him develop and patent the airport security device that had made him a mint. Once he took his business to the next level, funding and overstretched government budgets wouldn't be an issue...

So damn close to achieving all his business dreams.

Yet, still he was restless. "Let's forget arguing about tomorrow and business. We can hash that out later. Right now, I'm off the clock. I want to make the most of our time left in St. Augustine tonight."

"What exactly did you have in mind?" She eyed him suspiciously.

Had he imagined her softening on the all-business stance? There was only one way to find out.

Standing, he snagged his suit coat. "We're going to spend the evening out."

"With twins? Don't you think breakfast was pushing our luck?"

He grinned, scooping up his groggy daughter. "Trust me. I can handle this."

"All right, if you're sure."

"Absolutely." He palmed his daughter's back as she wriggled in his arms and tugged at his collar. "Wait until you see what I have planned. You'll want to dress comfortably, though. And we should probably pack extra clothes for the kids in case they get dirty."

Alexa pulled up alongside him, Owen in her arms. Seth reached for the door inside—

Until her gasp stopped him short.

"Did you forget something?" he asked.

When Alexa didn't answer, he glanced and found her

staring back at him with horror. What the hell? Except as she raised a shaking hand to point, he realized she wasn't looking at him. Her attention was focused fully on Olivia.

More precisely, on Olivia's bulging left nostril.

Sitting on the edge of the hotel sofa in their suite, Alexa struggled to contain the squirming little girl in her lap while pushing back the welling panic. The whole ride up in the elevator had been crazy, with Seth attempting to check his daughter's nose and the child growing more agitated by the second.

How in the world had Olivia wedged something up her nostril? More importantly, *what* had she shoved into there?

Alexa winced at the baby's bulging left nostril. She hadn't taken her eyes off Olivia for a second during their time at the pool—except when Olivia had been sleeping. Had she woken up? Found something in the playpen? Perhaps something blew inside the pen with her?

Panic gripped her. What the hell had she been thinking, allowing herself to believe she could care for these two precious children? She willed herself to stop shaking and deal with the crisis at hand.

Seth knelt in front of her, trying to grasp his daughter's head between his palms. "I can get this out if you will just hold her still long enough for me to push my thumb down the outside of her nose."

"Believe me, I'm trying my best." Alexa's heart pumped as hard and fast as Olivia's feet as the little girl screamed, kicking her father in the stomach. Her face turned red; her skin beaded with sweat from hysteria.

Sinking back on his haunches, Seth looked around their suite. "Is there any pepper left from last night's dinner?"

"Housekeeping cleared away everything. Oh, God, I am so sorry. I don't know how this happened—"

A crash echoed through the room.

Alexa looked at Seth, her panic mirrored in his eyes. "Owen!"

They both shot to their feet just as a pitiful wail drifted from behind the velvet sofa. Holding Olivia around the waist, Alexa ran fast on Seth's heels, only to slam against his back when he stopped short.

Owen sat on the floor, blessedly unharmed, just angry. His "tower"—which consisted of a chair, a pillow and the ice bucket—now lay on its side by the television. Handprints all over the flat screen testified to his attempt to turn on the TV by himself.

Seth knelt beside his son, running his hands along the toddler's arms and legs. "Are you okay, buddy? You know you're not supposed to climb like that." His thumb brushed over his son's forehead, along the eyebrow that still carried a scar from past stitches. "Be careful."

Picking up Owen, Seth held him close for a second, a sigh of relief racking through his body so visibly Alexa almost melted into the floor with sympathy. God, this big manly guy who plowed through life and through the skies alone had the most amazing way of connecting with his kids.

What would it have been like to grow up with a father like him? A dad so very present in his children's lives?

Standing, Seth said, "I'm going to have to take Olivia to the emergency room. Swap kids with me. You can stay here with Owen."

"You still trust me?"

"Of course," he responded automatically even though his mouth had gone tight. With frustration? Fear?

Or anger?

He leaned toward her. Olivia let out a high-pitched shriek and locked her arms tighter around Alexa's neck, turning her face frantically from her father.

Seth frowned. "It's okay, kiddo. It's just me."

Patting Olivia's back, Alexa swayed soothingly from side to side. "She must think you're going to pinch her nose again."

"Well, we don't have much choice here. I need to take her in." He set down Owen and clasped his daughter.

Olivia's cries cranked up to earsplitting wails, which upset her brother who started sobbing on the floor. If Olivia kept gasping would whatever was in her nose get sucked in? And then where would it go? Into a lung? The possibilities were horrifying. This parenting thing was not for the faint of heart.

"Seth, let me hold her rather than risk her becoming even more hysterical." She cradled the little girl's head, blond curls looping around Alexa's fingers as surely as the child was sliding into Alexa's heart. "You and I can go to the emergency room and take both kids."

Plowing a hand through his hair, Seth looked around the suite again as if searching for other options. Finally he nodded and picked up his son. "That's probably for the best. We just have to get a car." He grabbed the room phone and dialed the hotel operator. "Seth Jansen here. We need transportation to the nearest E.R. waiting for us. We're headed to the elevator now."

She jammed her feet into the flip-flops she'd worn to the pool, grateful she'd at least had time to change out of her swimsuit, and followed Seth out into the hall. The elevator opened immediately—thank God—and they plunged inside the empty compartment. He jostled his restless son while she made *shhh, shhh, shhh* soothing sounds for Olivia, who was now hiccupping. But at least the little girl wasn't crying.

The floors dinged by, but not fast enough. The doors parted and the elderly couple they'd seen on their way down to breakfast stepped inside.

Dressed to the nines in jewels and evening wear, the woman wasn't carrying her canvas bag made by her grandchildren, but she still radiated a grandma air. She leaned toward Olivia and crooned, "What's the matter, sweetie? Why the tears?"

Lines of strain and worry pulled tighter at the corners of Seth's mouth. "She shoved something up her nose," he said curtly, his gaze locked in on the elevator numbers as if willing the car to move faster. "We're headed to the E.R."

As if sensing her dad's intent, Olivia pressed her face into Alexa's neck.

The grandmother looked back at her husband and winked knowingly. The older gentleman, dressed in a tuxedo, reached past Alexa so quickly she didn't have time to think.

He tugged Olivia's ear. "What's that back there behind your ear, little one?" His hand came back around with a gold cuff link in his palm. "Was that in your ear?"

Olivia peeked around to see and like lightning, the grandmother reached past and swiped her finger down Olivia's nose. A white button shot out and into the woman's hand. She held it up to Seth's shirt. A perfect match. They hadn't even noticed he was missing one from near his neck.

Surprise stamped on his handsome face, Seth stuffed the button into his pocket. "She must have pulled it off when I picked her up by the pool."

Alexa gasped in awe at how easily the couple had handled mining the button from Olivia's nose. "How did you two manage that so smoothly?"

The grandpa straightened his tuxedo bow tie. "Lots of practice. You two will get the knack before you know it."

In a swirl of diamonds and expensive perfume, the couple swept out of the elevator, leaving Alexa and Seth inside. The doors slid closed again. She sagged back against the brass rail. Relief left her weak-kneed all the way back to the penthouse floor while Seth called downstairs on his cell to cancel their ride to the E.R.

Stopping just outside their door, he tucked his phone in his pocket and slid a hand behind her neck. "Thank you."

"For what? I feel like I've let you down." The emotions and worry after the scare with Olivia had left her spinning. She could only imagine how he must feel.

"Thank you for being here. Chasing these two is more challenging than flying a plane through a thunderstorm." He scrubbed a hand over his jaw. "My family tells me I'm not too good at asking for help. But I gotta admit having an extra set of hands and eyes around made things easier just now."

His emerald-green gaze warmed her along with his words. Given her history with men, the whole trust notion was tough for her. But right now, she so desperately wanted to believe in the sincerity she saw in his eyes. She felt appreciated. Valued as a person.

Giving that much control to another person scared her spitless. "You're welcome."

She thought for a moment he was going to kiss her again. Her lips tingled at the prospect. But then he glanced at the two children and eased back. "Let's get the diaper bag so we can move forward with our night out on the town."

Blinking fast, she stood stock-still for a second, barely registering his words. They still had a whole night ahead of them? She was wrung out, as if she'd run an emotional marathon. With her defenses in the negative numbers, an evening out with Seth and his children was too tantalizing, too tempting a prospect. Hell, the man himself was too tempting. Not that she had the choice of opting out.

She just really hoped the evening sucked.

The evening hadn't sucked.

In fact, Seth had followed through with the perfect plans so far, starting off with a gourmet picnic at a park near a seventeenth century fort by the harbor. The children had toddled around, eaten their fill and gotten dirty. So precious and perfect and far more normal than she would have expected.

Then Seth had chartered a carriage ride through the historic district at sundown. Olivia and Owen had squealed with delight over the horse. And the last part of the outing hadn't ended in a half hour as she'd expected.

Once the kids' bedtime arrived, Seth had simply paid the driver to continue down the waterside road while the children slept in their laps. The *clop, clop, clop* of the Belgian draft's hooves lulled Alexa as she cuddled the sweet weight of Owen sleeping in her arms.

The night was more than Cinderella-perfect. Cinderella only had the prospect of happily ever after. For tonight, Alexa had experienced the magic of being a part of a real family during this outing with Seth and his children.

Although Cinderella's driver likely wasn't sporting ear buds for an iPod. Alexa appreciated the privacy it offered as she didn't have to worry about him eavesdropping.

Being a part of a family taking a magical moonlit carriage ride presented a tableau she'd dreamed about. The way Olivia nestled so trustingly against her father's chest. The obvious affection between him and his children during their picnic. He'd built a relationship with them, complete with familiar games and songs and love.

But even as she joined in this family game for now, she couldn't lose sight of her real role here. Or the fact that Seth Jansen was a sharp businessman, known for his drive for perfection and no-nonsense ways.

She knew he wanted her. Could he be devious enough to use his children to keep her here? She thought of earlier, by the pool, how he'd focused all that intensity on her. His eyes had stroked over her, hot and hungry.

Exciting.

There'd been a time when she couldn't show her body in a bathing suit—for fear people would find out her secret, because of her own hang-ups. She'd worked past that. She'd come to peace with herself. But as her thoughts drifted toward the possibility of intimacy with another person, she faced the reality of sharing that secret part of herself, to explain why she had such extensive stretch marks in spite of never having had a child.

Even though she'd found resolution inside, it wasn't something she enjoyed revisiting.

She rested her chin on Owen's head, Seth sitting across from her holding Olivia. "How did your business meeting go?"

"We're moving forward, closer to a deal than before. My gut tells me there's a real possibility I can land this one."

"If he hasn't ended the negotiations, that's got to be a positive sign." She settled into the professional discussion, thinking of how far she'd come from her teenage years of insecurity.

"That's my take." He nodded, then something shifted in his eyes. "It appeared you had fun with Victoria today."

More memories of his interest at the pool, of his kiss last night steamed through her as tangibly as the heat rising from the paved road. A cooling breeze rolled off the harbor and caressed her shoulders, lifting her hair the way his fingers had played through the strands.

Her hand lifted to swipe back a lock from her face. "I feel guilty calling this work when it really has been more of a vacation."

"You've had twins to watch over. That's hardly a holiday."

"I've had a lot of help from you and Victoria." The carriage driver tugged the reins at a stop sign, a towering adobe church on the corner. "Not that any of us could stop that oatmeal incident."

He chuckled softly. "Thank goodness Javier's more laid back than I would have given him credit for."

"It was gracious of him to acknowledge that the breakfast with toddlers was his idea." She shuffled Owen into a more comfortable position as the baby settled deeper into sleep. "What made you think of taking a carriage ride to help the twins wind down?"

"I spent so much time outdoors growing up." He patted his daughter's back softly. "I try to give that to my kids when I can."

"Well, this was a great idea…" The moonlight played across the water rippling in the harbor. "The night air, the gorgeous scenery, the water, it's been quite a break for me, too."

"I never get tired of the year-round good weather here." As he sat across from her, he propped a foot beside her on the seat.

"What about January through March?" She shivered melodramatically. "The cold wind off the water is biting."

His laugh rode the ocean breeze as he opened up more as the evening wore on. "You've obviously never visited North Dakota. My uncle would get icicles in his beard in the winter."

"No kidding?"

"No kidding." He scratched his chin as if caught in the memories. "My cousins and I still went outside, no matter how far the temperature dropped, but it's a lot easier here when it doesn't take a half hour to pull on so many layers of clothes."

"What did you like to do in North Dakota?" she asked, hungry for deeper peeks into this intriguing man.

"Typical stuff, snowmobiling, hiking, horseback

riding on the farm. Then I discovered flying..." He shrugged. "And here I am now."

Yet there was so much more to him than that, this man who'd come from a North Dakota farm and made billions off his interest in airplanes.

The carriage shocks squeaked as the large wheels rolled along a brick side-road. How was it she felt tipsy when she hadn't even had so much as a sip of alcohol?

He nudged the side of her leg with his foot. "What about you? What did you want to do when you were a kid?"

"Art history, remember?" she said evasively.

"Why art history?"

"An obsession with creating beauty, I guess."

And now they were dancing a little too close to uncomfortable territory from her past. She pointed to the old-fashioned sailboat anchored near the shore with the sounds of a party carrying across the water. "What's up with that?"

He hesitated for a moment as if he understood full well she was trying to redirect the conversation. "It's a pirate ship. The *Black Raven*. They do everything from kids' parties to the more adult sort." He gestured toward a couple in buccaneer and maid costumes strolling down the sidewalk. "Then there are regular bar hours. People come in costume. I thought about having a party for the kids there someday—during regular hours, of course."

"I can envision you in a Jack Sparrow-style pirate shirt so you wouldn't have to tug at your tie all the time."

"You've noticed that?"

She shrugged, staying silent.

"There are lots of things I hope to teach my kids." He pointed toward the sky. "Like showing them the Big Dipper there. Or my favorite constellation, Orion's belt. See the orange-looking star along the strand? That's Betelgeuse, a red star. There's nothing like charting the sky."

"Sounds like you have a pirate's soul. If you'd been born before airplanes..."

"Star navigation can be helpful if you're lost," he pointed out. "Betelgeuse saved my ass from getting lost more than once when the navigational instruments went on the fritz during a search."

She thought back to her research on him from when she'd put together her proposal. "You started your company doing search and rescue."

"I'm still active in that arena."

"Really?" Why hadn't she seen information about that kind of work? That could have been useful in her proposal. She wanted to kick herself for falling short. "I didn't realize that."

"SAR—search and rescue—was my first love. Still is," he said with undeniable fire.

"Then why do you do the corporate charter gig?" The image of Seth Jansen was more confusing with each new revelation. She hadn't expected so many layers, so much depth.

"Search and rescue doesn't pay well. So the bigger my business..."

"The more good you can do." And just that fast the pieces came together, the billionaire, the father, the philanthropist. And on top of everything he was hot?

God, she was in serious deep water here.

His gaze slid to hers, held and heated. In a smooth

move, he shifted off the seat across from her to sit beside her. The scent of his crisp aftershave teased her nose, while his hulking magnetism drew her. Before she could think, she swayed toward him.

They still held both sleeping children, so nothing could or would happen. But the connection between them was tangible. His eyes invited her to lean against him and his arm slid around her shoulders, tucking her closer as the carriage rolled on.

How far did she want to take this? She hadn't forgotten his request that she extend her stay, even if he hadn't brought it up again. Then there was the whole tangle of her wanting to work for him...

And there were these two beautiful children who obviously came first with him, as they should. She understood how deeply a child could be affected by their growing up years. She carried the scars of her own childhood, complete with fears about opening herself to another relationship, making herself vulnerable to a man by baring her secrets as well as her body.

The carriage jerked to a halt outside their hotel, and her time to decide what to do next came to an end.

Seth set his iPod in the hotel's docking station and cued up the twins' favorite Mozart for tots music. The babies had been too groggy for baths after the carriage ride, so he and Alexa had just tucked them into their cribs, each wearing a fresh diaper and T-shirt.

Leaving him alone with Alexa—and completely awake.

Their evening together had given him an opportunity to learn more about her, the person, rather than the businesswoman. Guilt tweaked his conscience. She had a life and a company and a tender heart. She also had some misguided notion she could persuade him to sign a contract with her cleaning service. He'd told her otherwise, but he suspected she believed she could change his mind.

He needed to clear that up now, before things went further.

While he would do anything for his kids, he had other options for their care now and he couldn't deny the truth. He was keeping her here because he wanted to sleep with her, now, away from Charleston, in a way that wouldn't tangle their lives up with each other. Because, damn it all, no matter how much he wanted her in his bed, he didn't have the time or inclination to start a full out relationship. He would not, under any circumstances put his children through the upheaval of another inevitable breakup.

He plowed his fingers through his hair. He was left with no choice. He had to come clean with Alexa. He owed it to her. If for no other reason than because of the way she'd been so patient with his children, more than just watching over them, she'd played with them.

Rolled a ball.

Kissed a minor boo-boo.

Wiped away pudding smudges from their faces.

Rested her cheek on a sleeping baby's head with such genuine affection while they rode in the carriage like an honest to God family.

A dark cloud mushroomed inside him. He pivoted toward the living room—and found her waiting in the open doorway. She still wore the tan capris and flowing blouse she'd had on for their picnic, except her feet were bare.

Her toes curled into the carpet. "Earlier tonight, you mentioned extending our stay. What was that all about?"

He should be rejoicing. He had achieved exactly what he wanted in enticing her to stay.

Yet now was his time to man-up and tell her the whole story. "There's been a change in plans. I'm not returning to Charleston in the morning."

"You're staying here?" Her forehead crinkled in confusion.

He glanced back at his kids, concerned with waking them, and guided Alexa into the living area, closing the bedroom door behind him.

"Not exactly." He steered her to the blue velvet sofa and sat beside her. "Tomorrow, Javier and I are moving negotiations to the king's island to peruse his landing strip and discuss possibilities for increasing security measures."

"That's great news for you." She smiled with genuine pleasure.

Her obvious—unselfish—happiness over his success kicked his guilt into high gear. "I need to be up-front with you."

"Okay—" her eyes went wary "—I'm listening."

"I want you to come with me to the island." He tucked a knuckle under her chin, brushed his mouth over hers. The connection deepened, crackled with need. "Not because of business or the kids. But because I want *you*. I want *this*."

He hesitated. "And before you ask, I do still intend to introduce you to the contacts just like I promised on day one. And I will listen to your business proposal and give you advice. But that's all I can offer."

Small consolation to his burning conscience right

now. He truly wished he could do more for her and for her business.

Realization dawned in her eyes, her face paling. "I'm not going to land the Jansen Jets contract, no matter what I say."

"I'm afraid not. Your company is simply not large enough. I'm sorry."

She gnawed her plump bottom lip, then braced her shoulders. "You don't have to apologize. You told me as much that first day, and I just didn't want to hear you."

"The way your service is growing shows promise, and if this had been a year from now, the answer might have been different." That made him wonder what it would have been like to meet her a year from now, when his kids were older and the sting of his divorce had lessened.

"Then I go home now."

Was that anger or regret he saw chasing across her expression? It looked enough like the latter that he wasn't going to miss the opportunity to press what little advantage he had. "Or you could go with me to the island. Just for the weekend."

Her lips pressed tightly, thinning. "You may always get weekends free, but Bethany and I trade off every other one. I've already taken two days off work in the hope of a business proposition you never intended to fulfill. I can't keep imposing on her indefinitely."

"I meant what I said. I do intend to make good on introducing you to new connections and helping you beef up your presentation. Damn it, I'm trying hard to be honest with you." He reached to loosen his tie and then realized he wasn't wearing it anymore. "I'll pay the difference you need to hire temporary help while you're away—"

Her eyes went wide with horror. "You've already paid me enough. It's not about the money."

"Take it anyway. Consider it an exchange for your help with the kids. And I do need your help."

"You want me to stay for the twins?" She crossed her arms defensively.

"It's not that simple. I can't untangle my kids from what's going on between us. So yeah, they factor into this decision." They had to factor into every decision he made. "My children like you. That counts for a lot. They've seen too much upheaval in their lives already. I try to give them as much stability as I can."

"They've only known me for a couple of days and then I'll be gone." Her fingers dug into her elbows.

She had a point there. The thought of them growing too attached…

Shaking his head, he refocused. His plan for the weekend was solid. Second-guessing himself would only derail things. He loosened her grip and held her soft hands in his. "I like how happy Owen and Olivia are with you."

"I adore them, too." Obvious affection tinged her words, along with regret. "But even if I agree to this crazy proposition of yours, I'll be leaving their lives when we all go home."

"Maybe. Maybe not." Where had that come from? Only seconds ago he'd been thinking about how he needed to have an affair now because indulging in more once they returned home wasn't an option.

Was it?

She tugged her hands from his. "I'm not ready for

any kind of relationship, and I'm still not happy about the business end of things between us."

He should be rejoicing at those words. Should be. He cradled her face in his palm. "Then consider having a fling with me."

"A fling?" She gnawed her bottom lip slowly as she repeated the word. "Fling? No attachment or expectations. Just pure indulgence in each other?"

Already her suggestive words sent a bolt of lust straight to his groin. If she could seduce him this thoroughly with just a few words, what more did she hold in store with her hands, her body?

"That's the idea," he growled softly in agreement. "We pick up where we left off last night at dinner."

So he waited for her decision, the outcome more important than it should have been for someone of such brief acquaintance. But then she smiled, not full out, just a hint of possibility.

She reached, skimming her fingers down the front of his chest lightly as if still making up her mind. The feel of her featherlight touch made his erection impossibly harder.

Her hand stopped just shy of his belt, her eyes assessing, yet still holding the briefest hint of reservation. "For how long?"

He clasped her hand and brought her wrist to his mouth. Her pulse leaped under his kiss.

"For the weekend." Or more. He wasn't sure of a hell of a lot right now. But he was certain of one thing. He wanted Alexa. "Starting now."

Six

Alexa leaned into the restrained strength of Seth's touch. He was such a giant of a man with amazing control. She'd been aching for the feel of his hands on her skin since she'd first seen him. Yes, she was angry over the doused hopes of signing a contract with his company. However, in other ways, she was relieved. The end of their business acquaintance freed her to pursue the attraction between them.

As much as she wanted to attribute the power of her desire to months of abstinence, she knew she hadn't felt anything near this compulsion for other attractive men who'd crossed her path. She wanted him, deeply, ached to have him with such a craving it was all she could do not to fling herself onto him.

Even in her spoiled princess days, she'd guarded her body closely. She'd only slept with two men before her husband and no one since. Each relationship had come after months of dating. This was so out of character for her, which emphasized the tenacious attraction all the more.

The prospect of a no-strings affair with Seth, especially now that she wasn't trying to win a contract with him, was more temptation than she could resist.

She angled her face into his hard hand, turning to press a kiss into his palm. A primitive growl of desire rumbled from him in response, stirring and stoking molten pleasure deep in her belly.

Without moving his hand from her face, he leaned to kiss her bared neck. The glide of his mouth sent delicious shivers down her spine. Her head lolled back to give him fuller access.

He swept her hair aside with a large confident hand that skimmed down to palm her waist. Nipping, kissing, his mouth traced along her throbbing pulse. His chin nudged aside one shoulder of her blouse, his late-day beard raspy and arousing against her flushed skin.

His body hummed with restraint. Straining tendons along his neck let her know just how much it cost him to go slowly. His meticulous attention to detail sent a fresh shiver of anticipation through her.

She grabbed his shirt, her fist twisting in the warm cotton as she hauled him closer, urged him on. He shot to his feet and scooped her into his arms. Her fingers linked behind his neck as she steadied herself against his chest. Part of her warned that she should stop, now; but an even more insistent part of her urged her to see this through. Then maybe she would be free of the frenetic lure of this man. She could get back to the carefully planned, safe life she'd built for herself.

Seth angled sideways through the door into the spare room. Gauzy curtains hung from rings around the wrought-iron canopy frame overhead. He lowered her gently into the poofy white spread. Stepping back, he began unbuttoning his shirt while she watched—not that he seemed the least concerned with her gaze clinging to him.

In fact, he appeared all the more aroused by her appreciation. He shrugged off the shirt and unbuckled his belt, the low lighting from the bedside lamp casting a warm glow over his bared flesh.

One long zip later... Oh, yeah, he was most definitely as turned on as she was. The rigid length of his arousal reached up his rock solid abs. Golden hair sprinkled along his defined chest. He was a sculpted god of a man, and for tonight, he was all hers...

But as she devoured him with her eyes, unease skittered up her spine at the prospect of turning the tables. While she'd conquered the eating disorder of her teenage years, her body still carried marks and signs of how close she'd come to dying.

Twisting sideways, she reached to turn off the lamp and prayed he wouldn't argue. She truly didn't want to have this discussion right now. *Click*. The room went dark then shadowy as her eyes adjusted to the moonlight streaming through the sheers on the window, the thicker brocade curtains pulled back.

She waited and thank God, Seth stayed silent. Brows pinching together, his head tilting to the side offered the only signs he'd registered her turning off the light.

Swallowing the patter of nerves, she sat up and swept her loose shirt upward and over her head. As she shook her hair free, he kicked aside his pants and leaned over her, angling her back to recline against the piled pillows. His hand fell to the top button on her capris. Up close, she could see the question in his eyes as he waited for her consent.

Arching upward, she slid her fingers into his hair and tugged his mouth toward hers. The feel of him was becoming familiar as they deepened contact, her lips parting, opening, welcoming him. Losing herself in the kiss, she barely registered his deft work pushing aside her pants and freeing the front clasp of her bra.

The cool air contrasted with the warmth of his hard muscled body. Tension built inside her, a need to take this farther, faster. She tugged at Seth's shoulders, whispering her need, her desires, but he wouldn't be rushed.

He nipped, licked, laved his way down her neck and to her breasts, drawing on her tightening nipples with the perfect mixture of tongue and tug. Her fingernails grazed down his back, tendons and muscles flexing under her stroke in response.

The glide of his hand between them sent her stomach muscles tensing. He slowed, pausing to flick her belly button ring. "This drove me insane when I saw it earlier, exposed by that sexy deep V of your bathing suit. Ever since, all I could think of was touching it. Touching you."

"Then I like the way you think," she whispered, then gasped.

His tender torment continued until her head thrashed along the deep downy pillow. She hooked her leg around his, bringing his stony thigh to rest against her aching core. Rocking against him only made her more frustrated, liquid longing pulsing through her veins and flushing her skin.

The air conditioner swirled the scents of his aftershave, her shampoo and their desire into a perfume of lust, intoxicating her with each gasping breath. He angled off her, and she moaned her frustration.

"Shh." He pressed a finger to her mouth. "Only for a second."

His hand dipped into a drawer in the bedside table. He came back with a box of condoms. Thank heaven, someone had the foresight to plan ahead. She couldn't even bring herself to condemn him for assuming this could happen...because here they were, the only place she wanted to be at the moment.

Then the thick pressure of him between her thighs scattered any other thoughts as he pushed inside her. Large and stretching and more than she'd expected. She hooked her legs around his waist, opening for him, welcoming him and the sensation of having him fully inside her.

Smoothly, he rolled to his back while their bodies stayed connected. She lay sprawled on top of him. Bowing upward, she straddled him, taking him impossibly deeper. His eyes flamed as he watched her with the same intensity she knew she'd lavished on him when he'd undressed for her. He gripped her waist, and she rolled her hips against him.

Her head flung back at the pure sensation, the perfect angle as he nudged against the circle of sensitivity hidden inside her. And again, he moved, thrusting, pumping, taking her need to a whole new level of frenzy until she raked her nails down his chest, desperate for completion. She didn't know herself, this out of control woman all but screaming for release. She'd thought she knew her body and the pleasures to be found in bed. But nothing came close to this…this fiery tingle along her every nerve.

Then they were flipping position again and he was on top of her, pumping faster, the head of his arousal tormenting that special spot inside her again and again until…

Sensation imploded, sparks of white light dotting behind her eyes. His mouth covered hers, taking her gasps and moans and, yes, even her cries of pleasure into him the way she still welcomed him into her body.

The bliss rippled through her in tingling aftershocks even as he rolled to his side, tucking her against his chest. He drew the covers over them and kissed the top of her head tenderly, stroking her back. His heart thumped hard and loud against her ear in time with her own racing pulse.

What the hell had just happened?

The best sex of her life.

And as the wash of desire cooled inside her that thought scared her more than a little. Already she wanted him again. Far too much. She needed distance to shore up her own defenses. Establishing her independence after her divorce had been damn difficult. She couldn't allow herself to turn clingy or needy again—no matter how amazing the orgasm.

Once his breathing evened out into a low snore, she eased herself from his arms, needing to think through what had just happened between them. She inched off the bed, slowly, carefully, her feet finally touching the carpet.

She tugged on her shirt and panties, the fabric gliding

across her well-loved body still oversensitized from the explosiveness of her release. She pulled open the door to the sitting area with more than a little regret.

"You're leaving?" His voice rumbled softly from the bed.

She turned toward him, keeping her head high. "Just returning to my room for the night."

Gauzy white curtains and his large lounging body gave off the air of a blond sheikh.... Good Lord, her mind was taking fanciful routes and fantasies.

"Uh-uh." He shook his head, sliding his hands behind his neck, broad chest all but calling to her to curl right back up again. "You're not ready to sleep together."

"I want to." God, did she ever want to.

"Glad to hear it. Hold on to that thought for our weekend together." He swung his feet to the floor and was beside her in a heartbeat. He kissed her just once, firmly but without moving, as if simply sealing his imprint on her.

As if she didn't already carry the feel of him in her every thought right now.

He stepped back into his room. "Sleep well, Alexa. We leave early for the island. Good night."

The door closing after him, he left her standing in the middle of the sitting room ready to burst into flames all over again.

From inside the chartered jet, Alexa felt the blazing sun flame its way up the morning sky on her way to a king's getaway. The Atlantic Ocean stretched out below, a small dot of an island waiting ahead.

Their destination.

Waking up late, she and Seth had been too rushed for

conversation. They'd dressed the kids and raced to the lobby just as the limousine arrived to pick them up along with Javier and his wife. The luxury ride to the small airport had given her the opportunity to double-check with Bethany and clear the schedule change. Bethany seemed so excited at the prospect of new contacts, she gave two thumbs-up. So there were no obstacles to Alexa's leaving. The ride had been so smooth and speedy she'd been whisked onto the jet before she'd even fully wiped the sleep from her eyes.

Breakfast had been waiting for them on the flight, although she'd been told they would land within a half hour. She had monitored the babies plucking up Cheerios, while nibbling on a *churro*—a Spanish doughnut. It had all seemed so normal, as if her insides weren't still churning from what had happened between her and Seth the night before.

And wondering what would happen when they landed on the isolated island for the weekend.

Her eyes gravitated to the open door leading to the cockpit where Seth flew the jet, Javier sitting in the copilot's seat. Their night together scrolled through her mind in lush, sensual detail. He'd touched her, aroused her, fulfilled her in ways she'd never experienced before. And while she was scared as hell of where this intense connection might lead her, she couldn't bring herself to walk away. Not yet.

Victoria touched her arm lightly. "They're both loners, but I think they're going to work well together."

"I'm sure they will." Loner? She hadn't thought of Seth quite that way, more brusque and businesslike. Except when he was around his kids, then he really opened up. Like he had when talking to her during their carriage ride.

And while making love, he'd held nothing back.

"Are you all right?" Victoria asked.

Alexa forced a smile. "Sorry to be so quiet." She searched for something to explain her preoccupation with a certain hot pilot only a few feet away. "It's just surreal that we would go to a king's home with babies in tow."

"Deposed king—and indulgent grandfather. If it makes you worry less, he's not in residence at the moment. He's visiting his doctors on the mainland, follow-ups on some surgery he had. We'll have the island all to ourselves, other than the staff and security, of course." She replenished the pile of Cheerios on Olivia's tray. The company that had stocked and cleaned the jet had done their job well. "The twins will find anything they need already there. He even keeps a sitter on staff."

"So none of the king's family is in residence at the moment? No other children?"

"None. The other family members have their own homes elsewhere. Since the family has reconciled, they're all visiting more often."

"More air travel." That explained why they were courting Jansen Jets.

"And more need for security with all these extra trips."

That also explained how Seth fit the bill all the better with his background in search and rescue, and security devices for airports. "How scary to have to worry so much about a regular family vacation."

Victoria huffed her blond bangs from her forehead.

"The press may have eased up from the initial frenzy, but they haven't backed off altogether. Even relatives have to be on guard—and stay silent at all times."

Alexa struggled not to squirm. She was used to the background checks that accompanied working at an airport. "I hear you. No speaking to the press."

"Their cousin Alys is still persona non grata after speaking to the press. She moved back to another family compound in South America. I guess you could say she's even in exile from the exiled."

"That's so sad, but understandable." Alexa had grown up in a privileged world, but these people took privileged to a whole new level.

When the silence stretched, she followed Victoria's puzzled stare and realized...Alexa closed her fist around her napkin. She'd been scrubbing a smudge on the silver tray obsessively. Her flatware was lined up precisely and she'd even brushed some powdered sugar into a tiny pile.

Smiling sheepishly, she forced her fists to unfurl and still. "When I'm nervous, I clean."

Victoria covered Alexa's hand with her own. "There's nothing to sweat, really."

Easier said than done when she'd barely survived her home life growing up. It was one thing to stand on the periphery of that privileged world, restoring order to the messes made by others. It was another thing entirely to step into the lushness of overindulgence that had once threatened to swallow her whole. But she was committed to this weekend. Literally. There was no escape.

She stared out the window at the island nestled in miles and miles of sparkling ocean. Palm trees spiked from the lush landscape. A dozen or so small outbuildings dotted a semicircle around a larger structure.

The white mansion faced the ocean in a U shape, constructed around a large courtyard with a pool. Details were spotty but she would get an up close view soon enough. Even from a distance she couldn't miss the grand scale of the sprawling estate, the unmistakable sort that housed royalty.

The plane banked as Seth lined up the craft with a thin islet alongside the larger island. A single strip of pristine concrete marked the private runway. As they neared, a ferry boat came into focus. To ride from the airport to the main island? They truly were serious about security.

She thought she'd left behind this kind of life when she'd cut ties with her parents. She'd been happy with her peripheral role, knowing what the rich needed but free of the complications of that life for herself.

Yet here she was.

Did she really want to even dip her toe in this sort of affluent world again? What choice did she have at the moment? Her gaze slid back to Seth. No choice really given how deeply she ached to be with him again.

Or maybe she had a choice after all: the option to take control on their next encounter rather than simply following his lead.

And she would make damn sure he was every bit as knocked off balance by the experience as she'd been.

The night unfolded for Seth, full of opportunities.

He'd concluded his deal with Javier and would spend tomorrow formulating plans for the future. He was ready to celebrate. With Alexa. Hopefully she would be in the same mindset.

He closed the door to the nursery where the twins would spend the night under the watchful eye of one of the resident nannies.

Just before their bedtime, he'd tried Pippa again, on the off chance she would pick up and could wish the kids good-night. She'd actually answered, sounding overly chipper, but cut the call short once he'd attempted to put Owen and Olivia on the line. Something about the whole conversation had been "off" but he couldn't put his finger on the exact problem.

Most likely because all he could think about right now was getting Alexa naked again.

He entered their quarters. More like a luxurious condominium within the mansion. He and Alexa had been given separate rooms in the second floor corner suite, but he hoped he could keep her distracted through the night until she fell asleep in his arms, exhausted by good sex.

Great sex.

Searching the peach and gray room, he didn't see signs of her other than her suitcase open on her bed. His shoes padded softly against the thick Persian rug past a sitting area with an eating space stocked more fully than most kitchens.

The quiet echoed around him, leaving him hyperaware of other sounds…a ticking grandfather clock in the hall…the crashing ocean outside… Through the double doors, the balcony was as large as some yards.

And Alexa leaned on the railing.

A breeze gusted from the ocean plastering her long

tiered sundress to her body, draping her curves in deep purple.

He stopped beside her. "Penny for them?"

She glanced at him sideways, the hem of her dress brushing his leg like phantom fingers. "No money for no work, remember? I've done nothing here to earn even a cent. The nanny takes over the kids, and I have to admit, she's good at charming them."

"You would rather they cried for you?"

"Of course not! I just...I like to feel useful. In control."

"Most women I know would be thrilled by an afternoon with a manicurist and masseuse."

"Don't get me wrong, I enjoy being pampered as much as anyone. In fact, I think you deserve a bit of relaxation yourself." She tapped a pager resting on the balcony wall. "The nanny can call if she needs us. What do you say we head down to the beach? I found the most wonderful cabana where we can talk."

Talk?

Not what he'd been fantasizing about for their evening together. But Alexa apparently had something on her mind, given the determined tilt of her chin. He took her hand in his. Her short nails were shiny with clear polish. The calluses on her fingers from cleaning had been softened and he felt the urge to make sure she never had to pick up a scrub brush ever again.

Keeping his hand linked with hers, he followed her down the winding cement steps toward the beach. She kicked off her sandals and waited for him to ditch his shoes and socks.

Hand in hand, they walked along the shore, feet sinking into the sand as they made their way toward a white cabana. With each step closer he could feel the tension ramping up in her body.

"I'd hoped today would offer you breaks, be a sort of vacation."

She glanced up, a smile flickering. "This is paradise. I've been in some impressive mansions over the years, but even I'm a floored by this place. No kidding royalty. Your business is going to a whole new level with this deal."

"That's the plan." So why did he still feel so... unsettled? He gestured inside the cabana where she'd ordered two low lounge chairs with a small table of refreshments between them.

Her eyes flickered wide for a second before she plunged inside, choosing a chair and eyeing the wine, cheese and grapes. She'd obviously planned this chance to...talk?

She wriggled her toes in the sand and plucked a grape. A wave curled up closer and she stretched her legs out until the water touched the tips of her feet. "This truly is paradise."

He dropped into the chair beside her. "Then why are you so tense?"

"Why do you want to know?"

"Why do you think?" He poured deep red wine into two crystal glasses and let his eyes speak as fully as his words.

She took one of the drinks by the stem and sipped. "Victoria called you a loner."

"Interesting." And he wasn't sure what that had to do with anything.

"You have so much family in Charleston, I hadn't thought of you that way." The wind rippled and flapped the three canvas walls of the cabana. "You do have family there, right? You called them when you found the babies, to ask for help."

"I have two cousins—Vic and Paige. I grew up with them in North Dakota when my parents died in a car accident." He reached for his wine. "Their SUV slid off the road in a storm when I was eleven." He downed half of the fine vintage as if it was water.

"I'm so sorry." She touched his wrist lightly as he replaced his drink.

"No need to feel sorry for me. I was lucky to have family willing to take me in." He hesitated. "My parents didn't have any assets when they died. My aunt and uncle never said anything about the extra mouth to feed, but I vowed I would pay them back."

"Look at you now. You've truly accomplished the amazing."

He stared out over the dark water and the darker night sky. "Too late to give anything to them… It took me a while to find my footing. Too long."

"Good God, Seth, you're all of what…"

"Thirty-eight."

"A self-made billionaire by thirty-eight." Her laugh stroked over his senses like the ocean breeze. "I wouldn't call that a slow start."

But he was still chasing dreams around the country. "I didn't set out on this path. I wanted to fly for the Air Force, even started ROTC at the University of Miami, but lost out on a medical snafu that isn't an issue anywhere but the Air Force. So I finished my degree and came home. Ran a flight school while flying my veterinarian cousin around to farms until the family all relocated to South Carolina."

He could feel her undivided attention on him. He wasn't sure why he was spilling all of this about himself, but somehow the words kept coming out. Strange as hell since she'd been on the mark in calling him a loner in spite of his large family.

"I wrestle with wanting to give my kids everything while worrying about teaching them working class values. I think about it a lot, how to help them have their own sense of accomplishment."

"The fact that you're even thinking about it says you're ahead of the game." She reached for his hand this time, linking her fingers and squeezing. "You do well by them."

He lifted her hand to kiss her wrist. "You grew up in a privileged world but came out with a strong work ethic. Any tips?"

She laughed bitterly. "My parents had shallow values, spending every penny they inherited to indulge themselves. My father bankrupted the family trust fund, or rather I should say they both did. Now, I have to work in order to eat like most of the rest of the world, which isn't a tragedy or sob story. Just a reality."

He'd known about her father's crappy management of the family's finances and sportswear line. But... "What about your marriage settlement?"

"We signed a prenup. My father's lawyers were worried Travis was a fortune hunter. I told Travis I didn't care about any contracts but he insisted." She spread her arms without letting go of his hands. "No alimony for either of us."

Frustration spiked inside him. "He doesn't care that you were left penniless? The jackass."

"Stop right there." She squeezed his hand insistently.

"I signed the prenup, too, and I don't want your sympathy."

"Okay, I hear you."

What was she thinking right now? He wished he was better at understanding the working of a woman's mind. He'd brought her to the island for seduction, and somehow, out here tonight, they'd ended up talking about things he didn't share with others. But Alexa had a way of kicking down barriers, and he'd had as much sharing as he could take for one night.

The rush of the ocean pulling at the sand under his feet seemed as if it tugged the rest of the world with it. He'd brought Alexa to this island for a reason: to seduce her so thoroughly he could work through this raw connection they felt.

Except, as he leaned in to kiss her, he was beginning to realize the chances of working her out of his system was going to be damn near impossible.

Her hand flattened to his chest. "Stop."

"What?" His voice came out a little strangled, but he held himself still. If a woman said no, that meant no.

"Last time we did this, you were the boss." She slid from her lounger and leaned over to straddle his hips. The warm core of her seared his legs even through her cotton dress and his slacks. "This time, Seth, I'm calling the shots."

Seven

Seth's brain went numb.

Did Alexa actually intend to have sex with him outside, in a seaside cabana? If so, she wouldn't get an argument from him. He was just surprised, since she'd insisted on leaving his bed the night before. He'd assumed she was more reserved given how she'd wanted to keep the light off.

Although the way she tugged at his shirttails, he couldn't mistake her intent, or her urgency.

Moonbeams bathed her in a dim amber glow. Still straddling his hips, Alexa yanked the hem free then ripped, popping the buttons, sending them flying into the sand. Surprise snapped through him just as tangibly. Apparently he'd underestimated her adventurous spirit.

Wind rolled in from the ocean across his bare chest. His body went on alert a second before her mouth flicked, licked and nipped at his nipple the way he'd lavished attention on her the night before.

He cupped her hips, his fingers digging into the cottony softness of her bunched dress. "I like the way you think, Alexa."

"Good, but you need to listen better." She clasped his wrists and pulled them away. "This is *my* turn to be in control."

"Yes, ma'am." Grinning at her, he rested his hands on the lounger's armrests, eager to see her next move.

Wriggling closer, she sketched her mouth over his, over to his ear. "You won't be sorry."

Her hands worked his belt buckle free, her cool fingers tucking inside to trace down the length of his arousal. He throbbed in response, wanted to ditch their clothes and roll her onto the sandy ground. The more she stroked and caressed, the more he ached to do the same to her. But every time he started to move, she stopped.

Once he stilled again, she nipped his ear or his shoulder, her fingers resuming the torturously perfect glide over him. His fingers gripped the rests tighter, until the blood left his hands.

Alexa swept his pants open further, shifting. As he started to move with her, she placed a finger over his lips. "Shh… I've got this."

Sliding from his lap, she knelt between his legs and took him in her mouth, slowly, fully. Moist, warm ecstasy clamped around him, caressed him. His head fell back against the chair, his eyes closing, shutting out all other sensation except the glide of her lips and tongue.

Her hands clamped on his thighs for balance. With

his every nerve tuned into the feel of her, even her fingers digging into his muscles ramped his pulse higher. Wind lifted her hair, gliding it over his wrist. The silky torment almost sent him over the edge.

The need to finish roared inside him, too much, too close. He wasn't going there without her. Time for control games to come to an end.

He clasped her under her arms and lifted her with ease, bringing her back to his lap.

"Condom," he growled through clenched teeth. "In my wallet. Leftover from the hotel."

Laughing softly, seductively, she reached behind him and tucked her fingers into his back pocket. The stroke of her hand over his ass had him gritting his teeth with restraint. Then she pitched his wallet to the ground with a wicked glint in her eyes.

What the hell?

She leaned sideways, toward the table of wine and cheese. Pitching aside a napkin, she uncovered a stack of condoms. "I came prepared."

His eyebrows rose at the pile of condoms, a dozen or so. "Ambitiously so."

"Is that a problem?" She studied him through her lashes.

God, he loved a challenge and this woman was turning out to be a surprise in more ways than one since she'd blasted into his life such a short time ago. "I look forward to living up to your expectations."

"Glad to hear it." She tore open one of the packets and sheathed him slowly.

Backlit by the crescent moon, she stood. She bunched the skirt of her dress and swept her panties down, kicking them aside. A low growl of approval rumbled inside him as he realized her intent. She straddled him again, inching the hem of her dress up enough so the hot heat of her settled against his hard-on.

Cradling his face in her hands, she raised up on her knees to kiss him. Her dress pooled around them, concealing her from view as she lowered herself onto the length of his erection. The moist clamp of her gripped him, drew him inside until words scattered like particles of sand along the beach.

The scent of the ocean clung to her skin. Unable to resist, he tasted her, trekking along her bared shoulder and finding the salty ocean flavor clung to her skin. He untied the halter neck of her dress, the fabric slithering down to reveal a lacy strapless bra. Her creamy breasts swelled just above the cups and with a quick flick of his fingers, he freed the front clasp.

Freed her.

Lust pumped through him along with anticipation. He filled his hands with the soft fullness, the shadowy beauty of her just barely visible in the moonlight.

His thumbs brushed the pebbly tips. "Someday we're going to make love on a beach with the sun shining down, or in a room with all the lamps on so I can see the bliss on your face."

"Someday…" she echoed softly.

Were those shadows in her eyes or just the play of clouds drifting past?

Her face lowered to his, blocking out the view and his thoughts as she sealed her mouth to his, demanding, giving and taking. With the lighting dim, his other senses heightened. The taste of her was every bit as intoxicating as the lingering hint of red wine on her tongue. Burying himself deep inside her, deeper still, he reveled in the purr of pleasure vibrating in her throat.

He stroked down her spine until his hands tucked under her bottom. Her soft curves in his palms, he angled her nearer, burning for more of her, more of them together. Her husky sighs and moans grew louder and closer together. Damn good thing since he was balancing on the edge himself, fulfillment right there for the taking.

Waves crashed in the distance, echoing the rush of his pulse pounding in his ears. Sand rode the air and clung to the perspiration dotting their skin, the gritty abrasion was arousing as she writhed against him. He tangled his hand into her satiny hair and gently tugged her head back. Exposing her breasts to his mouth, he took the tip of one tight bud and rolled it lightly between his teeth.

She sighed, her back arching hard and fast, her chanted "yes, yes, yes," circling him. Wrapping and pulsing around him like the moist spasms of her orgasm. Her cries of completion mingled with the roar of crashing waves.

Blasting through his own restraint.

Thrusting through her release, he triggered another in her just as he came. The force slammed through him, powerful and eclipsing everything else as he flew apart inside her into a pure flat spin nosedive into pleasure. His arms convulsed around her with the force of his completion.

He forced his fist open to release her hair even though she hadn't so much as whimpered in complaint. In fact, her head stayed back even as he relinquished her hair, the locks lifted and whipped by the wind into a tangled mass.

Gasping, she sagged on top of him, her bared breasts against his heaving chest. He didn't have a clue how long it took him to steady his breathing, but Alexa still rested in his arms. He retied the top of her sundress with hands not quite as steady as he would like. She nuzzled his neck with a soft, sated sigh.

He slid from under her, smoothing her dress over her hips, covering her with more than a little regret. With luck, though, there would be more opportunities to peel every stitch of clothing from her body.

For now, though, it was time to go inside. He refastened his pants and tucked the remaining condoms in his pocket. Not much he could do about his shirt since the buttons were scattered on the beach. He snagged the nursery pager and clipped it to his waistband before turning back to Alexa.

Scooping her in his arms, he started barefoot toward the mansion. She looped her arms around his neck, her head lolling onto his shoulder. Climbing the steps to their second floor suite, he walked through the patio filled with topiaries, ferns and flowering cacti. He'd enjoyed her power play on the beach. It had certainly paid off for both of them. But that didn't mean he was passing over control completely.

Tonight, she would sleep in his bed.

Alexa stretched in the massive sleigh bed, wrapped in the delicious decadence of Egyptian cotton sheets and the scent of making love with Seth. She stared around the unfamiliar surroundings, taking in oil paintings and heavy drapery.

She dimly remembered him carrying her from the beach to his bed. For a second, she'd considered insisting he take her to her room and leave her there. But his arms felt so good around her and she'd been so deliciously sated from their time in the cabana, she'd simply cuddled against his chest and slept.

God, had she ever slept. She couldn't remember when she'd last had eight uninterrupted hours. Could be because every muscle in her body had relaxed.

Yes, she knew she hadn't turned on the glaring lights, literally and in theory, by avoiding telling him about the issues in her past. But taking control last night had given her the confidence to invite Seth the rest of the way into her life.

Through the thick wood door, she heard voices in the other room; Seth's mingled with the babble of the twins. She smiled, looking forward to the day already. Except her suitcase and other clothes were in her bedroom, and she couldn't walk out there as is with the children nearby.

Swinging her feet to the floor, she grabbed her dress off the wing chair and pulled it on hastily. The crumpled cotton shouted that she'd spent the night with a man, but at least the twins wouldn't pick up on that. She could say "good morning" to them and then zip into her room to put on something fresh before she greeted the rest of the household.

At the door, she paused by a crystal vase of lisianthus with blooms that resembled blue roses. She plucked one out, snapped the stem and tucked the blossom behind her ear. Her hands gravitated to the flowers, straightening two of the blooms again so they were level with the rest, orderly. Perfect. She pulled open the door to the living area.

Another voice mingled in the mix.

An adult female voice.

Alexa froze in the open doorway. She scoured the room. Seth sat in a chair at the small writing desk, a twin on each knee as they faced the laptop computer in the middle of a Skype conversation.

A young woman's face filled the screen, her voice swelling from the speakers. "How are my babies? I've missed you both so very, very much."

Oh, God. It couldn't be. Not right now.

If Alexa had harbored any doubts as to the woman's identity, both babies chanted, "Ma-ma, Ma-ma, Ma-ma."

"Olivia, Owen, I'm here." Her voice echoed with obvious affection.

Pippa Jansen wasn't at all what she'd expected.

For starters, the woman didn't appear airheaded; in fact she had a simple, auburn-haired glamour. She wore a short-sleeved sweater set and pearls. From the log cabinlike walls and mountainous backdrop behind Pippa, she didn't appear to be at a plush spa or cruise ship getaway as Alexa had assumed.

Pippa didn't look to be partying or carefree. She appeared...tired and sad. "Mommy's just resting up, like taking a good nap, but I'll see you soon. We'll have yogurt and play in the sandbox. Kisses and hugs." She pressed a hand to her lips then wrapped her arms around herself. "Kisses and hugs."

Olivia and Owen blew exuberant baby kisses back. Both babies were so happy, so blissfully unaware. Alexa's heart ached for both of them. Her hands twitchy, she straightened a leather-bound volume of *Don Quixote* on a nearby end table.

Tension radiated from Seth's shoulders as he held a baby on each knee. "Pippa, while I understand your need for a break, I need some kind of reassurance that you're not going to drop off the map again once we hang up. I need to be able to reach you if there's an emergency."

"I promise." Her voice wavered. "I'll check in regularly from now on. I wouldn't have left this way if I wasn't desperate. I know I should have stayed to tell you myself, but I was scared you would say no, and I really needed a break. I watched through an airport window until you got on your plane. Please don't be angry with me."

"I'm not mad," he said, not quite managing to hide the irritation in his voice. "I just want to make sure you're all right. That you never feel desperate."

"This time away is good for me, really. I'll be back to normal when I come back to Charleston."

"You know I would like to have the children more often. When you're ready to come back, we can hire more help when they're with you, but we can't have a repeat of what happened at the airport. The twins' safety has to come first."

"You're right." She fidgeted with her pearls, her nails chewed down. "But I don't think we should talk about this now, in front of the babies."

"You're right, but we do have to discuss it. Soon."

"Absolutely." She nodded, almost frantically, pulling a last smile for the babies. "Bye-bye, be good for Daddy. Mommy loves you."

Her voice faded along with her picture as the

connection ended. Olivia squealed, patting the screen while Owen blew more kisses.

Alexa sagged against the door frame. She'd been prepared to hate Pippa for the way she'd been so reckless with her kids. And while she still wasn't ready to let the woman off the hook completely, she saw a mother running on fumes. Someone who was stressed and exhausted. She saw a mother who genuinely loved her children. Pippa had obviously reached her breaking point and had wisely taken them to their father before she snapped.

Of course sticking around to explain that to him would have been a far safer option. But life wasn't nearly as black and white as she'd once believed.

She'd seen Seth angry, frustrated, driven, affectionate, turned on… But right now, as Seth stared at the empty computer screen, she saw a broad-shouldered, good man who was deeply sad.

A man still holding conflicted feelings for his ex-wife.

Seth set each of his kids onto the floor and wished the weight on his shoulders was as easy to move.

Talking to Pippa had only made the situation more complicated just when he really could have used some simplicity in his personal life. He and Alexa had taken their relationship to a new level last night, both with the sex and sharing the bed. And he'd looked forward to cementing that relationship today—and tonight.

The call from Pippa had brought his life sharply back into focus. She was clearly at the end of her rope. While he wanted more time with his children, he didn't want to get it this way.

And this certainly wasn't how he'd envisioned kicking off his day with Alexa.

Glancing back over his shoulder at her in the doorway, he said, "You can come in now."

He'd sensed her there halfway through the conversation with his ex. Strange how he'd become so in tune with Alexa so quickly.

"I didn't mean to eavesdrop." She stepped deeper into the room, a barefoot goddess in her flowing purple dress with a flower behind her tousled hair.

Gracefully she sank down to the floor in front of the babies and a pile of blocks. He took in her effortless beauty, her ease with his kids. She was his dream woman—who'd come into his life at a nightmare time.

Right now, he couldn't help but be all the more aware of her strength, the way she met challenges head-on rather than running from her troubles. She'd rebuilt her entire life from the ground up. He admired that about her. Hell, he just flat out liked her, desired her and already dreaded the notion of watching her walk away.

"The conversation wasn't private." He shoved up from the chair and sat on the camelback sofa. "Olivia and Owen were just talking with their mother. Raising a baby is tough enough. The added pressure of twins just got to her. She's wise to take a break."

She glanced up sharply. "Even though she left them unattended on the airplane?"

"I'm aware that the way she chose to take that break left more than a little to be desired in the way of good judgment." He struggled to keep his voice level for the kids. For Alexa, too. He couldn't blame her for voicing the truth. "I'll handle it."

"Of course. It's really none of my business." She gnawed her bottom lip, stacking blocks then waiting for Olivia to knock the tower over. "Why don't I take the kids for a couple of hours? Give you some time to—"

"I've got them." He watched his son swipe his fist through the plastic blocks with a squeal of delight. "I'm sure you want a shower or a change of clothes."

In a perfect world he would have been joining her in that shower. As a matter of fact, in his screwed up, imperfect world he needed that shower with her all the more. What he would give for twenty minutes alone with her under the spray of hot water with his hands full of soap suds and naked Alexa. He swallowed hard and filed those thoughts away at the top of his "to do" list.

Although to get to everything on that list he would need more time. A lot more time.

"Really, it's no trouble." She patiently stacked the blocks again in alphabetical order while Olivia tried to wedge one, the *w*, in her mouth. "I'm getting good at balancing them on both hips. They can run out some energy on the beach while you finish up last minute busi—"

"I said I have them. They are my children," he snapped more curtly than he'd intended, but the discussion with Pippa had left him on edge. Wrestling for control was tough as hell with anger and frustration piling up inside him faster than those blocks made a Leaning Tower of Pisa.

Hurt slashed across her face before she schooled her features into an expressionless mask. "I'll change then, and take care of my own packing. How much longer until we leave the island?"

"We're flying out in an hour." Not that he intended to let that stop him from pursuing her. As much as he'd hoped to win her over during their trip, he now realized that wasn't going to be enough. He needed more—more time with her, more *of* her. While his relationship with Pippa had been a disaster, he was wiser for the experience now. He could enjoy Alexa in his life without letting himself get too entangled, too close.

Staring at his babies on the floor, he listened to the echo of tread as she walked away. Thought harder on the prospect of her walking away altogether.

Away, damn it.

He was going to lose Alexa if he didn't do something. He was fast realizing that no matter what his concerns about bringing a new woman into his children's lives, he couldn't let her leave.

"Alexa?"

Her footsteps stopped, but she didn't answer.

God, for about the hundredth time he wished they'd met a year from now when this would have been so much easier. But he couldn't change it. The time was now.

He wanted Alexa in his life.

"I'm sorry for being an—" He paused short of cursing in front of his children. "I'm sorry for being a jerk. I know you didn't sign on for this, but I hope you'll give me a chance to make it up to you."

She stayed silent so long he thought she would tell him to go to hell. He probably deserved as much for the way he was botching things with her right now. Her lengthy sigh reached him, heaping an extra dose of guilt on his shoulders.

"We'll talk later, after you have your children settled."

"Thanks, that's for the best." Problem was, with Pippa, he wasn't sure how or when things in his life would ever be *settled*. All the more reason to keep his emotions in check when dealing with either woman in his life. Starting now.

Because, their island paradise escape was over. It was time to return to the real world.

Riding on the ferry out to the king's private airstrip, Alexa gripped the railing as they neared Seth's plane on the islet runway. The twins, buckled into their safety seats, squealed in delight at the sea air in their faces as they waved goodbye to the tropical paradise.

She feared she was saying goodbye to far more than that.

Her eyes trekked to Seth, who was standing with the boat captain. Not surprising, since Seth had all but shut down emotionally around her since his conversation with his ex-wife.

Alexa twirled the stem of a sea oat in her hand, then tickled the twins' chins with it. They were cute, but it would be helpful if they spoke a few more words so they could hold up the other end of a conversation. There was no one else to talk to. Javier and his wife had opted to stay on the island for a couple of extra days. Alexa envied them. Deeply. The time here with Seth before that Skype call had been magical, and she wanted more.

As smoothly as the ferry moved along the marshy water, her mind traveled to dreams of extending her relationship with Seth. Could what they'd shared be just as powerful under the pressure of everyday life?

A daunting thought to say the least, especially when he had begun pulling away after his conversation with Pippa.

Thinking of that call, Alexa reached for her own phone. She should check for messages from Bethany. She'd turned her cell off last night and let it recharge—and, yes, probably because she didn't want interruptions. The way she'd made love with Seth on the beach…the way he'd made love to her afterward…

Heat pooled inside her, flushing her skin until she could have sworn she had an all-over sunburn.

Her phone powered up and she checked… No messages from Bethany, but the expected nine missed calls from her mother. Just as she started to thumb them away, the phone rang in her hand.

Her mom.

She winced.

Was her mother's perfectly coiffed blond hair actually a satellite dish that detected when her daughter turned on her phone?

Wind tearing at her own loose hair, she considered ignoring that call altogether as she had the others. But Olivia giggled and Alexa's heart tugged. If she felt this much for these two little ones so quickly, how much more must her mother feel for her?

Guilt nudged her to answer. "Hey, Mom. What's up?"

"Where are you, Lexi? I have been calling and calling." Laughter and the clank of dishes echoed over the phone line. Her parents had taken what little cash they had left and bought into a small retirement community chock-full of activities. How they continued to pay the bills was a mystery. "Lexi? Are you listening?

I took a break from my 'Mimosas and Mahjong' group just to call you."

God, why couldn't her mother call her Alexa instead of Lexi? "Working. In Florida."

Crap. Why hadn't she lied?

And was the island even part of Florida? Or was it the royal family's own privately owned little kingdom? She wasn't sure and didn't intend to split hairs—or reveal anything more than necessary to her mother.

"Oh, are you near Boca? Clear the rest of your day," her mother ordered. "Your dad and I will drive over to meet you."

"I really am working. I can't just put that on hold. And besides, I'm in Northern Florida. Very far away." Not far enough at the moment.

"You can't be working. I hear children in the background."

She hated outright lying. So she dodged with, "The boss has kids."

"Single boss?"

Not wading into those waters with her mother. "Why was it that you called?"

"Christmas!"

Huh? "The holidays are months away, Mom."

"I know, but we need to get these things pinned down so nothing goes wrong. You know how I like to have everything perfect for the holidays."

And that need for perfection differed from the rest of the year how, exactly? "I'll do my best to be there."

"I need to know, though, so we have an even number of males and females at the table. I would just hate to have the place setting ruined at the last minute if you cancel."

So much for her mother's burning need to see her only child. She just needed an extra warm body at the table, a body with female chromosomes. "You know what, Mom, then let's just plan on me not being there."

"Now, Lexi, don't be that way. And wipe that frown off your face. You're going to get wrinkles in your forehead early, and I can't afford collagen treatments for you."

Deep breaths. She wasn't her mother. She'd refused to let her mom have power over her life.

But control seemed harder to find today than usual after she'd lowered so many barriers with Seth last night.

Her mother had her own reasons for the way she acted, most of which came from having a control freak mother of her own. Holiday photos were always color-coordinated, perfectly posed and very strained.

But understanding the reasons didn't mean accepting the hurtful behavior. Alexa had worked hard to break the cycle, to get well and make sure that if she ever had a child of her own, the next generation would know unconditional love, rather than the smothering oppression of a parent determined to create a perfectly crafted mini-me.

Her eyes slid down to Olivia who was trying her best to stuff her sock in her mouth. God, that kid was adorable.

Alexa's hand tightened around the phone, another swell of sympathy for her mom washing over her. She could do this. She could talk to her mother while still keeping boundaries in place. "Mom, I appreciate that you want to have me there for the holidays. I will get back to you at the end of the month with a definite answer one way or the other."

"That's my good girl." Her mother paused for a second, the background chatter and cheers the only indication she was still on the line. "I love you, Alexa. Thanks for picking up."

"Sure, Mom. I love you, too."

And she did. That's what made it so tough sometimes. Because while love could be beautiful, it also stole control, giving another person the power to cause hurt.

As the ferry docked at the airstrip and Alexa dropped the phone back into her bag, her eyes didn't land on the kids this time. Her gaze went straight to Seth.

Eight

Her stomach knotted with each step down the stairway leading from the private jet. Back where she'd started in Charleston a few short, eventful days ago.

The flight hadn't given them any opportunity to discuss what they would do after landing. The kids had been fussy for most of the journey, not surprising given all the upheaval to their routine. Seth had been occupied with flying the plane through bumpy skies.

And all those pockets of turbulence hadn't helped the children's moods. Or hers for that matter. Her nerves were shot.

Alexa hitched Olivia on her hip more securely. The early morning sun glinted off the concrete parking area of the private airport that housed Jansen Jets. She saw Seth's world with new eyes now. Before she'd viewed him and his planes from a business perspective. She'd seen his hangars at the private airport and his jets, and thought about what a boon it would be to service his fleet. Now, she took in the variety of aircraft, in awe of how much he'd acquired in such a short time.

From her research on him she'd learned that about ten years ago he'd purchased the privately owned airport, which, at that time, sported two hangars. Now there were three times as many filled with anything from the standard luxury Learjets to Gulfstreams like the one she'd flown in today. In fact, one of those Lears taxied out toward the runway now.

As she looked back at the hangars, she also saw smaller Cessnas. Perhaps for flight training like he'd done back in North Dakota? Or was that a part of the search and rescue aspect he obviously felt so passionately about?

There was so much more to Seth than she'd originally thought.

An open hangar also gave her a peek of what appeared to be a vintage plane, maybe World War II era. Not exactly what she expected a buttoned-up businessman to own. But a bold, crop-dusting North Dakota farm boy who'd branched out to South Carolina, who'd built a billion-dollar corporation from the ground up? That man, she could envision taking to the skies in the historic craft.

She'd wanted to get to know more about Seth, to understand him, at first to win his contract and then to protect herself from heartache. Instead she was only more confused, more vulnerable, and unable to walk away.

Her feet hit solid ground just as she heard a squeal from the direction of the airport's main building, a

one-story red brick structure with picture windows.
An auburn-haired woman raced past a fuel truck toward
the plane, her arms wide.

Pippa Jansen.

The beauty wore the same short-sleeve sweater set
she'd had on during the Skype conversation earlier. She
raced toward them, a wide smile on her face.

Olivia stretched out her hands, squealing, "Ma-ma,
Ma-ma..."

Pippa gathered her daughter into her arms and spun
around. "I missed you, precious girl. Did you have fun
with Daddy? I have your favorite *Winnie the Pooh* video
in the car."

She slowed her spin, coming face-to-face with
Alexa. A flicker of curiosity chased through Pippa's
hazel eyes. The Learjet engines hummed louder in
the background as the plane accelerated, faster, faster,
swooping smoothly upward. Owen pointed with a grin
as he clapped.

Her son's glee distracted her and she turned to kiss
his forehead. "Hello, my handsome boy."

His face tight with tension, Seth passed over his son.
"I thought we were going to talk later today?"

"I decided to meet you here instead. After I heard the
children's voices this morning, I just couldn't stay away
any longer. I missed them too much, so I flew straight
home. Your secretary gave me your arrival time since
it related to the children." She kissed each child on top
of the head, breathing deeply before looking up again,
directly at Alexa. "And who might you be?"

Seth stepped up, his face guarded. "This is my friend
Alexa. She took time off work to help me with the twins
since I had an out of town business meeting I couldn't

cancel. Your note said you were going to be gone for two weeks."

"The weekend's rest recharged me. I'm ready to be with my children again." Her pointy chin jutted with undeniable strength. "It's my custodial time."

He sighed wearily, guiding them toward the building, away from the bustle of trucks and maintenance personnel. He stopped outside a glass door at the end of the brick building. "Pippa, I don't want a fight. I just want to be sure you won't check out on them again without notice."

"My mother's in the car. I'm staying with her for a while." She adjusted the weight of both babies, resettling them. "Seth, I'm going to take you up on the offer to hire extra help when I'm with them, and I'd like to write up more visitation time into our agreement. They've been weaned for a couple of months, so the timing is right. Okay?"

He didn't look a hundred percent pleased with the outcome but nodded curtly. "All right, we'll meet tomorrow morning in my office at ten to set that in motion."

"Good, I'm so relieved to see them. My time away gave me a fresh perspective on how to pace myself better." She passed Olivia to Seth. "Could you help me carry them out to the car? You'll get to see my mom and reassure yourself." She glanced at Alexa. "You won't mind if I borrow him for a minute?"

"Of course not." It was clear Alexa wasn't invited on this little family walk.

Seth slid an arm around Alexa's shoulder. "This won't take long." He pulled out a set of keys and unlocked the glass door in front of him. "You can wait in my office space here where it's cooler."

An office here? Jansen Jets Corporate was located downtown. But then of course he would have an office here as well.

"I'll be waiting."

He dropped a kiss on her lips. Nothing lengthy or overtly sexual, but a clear branding of their relationship in front of his ex. Surprise tingled through her along with the now expected attraction.

Pippa looked at her with deepening curiosity. "Thank you for being there for my babies when Seth needed an extra set of hands."

Alexa didn't have a clue how to respond, so she opted for a noncommittal. "Owen and Olivia are precious. I'm glad I could help."

Stepping into the back entrance to Seth's office, she crossed to a corner window and watched the couple carrying their children toward a silver Mercedes sedan parked and idling. Pippa's older "twin" sat behind the wheel. Her mother, no doubt.

A sense of déjà vu swept over Alexa at the mother-daughter twin look. It could have been her with her own mom years ago. More than the outward similarity, Alexa recognized a fragility in Pippa, something she'd once felt herself, a lack of ego. Having rich parents provided a lot of luxuries, but it could also rob a person of any sense of accomplishment. Her parents bought her everything, even bought her way out of bad grades... which had been wrong.

Just as it would be wrong to write off Pippa's reckless escape from motherhood for the weekend. Yes, she was an overwhelmed mom, but she was also a parent with resources. She could hire help. There were a hundred better options than leaving her children unattended on an aircraft. Pippa's excuse about watching through a window was bogus. How could she have helped them from so far away if something had gone wrong?

Alexa's fists dug into the windowsill, helplessness sweeping over her. There was nothing she could do. These weren't her children. This wasn't her family. She had to trust Seth to handle the situation with his ex-wife.

Spinning back to the office, she studied the space Seth had created for himself. It was a mass of contradictions, just like the man himself. High-end leather furniture filled the room, a sofa, a wing recliner and office chair, along with thick mahogany shelves and a desk.

She also saw a ratty fishing hat resting on top of a stack of books. The messy desktop was filled with folders and even a couple of honest to God plastic photo cubes—not exactly what she'd expected in a billionaire's space. It was tough for her to resist the desire to order the spill of files across the credenza.

Forcing her eyes upward, she studied the walls packed with framed charts and maps, weathered paper with routes inked on them. In the middle of the wall, he'd displayed a print of buffalo on the plains tagged Land of Tatanka.

The land looked austere and lonely to her. Like the man, a man who'd been strangely aloof all day. Her fingers traced along the bottom of the frame. Even as he embraced the skies and adventure here, there was still a part of him that remembered his stark North Dakota farm boy roots.

The opening door pulled her attention off the artwork

and back to the man striding into the room. His face was hard. His arms empty and loose by his sides.

She rested her hand on his shoulder and squeezed lightly. "Are you okay?"

"I will be." He nodded curtly, stepping away.

Only a few minutes earlier he'd kissed her and now he was distant, cold. Had it been an act? She didn't think so. But if he didn't want her here, if he needed space, she could find her own way home. She started toward the door leading out of his office and into the building.

"Alexa," he called out. "Hold on. We have some unfinished business."

Business? Not what she was hoping to hear. "What would that be?"

He walked to the massive desk and pulled a file off the corner. "I made a promise when you agreed to help me. Before I spoke to Pippa this morning, I put in some calls, arranged for you and your partner to interview with four potential clients who commute into the Charleston area, both at the regional airport and here at my private airstrip." He passed her the folder. "Top of the list, Senator Matthew Landis."

She took the file from his hand, everything she could have hoped for when she'd first stepped onto his plane, cleaning bucket in hand. And now? She couldn't shake the sense he was shuffling her off, giving her walking papers. While, yes, that's what they'd agreed upon, she couldn't help worrying that he was fulfilling the deal to the letter so they could be done, here and now.

Her grip tightened on the file until the edges bent. "Thank you, that's great. I appreciate it."

"You still have to seal the deal when you meet them, but I had my assistant compile some notes I made that I believe will help you beef up your proposal." He sat on the edge of the desk, picked up a photo cube and tossed it from hand to hand. "I also included some ways I think you may be missing out on expansion opportunities."

He hadn't left money on the dresser, by God, but somehow the transaction still felt cheap given the bigger prize they could have had together.

"I don't know how to thank you." She clasped the folder to her chest and wondered why this victory felt hollow. Just a few days ago she would have turned cartwheels over the information in that folder.

"No. Thank *you*. It was our agreement from the start, and I keep my word." *Toss, toss,* the cube sailed from hand to hand. "And while I am genuinely sorry I can't pass over my fleet to A-1, I have requested that your company be called first for any subcontracting work from this point on."

His words carried such finality she didn't know whether to be hurt or mad. "That's it then. Our business is concluded."

"That was my intention." He pitched the cube side to side, images of Owen and Olivia tumbling to rest against a paperweight.

Okay, she was mad, damn it. They'd slept together. He'd kissed her in plain view of his ex-wife. She deserved better than this.

She slapped the file down on his messy desk and yanked the cube from midair. "Is this a brush-off?"

He did a double take and took his photos back from her. "What the hell makes you think that?"

"Your ice cold shoulder all day, for starters." She crossed her arms over her chest.

"I'm clearing away business because from this point

on, if we see each other, it's for personal reasons only."
He clasped her shoulders, skimming his touch down
until she stepped into his embrace. "No more agendas.
Holding nothing back."

She looked up at him. "Then you're saying you want
to spend more time together?"

"Yes, that's exactly what I'm telling you. You've
cleared your calendar until tomorrow, and it's not even
lunchtime yet. So let's spend the day together, no kids,
no agendas, no bargains." He brushed her hair back with
a bold, broad palm. "I can't claim to know where this
is headed, and there are a thousand reasons why this
is the wrong time. But I can't just let you walk away
without trying."

Being with this guy was like riding an emotional
yo-yo. One minute he was intense, then moody, then
happy, then sensual. And she was totally intrigued by
all of him. "Okay then. Ask me out to lunch."

A sigh of relief shuddered through him, his arms
twitching tighter around her waist. "Where would you
like to go? Anywhere in the country for lunch. Hell, we
could even go out of the States for supper if you can lay
hands on your passport."

"Let's keep it stateside this time." This time? She
shivered with possibility. "As for the place? You pick.
You're the one with the airplanes."

With those words, reality settled over her with
anticipation and more than a little apprehension. She'd
committed. This wasn't about the babies or her business
any longer. This was about the two of them.

She'd explored the complex layers of this man, and
now she needed to be completely open to him as well.

They had one last night away from the real world to decide where to go next.

One last night for her to see how he handled knowing everything about her, even the insecure, vulnerable parts that were too much like those she'd seen in his ex-wife.

Seth parked the rental car outside the restaurant, waiting for Alexa's verdict on the place he'd chosen.

He could have taken her to Le Cirque in New York City or City Zen in D.C. He could have even gone the distance for Savoy's in Vegas. But thinking back over the things she'd shared about her past, he realized she wasn't impressed with glitz or pretension. They'd just left a king's island, for Pete's sake. Besides, she'd grown up with luxurious trappings and, if anything, seemed to disdain them now.

The North Dakota farm boy inside him applauded her.

So he'd fueled up one Cessna 185 floatplane and taken off for his favorite "hole-in-the-wall" eating establishment on the Outer Banks in North Carolina. A seaside clapboard bar, with great beer, burgers and fresh catch from the Atlantic.

A full-out smile spread across her face. "Perfect. The openness, the view... I love it."

Some of the cold weight he'd been carrying in his chest since saying goodbye to his kids eased. He sprinted around the front of the 1975 Chevy Caprice convertible—special ordered, thanks to his assistant's speedy persistence. He opened the door for Alexa. She swept out, her striped sundress swirling around her knees as she climbed the plank steps up to the patio dining area. The Seat Yourself sign hammered to a wooden column was weatherworn but legible.

He guided her to a table for two closest to the rocky shoreline as a waitress strolled over.

"Good to see you, Mr. Jansen. I'll get your Buffalo blue-water tuna bites and two house brews."

"Great, thanks, Carol Ann." Seth passed the napkin-rolled silverware across the table. Alexa fidgeted with the salt and pepper shakers until he asked, "Something wrong? Would you like to go somewhere else after all?"

She looked up quickly. "The place is great. Really. It's just... Well... I like to order my own food."

"Of course. I apologize. You're right, that was presumptuous of me." He leaned back in his chair. "Let me get Carol Ann back over and we can add whatever you would like."

"No need. Truly. It's just for future reference. And I actually do like the sound of what you chose, so it's probably silly that I said anything at all." She smiled sheepishly. "You may have noticed I have some... control issues."

"You appreciate order in your world. Plenty to admire about that." God knows, his world could stand a little more order and reason these days. The unresolved mess with Pippa still knocked around in his head. "That's a great asset in your job—"

He stopped short as the waitress brought their plates of Buffalo tuna bites, mugs of beer and glasses of water.

Alexa tore the paper off her straw and stirred her lemon wedge in her water. "Control's my way of kicking back at my childhood."

"In what way?" He passed an appetizer plate to her.

"When I was growing up there wasn't a lot I could

control without bringing down the wrath of Mom." She speared the fish onto her plate. "She may have depended on those nannies to free up her spa days and time on the slopes but her expectations were clear."

"And those were?"

"Great grades, of course, with all the right leadership positions to get into an Ivy League school. And in my 'spare time' she expected a popular, pretty daughter. Perfectly groomed, with the perfect boyfriend." She stabbed a bite and brought it to her mouth. "Standard stuff."

"Doesn't sound standard or funny to me." Out of nowhere, an image flashed through his mind of Pippa sitting in the front seat of the car with her mother, both women wearing matching sweater sets and pearls with their trim khakis.

"You're right. That kind of hypercontrol almost inevitably leads to some kind of rebellion in teens. Passive aggressive was my style in those days. The problem started off small and got worse. I controlled what I ate, when I ate, how much I ate." She chewed slowly.

A chill shot through him as he recalled her ordering the blocks for his kids. Her careful lining up of her silverware. Little things he'd written off as sweet peculiarities of a woman who liked the proverbial ducks in a row.

Now, his mind started down a dark path and he hoped to God she would take them on a detour soon. He didn't know what to say or do, so he simply covered her other hand with his and stayed quiet.

"Then I learned I could make Mom happy by joining the swim team. And what do you know? That gave me another outlet for burning calories. I felt good, a real rush of success." She tossed aside her fork. "Until one day when I peeled away my warm-up suit and I saw the looks of horror on the faces of the people around me..."

Squeezing her hand softly, he wished like hell he could have done something for her then. Wishing he could do something more now than just listen.

"I'm lucky to be alive actually. That day at swim practice, right after I saw the looks on their faces, I tried to race back to the locker room, but my body gave out... I pretty much just crumpled to the ground." She looked down at her hands fidgeting with the silverware. "My heart stopped."

He clasped her hand across the table, needing to feel the steady, strong beat of her heart throbbing in her wrist. There were no words he could offer up right now. But then he'd always been better at listening than talking anyway.

"Thank goodness the coach was good at CPR," she half joked, but her laugh quickly lost its fizz. "That's when my parents—and I—had to face up to the fact that I had a serious eating disorder."

She pulled away from him and rubbed her bare arms in spite of the noonday sun beating overhead. "I spent my senior year in a special high school—aka hospital— for recovering bulimics and anorexics." She brushed her windswept hair back with a shaky hand. "I was the latter, by the way. I weighed eighty-nine pounds when they admitted me."

This was more—worse—than he'd expected and what he'd expected had been gut-twisting enough. He thought of his own children, of Olivia, and he wanted to wrap her up in cotton while he read every parenting book out there in hopes that he could spare his kids this kind of pain. "I'm so damn sorry you had to go through that."

"Me, too. I'm healthy now, completely over it, other than some stretch marks from the seesawing weight loss and gain."

"Was that why you preferred to keep the lights off?"

"When we were making love? Yes." She nodded, rolling her eyes. "It's not so much vanity as I wasn't ready to tell you this. I fully realize those lines on my skin are a small price to pay to be alive." She reached for her beer, tasted the brew once, and again, before placing the mug on the red-checkered cloth. "My stint in the special high school cost me a real prom, sleepovers with ice cream sundaes and dates spent parking with a boyfriend. But it also screwed up Mom's Ivy League aspirations for me. So I won control of something for a while, I guess."

"What happened after you graduated?"

"Dad bought my way into a college, and I married the man of their choice." She patted her chest. "A-1 Cleaning is the first independent thing I've done on my own, for me."

Admiration for her grew, and he'd already been feeling a hefty dose where she was concerned. But she'd broken away from every support system she had in place—such as they were—to forge her own path. Turning her back on her family had to be tough, no matter how strained the relationship. He could also see she'd grown away from the world Pippa still seemed to be suffocating in.

He hadn't been expecting this kind of revelation from her today. But he knew he'd better come up with the right response, to offer the affirmation she should have gotten from those closest to her.

"What other things would you like to do? Anything... I will make it happen."

She leaned back in her chair, her eyes going whimsical. "That's a nice thought. But the things I regret? I need to accept I can't have them and be at peace with that."

"Things such as?"

"I can't go back and change my teenage years. I need to accept that and move forward."

The sadness in her voice as she talked about her lost past sucker punched him with the need to do something for her. To give her back those parts of her life her parents had stolen by trying to live out their own dreams through their kid. He couldn't change the past.

But he could give her one of those high school experiences she'd been denied.

Nine

Alexa shook her hair free as they drove along the seaside road with the convertible top down. She adored his unexpected choices, from the car to the restaurant. The red 1975 Chevy Caprice ate up the miles down the deserted shore of the Outer Banks. She'd marveled at how lucky they were to get such a classic car, but then learned Seth's assistant had taken care of the arrangements.

How easy it was to forget he was a billionaire sometimes, with all the power and perks that came with such affluence.

The afternoon sun blazed overhead, glinting on the rippling tide. Sea oats and driftwood dotted the sandy beach along with bare picket fences permanently leaning from the force of the wind. Kind of like her.

Leaning and weathered by life, but not broken, still standing.

She studied the brooding man beside her. Seth drove on, quietly focused on the two-lane road winding ahead of them. What had he thought of her revelations at lunch? He'd said all the right things, but she could see his brain was churning her words around, sifting through them. She couldn't help but feel skittish over how he would treat her now. Would he back away? Or worse yet, act differently?

Tough to tell when he'd been in such an unpredictable mood since talking with Pippa. That made Alexa wonder if she should have waited to dish out her own baggage? But she couldn't escape the sense of urgency pushing her, insisting they had only a narrow slice of time. That once they returned to Charleston permanently, this opportunity to fully know him would disappear.

She hooked her elbow on the open window, her own face staring back at her in the side mirror. "Seth? Where are we going? I thought the airport was the other way."

"It is. I wanted to make the most of the day before we leave." He pointed ahead toward a red brick lighthouse in the distance. "We're headed there, on that bluff."

The ancient beacon towered in the distance. She could envision taking the kids there for a picnic, like the one they'd shared at the fort in St. Augustine. "It's gorgeous here. I love our South Carolinian low country home, but this is special, too, different. I can't believe I've never been here before."

Her parents had always opted for more "exotic" vacations.

"I thought you would appreciate it. You seem to have

an eye for the unique, an appreciation for entertainment off the beaten path."

"I'm not sure I follow what you mean."

"Like when we had the picnic at the old fort. You saw it with an artist's eye rather than looking for an up-to-date, pristine park. Must be the art history major in you. This place and this car are certainly pieces of history. Did I read you right on that?"

"You did, very much so." The fact that he knew her this well already, had put so much thought into what she thought, made her heart swell. The twisting road led higher over the town, taking them farther away and into a more isolated area.

When she looked around her, she also realized… "You brought me here to make out, didn't you?"

"Guilty as charged."

"Because of what I said at the restaurant about missing the high school experience of parking and making out with a guy."

"Guilty again. It's private, bare, stripped away nature, which in some ways reminds me of North Dakota as a whole. There's something…freeing about leaving civilization behind." He steered the car off the paved road, onto a dirt trail leading toward the lighthouse. "It's good to leave baggage behind, and it's safe to say we both have our fair share."

Nerves took flight in her belly like the herons along the shore. "Like what I told you at lunch?"

"In part. Yes." Tires crunched along the rocky road, spitting a gritty cloud of dirt behind them. "It's clear we're both members of the Walking Wounded Divorce Club, both with hang-ups. But we have something else in common, an attraction and a mutual respect."

The way he'd analyzed them chilled her in spite of the bold shining sun overhead and the thoughtfulness of his gesture. He'd pinpointed them so well, and yet... "You make it sound so logical. So calculated. So... coldly emotionless."

Stopping the car at the base of the lighthouse, the top of the bluff, he gripped the steering wheel in white-knuckled fists. "Believe me, there's nothing cold about the way I'm feeling about you. I want you so much I'm damn near ready to explode just sitting beside you."

Breathless, she leaned against her door, the power of his voice washing over her as tangibly as the sun warming her skin.

He turned toward her, leather seat squeaking, his green eyes flinty. "Just watching you walk across the room, I imagine resting my hands on your hips to gauge the sway." His fingers glided along her shoulder. "Or when I see the wind lift your hair, I burn to test the texture between my fingers. Everything about you mesmerizes me."

Tension crackled between them like static in her hair, in his words. "Before this past weekend, I'd been celibate for over six months. Attractive women have walked into my life and not one of them has tempted me the way you do."

There was no missing the intensity of his words— or the intent in his eyes. His fingers stroked through her hair, down to the capped sleeves of her sundress, hovering, waiting. "Did anyone ever tell you what a truly stunning woman you are, how beautiful you will still be when you're eighty-five years old? Not that it matters what the hell I, or anyone else, thinks."

While she was flattered, his words also left her blushing with self-consciousness.

She resisted the urge to fidget. "Okay, I hear you. Now could you stop? I don't need you to flatter me because of what I said earlier. I'm beyond needing affirmation of my looks."

"I'm not flattering. I'm stating facts, indisputable, beyond perceptions."

She realized now that he'd brought her out to this place for a private conversation, a better place to discuss her past than a crowded restaurant. She should have realized that earlier.

"Thank you and I hear you. Skewed perceptions played a part in what I went through." Her hands fell to his chest. "But I'm over that now. It was hard as hell, but I'm healthy and very protective of that particular fact."

"Good. I'm glad to hear it, and I don't claim to be an expert on the subject. I only know that I want to tell you how beautiful, how sexy you are to me. Yet, that seems to make you uncomfortable."

The ocean breeze lifted her hair like a lover's caress, the scent so clean and fresh that the day felt like a new beginning.

"Maybe I like to speak with actions."

"I'm all about that, too." His hands brushed down the sleeves of her dress. "When I touch you, it turns me inside out to feel the curves, the silky softness, the way you're one hundred percent a woman."

He inched the bodice down farther, baring the top of her breasts.

Realization raised goose bumps along her skin as she

grasped his deeper intent for bringing her here… "Are you actually planning for us to make love, here?"

He nuzzled the crook of her neck. "Do you think you're the only one who can initiate outdoor sex?"

"That was at night."

"Hidden away where no one could see us." Where they could barely see each other.

Her thoughts cleared as if someone had turned the sun up a notch. Out here, there was no turning off the lamp or shrouding herself in darkness. Oh hell, maybe she wasn't as over the past as she'd thought. She'd controlled everything about their lovemaking before.

This place, now, out in the brightest light of all, meant giving over complete control. That sent jitters clear through her. But the thought of saying no, of turning down this chance to be with him, upset her far more.

He cupped her face in both hands. "Do you think I would ever place you at risk? I chose this place carefully because I feel certain we're completely alone."

Alone and yet so totally exposed by the unfiltered sunshine. Seth was asking for a bigger commitment from her. He was requiring her trust.

Toying with his belt, she said, "Out here, huh? In full daylight. No drawing the shades, that's for sure."

"Sunscreen?" He grinned.

She raised an eyebrow and tugged his belt open. "You expect to be naked that long? You're a big talker."

His smile faded, his touch got firmer. "So you're good with this."

"I'm good with *you*," she murmured against his lips.

"I like the sound of that." He slanted his mouth over hers.

The man knew how to kiss a woman and kiss her well. The way he devoted his all to the moment, to her, in his big bold way, made her want to take everything he offered here today. She'd shared everything about herself at lunch. Giving all here seemed the natural extension of that if she dared.

And she did.

Easing back from him, she shrugged the sleeves of her dress down, revealing herself inch by inch, much the way he'd undressed for her their first time together. In some ways, this was a first for them. A first without barriers.

Her bodice pooled around her waist. With the flick of her fingers, she opened the front clasp on her lacy bra. And waited. It was one thing to bare herself in the dark, but in the daylight, everything showed, her journey showed. Her battle with anorexia had left stretch marks. Regaining her muscle tone had taken nearly six years.

Meeting his gaze, she saw…heat…passion…and tenderness. He touched her, his large hands so deft and nimble as they played over her breasts in just the ways she enjoyed best, lingering on *her* erogenous zones, the ones he must have picked up on from their time together.

She arched into his palms, her grip clenching around his belt buckle. Her head fell to rest against the leather seat. The sun above warmed every inch of her bared flesh as fully as his caresses, his kisses.

His hands swept down to inch the hem upward until he exposed her yellow lace panties. Just above the waistband, he flicked a finger against her belly button ring.

She smiled at a memory. "That was my treat to myself the first time I wore a bikini in public."

"I'll buy you dozens, each one with a different jewel."

Laughing softly, she traced his top lip with the tip of her tongue. He growled deeply in his throat. But he only allowed her to steal control for an instant before he stroked lower, dipping a finger inside her panties, between her legs, finding her wet and ready.

Her spine went weak and he braced her with an arm around her waist, holding her. She unbuttoned his shirt, sweeping it aside and baring his brazened chest to her eyes, her touch. The rasp of his crisp blond hair tantalized her fingertips.

She inhaled the scent of leather and sea, a brand-new aphrodisiac for her. "We should move this to the backseat where we can stretch out somewhat."

"Or we can stay here and save the backseat for later."

She purred her agreement as she swung her leg over to straddle his lap. The steering wheel at her back only served to keep her closer to him. Everything about this place was removed from the real world, and she intended to make the most of it. She opened his pants and somehow a condom appeared in his hand. She didn't care where or how. She just thanked goodness he had the foresight.

His hands palmed her waist, her arms looping around his neck. He lowered her onto him, carefully, slowly filling her. Moving within her. Or was she moving over him? Either way, the sensation rippled inside her, built to a fever pitch. Every sensation heightened: the give of the butter-soft leather under her knees, the rub of his trousers against the inside of her thighs.

The openness of the convertible and the untouched

landscape called to her. The endless stretch of ocean pulled at her, like taking a skein of yarn and unraveling it infinitely. Moans swelled inside her, begging to be set free to fly into that vastness.

He thrust his hands into her hair and encouraged her in a litany detailing how damn much he wanted her, needed her, burned to make this last as long as he could because he was not finishing without her. The power of his words pulsed through her, took her pleasure higher.

Face-to-face, she realized there wasn't a battle for control. They were sharing the moment, sharing the experience. The insight exploded inside her in a shower of light and sensation as she flew apart in his arms. Her cries of completion burst from her in abandon, followed by his. Their voices twined together, echoing out over the ocean.

Panting, she sagged against his chest, perspiration bonding their bodies. Their time together here, away from the rest of the world, had been perfect. Almost too much so.

Now she had to trust in what they'd shared enough to test it out when they returned home.

Seth revved the Cessna seaplane's engines, skimming the craft along the water faster and faster until finally, smoothly...*airborne.*

A few more days on the Outer Banks would have been damn welcome to give him a chance to fortify his connection with Alexa. To experience more of the amazing sex they'd shared in the front seat of the convertible, then the backseat. Except he was out of time.

He had to meet with Pippa tomorrow and hammer

out a new visitation schedule. That always proved sticky since the ugly truth lurked behind every negotiation that he might not be the twins' biological father. If Pippa ever decided to push that, things could go all to hell. He would fight for his kids, but it tore him up inside thinking of how deep it would slice if he lost. Acid burned in his gut.

If only life could be simpler. He just wanted to enjoy his children like any parent. The way his cousin Paige enjoyed hers. The way his cousin Vic was celebrating a new baby with his wife, Claire. That reminded him of what a crappy cousin he'd been in not calling to congratulate them. Paige had texted him that Claire was staying in the hospital longer because of the C-section delivery. He needed to stop by and do the family support gig.

That also meant introducing Alexa to the rest of his family. Soon. His relatives were important to him. He wasn't sure how he was going to piece together his crazy ass life with hers, but walking away wasn't an option. He also wasn't sure how Alexa would feel about his big noisy family, especially given how strained her relationship was with her own.

If only life was as easy to level out as an airplane.

Easing back on the yoke, he scanned his airspeed, along with the rest of the control panel.

Alexa touched the window, an ocean view visible beyond. "I grew up with charter jets, but I've never flown on one of these before. And I certainly didn't have a fleet of planes at my fingertips 24/7."

"This wasn't among my more elite crafts, but, God, I love to fly her."

"I can tell by how relaxed you are here versus other

times." She trapped the toy bobble head fisherman suction-cupped to the control panel. Her finger swayed the line from the fishing pole. "I can hardly believe how much we've done since waking up. Starting in Florida, stopping in South Carolina, North Carolina by lunch. Now home again."

"I still owe you supper, although it'll be late."

"Can we eat it naked?"

"As long as I have you all to myself."

She laughed softly. "While I enjoyed our time in the convertible, I haven't turned into that much of an exhibitionist."

"Good," he growled with more possessiveness than he was used to feeling. "I don't share well."

She toyed with the sleeve of her dress, adjusting it after the haphazard way they'd thrown on their clothes as the sun started to set. "I appreciate that you didn't get weirded out by what I shared with you at the restaurant."

"I admire the way you've taken everything life threw at you and just kept right on kicking back," he answered without hesitation.

He meant every word.

"I'm determined not to let other people steal anything more from me—not my parents or my ex."

"That attitude is exactly what I'm talking about."

"I'm not so sure about the kick-ass thing." Her hand fell to her lap. "It's wacky the way a piece of cheesecake can sometimes still hold me hostage. Sounds strange, I know. I don't expect you to understand."

"Explain it to me." He needed to understand. He couldn't tolerate saying or doing something that could hurt her.

She sagged back in her seat. "Sometimes I look at it

and remember what it was like to want that cheesecake, but then I would measure out how many calories I'd eaten that day. Think how many laps I would need to swim in order to pick up that fork for one bite. Then I would imagine the disappointment on my mother's face when I stepped on the scale the next morning."

What the hell? Her mother made her weigh in every morning? No wonder Alexa had control issues.

He wrestled to keep his face impassive when he really wanted to find her parents and… He didn't know what he would do. He did know he needed to be here for Alexa now. "I wish I'd known you then."

She turned to look at him. "Me, too."

Suddenly he knew exactly where he wanted to take Alexa tonight. "Do you mind staying out late?"

"I'm all for letting this day last as long as possible."

"Good. Then I have one more stop to make on my way to take you home."

Of all the places she thought Seth might take her, Alexa wouldn't have guessed they would go to a hospital.

Once they'd landed, Seth had said he wanted to visit his cousin's new baby. Her heart had leaped to her throat at the mention of an infant. A newborn.

Her skin felt clammy as she rubbed her arms. Was she freaked out because of the baby or because of her own hospital stay? Right now, with her emotions so close to the surface, she couldn't untangle it all.

Damn it, she was being silly. It wasn't like she would even go in to see the new mom. This visit would be over soon and she could clear the antiseptic air with deep breaths outside. Seth was walking in on his own while she hung out at the picture window looking into a nursery packed full of bassinets. Her gaze lingered on one in particular, front row, far left.

Baby Jansen.

She could barely see anything other than a white swaddling blanket and a blue-and-yellow-striped cap. But she could tell the bundle was bigger than most of the others, nearly ten pounds of baby boy, according to Seth. Alexa touched the window lightly, almost imagining she could feel the satiny softness of those chubby newborn cheeks.

A woman stepped up alongside her and Alexa inched to the side to make room.

The blonde woman—in her late thirties—wore a button that proclaimed Proud Aunt. "Beautiful little boy." She tapped the glass right around Baby Jansen territory. "Can you believe all that blond hair? Well, under the hat there's lots of blond hair."

Alexa cocked her head to the side. "Do I know you?"

The woman grinned, and Alexa saw the family resemblance so strongly stamped on her face she might as well have pulled back her question.

"I'm Paige, Seth's cousin. While I was getting coffee, I saw you walking in with him. My brother, Vic, is this baby's daddy."

It was one thing meeting his family with Seth there to handle the introductions, to define their still new relationship. This was awkward to say the least. Why, why, why hadn't she waited in his SUV outside? "Congratulations on your new nephew."

"Thank you, we have lots to celebrate. Hope you'll join us at the next family get-together." She cut her brown eyes toward Alexa. "How did the trip with

Seth and the twins go? They're sweet as can be, but a handful, for sure."

Seth had told his family about her? Curiosity drowned out the rattle of food carts, the echo of televisions, even the occasional squawk of a baby.

"Nice trip. But it's always good to be home," she answered noncommittally. "The twins are back with their mother now."

Paige nodded, tucking her hair behind her ears. "Pippa's, well…" She sighed. "She's Pippa, and she's the twins' mom. And Seth's such a good daddy. He deserves to have a good woman to love him, better than…well…you know."

Sort of. Not really. And she should really cut this short and get all of her answers from Seth. "I'm not in a position to—"

Pivoting, Paige stared her down with an unmistakably protective gleam in her golden-brown eyes. "I'm just asking you to be good to my cousin, to be fair. Pippa screwed him over, literally. There are days I would really like to give her a piece of my mind, but I hold back because I love those kids regardless of whether they're my blood or not. But I don't think I could take seeing him betrayed like that again. So please, if you're not serious, walk away now."

Whoa, whoa, whoa. Alexa struggled to keep up the barrage of information packed into that diatribe. "I don't know what to say other than your family loyalty is admirable?"

"Crap. Sorry." Paige bit her bottom lip. "I should probably hush now. I'm rambling and being rude. Hormones are getting the best of me, compounded even more by the nursery and being pregnant—a whoops, but a happy whoops. And I already get so emotional with how Pippa used Seth, the way she still uses him. I'm sure you're lovely, and I look forward to seeing you again."

Paige squeezed her arm once, before rushing away in a flurry of tissues and winces, leaving Alexa stunned. She looked back into the nursery, then at the departing woman, going over what she'd said, something about whether or not the twins were related to her. And how Pippa had screwed Seth over. Literally.

What the hell? Had Pippa actually cheated on Seth? But he'd said they split before the twins were even born. Not that a pregnant woman couldn't have an affair, but it seemed less likely... Unless... Pippa had the affair while she and Seth were dating, and it only came out later?

An awful possibility smoked through her mind—perhaps the twins weren't his biological children?

She dismissed the thought as quickly as it came to her. He would have shared something like that with her.

Her perceptions of the man jumbled all together. At first, she'd assumed he was like her wealthy parents, too often looking for a way to dump off their kids on the nearest caregiver. Yet, she'd seen with her own eyes how much he loved them, how he spent every free waking moment with them.

If what she suspected was true, why hadn't he said something to her when they'd deepened their relationship? Sure they'd only known each other a short time, but she'd told him everything. He'd insisted on her being open, vulnerable even, when they'd made love by the lighthouse.

Had he been holding back something this important?

She wanted to believe she'd misunderstood Paige. Rather than wonder, she would ask Seth once the timing was right. They would laugh together over how she'd leaped to conclusions. She wanted to trust the feelings growing between her and Seth. More than anything, she wanted this to be real.

And if she was right in her suspicions that he was holding back?

Her eyes skipped to a family at the far end of the picture window. A grandma and grandpa were standing together, shoulder to shoulder, heads tilted toward each other in conversation as they held two older grandchildren up to see their new sister. The connection, the family bond, was undeniable.

She'd seen it earlier today when Seth and Pippa discussed their children. Yes, there was strife between them, but also a certain connection, even tenderness. Disconcerting, regardless. But if they still felt that way after such a betrayal…it gave Alexa pause. It spoke of unresolved feelings between them.

Steadying herself, she pressed her hand to the window. She'd ached for a real family connection growing up, yearned to create such a bond in her marriage. She knew what it felt like to stand on the outside.

And she refused to live that way ever again.

Ten

He wanted Alexa in his life, as well as in his bed.

As Seth drove Alexa home to her downtown Charleston condo after seeing his new nephew, he kept thinking about how right it felt having her sit beside him now. How right it had felt earlier taking her to the hospital with him. Having Alexa with him at such an important family moment made the evening even more special. He hoped when they got to her place, he could persuade her to just pick up some clothes and go with him to his house.

Beams of light from late night traffic streaked through the inky darkness as they crossed the Ashley River. The intimacy of just the two of them in his Infiniti SUV reminded him of making love in the classic Chevy convertible on the Outer Banks. God, was that only a few hours ago? Already, he wanted her again.

And what did she want?

He glanced out of the corner of his eye. She rested her head on the window, cool air from the vent lifting her hair. Shadows played along the dark circles under her eyes, in the furrows along her forehead. He was surprised—and concerned.

"Tell me." He skimmed a strand of hair behind her ear. "What's bothering you?"

She shook her head, keeping her face averted with only the glow of the dashboard lights to help him gauge her mood. She hugged her purse to her chest until the folder inside crackled.

"Whatever it is," he said, "I want to hear it, and don't bother saying it's nothing."

"We're both exhausted." She looked down at her hands, at least not staring out the window but still not turning to him. "It's been an emotional ride since we met, a lot crammed into a short time. I need some space to think."

Crap. She'd asked him earlier if he was giving her the brush-off and now he wondered the same thing. "You're backtracking."

"Maybe."

"Why?" he demanded, considering pulling off the six-lane highway so he could focus his full attention on her.

"Seth, I've worked hard to put my life back together again, twice. As a teenager. And again after my divorce. I'm stronger now because of both of those times. But I still intend to be very careful not to put myself in a dangerous position again."

What the hell? This wasn't the kind of conversation

they should have with him driving. He needed his focus planted firmly on her.

He eyed the fast food restaurant ahead and cut over two lanes of traffic, ignoring the honking horns. He pulled off the interstate and parked under the golden arches.

Hooking his arm on the steering wheel, he pinned her with his gaze. "Let me get this straight. You consider me *dangerous?* What have I done to make you feel threatened?"

"A relationship with you, I mean—" the trenches in her forehead dug deeper "—could be…maybe the better word is chancy." Headlights flashed past, illuminating her face with bright lights in quick, strobelike succession.

Some of the tension melted from his shoulders. His arm slid from the wheel and he took her hand in his. "Any relationship is risky. But I believe we've started something good here."

"I thought so, too, especially this afternoon. I opened up to you in ways I haven't to anyone in as long as I can remember." Her hand was cold in his. "But a relationship has to be a two-way street. Can you deny you're holding back?"

Holding back? Hell, he was giving her more than he'd imagined shelling out after the crap year he'd been through. What more did she want from him? A pint of blood? A pound of flesh?

But snapping those questions at her didn't seem wise. "I'm not sure what you mean."

"You have reservations about us as a couple." She didn't ask. She simply said it.

He couldn't deny she was right on the money.

Now he had to figure out how to work around that in a way that would still involve her packing a sleepover bag to go to his place. "Would it have been better for us to meet a year from now? Absolutely."

"Because?" she pressed.

Damn, he was tired and just wanted to take Alexa to his bed. This wasn't a conversation he wanted to have right now. He didn't much want to have it ever. "A year from now, my divorce wouldn't be as fresh—neither would yours. My kids would be older. Your business would have deeper roots. Can you deny the timing would be better for both of us?"

She shook her head slowly, the air conditioner vent catching the scent of her shampoo. "You know all the reasons why I have issues. I've been completely open with you, and I thought you'd been the same with me."

A buzz started in his brain. She couldn't be hinting at what he thought...

"Your cousin told me about Pippa, how she cheated on you. I can understand why that would make you relationship wary and it would have been helpful to know that."

The buzz in his head increased until he felt like he was being stung by hundreds of bees. Angry bees. Except the rage was his. "Paige had no business telling you that."

"Don't blame her. She thought I already kn—"

"How exactly was I supposed to work that into conversation? Hey, my ex-wife doesn't know for sure if my children are actually mine." His hands fisted. "In fact, she lied to me about that all the way to the altar. Now where would you like to go for dinner?"

Her face paled, her eyes so sympathetic her reaction slashed through all the raw places inside him.

"Seth, I am so sorry."

"I am their father in every way that matters." He slammed his fist into the dash. "I love my kids." His voice cracked.

"I realize that," she said softly, hugging her purse to her stomach.

"It doesn't matter to me whose blood or biology flows through their veins." He thumped his chest right over his heart that he'd placed in two pairs of tiny hands nearly a year ago. "They're *mine*."

"I'm sure they would agree." She paused then continued warily, "Have you taken a paternity test? They certainly look like you."

He didn't need any test to validate his love for those kids. "Back off. This isn't your business."

Her blue eyes filled with tears. "That's my whole point. We may have baggage, but I'm ready to be open about mine. You're not."

"Good God, Alexa, we've barely known each other for a week and you expect me to tell you something that could cripple my kids if they ever found out?"

"You think I would go around telling people? If so, you really don't know me at all." She held up her hands. "You know what? You're one hundred percent correct. This is a mistake. *We* are a mistake. The timing is wrong for us to have a relationship."

The thought of her backing out blindsided him. "Well, there's nothing I can do about the timing."

"My point exactly. Seth, I want to go home now, and I don't want you to follow me inside, and I don't want you to call me."

That was it? Even after their encounter on the Outer Banks, the way they'd come together so magnificently, she was slamming the door in his face? "Damn it, Alexa. Life isn't perfect. I'm not perfect, and I don't expect you to be, either. It's not about all or nothing here."

She chewed her bottom lip and he thought he might be making headway until she looked out the window again without answering.

"What do you want from me, Alexa?"

She turned slowly to him, blue eyes clouded with pain and tears. "Just what I said. I need you to respect my need for space."

Her mouth pursed shut, and she turned her head back toward the window. He waited while four cars cleared the fast food drive-through window and still she wouldn't look at him. He knew an ice-out when he saw one.

Stunned numb, he drove the rest of the way to her condo, a corner unit in a string of red brick buildings made to fit in with the rest of the historic homes. Her place. Where she belonged and he wasn't welcome.

How the hell had it gone so wrong so quickly? So he hadn't told her about Pippa cheating. He would have gotten around to it soon enough.

"Goodbye, Seth." She tore open the door and ran up the walkway into her apartment before he could make it farther than the front of the car.

Frustration chewed his gut as he settled behind the wheel again. He was doing his best here and she was cutting him off at the knees. The way she'd clutched her purse to her chest, she looked like she couldn't get out of the car fast enough. She had probably mangled the folder he'd given her.

An ugly, dark thought snaked through him. That she'd wanted her new contacts and now that she had them, she was looking for a way out. She'd used him. Just as Pippa had used him.

And just that quickly the thought dissipated. He knew Alexa was nothing like Pippa. Sure, they'd come from similar backgrounds, but Alexa had broken free of the dependent lifestyle. She was making her own way in the world. Honestly. With hard work. And she'd been up-front with him from the very start.

If anything, he was the one who'd held back.

Damn it.

She was right.

His head *thunked* against the seat. He'd been carrying so much baggage because of Pippa that he might as well have been driving one of those luggage trucks at the airport. He'd screwed up in that relationship in so many ways and felt the failure all the more acutely in the face of his cousins' marital bliss. To the point that he'd even held back from fully participating in their lives. Sure he'd moved here to be with them, but how close had he let anyone get? How many walls had he built?

None of which was fair to his cousins. And it most definitely wasn't fair to Alexa.

So where did he go from here? Talking to her now would likely only stoke her anger, or worse, stir her tears. Once she had a chance to cool down, he needed to approach her with something more than words. He needed strong actions to show Alexa how special, how irreplaceably important she was to him.

How very much he loved her.

Love.

The word filled his head and settled in with a flawless landing. Damn straight he loved her, and she deserved to know that.

And if she still said no? Then he would work harder. He believed in what they'd shared these past days, in what they'd started to build together.

He hadn't given up in his professional life. Against the odds, regardless of what people told him about waiting until he was older, more established, he'd accomplished what he set out to do.

Now it was time to set his sights on winning over Alexa.

Alexa Randall had accumulated an eclectic box full of lost and found items since opening her own cleaning company for charter jets. There were the standard smart phones, portfolios, tablets, even a Patek Philippe watch. She'd returned each to its owner.

Then there were the stray panties and men's boxers, even the occasional sex toys from Mile High Club members. All of those items, she'd picked up with latex gloves and tossed in the trash.

But the pacifier lying beside a seat reminded her too painfully of the precious twins she'd discovered nearly two weeks ago. Memories of their father pierced her heart all the more.

Her bucket of supplies dropped to the industrial blue carpet with a heavy thud. Ammonia fumes from the rag in her fist stung her eyes. Or maybe it was the tears. Heaven knew, she'd cried more than her fair share since leaving Seth's car after their awful argument a week ago. God, this hurt more than when she'd divorced.

The end of her marriage had been a relief. Losing Seth, however, cut her to the core. So much so, she couldn't escape the fact that she loved him. Truly, deeply loved him.

And he'd let her go.

She'd half expected him to follow her or do something cliché like send bunches of flowers with stock apologies. But he'd done none of that. He'd stayed quiet. Giving her the space she'd demanded? Or walking away altogether?

Her husband and parents would have shouted her down, even going so far as to bully her until she caved.

That made her question how she'd reacted that night to his news about the children. She may have grown in how she stood up for herself since the days when she'd tried to control stress through her eating habits. While she was happy for that newfound strength, perhaps she needed to grow even more to be able to return to a problem and fix it. Real strength wasn't about arguing and stomping away. It was going back to a sticky situation and battling—compromising—for a fair resolution.

And she had no one to blame but herself for condemning him because he hadn't told her all his secrets right away. How fair had that been?

Yes, he'd held back. Yet to the best of his ability, he'd lived up to everything he'd promised, everything he was able to give right now. Why was she realizing this now rather than days ago when she could have saved herself so much pain?

Most likely because she'd hidden her head in the sand the past few days, crying her eyes out and burying herself in paperwork at the office. Today was her first day actually picking up a bucket—and what a day it was with so many reminders of Seth and his kids.

She looked around the private luxury jet owned by Senator Landis, parked at the Charleston airport—not Seth's private field. But still, with that pacifier in hand from one of the Landis babies, she couldn't help but think of Owen and Olivia, and wonder how they were doing. She'd missed their sweet faces this week as well, and she liked to think they'd felt a connection to her, too, even during their short time together.

Her ultimatum had hurt more than just her. She stared into the bucket, more of those tears springing to her eyes. Blaming them on ammonia wouldn't work indefinitely.

She sank down onto the leather sofa, her mind replaying for the millionth time the harsh words they'd shared. She looked around the pristinely clean aircraft and wished her life was as easy to perfect.

Perfect?

Her mind snagged on the word, shuffling back to something Seth had said about it not being the perfect time, but life wasn't perfect. He didn't expect her to be perfect... And... What? She reached for the thought like an elusive pristine cloud until—

An increasing ruckus outside broke her train of thought. The sound of trucks and people talking in a rising excited cacophony of voices. She stood and walked toward the hatch. Bits of conversation drifted toward her.

"What's that up—?"

"—airplane?"

"P-47 Thunderbolt, I th—"

"Can you read what—?"

"—wonder who is Alexa?"

Alexa? Airplane?

A hope too scary to acknowledge prickled along her skin. She stepped into the open hatch, stopping at the top of the metal stairs. Shading her eyes, she scanned the crowd of maintenance workers and aircraft service personnel. She followed the path of their fingers pointing upward.

A World War II-era plane buzzed low over their section of the airfield, a craft that looked remarkably like the one she'd seen in Seth's hangar. Trailing behind, a banner flapped against the bright blue sky. In block red letters, it spelled out:

I Love You, Alexa Randall!

Her breath hitched in her throat as she descended the steps one at a time, rereading the message. By the time her feet hit concrete, it had fully sunk in. Seth was making a grand gesture to win her back. Her. Alexa Randall. At an imperfect time. In spite of her frustrated fears that were far from rational.

She'd thought she'd left her growing up years behind her, but she'd been hanging on to more than a need to make the world around her perfectly in order. She'd still subconsciously held onto the old, misguided mantra that *she* had to be perfect as well.

Seth had told her that didn't matter to him.

Maybe she needed to remember Seth didn't need to be perfect, either.

And she couldn't wait for him to land so she could tell him face-to-face.

The plane circled once more, message rippling for the entire airport to see. Then the craft descended, drifting downward into a smooth landing only twenty feet away from her.

The engine shut off with a rattle. The whirring rotor on the nose slowed and finally *click, click, clicked* to a stop. And there he was. *Seth.* Big, blond, bold and all *hers.*

He jumped out of the old craft, wearing khakis, hiking boots and a loose white shirt. His broad shoulders blocked out the sun and the crowd. Or maybe that was just because when he walked into her world, everything else went fuzzy around the edges.

She threw away the rag in her hand and raced toward him. A smile stretched across his face, his arms opening just as wide. She flew into his embrace, soaking up the crisp, clean scent of him.

She kissed him. Right there in front of the cheering crowd of airport personnel as he spun her around. The other voices and applause growing dimmer in her ears, she lost herself in the moment and just held tight to Seth. Even after her feet touched ground again, her head still twirled.

Moisture burned behind her eyelids, the happy kind of tears. How amazing to find her perfect love in accepting their imperfections.

He whispered in her ear. "Now maybe we can take this conversation somewhere a bit more private."

"I happen to be cleaning that plane right behind you and no one's due to show up for at least a half hour."

He scooped her into his arms—which launched another round of applause from the crowd—and he jogged up the steps, turning sideways to duck into the plane. He set her on her feet and right back into his arms.

Holding him closer, she laughed into his neck, his shirt warm against her cheek. "How did you know I was here?"

"I had an inside track on your work schedules. Senator Landis is a cousin of mine, sort of, with his wife being the foster sister of my cousin's wife... My family. There are a lot of us." He guided her to the leather sofa. "Before we talk about anything else, I need to tell you a few things."

Good or bad? She couldn't tell from the serious set of his face. "Okay, I'm listening."

"I've spent the past week working out some new custody arrangements with Pippa. The twins will be spending more time with me, and we've hired a new nanny for when they're with her." He looked down at their joined hands, his fingers twitching. "I'm not ready to run that paternity test. I don't know if I ever will be. The other guy who could be their biological father doesn't want anything to do with them. So, I want to leave things as they are for now. I just want to enjoy watching my kids grow up."

"I can understand that." She wanted that same joy in her life. The way he loved the twins made total sense to her. She'd been completely certain she would love an adopted child during her first marriage. "I'm sorry for pushing you away."

His knuckle glided gently along her cheekbone. "And I'm sorry for not being more open with you."

She cradled his face in her hands. "I can't believe the way you flew out there. You're crazy, did you know that?"

"When it comes to you, yes I am." He pressed a

lingering kiss into her palm, before pointing a thumb toward his airplane outside. "Did you get my message?"

"There wasn't any missing it." She tipped her face to his.

"I meant it, every word." His emerald eyes glinting with a gemstone radiance and strength. "I should have said them to you that night. Even before that. I was so zeroed in on my need to keep my kids' lives stable I focused on the idea of making sure they didn't have a parade of women through their lives. I almost missed the bigger message knocking around in my brain."

Her arms around his neck, she toyed with his sun-kissed hair. "And that message would be?"

"Marry me, Alexa." He pressed a hand to her lips, his fingertips callused. "I realize this is moving too fast in some ways and in other ways I haven't moved quickly enough. But if you need to wait a while, I can be patient. You're worth it."

"I know," she said confidently, realizing for maybe the first time she did deserve this man and his love. They both deserved to be happy together. "And I love you, too. The bold way that you touch me and challenge me. How tenderly you care for your children. You are everything I could want, everything I never even knew I could have."

"I love you, Alexa." He stroked her hair back from her face. "You. The beautiful way you are with my kids. The way you try to take care of everyone around you. But I also want to be here to take care of you when you demand too much of yourself. I love the perfect parts of us being together—and even the parts of us that aren't perfect but somehow fit together. Bottom line, you have to trust me when I say I love you and I want to be with you for the rest of my life."

"Starting now," she agreed.

"Starting right this second, if you're done here."

She scooped up her bucket. "As a matter of fact, I am. What did you have in mind?"

"A date, an honest to God, going out to dinner together date—" he punctuated each plan with a kiss "—followed by more dates and making out and sex— lots of sex—followed by more romancing your socks off."

She sighed against his mouth, swaying closer to him. "And we get married."

"Yes, ma'am," he promised, "and then the real romancing begins."

Epilogue

A year later

She couldn't have asked for a more romantic wedding.

And it had nothing to do with pomp and circumstance. In fact she and Seth had bypassed all of that and planned a beach wedding in Charleston that focused on family. A very *large* family, all in attendance.

Her bouquet in one hand, Alexa looped her other arm around her husband's neck and lost herself in the toe-tingling beauty of their first kiss as man and wife. Her skin warmed from the late day sun and the promise of their honeymoon in the outer banks—of Greece.

The kiss still shimmering to the roots of her upswept hair, Alexa eased back down to her toes. Applause and cheers echoed with the rustle of sea oats. She scooped up Olivia and Seth hefted up Owen. Arm in arm with her husband, she turned to face the hundred guests. Waves rolled and crashed in time with the steel drums playing as they walked back down the aisle lined with lilies and palm fronds. The sun's rays glittered off the sand and water like billions of diamonds had been ordered special for the day.

The twins, now nearly two and nonstop chatter bugs, clapped along with the guests. Shortly before the wedding, Seth had quietly seen the doctor about running a paternity test. As Alexa had suspected all along, the babies were Seth's biological children. His relief had been enormous. He'd credited her love with giving him the strength to take that step.

A love they were celebrating today.

Sand swirled around her ankles, the perfume of her bouquet swelling upward—a mix of calla lilies, orchids and roses, with trailing stephanotis. The attire had been kept casual, with pink flowing sundresses for both bridesmaids. For the men, khakis with white shirts— and rose boutonnieres that had arrived in the *wrong* color. But she knew it was a sign that they were ideal for her wedding because the deep crimson rose was a lovely wink and nod to the beauty of the imperfect.

And her dress… White organza flowed straight down from the fitted bodice with diamond spaghetti straps. No heels to get caught in the sand, just bare feet, miles of pristine beach and crystal blue waters. A very familiar and dear World War II vintage aircraft flew overhead carrying a banner for the entire wedding party to see.

Congratulations, Mr. and Mrs. Seth Jansen.

Cabanas with dining tables filled the beach, complete with a large tent and jazz band for dancing later. She'd let her new caterer-cousin choose the menu and design a detailed sandcastle wedding cake fit for a princess. And ironically enough, she had an entire Medina royal family in attendance as well as the Landises, considered by some to be American political royalty.

A play area with babysitters on hand had been roped off for children with their own special menu and cupcakes with crystallized sugar seashells on top. Although already kids were playing outside the designated area carefully arranged for them. They were happily building a sandcastle town with new moms Paige and Claire overseeing them. Just the way it should be—with everyone enjoying the day.

She and Seth had wanted their wedding to celebrate family, and they'd succeeded. Even her family was in attendance. While their relationship would likely never be close, enjoying a peaceful visit with them went a long way in soothing old hurts.

She and Seth had spent the past year building their relationship, strengthening the connection they'd felt so tangibly from the start. She'd also spent the past twelve months building her business and confidence. Her favorite work? Servicing the search and rescue planes on the philanthropic side of Jansen Jets. It was not the whole company, but certainly the part most near and dear to Seth's heart.

They were both living out their dreams.

She looked from their applauding relatives to her new husband. And what do you know?

He was already staring right back at her, his eyes full of love. "Is everything turning out the way you wanted today?"

She toyed with his off-color rose boutonniere. "The day couldn't be any more perfect."

And the best part of that? She knew each of their tomorrows promised to be even better.

* * * * *

THE PREGNANCY AFFAIR

ELIZABETH BEVARLY

For my grandmother,
Ruth Elizabeth Hensley Bevarly,
who told me some really great stories
when I was a kid.
I miss you, Nanno.

One

Renny Twigg threw her car into Park and gazed at the Tudor-style house beyond her windshield. Or maybe she should say Tudor-style *castle* beyond her windshield. Its walls were made of majestically arranged stones and climbed a full three stories, and they were tatted here and there with just the right amount of ivy. Its stained glass mullion windows sparkled in the late-morning sunlight as if they'd been fashioned from gemstones, and its turrets—one on each side—stretched even higher than the slate roof, looking as if they'd been carved by the hand of a Renaissance artist. The lot on which the mansion sat was nearly a city-state unto itself, green and glorious and landscaped with more flowering shrubs than a Spring Hill catalog.

There was rich, and then there was *rich*. The first

was something with which Renny had a more-than-nodding acquaintance. She'd come from a long line of powerful attorneys, financiers and carpetbaggers, the first of whom had arrived in this country hundreds of years ago to capitalize on the hugely exploitable land and its even more exploitable colonists. The Twiggs who followed had adopted the tradition and run with it, fattening the family coffers more with each ensuing generation. She'd grown up in a big white Cape Cod in Greenwich, Connecticut, had donned tidy blue uniforms for tony private schools before heading off to be a Harvard legacy, and had worn a sparkly tiara—with real diamonds—for her debut eleven years ago. Renny Twigg knew what it was to be rich.

She eyed the massive structure and its imperious gardens again. Tate Hawthorne was obviously *rich*.

She inhaled a fortifying breath and tucked an unruly dark brown tendril back into the otherwise flawless chignon at her nape. Then she checked her lipstick in the rearview mirror, breathed into her hand to ensure that there were no lingering traces of her breakfast burrito and smoothed a hand over her tan linen suit. Yep. She was perfectly acceptable for her meeting with the man her employer had assigned her to locate. *So go ahead, Renny. What are you waiting for?*

She eyed the massive mansion again. What she was waiting for was to see if a dragon would come swooping down from one of those turrets to carry her off for his own breakfast. In spite of the colorful landscaping and bright blue summer sky that framed it, the place just had that look about it. As if its owner were some brooding, overbearing Rochester who might very well lock her away in his attic.

Oh, stop it, she told herself. Tate Hawthorne was one of Chicago's savviest investors by day and one of its most notorious playboys by night. From what she'd learned of him, the only thing he dedicated more time to than making money was spending it. Mostly on fast, lustrous cars and fast, leggy redheads. Renny was five foot three in her kitten heels and had driven up in a rented Buick. She was the last kind of woman a man like him would want to stash away for nefarious purposes.

Even if his origins were pretty freakin' nefarious.

She opened the car door and stepped out onto the cobbled drive. Although it was only June, the heat was oppressive. She hurried to the front door, rehearsing in her head one last time the most tactful way to relay all the news she had for Tate Hawthorne.

Like how he wasn't really Tate Hawthorne.

Renny's employer, Tarrant, Fiver & Twigg—though the Twigg in the name was her father, not her—was a law firm that went by many descriptions. Probate researchers. Estate detectives. Heir hunters. Their services were enlisted by the state of New York when someone died without a will and no next of kin was known or when the next of kin was known but his or her whereabouts were not.

That second option had brought her to Highland Park, a suburb of Chicago for people who were *rich*. Bennett Tarrant, president and senior probate researcher, had given the job to Renny because she always found the heir she was looking for. Well, except for that one time.

And also because she was the only probate researcher available at the time who didn't have anything on her plate that couldn't be scraped off with a quick fork to the archives room. For lack of a better analogy. That breakfast burrito had, after all, been hours ago.

And although he hadn't said so specifically, she was pretty sure another reason Bennett had assigned her the job was to offer her a chance to redeem herself for that one time she hadn't been able to find the heir she was looking for. Locating someone who would be extremely hard to locate—like Tate Hawthorne—and doing so without screwing it up would make Renny a shoo-in for the promotion that had been eluding her, something that would make her father very proud. Not to mention make him stop looking at her as if she were a complete screwup.

In the meantime, Renny was proud of herself. It took skill and talent to find someone who had been buried in the federal Witness Protection Program along with the rest of his immediate family nearly three decades ago. Well, it took those things and also a friend from high school who had mad hacking skills and could find anything—or anyone—on the internet. But that was beside the point. The point was Renny had found the heir she was looking for, thanks to said friend. Which would, she hoped, put her back on the fast track at Tarrant, Fiver & Twigg and get her father off her back for that one tiny blip that had changed the company's 100% find rate to a 99.9999% find rate, and jeez, Dad, it wasn't like she'd lost that one on purpose, so just give her a break. *Man.*

She rang the doorbell and fanned herself with her

portfolio as she waited for a response, since, judging by the size of the house, it could be days before anyone made their way to the front door. So she was surprised to be caught midfan when the door opened almost immediately. Thankfully, it wasn't Tate Hawthorne who answered. It was a liveried butler, who looked to be about the same age as one of the founding fathers. If the founding fathers were still alive, she meant.

"Good morning," Thomas Jefferson greeted her. "Miss Twigg, I presume?"

She nodded. She had contacted Tate Hawthorne earlier this week—or, rather, she had contacted his assistant Aurora, who, Renny hadn't been able to help thinking, sounded like a fast, leggy redhead—and set up a meeting with him for the only fifteen minutes the guy seemed to have available for the entire month of June. And that was only because, Aurora had told her, he could cut short by a teensy bit his preparation for his regular Saturday polo match.

"Hello," Renny replied. "I'm sorry to be a bit early. I was hoping Mr. Hawthorne might be able to squeeze in another ten or fifteen minutes for our meeting. What I have to tell him is kind of—" *life changing* was the phrase that came to mind, but it sounded a little melodramatic "—important. What I have to tell Mr. Hawthorne is kind of important." And also life changing.

"All of Mr. Hawthorne's meetings are important," Thomas Jefferson said indulgently.

Of course they were. Hence his having only fifteen minutes in the entire month of June for Renny. "Nevertheless," she began.

"It's all right, Madison," a booming baritone interrupted her.

Renny gazed past the butler at a man who had appeared behind him and who had to be Tate Hawthorne.
She knew that, because he looked really, really *rich*.

His sable hair was cropped short, his skin was sun
burnished to the color of a gold doubloon and his gray
eyes shone like platinum. He was dressed in a polo uniform—equestrian, not water, unfortunately, because a
body like his would have seriously rocked a Speedo—
in hues of more precious materials, from the coppery
shirt to the chocolate-truffle jodhpurs, to the front-zip-
per mahogany boots that climbed up over his knees
with their protective padding. All of it skintight over
taut thighs, a sinewy torso, salient biceps and shoulders
broader than the Brooklyn Bridge. It was all Renny
could do to not drool.

Unfortunately, she wasn't as lucky in keeping herself
from greeting him less than professionally. "Hiya." Immediately, she realized her loss of composure and pheromones and amended, "I mean…hello, Mr. Hawthorne."

"Hello yourself, Ms…" He halted. "I'm sorry. Aurora included your name with the appointment, but I've
been working on something else this morning, and it's
slipped my mind. And, well…you are a bit early."

He seemed genuinely contrite that he was at a loss
for her name, something for which Renny had to give
him credit. Not just because he was being so polite
about her having impinged on his time after being told
he didn't have much to spare, but because, in her experience, most high-powered business types didn't feel

contrite about anything, least of all forgetting the name of a junior associate from a law firm they never had dealings with.

Madison the butler moved aside, and she murmured her thanks as she stepped past him into the foyer. She withdrew a business card from inside her jacket and extended it toward Tate Hawthorne.

"I'm Renata Twigg," she said. Not that she'd felt like a *Renata* a single day in her life, because Renata sounded like, well, a tall, leggy redhead. Renny had no idea what her mother had been thinking to want to name her that, or what her father had been thinking to insist it be the name she used professionally. "I represent Tarrant, Fiver & Twigg, attorneys," she concluded.

He took the card from her but didn't look at it. Instead, he looked at Renny. With way too much interest for her sanity and saliva glands. And—okay, okay—her pheromones, too.

"Renata," he said, fairly purring the word in a way that reminded her of velvet and cognac. And suddenly, for some reason, Renny didn't mind her given name at all.

"Thank you so much for making time to meet with me this morning," she said. "I know you must be very busy." Duh.

She drove her gaze around the massive black-and-white-tiled foyer to the half-dozen ways out of it—two doors to her right, two doors to her left, and one more framed by a curving staircase that led to the second floor.

"Um, is there someplace we can talk?" she asked.

For a moment, Tate Hawthorne said nothing, only continued to gaze at her in that mind-scrambling, gland-addling way. Finally, he said, "Of course."

He extended a hand to his left to indicate Renny should precede him. Which she would have done, had she had a clue where he wanted her to go. He could have been gesturing at the doors to her left, the staircase, or to the exit behind himself. He seemed to realize the ambiguity of his action, too, and threw her an apologetic smile that just made him even more charming. As if he needed that. As if *she* needed that.

"My office is this way," he told her.

He opted for the exit behind himself, and Renny followed. They passed another eight or nine—hundred—rooms before he finally turned into one that looked more like a library than an office, so stuffed to the ceiling was it with books. There was a desk tucked into a corner, facing to look out the window at a green space behind the house that was even more idyllic than the scene in front, and topped with a state-of-the-art computer and tidy piles of paperwork. Also sitting there was a polo helmet that matched his uniform, so she gathered he was in here when she arrived, trying to cram in more work before heading out to play. The guy clearly took both his business and his pleasure seriously.

"Please, have a seat," he said, gesturing toward a leather-bound chair that had probably cost more than the gross national product of some sovereign nations. Then he spun around his desk chair—also leather, but smaller—and folded himself into it.

Renny tried not to notice how his clothing seemed

to cling even more tightly when he was seated, and she tried not to think about how much she suddenly wanted to drop to her knees in front of him to unzip his boots. With her teeth. Instead, she opened her portfolio and withdrew the handful of documents she'd brought with her to support what was sure to sound like a made-for-cable movie on one of the channels that was *way* high up the dial.

"Mr. Hawthorne," she began.

"Tate," he corrected her.

She looked up from her task, her gaze fastening with his again. Those eyes. So pale and gray and cool for a man who seemed so deep and dark and hot. "Excuse me?" she said without thinking.

He smiled again. She tried not to spontaneously combust. "Call me Tate," he said. "'Mr. Hawthorne' is what they call me at work."

This wasn't work? she wanted to ask. It was work to her. At least, it had been before he smiled in a way that made clear his thoughts were closer to pleasure at the moment than they were to business. And, thanks to that smile, now Renny's were, too.

"Ah," she started again. Probably best not to call him anything at all. Especially since the only thing coming to mind at the moment was… Um, never mind. "Are you familiar with the name Joseph Bacco?" she asked.

A spark of something flickered in his eyes, then disappeared. "Maybe?" he said. "Something in the news a while back? I don't remember the context, though."

Renny wasn't sure how far Joseph Bacco's influence might have traveled beyond New York and New Jersey, but he'd been a colorful-enough character in his time to warrant the occasional story in magazines or true-crime shows on TV. And his death had indeed made national news. She tried another tack.

"How about the name 'Joey the Knife?'"

Tate's smile this time was tinted more with humor than with heat. And, gee, why was it suddenly so easy for her to think of him as *Tate*?

"No," he replied.

"'Bulletproof Bacco'?" she asked, trying another of Joseph Bacco's distinctive monikers.

"Ms. Twigg—"

"Renny," she said before she could stop herself. And immediately regretted not being able to stop herself. What was she thinking? She never invited clients to use her first name. And only Bennett Tarrant and her father called her Renny at work, because they'd both known her since the day she was born.

Tate's gaze turned hot again. "I thought you said your name is Renata."

She swallowed hard. "It is. But everyone calls me Renny."

At least everyone who wasn't tied to her by business. Which Tate most certainly was. So why had she extended the invitation to him? And why did she want to extend more invitations to him? None of which included him calling her by name and all of which had him calling her hot, earthy things as he buried himself inside her and drove her to the brink of—

"You don't seem like a Renny," he said. Just in the nick of time, too. The last thing she needed was to have an impromptu orgasm in front of a client. Talk about a black mark on her permanent record.

"I don't?" she asked, in a voice normally used only when having an impromptu orgasm. Maybe he wouldn't notice.

Judging by the way his pupils dilated, though, she was pretty sure he did. Even so, his own voice was level—if a tad warm—when he said, "No. You seem like a Renata to me."

Well, this was news to Renny. No one thought she was a Renata. Even her own parents had given up calling her that the day she stripped off her pink tutu in ballet class and decreed she would instead play football, like her brothers. Ultimately, she and her parents had compromised on archery, but still. *Renata* had gone the way of the pink tutu decades ago.

"Uh…" she said eloquently. Damn. What had they been talking about?

"Bulletproof Bacco," he repeated.

Right. Joey the Knife. Nothing like references to ammunition and cutlery to put a damper on thoughts of… Um, never mind.

"That doesn't sound like the name of someone I'd run into at the Chicago Merc," he continued.

She tried one last time. "How about the 'Iron Don'?" she asked. "Does that name ring a bell?"

The light came back into his eyes, and this time it stayed lit. "Right," he said. "The mobster."

"*Alleged* mobster," Renny corrected him. Since no one had ever been able to pin any charges on Joey the Knife that hadn't slid right off him like butter from a hot, well, knife. Though she was reasonably sure that wasn't why he'd earned that particular nickname.

"From New York, I think," Tate said. "His death was in the news a couple of months ago. Everyone kept commenting that he'd lived to be the oldest organized-crime figure ever and died of old age instead of…something else."

"*Alleged* organized-crime figure," Renny corrected him again. "And, yes, he's the man I'm talking about."

Tate glanced at his watch, then back at Renny. All heated glances and flirtation aside, the man was obviously on a schedule he intended to keep. "And he has bearing on this meeting…how?"

Renny handed him the first of the records she'd brought with her—a copy of his original birth certificate from New Jersey, much different from the one he had now from Indiana, which he'd been using since the fifth grade. The name printed on it, however, wasn't Tate Hawthorne, as he had come to be known after his stepfather adopted him. Nor was it Tate Carson, as he had been known before that. The name on this record was—

"Joseph Anthony Bacco the Third?" he asked.

"Grandson of Joseph Anthony Bacco Senior," Renny said. "Aka Joey the Knife. Aka Bulletproof Bacco. Aka the Iron Don."

"And why are you showing me a birth certificate that belongs to a mobster's grandson?"

Renny started to correct him, but he hastily amended, "*Alleged* mobster's grandson. What does Joseph the Third, or Joseph Senior, for that matter, have to do with me?"

She withdrew from her portfolio a photograph, one of several she had from the 1980s. In it, a man in his sixties was seated on a sofa beside a man in his twenties who was holding a toddler in his lap. She handed it to Tate, who accepted it warily. For a moment, he gazed at her through narrowed eyes, and somehow she sensed there was a part of him that knew what was coming. But he only dropped his gaze to the photo.

"The picture is from Joseph Bacco's estate," Renny said. "The older man is Joseph Anthony Bacco Senior, and the younger man beside him is—"

"My father," Tate finished for her. "I don't remember him very well. He died when I was four. But I have some photographs of him and recognize him from those. I assume the little boy he's holding is me."

"Yes."

"Meaning my father was an acquaintance of the Iron Don," he gathered, still looking at the photograph.

"He was more than an acquaintance," she told him. "Your father was Joseph Anthony Bacco Junior."

At this, Tate snapped his head back up to look at her. "That's impossible. My father's name was James Carson. He worked in a hardware store in Terre Haute, Indiana. It burned down when I was four. He was killed in the fire."

Renny sifted through her documents until she located two more she was looking for. "James Carson was the name your father was given by the federal marshals before they placed him and your mother and you in the Witness Protection Program when you were two years old. Your family entered WITSEC after your father was the star witness at a murder trial against one of Joseph Bacco's capos, Carmine Tomasi. Your father also gave testimony against a half-dozen others in the organization that led to a host of arrests and convictions for racketeering crimes."

She glanced down at the record on top. "Your mother became Natalie Carson, and you became Tate Carson. You all received new Social Security numbers and birth dates. The feds moved the three of you from Passaic, New Jersey, to Terre Haute, and both your parents were given new jobs. Your father at the hardware store and your mother at a local insurance company."

Renny handed him copies of documents to support those assertions, too. She'd received everything she had to support her story via snail mail at her condo a few days ago, from her high school friend with the mad hacking skills. They were records she was reasonably certain she wasn't supposed to have—she'd known better than to ask where they came from. The only reason Phoebe had helped her out in the first place was because Renny (A) promised to never divulge her source and (B) pulled in a favor she'd been owed by Phoebe since a sleepover thirteen years ago, a favor that might or might not have something to do with a certain boy in homeroom named Kyle.

These records, too, Tate accepted from her, but this time, his gaze fell to them immediately, and he voraciously read every word. When he looked up again, his pale gray eyes were stormy. "Are you trying to tell me...?"

She decided it would probably be best to just spill

the news as cleanly and quickly as possible and follow up with details in the inevitable Q&A.

"You're Joey the Knife's grandson and legal heir. In spite of your father's having ratted out some of his associates, your grandfather left his entire estate to you, as you're the oldest son of his oldest son, and that's what hundreds of years of Bacco tradition dictates. What's more, it was Joey's dying wish that you assume his position as head of the family and take over all of his businesses after his death.

"In short, Mr. Hawthorne," Renny concluded, "Joseph Anthony Bacco Senior has crowned you the new Iron Don."

Two

It took a minute for Tate to process everything Renata Twigg had dropped into his lap. And even then, he wasn't sure he was processing it correctly. It was just too far outside his scope of experience. Too hard to believe. Too weird.

Renata seemed to sense his state of confusion, because she said, "Mr. Hawthorne? Do you have any questions?"

Oh, sure. He had questions. A couple. Million. Now if he could just get one of them to settle in his brain long enough for him to put voice to it...

One that finally settled enough to come out was "How could a mobster want to leave his fortune to the son of a man who double-crossed him?"

"*Alleged* mobster," Renata corrected him. Again.

Not that Tate for a moment believed there could be any shades of gray about a guy named Joey the Knife.

"If I really am Joseph Bacco's grandson," he began.

"You are definitely Joseph Bacco's grandson."

"Then why would he want to have anything to do with me? My father—his son—turned him in to the feds. Wouldn't that kind of negate any familial obligation that existed prior to that? Or…I don't know…put a contract on my father's head?"

"Actually, your father didn't turn Joey in to the feds," Renata said. "Or any other member of the immediate Bacco family. All the information he gave to the feds had to do with other members of the organization. And he only gave up that information because the feds had enough evidence of his own criminal activity to put him away for forty years."

"*My* father?" Tate said incredulously. "Committed crimes worthy of forty years in prison?"

Renata nodded. "I'm afraid so. Nothing violent," she hastened to reassure him. "The charges against your father were for fraud, bribery, embezzlement and money laundering. Lots and lots of fraud, bribery, embezzlement and money laundering. There was never any evidence that he was involved in anything more than that. He was highly placed in your grandfather's business. Wise guys that high up… Uh…I mean…*guys* that high up don't get their hands that dirty. But your father didn't want to go to prison for forty years." She smiled half-heartedly. "He wanted to watch his little son grow up."

Tate tried to take some comfort in that. Even so, it

was hard to imagine James Carson involved in corruption. His memories of his father were hazy, but they evoked only feelings of affection and warmth. His dad, from what he recalled, was a good guy.

"Anyway," Renata continued, "because your father never fingered anyone in the Bacco family proper—in fact, his agreement with the feds stated he would absolutely not, under any condition, incriminate his family—Joey the Knife never sought a vendetta. He really loved his son," she added. "I think a part of him kind of understood why your father did what he did, so he could be with his son. But even more important, I think Joey really loved you—his first grandson. And since you had nothing to do with what your father did, he wanted you to come back and take your rightful place in the family."

As what? Tate wondered. What kind of nickname would suit the lifestyle he'd assumed instead? Bottom Line Bacco? Joey the Venture Capitalist? Somehow those just didn't have the same ring. Or did they? Renata had just said his grandfather had businesses. Maybe there was a bit of Bacco in Tate yet.

"You said my grandfather had businesses?" he asked.

She withdrew another collection of papers from her portfolio. "Several. He wants to put you in charge of Cosa Nostra, for one thing."

"Yeah, you just pretty much said that when you told me he wants me to be the new Iron Don."

She shook her head. "No, not that Cosa Nostra. That *alleged* one, I mean. Cosa Nostra is the name of a chain of Italian restaurants he owned up and down the Jersey shore."

Tate took this page from her, too, and quickly scanned the figures. Unless Cosa Nostra was a three-star Michelin restaurant that served minestrone for five hundred bucks a bowl, its profits were way too high to be on the up-and-up.

"Yeah, these places look completely legitimate," he said wryly.

"By all accounts, they are. Joey bought them with the proceeds from his waste-management business and his construction company."

Yep. Totally legit.

"Since your grandfather's death in the spring, everything's been run by his second in command, who—" she hesitated for a moment "—who's married to your father's sister."

Tate remembered then that Renata had mentioned there were other members of the "immediate" Bacco family. He'd been an only child all his life and had been under the impression that both of his parents were, too. At least, that was what his mother had always told him to explain why he didn't have any aunts or uncles or cousins, the way all his classmates did.

Of course, all these new revelations might also explain why she'd always seemed to go out of her way to ensure that he stayed an only child—not just in the birth sense but in the social sense, too. She'd never encouraged him to make friends when he was growing up and had, in fact, been wary of anyone who tried to get too close. Although he'd had a handful of friends at school, she'd never let him invite any of them home or allowed him to play at their houses. He'd never had birthday parties or sleepovers, hadn't been able to join Cub Scouts or play team sports or attend summer camp.

His childhood hadn't exactly been happy, thanks to his solitary state. He'd always thought his mother was just overprotective. Now he wondered if she'd spent the rest of her life watching their backs. He wished he could ask her about all this, but he'd lost her to cancer when he was in college. His stepfather—who might or might not have known about anything—had been quite a bit older than his mother and had died less than a year later. There was no one around who could verify any of this for Tate. No one except Renata Twigg.

"I have other family members?" he asked.

She nodded. "Your father had two sisters, both older than him. Denise is married to Joseph Bacco's second in command, Nicholas DiNapoli, aka Nicky the Pistol."

"My aunt is mobbed up, too?"

"Allegedly. His other sister, Lucia, is married to Handsome Mickey Testa, the manager of one of Joey's casinos."

Did anyone in the mob *not* have a nickname? "Do I have cousins by them?" Tate asked.

She flipped another page. "Yes. Denise and Nicky have Sal the Stiletto, Dirty Dominic and... Oh. This is different."

"What?"

"Angie the Flamethrower. Gotta give a girl credit for that. And Lucia and Mickey have Concetta."

"Who I assume is Connie the something."

"Well, right now she's Connie the economics major at Cornell. But I wouldn't rule anything out."

"So my entire family are mobsters."

"Alleged mobsters. And an economics major."

Renata gazed at him with what could have been compassion or condemnation. He had no idea. She was very good at hiding whatever she was thinking. Well, except for a couple of times when he was pretty sure she'd been thinking some of the same things he'd been thinking, most of them X-rated. Her espresso eyes were enormous and thickly lashed, her dark hair was pulled back into the most severe hairstyle he'd ever seen and her buff-colored suit was conservative in the extreme.

Even so, he couldn't shake the feeling that the image she presented to the world had nothing to do with the person she really was. Although she looked professional, capable and no-nonsense, there was something about her that suggested she wanted to be none of those things.

"So this law firm you work for," Tate said. "Does it handle a lot of, ah, *alleged* mob work?"

She shook her head. "Tarrant, Fiver & Twigg is about as white-shoe a firm as you're going to find. But, according to my father—who's the current Twigg in the name—Joey the Knife and Bennett Tarrant's father had some kind of shared history when they were young. No one's ever asked what. But it was Bennett's father who took him on as a client back in the sixties, and Bennett honored his father's wish that he always look after Joey."

"So Joey must have had some redeeming values then."

"He loved his son. And he loved his grandson. I'd say that makes up for a lot."

Tate looked down at the sheet that had his mother's original information on it. She had been Isabel Danson before she married Joseph Jr.

When Renata saw where his attention had fallen, she told him, "For what it's worth, your mother's family wasn't connected. Allegedly or otherwise."

"Do I have family on that side, too?"

"I'm sorry, no. She was an only child."

At least something his mother had told him was true.

"Her parents, both deceased now, were florists."

Finally. Something beautiful to counter all the luridness of his heritage.

"So what do my aunts, uncles and cousins think of this?" Tate asked, looking up again. "Seems to me they might all be a little put off by Joey's wanting a total stranger to come in and take over. Especially when that stranger's father ratted out other members of the organization."

"Right now, I'm the only person who knows you're Joseph Anthony Bacco the Third," Renata assured him. "Because of the delicate nature of the situation, I haven't even told the senior partners of Tarrant, Fiver & Twigg who or where you are. Only that I found you and would contact you about Joey's final wishes. I haven't told the Baccos even that much."

"And if I decide I'd just as soon not accept my grandfather's legacy?" Tate asked.

Since it went without saying he wouldn't be accepting his grandfather's legacy. He wasn't sure yet how he felt about accepting his grandfather's family, though. The blood one, not the professional one. A lot of that depended on whether or not they were accepting of him. For all he knew, they were already dialing 1-800-Vendetta.

"The surviving Baccos were all aware of Joey's wishes," Renata said. "They've known all along that he wanted his missing grandson to be found and take over after his death. He never made any secret of that. But I don't know how they felt about that or if they even expected anyone to ever be able to find you. If you don't accept your grandfather's legacy, then Joey wants everything to go to Denise and her husband so they can continue the tradition with their oldest son. That may be what they've been assuming would happen all along."

"I don't want to accept my grandfather's legacy," Tate said plainly.

"Then I'll relay your wishes to the rest of the family," Renata told him. "And unless you decide to approach them yourself, they'll never know who or where you are. No one will. I'll take the secret of your identity to my grave."

Tate nodded. Somehow, he trusted Renata Twigg to do exactly that. But he still wasn't sure what he wanted to do about his identity. As a child, he'd often fantasized about having a family. Just not one that was quite so *famiglia*. He'd be lying, though, if he said there wasn't a part of him that was wondering what it would be like to be a Bacco.

"It's my aunt's and cousins' birthright as much as it is mine," Tate said. "They were a part of my grandfather's life and lifestyle. And I—"

He halted there, still a little thrown by everything he'd learned. He searched his brain for something that might negate everything Renata had told him. But his memories of his father were hazy. The only clear ones were of the day he died. Tate remembered the police coming to their house, his mother crying and a guy in a suit trying to console her. As an adult looking back, he'd always figured the guy was from the insurance company, there to handle his father's life-insurance policy or something. But after what Renata had told him, the guy might have been a fed, there to ensure that his mother was still protected.

He conjured more memories, out of sequence and context. His father swinging him in the ocean surf when he was very little. The two of them visiting an ancient-looking monkey house of some zoo. His father dancing him around in the kitchen, singing "Eh, Cumpari!," a song Tate had never heard anywhere else except for when…

Oh, God. Except for when Talia Shire sang it in *The Godfather, Part III*.

"There are more photos," he heard Renata say from what seemed a very great distance. "Joey had several framed ones of you and him on shelves in his office until the day he died."

Tate looked at the photo in his hand again. The Iron Don honestly looked like he could be anyone's grandfather—white hair and mustache, short-sleeved shirt and trousers, grinning at the boy in the picture as if he were his most cherished companion. There were no gold chains, no jogging suits, nothing to fit the stereotype at all. Just an old man happy to be with his family. Yet Tate couldn't remember him.

On some level, though, a lot of what Renata said explained his memories. He couldn't recall taking a long road trip anywhere until his mother married William Hawthorne. So how could he have been in the ocean when he was so young? Unless he'd lived in a state that had a coastline. Like New Jersey. And there were no ancient-looking monkey houses in this part of the country. But some zoos in the Northeast had lots of old buildings like that.

He looked at Renata Twigg. "I'm the grandson of a mobster," he said softly. This time, the remark was a statement, not a question.

"Alleged mobster," she qualified again, just as quietly.

"But real grandson."

"Yes."

So Tate really did have family out there with whom he would have grown up had things been different. He would have attended birthday parties and weddings and graduations for them. Vacationed with them. Played with them. He wouldn't have spent his childhood alone. Strangely, if his father had gone into the family's very abnormal business, Tate might have had a very normal childhood.

The pounding of footsteps suddenly erupted in the hall outside his office. Tate looked up just in time to see a man in a suit, followed by a harried Madison, come hurrying through the door. When he halted, the man's jacket swung open enough to reveal a shoulder holster with a weapon tucked inside. Tate was reaching for his phone to hit 9-1-1 when his presumed assailant flipped open a leather case in his hand to reveal a badge with a silver star.

"Inspector Terrence Grady," the man said. He reminded Tate of someone. An older version of Laurence Fishburne, maybe. "United States Marshals Service. Tate Hawthorne, you'll have to come with me immediately."

"Sir, he pushed right past me," Madison said. "I tried to—"

"It's all right, Madison," Tate said as he stood.

Renata stood at the same time, though she didn't cut quite as imposing a figure as Tate was trying to achieve himself. Actually, it was kind of hard to tell if she'd stood at all, because she barely came to his shoulder. Small women. He never knew what to do with small women. They were just so…small. But Renata Twigg had already inspired a few interesting ideas in his head. Given the chance—which, for some reason, he was hoping for—he was sure he could find a few more.

Instead of responding to Inspector Grady, Tate, for some reason, looked at Renata. He expected her to look as confused as he felt over the marshal's sudden appearance. Instead, a blush was blooming on her cheeks, and she was steadfastly avoiding his gaze.

He turned back to the marshal. "I don't understand. Why should I go anywhere with you?"

Grady—maybe not Laurence Fishburne, but he looked like *someone* Tate knew—said, "I can explain on the way."

"On the way where?"

"We need to get you someplace safe, Mr. Hawthorne." And then, just in case Tate had missed that part before, he added, more emphatically this time, *"Immediately."*

Tate straightened to his full six-three and leveled his most menacing gaze on the marshal. "I'm not going anywhere. What the hell does a federal marshal have to do with—"

Hang on. Didn't federal marshals run the Witness Protection Program? Tate looked at Renata again. She was looking at something on the other side of the room and fiddling with the top button of her shirt in a way that might have been kind of interesting in a different situation. Under the circumstances...

"Renata," he said softly.

She was still looking at the wall and twisting her button, but she lifted her other hand to the twist of dark hair at her nape, giving it a few little pats, even though not a single hair was out of place. "Yes?"

"Do you have any idea why a federal marshal would show up at my front door less than an hour after you did?"

"Mr. Hawthorne," Grady interrupted.

Tate held up a hand to halt him. "Renata?" he repeated.

Finally, she turned her head to look at him. This time he knew exactly what she was thinking. Her eyes were a veritable window to her soul. And what Renata's soul was saying just then was *Oh, crap.*

In spite of that, she said, "No clue."

"Mr. *Hawthorne*," Grady said again. "We have to leave. *Now.* Explanations can wait."

"Actually, Inspector Grady," Tate said, returning his

attention to him, "you won't have much to explain. I'm guessing you're here because my grandfather was Joseph Bacco, aka the Iron Don, and now that he's gone, he wants me to be the new Iron Don."

"You know about that?"

"I do."

Grady eyed him warily for a moment. "Okay. I wasn't sure you were even aware you had a WITSEC cover, if your mother ever made you privy to that or if you remembered that part of your life. The other thing I came here to tell you is that your WITSEC cover has been compromised, thanks to a hack in our files we discovered just this morning. We need to put you somewhere safe until we can get to the bottom of it."

Tate barely heard the second part of the marshal's comment. He was too focused on the first part. "You knew my mother?"

Grady was visibly agitated about his lack of compliance with the whole *leaving immediately* thing, but he nodded. "I was assigned to your father and his family after he became a state's witness. The last time I saw your mother or you was the day your father died."

Okay, *that* was why he looked familiar. The man in the suit that day must have been a younger Terrence Grady.

"Look, Mr. Hawthorne, we can talk about this in the car," he said. "We don't know that there's a credible threat to your safety, but we can't be sure there *isn't* one, either. There are an awful lot of people interested in taking over your grandfather's position—the one they know your grandfather wanted you to assume—and it's safe to say that few of them have your best interests at heart. Last week, someone accessed your federal file without authorization, so your WITSEC identity is no longer protected. That means I have to get you someplace where you *are* protected. *Immediately*."

"Um, Inspector Grady?" Renata said nervously. "I, uh… That is, uh… Funny story, actually…"

"Spit it out, Ms…" Grady said.

She began patting her bun again, but this time kept doing it the entire time she spoke. "Twigg. Renata Twigg. And, actually, the person who compromised Mr. Hawthorne's WITSEC identity? Yeah, that, um… that might have been, ah…me."

Grady eyed her flatly. "You're the one who told Mr. Hawthorne about his past?"

Something in his tone made Renata pat her bun harder. "Um…maybe?"

Tate was going to tell Grady that she absolutely had been the one to tell him about that, but he was kind of enjoying how her bun patting was causing strands of hair to come loose. Her hair was longer than it looked.

"You have access to federally protected files, have you?" Grady asked. "Or do you have hacking skills that allowed you to access those files? Because hacking a federal database is a Class B felony, Ms. Twigg. One that carries a sentence of up to twenty years."

She looked a little panicked by that. "Of course I don't have hacking skills," she said. "Are you kidding? I majored in English specifically so I wouldn't have to do the math."

"Well, which is it, Ms. Twigg?" Grady asked. "How

did you discover Mr. Hawthorne's identity? And why did you go looking for him in the first place?"

She bit her lip anxiously. Tate tried not to be turned-on.

Quickly, she told Grady about Joey the Knife's will and his intentions for his grandson. Grady nodded as she spoke, but offered no commentary.

When she finished, he asked again, "And just how were you able to locate Mr. Hawthorne?"

At first, she said nothing. Then, very softly, she asked, "Class B felony, you say? Twenty years?"

Grady nodded.

For a moment, Renata looked like the proverbial deer in the headlights, right down to the fawn-colored suit and doe eyes. Then her expression cleared, and she said, "Craigslist."

Grady looked confused. Tate wasn't surprised. He'd been confused since seeing Renata at his front door.

"Craigslist?" Grady echoed.

Renata nodded. "I found a computer whiz on Craigslist who said he could find anyone for anybody for the right price. He helped me locate Mr. Hawthorne."

"His name?" Grady asked. Dubiously, if Tate wasn't mistaken.

Renata briefly did the deer-in-the-headlights thing again. Then she told him, "John something, I think he said. Smith, maybe?"

Grady didn't look convinced. "And do you know if Mr., ah, Smith did anything else with this information he found for you? Like, I don't know…sold it to someone else besides you?"

"I'm sure he's totally trustworthy and kept it all completely confidential," Renata said.

Now Grady looked even less convinced. "A guy on Craigslist who says he can find anybody for anyone for money and calls himself John Smith is totally trustworthy," Grady reiterated. Blandly, if Tate wasn't mistaken.

Renata nodded with much conviction and repeated, "Totally."

Grady looked at her for a long time, as if weighing a number of scenarios. Finally he growled, "We don't have time for this right now. We need to get Mr. Hawthorne somewhere safe. And until it's all sorted out, you're coming, too, Ms. Twigg."

That finally stopped the bun patting. But it restarted the button fumbling. So much so that Renata actually undid the button, and then another below it, revealing a tantalizing glimpse of lace beneath. Which was weird, because in light of developments over the last several minutes, the only thing Tate should find tantalizing about Renata Twigg was thoughts of her having never entered his life in the first place.

"I'm sorry, but I can't go anywhere with you," she said to Grady. "I have a red-eye out of O'Hare tonight."

"You don't have a choice, Ms. Twigg," Grady said emphatically. He turned to Tate. "And neither do you. We're all leaving. Now. Once the two of you are settled in a safe house, we can get this all straightened out. But until we know there's no threat to Mr. Hawthorne, and until we get to the bottom of this security breach, both of you—" he pointed first at Tate, then at Renata "—are coming with me."

Three

Renny sat in the backseat of the black SUV with Tate, wishing she could wake up in her Tribeca condo and start the day over again. They'd been driving for more than two hours nonstop—pretty much due north, as far as she could tell—and Tate had barely said a dozen words to her during the entire trip.

He'd spoken to the marshal often enough early on—or, at least, tried to. Grady had responded to every question with a promise to explain once he was sure Tate and Renny were settled at a safe location. He'd replied the same way as he hustled the two of them out of the house earlier. He hadn't even allowed Tate time to change his clothes, hadn't allowed Renny to bring her handbag or portfolio and had made them both leave behind their electronics due to their GPS.

On the upside, the fact that Grady hadn't allowed them even basic necessities might be an indication he didn't intend to detain them for long. On the downside, the fact that they were still driving after two hours was a pretty decent indication that Grady planned on detaining her and Tate for some time.

She just wondered how far from Chicago Grady thought they had to be before they'd be considered safe. They'd crossed the Wisconsin state line less than an hour after leaving Tate's house and had kept driving past Racine, Milwaukee and Sheboygan. Like any good Northeasterner, Renny had no idea which states actually abutted each other beyond the tristate area, but she was pretty sure Wisconsin was one of the ones way up on the map beneath Canada. So they couldn't drive much longer if they wanted to stay in Grady's jurisdiction.

As if cued by her thoughts, he took the next exit off I-43, one that ended in a two-lane blacktop with a sign indicating they could head either west to a place called Pattypan or east to nowhere, because Pattypan was the only town listed. In spite of that, Grady turned right.

Okay then. Nowhere it would be.

The interstate had already taken them into a densely forested area, but the trees grew even thicker the farther they drove away from it. The sky, too, had grown darker the farther north they traveled, and the clouds were slate and ominous, fat with rain.

This day really wasn't turning out the way Renny had planned. She braved another look at Tate, who had crowded himself into the passenger-side door as if he wanted to keep as much space between them as pos-

sible. He wasn't turning out the way she'd planned, either. She was supposed to have gone to his house in
her usual professional capacity, relayed the terms of
his grandfather's will in her usual professional way and
handled his decision, whatever it turned out to be, with
professionalism.

Any personal arrangements Tate wanted to make
with the Bacco family would have been up to him. Then
Renny would have gone back to her life in New York
having completed what would be the most interesting
case she would ever handle in her professional career
and try not to think about how early she'd peaked.

Instead, all her professional responses had gone out
the window the moment she saw Tate, and every personal response had jumped up to scream, *Howdy do!*
And those responses hadn't shut up since, not even
when the guy was giving her enough cold shoulder to
fill a butcher's freezer.

The SUV finally turned off the two-lane blacktop, onto a dirt road that sloped sharply upward, into
even more trees. The ride grew bouncy enough that
Renny had to grab the armrest, but that didn't keep
her from falling toward Tate when they hit a deep rut.
Fortunately, she was wearing her seat belt, so she only
slammed into him a little bit. Unfortunately, when they
came out of the rut, he fell in the other direction and
slammed into her, too.

For one scant moment, their bodies were aligned
from elbow to shoulder, and Renny couldn't help thinking it was their first time. Um, touching, she meant.
Arms and shoulders, she meant. Fully clothed, she

meant. But the way her heart was racing when the two of them separated, and the way the blood was zipping through her veins, and the way her breathing had gone hot and ragged, they might as well have just engaged in a whole 'nother kind of first time.

She mumbled an apology, but he didn't acknowledge it. Instead, he gripped his armrest as if his life depended on it. After another few hundred jostling, friction-inducing feet of what may or may not have once been a road, the SUV finally broke through the trees and into a clearing.

A clearing populated by a motel that was clearly a remnant of mid-twentieth-century, pre-interstate travel culture—single story, brick and shaped like a giant L. There was a parking space in front of each room, but there wasn't a single car present. In fact, the place looked as if it had been out of business since the mid-twentieth-century, pre-interstate travel culture. The paint on the doors was peeling, the brick was stained with mold and a rusty, mottled sign in front read The Big Cheese Motor-Inn. In a small clearing nearby were a half-dozen stucco cottages shaped like wedges of cheese. It was toward one of those that Inspector Grady steered the SUV.

"Seriously?" Renny said when he stopped the vehicle and threw it into Park. "You're going to hide us in a cottage cheese?"

"We've used this place as a safe house since nineteen sixty-eight," Grady said. "That's when we confiscated it from the Wisconsin mob. These days, no one even remembers it exists."

"There's a Wisconsin mob?" Renny asked. "Like who? Silo Sal Schlitz and Vinnie the Udder?"

"There *was* a Wisconsin mob," Grady corrected her. "The Peragine family. Shipping and pizzerias."

Of course.

The marshal snapped off his seat belt, opened his door and exited, so Renny and Tate did, too. The moment she was out of the vehicle, she was swamped by heat even worse than in Chicago. Impulsively, she stripped off her jacket and rolled her shirt sleeves to her elbows. Her hair, so tidy earlier, had become a tattered mess, so she plucked out the pins, tucked them into her skirt pocket and let the mass of dark hair fall to the center of her back. Then she hastily twisted it into a pin-free topknot with the deftness of someone who had been doing it for years, drove her arms above her head and pushed herself up on tiptoe, closing her eyes to enjoy the stretch.

By the time she opened her eyes, Tate had rounded the back of the SUV and was gazing at her in a way that made her glance down to be sure she hadn't stripped off more than just her jacket. Nope. Everything was still in place. Though maybe she shouldn't have fiddled so much with her shirt buttons earlier, since there was a little bit of lace and silk camisole peeking out.

But come on. It was a camisole. Who thought camisoles were sexy these days?

She looked at Tate, who was eyeing her as if she were clad in feathery wings, mile-high heels and a two-sizes-too-small cubic-zirconia-encrusted bra. Oh. Okay. Evidently, there was still at least one guy in the world who found camisoles sexy. Too bad he also hated her guts.

As unobtrusively as she could, she rebuttoned the third and second buttons. Then she followed Grady to the giant cheese wedge, telling herself she only imagined the way she could feel Tate's gaze on her ass the whole time.

"Oh, look," she said in an effort to dispel some of the tension that had become thick enough to hack with a meat cleaver. "Isn't that clever, how they made some of the Swiss-cheese holes into windows? That's what I call functional design."

Unfortunately, neither man seemed to share her interest in architectural aesthetics, because they just kept walking. Grady pulled a set of keys from his pocket as he scanned the tree line for signs of God knew what, and Tate moved past her to follow the marshal to the front door, not sparing her a glance.

Renny deliberately lagged behind, scanning the tree line herself. Though for different reasons than Grady, she was sure. In spite of the weirdness of the situation, and even with the suffocating heat and teeming sky, she couldn't help appreciating the beauty surrounding her. The trees were huge, looking almost black against the still-darkening clouds, and there was a burring noise unlike anything she'd ever heard. She recognized the sound as cicadas—she'd heard them on occasion growing up in Connecticut—but here it was as if there were thousands of them, all singing at once.

The wind whispered past her ears, tossing tendrils of hair she hadn't quite contained, and she closed her eyes to inhale deeply, filling her nose with the scent of evergreen and something else, something that reminded her of summers at the shore. That vague fishy smell that indicated the presence of water nearby. If they really had traveled due north, it was probably Lake Michigan. She wondered if they were close enough to go fishing. She'd loved fishing when she was a little girl. And she'd always outfished her father and brothers whenever they went.

She listened to the cicadas, reveled in the warm breeze and inhaled another big gulp of pine forest, releasing it slowly. Then she drew in another and let it go, too. Then another. And another. Bit by bit, the tension left her body, and something else took its place. Not quite serenity, but something that at least kept her panic at bay. She loved being outdoors. The farther from civilization, the better.

She felt a raindrop on her forehead, followed by a few more; then the sky opened up and the rain fell in earnest. Renny didn't mind. Rain was hydrotherapy. The warm droplets cooled her heated skin and *tap-tap-tapped* on the leaves of the trees and the hood of the SUV, their gentle percussion calming her even more.

With one final breath, she opened her eyes. Tate stood inside the door of the cottage looking out at her, his expression inscrutable. He was probably wondering what kind of madwoman he was going to be stuck with for the rest of the day—maybe longer. Renny supposed that was only fair, since she was wondering a lot of things about him at the moment, too.

Like, for instance, if he enjoyed fishing.

* * *

As Tate gazed at Renata, so much of what had happened today became clear. The woman didn't even have enough sense to come in out of the rain.

He must have been nuts to have thought her professional, capable and no-nonsense. Then again, he'd also been thinking she didn't seem to want to be any of those things. Now he had his proof. Even when the rain soaked her clothing, she still didn't seem inclined to come inside.

On the other hand, her saturated state wasn't entirely off-putting. Her white shirt clung to her like a second skin, delineating every hill and valley on her torso. Just because those hills weren't exactly the Rockies—or even the Grassy Knoll—didn't make her any less undesirable. No, it was the fact that she'd disrupted his life and gotten him into a mess—then made a literal federal case out of it—that did that.

Actually, that wasn't quite true. She was still desirable. He just didn't like her very much.

He heard Grady in the cabin behind him opening and closing drawers, cabinets and closets, and muttering to himself. But the activity still couldn't pull his gaze from Renata in the rain.

Renata in the rain. It sounded like something by a French watercolorist hanging in the Musée d'Orsay. But there she was, a study in pale shades, and if he were an artist, he would be setting up his easel right now.

She really was very pretty. Not in the flashy, showy, don't-you-wish-you-were-hot-like-me way that the women he dated were. Her beauty was the kind that crept up on a man, then crawled under his skin and into his brain, until he could think of little else. A quiet, singular, unrelenting kind of beauty. When he first saw her standing at his front door that morning, he'd thought she was cute. Once they started talking, and he'd heard her breathless, whiskey-rough voice, he'd even thought she was kind of hot—in a sexy-librarian way. But now she seemed remarkably pretty. In a quiet, unrelenting, French-watercolorist kind of way.

"Mr. Hawthorne?" he heard Grady call out from behind him, raising his voice to be heard over the rain pelting the roof.

Yet still Tate couldn't look away from Renata. Because she started making her way to the door where he stood. She stopped long enough to remove her wet shoes, then continued barefoot. The dark hair that had been so severe was sodden and bedraggled now, bits of it clinging to her neck and forehead, and the suit that had been so efficient looking was rumpled and puckered. Somehow, though, that just made her more attractive.

"Mr. Hawthorne?" Grady said again, louder this time.

"What?" Tate replied over his shoulder. Because now Renata was only a few steps away from him.

"Sir, I'm going to have to go into town for some supplies. This place hasn't been used for a while, and I didn't have any notice that we'd be needing it. I did turn on the hot-water heater, so there should be hot water in a few hours. But the place is kind of light on fresh food. I shouldn't be gone long."

Renata was nearly on top of Tate now—figuratively,

not literally, though the literal thought was starting to have some merit. So he stepped just far enough out of the doorway for her to get by him, but not far enough that she could do it without touching him. She seemed to realize that, because she hesitated before entering, lifting her head to meet his gaze.

As he studied her, a drop of rainwater slid from behind her ear to glide down the column of her neck, settling in the divot at the base of her throat. He was so caught up in watching it, to see if it would stay there or roll down into the collar of her shirt, that he almost forgot she wasn't the kind of woman he found fascinating. It wasn't Renata that fascinated him at the moment, he assured himself. It was that drop of rainwater. On her unbelievably creamy, flawless, beautiful skin.

When he didn't move out of her way, she arched a dark eyebrow questioningly. In response, he feigned bewilderment. She took another small step forward. He stood pat.

"Do you mind?" she finally asked.

"Mind what?"

"Moving out of the way?"

Well, if she was going to speak frankly—another trait he disliked in women—there wasn't much he could do but move out of the way.

"Of course," he said. And moved a step as small as hers to the side.

She strode forward at the same time, but she moved farther and faster than he did so her shoulder hit him in the chest, and they both lost their footing. When Tate circled her upper arm with one hand, he discovered Renata Twigg had some decent definition in her biceps and triceps.

Muscles were another thing he wasn't crazy about finding on a woman. So why did finding them on Renata send a thrill of…something…shooting through his system?

"Sorry," he said.

"No problem," she replied. In a breathless, whiskey-rough voice that made him start thinking about sexy librarians again.

She kept moving, but even after she was free of him, his palm was still damp from her clothing, and there was a wet spot on his shirt where her shoulder had made contact. Those would eventually dry up and be gone. What wouldn't leave as quickly were the thoughts circling in his brain that were anything but dry.

He watched her as she continued into the cabin, noting how the rain had soaked her skirt, too. The skirt whose length barely passed muster for proper office attire. The dampness made it seem even shorter—though it could just be Tate's overactive imagination making it do that—and it, too, clung to her body with much affection. Whatever Renata lacked in the front—and, really, no woman ever lacked anything up front—she more than made up for behind. The gods might have made her small, but they'd packed more into her little package than a lot of women twice her size.

"Mr. Hawthorne?"

Reluctantly, he returned his attention to Grady. The marshal was looking at him in a way that indicated he knew exactly where Tate's gaze had been, and if he were Renata's father, he'd be hauling Tate out to the woodshed.

"Did you hear what I said?" he asked.

"You have to go into town for some supplies," Tate replied. See? He could multitask just fine, listening to Grady with the left side of his brain while ogling Renata with the right.

"And I won't be gone long," Grady added as he made his way to the front door. "There's a phone in the bedroom, but if either of you uses it to call anyone other than me, this is going to turn into a *much* longer stay than any of us wants. Get it?"

"Got it."

"Good." Without another word, Grady exited.

Leaving Tate and Renata truly alone.

Four

Renny watched Inspector Grady leave, then scanned the cottage and decided things could be worse. The place was actually kind of cute in a retro, Eisenhower-era kind of way. The walls were paneled in honey-colored wood, and a fireplace on one side was framed by creek stone all the way around. Doors flanked it on each side, one open and leading to a bedroom and the other closed, doubtless a bathroom. The wall hangings were amorphous metal shapes, and the rugs were textile versions of the same. The furniture was all midcentury modern—doubtless authentic—with smooth wood frames and square beige cushions. On the side of the cottage opposite the fireplace was a breakfast bar and kitchenette, whose appliances looked authentic to the middle of the last century, too.

The decor reminded her of James Mason's house on

top of Mount Rushmore in *North by Northwest*. Any minute now, Martin Landau ought to come sauntering in to mix up a pitcher of martinis for all of them. Of course, then he'd try to kill Renny and Tate the way he'd tried to kill Eva Marie Saint and Cary Grant, so…

"So," she said, turning to face Tate again, "pretty crazy day, huh?"

She had hoped to lighten the mood with the question. But he only glowered harder.

She sighed. "I'm sorry, okay? For like the hundredth time, I'm sorry. Will you please stop looking at me like I ruined your life?"

"You have ruined my life," he said. Still glowering.

"I have not!" she denied. "All I did was tell you the truth about your origins. *I'm* not the one who spawned you into an alleged mob family. *I'm* not the one who tried to make you an offer you couldn't refuse. The circumstances of your birth and your grandfather's wishes are facts of your life. They have nothing to do with me."

"Yeah, but the facts of my life you dumped on me today have ruined the facts of my life that existed before. Before today, my life was fine and would have remained that way if you'd stayed in New York. No, better than fine. Before today, my life was perfect."

"No one's life is perfect," Renny said. "There's always some—"

"My life was. Until you knocked on my door."

Well, technically, she had rung his doorbell, but it probably wasn't a good idea to argue that point. Not when they had so many others to argue instead. Not that Renny wanted to argue. Tate obviously did. And maybe, on some level, she deserved the dressing-down he was about to give her.

Although she really should have thought of another phrase than *dressing-down*, since she was pretty sure he'd been doing that to her long before he discovered the reason for her visit. So maybe, on some level, she deserved the tongue-lashing he was about to give her.

Um, no, that probably wasn't a good phrase to use, either. So maybe, on some level, she deserved the, uh…harangue—yeah, that was it—that he was about to give her.

He didn't disappoint.

"A few hours ago," he began, his anger barely in check, "my weekend was going to be great. After polo, I had a late lunch with some friends to tell them about an opportunity that would have netted us each a bundle. And tonight, I had a date with a gorgeous redhead."

Ha. Just as Renny suspected.

"Tickets for a show that's been sold out for months, followed by dinner at a restaurant where it's even harder to get a table. Then back to my place for a nightcap and hours of the obvious conclusion to a night like that."

Renny wasn't sure what bothered her more. That he assumed a woman would have sex with him just because he spent a zillion dollars on an evening out—even if it did sound like a supernice evening—or the fact that he was cocky enough to think he would last for hours. With a stunning redhead.

Okay, so maybe it was actually the stunning redhead that bothered her the most. And, okay, maybe the supernice evening, too, since the high point of Renny's weekend would have been a few episodes of *Bletchley Circle* and a bag of gummi bears.

Feeling a little haranguey herself, she said tartly, "Obvious conclusion to a night like that? So the two of you go back to your place to binge-watch British mysteries on Netflix all night? 'Cause that's what I consider an 'obvious conclusion' to a night like that."

She didn't bother to clarify that that was because (A) she generally spent her weekends alone lately, and (B) she really loved binge-watching British mysteries on Netflix.

He eyed her blandly. "Find yourself going out for evenings like that a lot, do you?"

"Sure. All the time." At least once a month. Okay, maybe more like once a year. Okay, maybe more like never. He didn't have to know that, either. "I'm sure you'll have a chance to make it up to the stunning redhead."

"Not when I can't call her and tell her I won't be there. I can't even give her the tickets to the show so she can go with someone else."

He wouldn't mind his girlfriend going to the play with someone else? Did that mean she really wasn't his girlfriend? And that he might maybe possibly perhaps be open to seeing someone else? Someone who *wasn't* a stunning redhead, but was more of an ordinary brunette and—

Oh, Renny, stop. You're embarrassing yourself.

It only meant the focus of his evening wasn't the woman he was with or where they were going or what they were doing. The focus of his evening was its obvious conclusion. Meaning Tate Hawthorne was a guy with a pretty face and a gorgeous body that housed a truly superficial brain. Renny hated guys like that.

Even if they did have pretty faces and gorgeous bodies.

"I'm sure she'll understand," Renny said, "once you get back and explain what happened."

He shook his head. "How do I explain something like this? It sounds like a bad movie."

"That I didn't write," she reminded him. "Don't blame me for this."

He slumped forward a bit, as if he'd been holding his entire body too tightly for too long. Then he crossed the room and folded himself into a chair by the fireplace.

"It's just been a lot to take in, you know?" he said.

Renny moved closer, opting for the sofa. Tate stared straight ahead, but his gaze was unfocused, as if he were seeing something other than a dated but really kind of charming venue. Since his question hadn't seemed to require an answer, she said nothing. Especially since he looked ready to answer it himself.

"I've always had a plan for my life," he said. "Even when I was a kid. After my dad died, my mom struggled so much to keep a roof over our head, and I wanted to grow up and make as much money as I could so she didn't have to worry anymore. So *I* wouldn't have to worry. I hate worrying. I never worry. Worrying is for people who don't know how to make life work for them."

He turned to Renny, and she braced herself for more scowling. Instead, he looked kind of...lost? Confused?

Uncertain? All of the above? Whatever it was, it was unsettling, because until now, Tate hadn't been any of those things. On the contrary, he'd been the most cocksure person she'd ever met.

"But now I'm worried," he said. "And I don't know how to handle it. Does that ever happen to you?"

She wanted to tell him no. She'd always had a plan for life, too, even when she was a kid. Attend the same high school as her parents. Get her BA in English from Vassar like her mother and graduate from Harvard Law like her father. Then go to work at his firm, since both of her brothers had opted to work in finance, and Renny had been his last hope. Eventually marry some as-yet-nameless up-and-comer like herself. At some point, squeeze out the requisite kid or two and hire a nanny like the one she'd had. Send the offspring to the same schools with the same majors so they could go to work at Tarrant, Fiver & Twigg, too, and start the cycle all over again. It was the upper-class, suburban way. Blah, blah, blah. She couldn't remember ever planning a life that was anything else.

But she could remember *wanting* a life that was anything else. She could remember that pretty well.

In spite of that, she told Tate, "No. It doesn't happen to me. I don't worry, either."

And she didn't. Because there was no uncertainty in her life. She had a job that paid well and guaranteed her a career—provided she didn't keep screwing up. She owned her condo and car outright. She carried no debt. Even if she did lose her job, she had trust funds from both sides of the family that would allow her to live comfortably for the rest of her life. There wasn't any uncertainty in Renny's life. She really didn't have anything to worry about.

Except for those days when she felt as if she'd ended up where she was through no thought or decision of her own. Except for those days when she carried around a knot in her stomach that couldn't be anything but, well, worry.

Days kind of like today.

She pushed the thoughts away. They were silly. Her life was fine. And it would stay fine. Fine was…fine. It was. It was totally, totally…fine. There were a lot of people who would kill to have lives that were fine. No way was she in any position to worry.

"I shouldn't be worried, though, right?" Tate asked, still sounding worried. "There's no way I'm going to take over my grandfather's position. And I don't have to meet my cousins or aunts or uncles if I don't want to, do I? They'd probably just as soon I stay out of their lives, right?"

"Maybe," Renny said. "But maybe not. Especially since you don't want to inherit your grandfather's estate or take his place in the business. Once the Bacco sisters and their families know you're not a usurper, they might want to reconnect with you."

Hey, it could happen. Joey the Knife had put an awful lot of importance on family, even family who had strayed. It was possible Tate's aunts still loved their brother as much as their father had. It was possible that, in spite of everything, they'd like to see how their little nephew turned out. A lot of things were possible at this point. When Tate remained silent, she said, "You have a lot to think about. Maybe being separated from your life for a few days will be a blessing in disguise. It will allow you to mull your options without your other daily distractions."

"A few days?" he echoed, sounding even more worried. "You think we'll actually be here for a few days?"

"I think it's pretty clear we're not going home tonight. Not if Inspector Grady had to go into town for supplies."

And not if Renny continued to hide the fact that she knew perfectly well who was responsible for the security breach that compromised Tate's WITSEC identity. She was no happier to be here than Tate was. But what was she supposed to tell Inspector Grady after he said hacking a federal database the way Phoebe had could land her in prison for twenty years? And probably Renny, too, as an accessory. She'd had no idea what to say at that point. She'd been too busy panicking. Tate wasn't the only person who had a lot to think about.

"You said 'a few days,'" he told her. "Not 'overnight.'"

"Well, it *is* the weekend," she said. "Not much gets done on Saturday or Sunday in the world of bureaucracy."

"So it could be Monday before we get the all clear?" he asked.

"Or maybe Tuesday," she hedged. "Everyone in Washington could be coming back to work after a weekend at the shore or something. Takes a while to get going again after a weekend like that. I mean, conceivably, it could even be Wednesday before we—"

"Wednesday?" he bellowed. "That's four days stuck here."

Well, only if they decided by then that the hack into the WITSEC system hadn't originated with someone in the Bacco family looking to off Tate to keep him from taking over his grandfather's position. Until someone at the Justice Department realized there was no danger to him—and Renny really, really hoped they could do that without discovering the true source of the hack—he and Renny could be stuck in this dated but really kind of charming venue for a while.

"I don't know," she said in response to his question. "We can ask Inspector Grady when he gets back how long he thinks we'll have to be—"

Out of nowhere, a crack of thunder shook the cottage, a burst of lightning flashed outside the windows and the single table lamp Grady had lit upon entry flickered off, then on again. It was only then that Renny realized how uncomfortably warm it had become inside.

"Mind a little air-conditioning?" she asked.

Tate still looked a little distracted—and a lot annoyed—but he shook his head. She glanced around for a thermostat, saw one by the front door and headed for it.

"It's only for heat," she said upon further inspection.

She checked the windows for an air conditioner. Nothing. She wandered into the bedroom, which was as retro as the living room—and which also had only one bed that didn't even appear to be queen-size—but there was no window unit in there, either.

Okay, so it was an old motel that was out of use, and it was Wisconsin, where maybe summers didn't usually get that hot, but still. It was hot. They'd just have to cool off the old-fashioned way. If nothing else, rain usually brought the temperatures down.

She returned to the living room and opened one of the windows in there…only to be pelted by rain, so she closed it again. Or, at least, she tried to. But it got jammed to the point where she was banging on the window sash with both hands as water streamed down her arms, making it too slippery to get the damned thing back in its groove.

Before she realized what was happening, Tate was behind her, leveraging his extra foot of height to wrestle the window back into place for her. He surrounded her completely, his entire body flush against hers, his front to her back, his arms over her shoulders, his legs pressed into her fanny. With every move he made—and he made a lot of them—he seemed to press closer still, until Renny felt as if he were crawling inside her. And still the rain came pouring in the window, drenching them both, doing nothing to cool her off. On the contrary, the air around them fairly sizzled as their bodies made greater contact, creating a blistering friction that made her feel as if she would spontaneously combust. Finally, Tate shoved the window back into place, leaving them both wet and panting and—

And *not* moving away from each other.

Five

In fact, Tate seemed to be moving closer still. And if Renny had thought it was hot and steamy in the cottage before, it was nothing compared to the way she felt with him surrounding her, clinging to her as snugly as her clothes. Good God, the man was tall. And broad. And hard. And hot. And—

And get a grip, Renny.

He was just a guy. Just a really sexy guy. With a beautiful face. And a gorgeous body. And millions—possibly billions—of dollars. Who, she was reasonably certain, didn't like her very much.

So why wasn't he moving away from her?

She discovered the answer when she tried to retreat first, by shifting her body to the right. The moment she did, she felt it—felt him—hard and ripe and ready against her back. She wasn't the only one who'd been affected by the friction of their bodies. The evidence of Tate's reaction was just a lot more obvious than her own, thanks to his anatomy. The anatomy that, some other time, she would take a moment to appreciate but that, at the moment… Oh, all right—she appreciated it now, too. What she didn't appreciate were the circumstances that had brought both their anatomies so close, in a situation where they couldn't do anything about it.

In an effort to relieve the tension—or whatever—they both must be feeling, she tried to move a little farther to the right. But he dropped his hands from the window to cup them over her shoulders.

"Don't," he said softly. "Just…don't move."

"But I—"

"Don't," he repeated, a little more roughly.

Reluctantly, Renny stopped, but she couldn't ignore the pressure of him behind her. For one long moment, they stood still, utterly aware of each other. Then, finally, he removed his hands from her shoulders. She waited for him to take a step backward, but he stayed where he was, dropping his hands to her waist, instead.

Okay, now he would move away—or at least move her away from him. But neither of those things happened, either. Instead, he dipped his head closer to hers. She felt a warm percussion of breath stir her hair from behind, then heard the soft sigh of his exhalation near her ear.

Unable to help herself, she turned her head toward the sound, only to find her mouth hovering within inches of his. Her gaze flew to his, but he had his lowered. At first she thought he was studying her mouth, and then she realized his eyes were too hooded for that, and his focus was even farther down. What he was really looking at was... She bent her own head to follow his gaze. He was looking at her shirt. More specifically, he was looking down her shirt. At the hint of camisole lace that still peeked out of the neckline. But when she looked back up at him, he had shifted his attention again, and this time he was definitely looking at her mouth. Then he was looking at her eyes. Then her mouth again.

And then his head was lowering more, his mouth drawing nearer to hers...nearer...nearer still. Renny held her breath as she felt his hands on her hips inching forward, one up along her ribs and the other down across her belly. She realized belatedly that she was still clinging to the windowsill, something that gave him free rein over her midsection. He curved one hand under her breast and pushed the other over her skirt at the juncture of her thighs.

She spun around to face him, opening her hands over his chest to push him away. Though she didn't push very hard, and he didn't go very far, it was enough for her to regain some semblance of sanity, enough to remember she barely knew him—even if it somehow felt as if she'd known him forever—enough to remind herself he didn't like her.

"Stop," she said quietly. "Just...stop."

Although the admonition echoed his own warning of a moment ago, the fact that she still had her hands splayed open over his chest—oh, wait, her fingers were actually curled into the fabric of his shirt, as if she intended to pull him forward again—didn't exactly put a fine point on her objection.

Tate seemed to notice that, too, because he cupped his hands over her hips, pulled her close and asked, "Why? We're obviously attracted to each other. You said yourself we're going to be stuck here for a while. It would be a nice way to pass the time."

Oh, and wasn't that what every woman wanted to be to a really hot, really sexy guy with millions—possibly billions—of dollars? A way to *pass the time*? Where did Renny get in line to sign up for that?

She forced herself to let go of his shirt—it actually would be a nice way to pass the time if it weren't for that pesky *he doesn't like you* thing—and covered his hands with hers to remove them from her hips.

"It's not a good idea," she said.

He circled her wrists with deft fingers and moved both their hands behind her back, then leaned in again. "Oh, I think it's a *very* good idea."

He started to lower his mouth to hers, and, God help her, Renny stood still for the merest of seconds and waited for him to make contact. He was just so unbelievably…so extremely…so totally, *totally*…

His lips brushed hers lightly…once, twice, three times, four. Heat splashed in her belly, spilling through her torso and into her limbs, warming parts of her she hadn't even realized were cold. Then he stepped closer and covered her mouth completely with his, and those parts fairly burst into flame. For another scandalous, too-brief moment, she reveled in the fantasy that was

Tate Hawthorne and the wild ride it promised. Then, nimbly, she tugged her hands free of his and somehow broke away to scurry to the kitchenette.

"Hey, are you as hungry as I am?" she asked when she got there.

Belatedly, she realized the glaring double entendre of the question. Because there was hunger, and then there was *hunger*. And, speaking for herself, anyway, she was feeling a lot more of the latter than she was the former.

In spite of that, she asked, "You want a sandwich? I could really go for a sandwich."

Then she remembered Grady had gone into town for supplies, which meant there probably wasn't much in the cottage for a sandwich.

She spun around so she wouldn't have the temptation that was Tate Hawthorne making her want a lot more than a sandwich and opened the refrigerator. It was empty save for a couple of bottles of water and a six-pack, minus two, of Spotted Cow beer. The freezer held only a handful of indeterminate foil-wrapped things all covered with frost. She tugged on one of the cabinet doors and found plates and glasses. Another offered a near-empty roll of paper towels. Then, finally, she found some food in one. Lots of food, actually. Lots of canned food. Lots of canned food that might be as midcentury modern as everything else in the place. She pushed herself up on tiptoe to reach one in front and flipped it over to inspect the date on the bottom. Then she smiled.

"Gotta love preservatives," she said. "This will still be good when I hit the big three-oh."

There was a long stretch of silence, then an even longer sigh of resignation, then the scrape of Tate's boots across the floor.

"And when will that be?" he asked impassively.

His voice came from so close behind her Renny actually jumped. She spun about to find him doing the surrounding thing again, though this time at least he gave her a couple of inches of space that allowed for some air circulation that might dry her clothes and some thought circulation that might clear her head.

"Um, a year," she told him. "Well, a year and two months."

He looked surprised. "I thought you were fresh out of law school."

She was grateful for the change of subject and clung to it, even though the subject was her, a topic she normally avoided. Still, when the alternative was thinking—or, worse, talking—about the mind-scrambling kisses they'd just shared…

"Nope," she said. "I passed the bar six years ago. So… Beefaroni?" She held up the can for his inspection.

He grimaced. "Really? You'd eat that?"

She gaped at him. "It was only my favorite dish the whole time I was in lower school. Of course I'll eat it. It's delicious."

He looked past her into the cabinet. "What else is in there?"

She turned around and started sorting through the cans, fairly certain that none of them would compare to what he would have found on the menu of a Chicago restaurant where it was nearly impossible to get a table, which he would have been perusing this evening if he wasn't stuck in a giant wedge of cheese with Renny and Chef Boyardee.

"Let's see," she said. "There's SpaghettiOs, Mini Raviolis, beef stew, baked beans, chili mac, a variety of soups... Anything sounding good?"

When she turned back for his reply, he somehow seemed even closer than he'd been before. Judging by the expression on his face, though, no, nothing sounded good. In fact, everything sounded revolting.

In spite of that, he asked, "What kind of soup?"

She turned to check. "Clam chowder, creamy potato, beef barley, chicken and stars—"

"Is it Campbell's chicken and stars?"

"Yep."

"Fine. I'll have that."

Before she could grab it, he reached over her head to pluck the can from the shelf. Then he moved to the stove to open the drawer beneath it and retrieve a serviceable saucepan. He turned the proper burner knob to medium high without even having to check which one it was, effortlessly popped the lid on the can and plopped its contents into the pan. His moves were quick and fluid, automatic enough to make it seem as if he made canned soup in a not particularly up-to-date kitchenette every day because he had one just like it at home in his ivy-encrusted, multimillion-dollar mansion.

The only thing he did wrong as far as Renny could tell was that he added only half a can of water to the condensed soup, instead of the full can she knew the directions called for. She knew that because chicken and stars had also been a fave of hers when she was a kid. Enough that she still bought it on a fairly regular basis and hid it in her cabinets behind the jars of organic tomatoes, the boxes of steel-cut oats, the tins of gourmet green tea and the bottles of extra-virgin, first cold-pressed olive oil. Right beside the cans of Beefaroni.

Anyway, she was just surprised he knew his way around a can of soup and an antiquated kitchen. Well, knew his way around an antiquated kitchen, anyway. As for the soup...

"You should add a full can of water," she said. "The directions call for—"

"A whole can," he finished in unison with her. "I know. But a whole can waters it down. A half can gives it more flavor."

Oh. Okay. So maybe he did know his way around a can of soup, too. It was still weird, because he seemed like the last kind of guy who would have even a nodding acquaintance with either.

As if he'd read her mind, he told her, "My mom and I lived on canned stuff for years when I was a kid. After my dad died, the two of us only had her income to live on. We made regular visits to the food bank. Almost everything there came in cans."

And a growing boy's hunger must have been voracious, she thought, filling in the blanks he didn't want to fill himself. Canned food probably barely made a dent in it. Maybe that was why he turned his nose up at canned stuff now. Because he'd paid his canned-food dues a long time ago. She honestly didn't know anything about him other than the name he'd been given from WITSEC and what she'd heard and observed today.

She'd been so happy when Phoebe had sent her the info about him, something that prevented Renny from screwing up again—ha—that she immediately looked up his most recent contact info, got in touch with his assistant and booked her flight to Chicago. And when she'd seen his house, she just assumed he must have lived that way forever.

"Lower school," he said.

"What?" she asked.

"You said Beefaroni was your favorite food when you were in lower school. Not 'grade school.' You said, 'lower school.'"

It took her a moment to rewind their conversation back to where she had used the phrase. But she didn't understand the distinction he was making. "Yes. So?"

"So you must have gone to private school. Only private schools use that 'lower school' designation. Anywhere else, you would have said 'grade school.' Or 'elementary school.'"

And if Tate had grown up on canned food and his mother's solitary paycheck, then he must not have gone to private school. Renny wondered if he was one of those people who'd been so driven to succeed as an adult because he'd been so deprived as a child.

"I did go to private school, actually," she told him. Without elaborating. Since there was really no reason to rub his nose in her privileged upbringing when he'd had what must have been a pretty challenging one himself. Even if he was superrich now, no one ever left their childhood far behind. Renny knew that, because every time she had to spend more than five minutes with either of her parents, she immediately regressed into that five-year-old disappointment shedding her pink tutu.

Tate, however, seemed to want her to elaborate, because he asked, "Was it one of those really tony private schools with marble floors and mahogany paneling and farm-to-table lunches?"

"Um, kind of," she admitted. She figured it wasn't necessary to add that it had also sat on acres and acres of gorgeously manicured green space that lent itself to some really beautiful pastoral afternoons when they sometimes held classes outdoors.

Instead, she said softly, "I'm sorry about your dad."

He'd located a spoon—also in the first drawer he checked—and was slowly stirring the soup, gazing into it as if it might offer him the answers he needed to get out of this mess.

"It was a long time ago," he replied just as softly. "I really don't remember him that well. My stepfather was more of a father to me than my dad was. Not that I'm saying my biological father was a bad father," he hastened to add, glancing up long enough to see if Renny had drawn the wrong conclusion. "Just…my stepfather is the only father I really knew, you know? My mom married him when I was ten. And he was a good guy. Good to my mom. Good for my mom."

Those last sentences—and Tate's absence from them—were awfully telling. Especially considering the way he'd sounded like a ten-year-old boy when he uttered them.

"Do you remember anything about your life before your parents went into the program?" she asked.

Still stirring the soup, he said, "A few impressions of isolated moments, but nothing that puts that life into perspective."

"And your mother never gave you any reason to think there was this secret past she and your father shared?"

He shook his head. "Nothing. I mean, she was an overprotective mother—wouldn't let me do a lot of the things I wanted to do. But lots of moms are like that. I just figured she was a worrier."

Renny could relate. Her mom had worried a lot about her, too. But the reason Melisande Desjardins Twigg had worried about her daughter was because she wasn't daughter-like enough. When her mother took her to the store to order Renny her first set of big-girl bedroom furniture, they'd gone straight to the French Provincial—sorry, that was *Provençal Français*—section. Renny had uttered something along the lines of "Ew, grody" and dragged her mother to the bunk beds and desks made out of much sturdier stuff. When Renny wanted to wear a suit—with pants—to her middle school graduation instead of the white dresses the other girls had to wear, her mother had about had a heart attack. And when Renny decorated her high school mortarboard with a quote from Tupac instead of the Swarovski crystals her mother suggested, well...

Suffice it to say Renny had a long tradition of giving her mother cause to worry. At least, that was what her mother had always thought. Anyway, she could kind of relate to Tate Hawthorne at the moment.

She tried again. "Is there any chance maybe—"

"Look, Renata," he interrupted. He stopped stirring

the soup and met her gaze. "I know you're just trying to help, but right now there's so much going on in my head I don't know what to think about any of it. I'd really rather not talk about it, okay?"

Not talking about it was another thing Renny understood. Her family were the hands-down champs of not talking about stuff. So were most of her ex-boyfriends, come to think of it.

"Okay," she said. "I understand. Just…when you're done with that pot, do you mind rinsing it out? I'll use it when you're finished."

He gazed at her in silence for another moment, as if he wasn't sure how to reply to what should be a simple question. "Sure," he said finally. "No problem."

A phone suddenly rang with the shrill retro ringtone used by so many today—except this one was shriller and more retro. When it sounded again, she realized it was coming from the bedroom. She and Tate hurried in that direction, but Renny had the lead on him and made it through the door first. She followed the ringing to the other side of the bed, where a plastic rotary phone sat on the lower shelf of the nightstand. She sprang for it as it rang again, landing on her stomach on the mattress, and snatched up the receiver.

"Hello?" she said breathlessly.

"Ms. Twigg?"

For some reason, she was disappointed to hear Inspector Grady's voice at the other end of the line. Who had she expected it would be? Her mother? The Publishers Clearing House Giveaway people? Walter, the guy who'd dumped her three weeks ago after two dates—

not that she'd minded much, since he'd been so, well, Waltery?

"Hi, Mr. Grady," she said.

She looked over her shoulder at Tate, only to find that he looked a little disappointed, too. Maybe he'd been expecting a call from his stunning redhead. Then his gaze skittered away from her face and landed… Well, there was no way to deny it. He was staring at her ass. Again. She grabbed the phone and maneuvered herself into a sitting position. When his gaze wandered to her face again, she did her best to glower at him. In return, he only smiled. Knowingly.

"Ms. Twigg? Are you there?"

"I'm here, Mr. Grady."

"Look, there's been a little trouble," he began.

Oh, duh, she wanted to reply. Instead, she listened as he told her how almost immediately after he arrived in town, the roads were closed behind him from flash flooding, and how he wouldn't be able to make it back to the cottage tonight, but there was some canned food and other stuff in the kitchen, enough to get them through till tomorrow, and blah, blah, blah, blah, blah. Renny didn't register much after that except for how Grady would get back as soon as he could, and he was sure Tate and Renny would be fine until he did, since nobody was getting out of Pattypan, Wisconsin, tonight, and nobody knew where she and Tate were, anyway.

All she could do was keep repeating, "Uh-huh…uh-huh…uh-huh." When she hung up the phone, Tate was still staring at her from the doorway, now with an expression that demanded, *Well?*

Gingerly, she set the phone back in its cradle. Nervously, she moved around the bed to return it to the nightstand. Anxiously, she tried to rouse a smile.

And then, very quietly, she said, "So. Looks like you and I are going to be on our own tonight. You know how to play Snap?"

Six

A raucous crack of thunder woke Tate from a dream about Renata. Or maybe not, he reconsidered when he saw her sleeping in a slant of moonlight in the chair near the sofa where he lay himself. She looked so fey and otherworldly, a part of him wondered if he might still be asleep. Once the thunder rolled off, the cottage was oddly quiet and, save for that one sliver of silver that had found her, very dark. He could still be dreaming. Any minute, he could wake up in his bed at home, with a belly full of sushi and champagne and a tumbled redhead sleeping beside him, waiting for him to wake her and tumble her again.

But if he woke in his own bed, it would mean Renata really had been nothing but a dream. And that would mean he'd never stood behind her wrestling with a window and his libido as he inhaled great gulps of her, a combination of immaculate sweetness and earthy sexiness that had nearly driven him mad. It would mean he'd never brushed her lips with his and been startled by the explosion of heat that rocked him, a reaction he hadn't had to a woman since... Hell, he didn't think he'd ever had a reaction like that to a woman. If Renata was nothing but a dream, and he woke up back in his real life, safe and sound, then that would mean he was back in his real life, safe and sound.

But that was what he wanted, wasn't it? His real life before she'd shown up at his front door? So why was he suddenly kind of relieved to realize he wasn't dreaming at all?

Lack of sleep, he told himself. It made people think crazy things. The rain had still been coming down in torrents when he and Renata ate a dinner of canned pasta just before sundown. Which, in hindsight, he had to admit hadn't been half-bad. The dinner or the company. Renata's incessant yakking had become less annoying as the day wore on. Maybe because trying to keep track of what she was nattering about had kept Tate from having to think about all the things he still wasn't ready to think about. Like not being who he'd always thought he was. Like having a family, regardless of how sketchy their origins might be. Like how tempting Renata smelled and how weird she made him feel.

The last thing he remembered before falling asleep, he'd been flipping through a years-old copy of *Esquire*, unable to sleep thanks to the storm raging outside, and Renata had been curled up in her chair with a tattered paperback she'd pulled from a bookcase in the bedroom. Something by Agatha Christie. He'd been surprised by her choice. It was so old-fashioned.

The book lay facedown in her lap now. One of her hands was curved loosely over its spine, and the other was dangling by the side of the chair. Her head was leaning back in a way that offered a tantalizing glimpse of her neck but guaranteed she would have a wicked ache in it when she woke. In spite of that, he was hesitant to rouse her. She just looked so...

He studied her again, the elegant line of her jaw, the sweep of dark lashes on her cheeks, the lush mouth. And the errant tresses of hair that fell from her ragged topknot, curving around the gaping shirt collar that still revealed a whisper of lace beneath.

Well, there was just something about moonlight that suited her. Who was Tate to mess with that?

What time was it? Automatically, he looked around for his phone, then remembered he didn't have it with him. Which naturally reminded him he didn't have anything with him. How the hell was anyone supposed to survive without even the most basic necessities? Like a cell phone? He rose and prowled around the cottage until he located a clock in the bedroom, one of those old plastic ones with glow-in-the-dark radium numbers. It was 1:57 a.m., according to the radioactive yet once common appliance. How had anyone survived the mid-twentieth century, anyway?

And just how much longer were they going to be stuck in this time warp of a place? Maybe he should be concerned about the fact that Grady had left the two of them alone, but the storm had worsened a lot after he left, so Tate hadn't been that surprised when the marshal was waylaid by flooding. He'd been heartened by Grady's assurance that he would be back tomorrow. Until the storm continued to lash for hours and the road they'd driven in on turned into a mud slide. Considering the lousy condition it was in when it was dry, he hated to think about how hard it would be to drive up the thing now, even with four-wheel drive. He and Renata could be living out of cans for a while.

Just like when Tate was a kid. Great. The last thing he wanted was to be reminded of that time in his life.

He returned to the living room and saw that Renata hadn't budged. Tate, on the other hand, was wide-awake. He seldom slept more than five hours a night, but he normally fell asleep much later than he did tonight. There was little chance he would be nodding off again any time soon. Normally, when he couldn't sleep, he went downstairs to his office to work. There was always plenty of that to catch up on. Here, though…

Well, he wasn't much of a reader. Not Agatha Christie, anyway. And as nice as it was to watch Renata sleep, to do that for any length of time put him in creepster territory. What did a man do in the middle of the night when he was locked up indefinitely with a beautiful woman who also had nothing to do?

Other than that?

Shower. Yeah, that was it. After spending the day in his polo uniform, he wasn't feeling exactly springtime fresh. Then again, once he showered, he was going to have to change back into the clothes on his back, since he'd left his house with nothing but, well, the clothes on his back. But if there was food in the cottage, maybe there were other provisions, too.

He returned to the bedroom and switched on a lamp by the bed. In the closet, he found a couple of shirts—off-the-rack and 100 percent polyester, he noted distastefully—and one pair of trousers that was four sizes too big for him. The shirts were all too big, too, save for one with long sleeves, but if he couldn't find anything else, he could make do.

He had better luck with the dresser. There was a sweater unsuited to swamp weather, but also a white cotton T-shirt. In another drawer, he discovered a pair of blue jeans, even if they were as midcentury as everything else in this place. The denim was soft and faded, and they had a button fly. But they were only one size too big, which at least made them workable. And it would make them more comfortable while he had to go commando waiting for his boxers to dry after washing them.

Just to be sure, he riffled through the rest of the drawers, but the only other clothes he found were some unspeakably ugly men's pajamas and some giant Bermuda shorts. Looked like Renata was out of luck. Evidently, the overwhelming majority of people who had to go into protective custody were men. Large men, at that.

Tate thought again about his parents. What had it been like for them, leaving everything behind and moving to a place they'd never visited before, having no clue what the future held? As bad as it was being stuck here with nothing, he at least knew that at some point he would be going back to his life and all that was familiar. His parents had had to build a new life in a new place with strangers they'd probably taken a long time to learn to trust—if they'd ever learned at all.

For some reason, that made him think again of Renata. In the moonlight. Looking soft and bewitching.

Shower, he reminded himself. He'd been about to take a shower. A nice, *long* shower. A nice, long, *cold* shower. He'd figure out the rest of it later.

Renny wasn't sure what woke her up. She only knew she was in semidarkness and wasn't in her own bed. When she lifted her head, her gaze fell on the book in her lap. Right, she recalled groggily. She was in King's Abbot with the recently deceased Roger Ackroyd. No, that wasn't right. She was in Wisconsin with Agatha Christie. No, that wasn't it, either. She was in Wisconsin with…

Tate Hawthorne. Right. It was all coming back to her now.

She rubbed her aching neck and sat up straighter, twisting to alleviate another ache in her back. Next time she fell asleep, it was going to be in bed. Then she remembered there was only one bed in the cottage. One bed that wasn't even queen-sized. Of course, there was also a sofa. Which didn't look very comfortable, the reason she'd chosen the chair for her reading.

Well, that and because Tate had been on the couch, surrounded by his cone of silence.

She heard what sounded like a metallic squeak, followed by the cessation of a humming she hadn't noticed until then, one she recognized as water rushing through pipes. Tate was in the shower. Or, more correctly, Tate was getting out of the shower. All naked and wet, and wet and naked, and covered in naked, wet skin. Like she really needed to have that information.

Thankfully, the only shower was in the bathroom adjacent to the bedroom, so he wouldn't come popping into the living room out of the other one all naked and wet, fumbling with a towel he couldn't quite get knotted around his waist, so it kept dipping low over his hips, under his flat waist and sculpted abs, low enough to reveal those extremely intriguing lines men had over their legs that curved and dipped down under the towel to frame what was sure to be a seriously impressive—

Anyway, that wouldn't be happening. For which Renny was exceedingly grateful. Really, she was.

She heard the bathroom door click open in the bedroom, and only then realized the reason the living room wasn't totally dark was because of the lamplight spilling in from that room. A great fist seized her insides and squeezed hard at the thought of Tate in there naked. She told herself she only imagined the scent of pine that seemed to permeate the entire cottage or the way the air suddenly turned all hot and damp. Then she heard the soft sound of bare feet on wood floor. She felt Tate moving closer behind her, then closer, then closer still.

She sat silently as he passed her chair—oh, yeah, that was definitely him causing the hot, steamy, piney thing—and seated himself on the couch. There was just enough light for her to see him, dressed now in a white V-neck T-shirt and faded blue jeans, a towel draped around his neck that he was using to scrub his close-cropped hair. She wondered where he'd found fresh clothes.

As if she'd asked the question aloud, his head snapped up, and his gaze met hers. "You're awake," he said.

"And you're clean," she replied, trying not to sound jealous. As uncomfortable as she'd been all day, it hadn't occurred to her to look for fresh clothes and get cleaned up. "You even shaved."

He lifted a hand to his beautiful jaw. "There are some disposable razors in the bathroom. If you're careful, you won't flay yourself alive with one. And there are some clothes in the bedroom that must have been left behind by previous visitors. A little big, but not too bad."

No, not too bad at all. As sexy as Tate had been in a skintight polo uniform, it was nothing compared to the jeans and T-shirt. Mostly because jeans and T-shirts were Renny's favorite attire for men. And when that T-shirt was V-necked enough to hint at the dark scattering of hair and sculpted muscle beneath, well...

"I don't suppose there was anything in my size, was there?" she asked in an effort to steer her brain in a new direction. "Something cute and comfy by Johnny Was, perhaps? Maybe some Tory Burch tomboy? Or some off-the-rack geek chic? I'd even settle for some sporty separates if they don't smell like swampland."

Because it was just Renny's luck to be trapped in the middle of nowhere with a rich, gorgeous, recently wet and naked playboy, and wearing the kind of clothes her mother would wear—which could only be made more off-putting by the added accessory of eau de quagmire.

Tate looked at her blankly. "The only part of that I understood was the word *tomboy*. If your definition of tomboy is men's shirts, trousers and pajamas that would swallow you, then, yeah. Have at it. Otherwise, the pickings are slim. But you might be able to figure out something."

Great. She could exchange clothes her mother would wear for clothes her father would wear. That was sure to make her less off-putting. Still, they would at least be clean and not stinky.

She looked at Tate again. At the curve of biceps peeking out from beneath the sleeve of his shirt. At the strong column of his throat. At the chiseled jaw now freshly shaved. And suddenly a shower seemed like a very good idea.

"Is there still some hot water?" she asked. Not that she would be using any hot water. Ahem.

"Oh, there's plenty," he said in a way that made her think he hadn't used any hot water, either. Hmm.

Without another word, she made her way to the bedroom. Tate's discarded polo uniform was folded loosely on the dresser, and his boots were on the floor below them. Quickly, she studied her apparel options in the closet and dresser, only to discover they were every bit as grim as he'd described. A gigantic man's shirt in the closet—in lavender, so apparently some criminals weren't afraid of a little color—would fall to her knees. But that was good, since she would have to wash out her underwear and let it air-dry, and she'd need something to cover her until then.

It took a minute for the significance of that to settle

into her brain, and it only did because she walked into the bathroom to see a pair of men's silk boxers slung over the towel rack, drying. If Tate's underwear was hanging in here, then what was he wearing under his blue jeans out—

There was no way Renny was going to let herself think any further about that. Or about how she would have to go panties-free herself, wearing nothing but a gigantic men's shirt that could easily be brushed aside for a quick—

Well, all righty, then. The less gigantic men's pajamas it would be. At least she could—probably—keep them hitched up by tying a knot in the waistband. A really tight knot. That would be virtually impossible for Tate *or* her to get untied.

Yeah. That's the ticket.

She snagged those from the dresser drawer—they were bilious green and patterned with little golf carts—escaped to the bathroom, closed and locked the door, turned the cold faucet handle to full blast, and stripped off her fetid clothing. So she and Tate would be without underwear for a few hours. So what? People went without underwear all the time in some parts of the world, and they did just fine.

She stepped into the cold shower and yelped.

Oh, yeah. That should do it. For now, anyway.

Seven

Tate heard a yelp from the bathroom and figured Renata was having a close encounter of the cold-shower kind much like his own. Obviously, he wasn't the only one who was thinking about the repercussions of two red-blooded adults who'd been dancing around an attraction to each other all day, being left alone for the night with no underwear.

Well, okay, maybe they hadn't been dancing around it the entire day, since he still couldn't shake the memory of that too-brief embrace. The question now was, had Renata opted for the obnoxious pajamas in the dresser, or one of the shirts in the closet? 'Cause the latter would make things infinitely easier.

Suddenly feeling restless, he rose and padded barefoot to the kitchen, forgetting until he opened the refrigerator that there wasn't much there to keep his mind off what Renata might or might not be wearing. Automatically, he grabbed one of the beers and twisted off the cap with a satisfying hiss. Then he enjoyed an even more satisfying swallow. As good as it tasted, though, it wasn't enough to keep his thoughts from wandering back to Renata. Who, at that very moment, was standing naked beneath a rush of water under the same roof he was.

He couldn't remember the last time he'd been this close to a naked woman when the two of them weren't taking advantage of that. Then again, Renata wasn't exactly his type, he reminded himself. Again. She was the last kind of woman he needed or wanted in his life. He'd survived a lot of women who showed up regularly on those "toxic types to avoid" lists—the diva, the control freak, the drama queen and his personal favorite, the material girl. But he'd never had a run-in with a member of Renata's tribe: the walking disaster.

And that one was probably the worst of the bunch for a man like him. The other types could be handled once a guy figured out which of their buttons to push or not push and where and when they liked best to be stroked. But the walking disaster? There were too many buttons with that type, and stroking the wrong part could be catastrophic. With a woman like that, there were too many things outside a man's control. Too many things that could go wrong. As had been the case with Renata from nearly the moment she'd walked into his life.

Okay, so maybe she wasn't responsible for the circumstances of his birth and had nothing to do with his biological family being a *famiglia*. She was still a disaster. There were still too many variables with her. There was still so much that could go wrong. And don't even get him started on her buttons.

He heard the click of the bathroom door and glanced at the bedroom in time to see a shadow fall across the bed. She turned off the bathroom light and, before exiting it, the bedroom light, as well, throwing the entire cottage into darkness.

He heard the whisper of bare feet, followed by a softly uttered "Ow, dammit" as she slammed something that sounded a lot like her knee into one of the tables by the sofa. Finally, she snapped on the lamp and threw the living room into warm golden light.

Okay, maybe she wasn't quite a walking disaster. Maybe she was more of a moseying disaster. She was still someone he needed to avoid.

Which was going to be even harder now than it had been before, because Renata looked... Even with her hair wrapped up in a towel like a suburban-dwelling, SUV-driving spa-goer, she looked... Even in ugly men's pajamas that would fit three of her, she looked...

Wow. Renata looked really, really... Wow.

"Sorry about that," she muttered as she steadied the lamp on the table. "I'm not so good in the dark."

Oh, Tate doubted that. She'd done pretty well in the dark so far. He'd love to see how well she did other things in the dark.

"No worries," he said.

No worries. Right. She'd rolled up the legs of the pajamas to her knees, and the sleeves to her elbows, meaning she was covered just fine, but was also intriguingly... not. And even with every button of the shirt fastened, the deep V of its placket and collar meant the garment was open to the center of her chest.

Tate was suddenly, oddly, grateful she wasn't better endowed. At least this way, he could pretend there wasn't a luscious woman underneath those little golf carts. A luscious woman who could make ugly golf-cart pajamas sexier than the skimpiest lingerie.

Renata smiled shyly at him—*shyly*, when he was thinking about things like barely there lingerie and even more barely there pajama necklines—and then, still wearing her terry-cloth turban, she moved back to her chair and picked up the book she'd left lying there. Then she thumbed through the pages until she found the one where she'd left off. And then, *then*, she did something really remarkable.

She continued with her reading. As if nothing had changed in the few minutes since she emerged from the bathroom in a cloud of prurience and pine soap and potential developments.

Fine. Two could play at that game.

"Beer?" he asked.

She threw him another sweet smile and shook her head. "No, thanks. I'm good."

Then she went back to reading. With her head still wrapped in a towel. And ugly golf-cart pajamas hiding every interesting part of her—except that tantalizing bit of skin between her breasts that had become even more tantalizing by how the shirt now gaped open enough to reveal she was better endowed than he'd first thought.

He moved back to the sofa and picked up the magazine he'd already flipped through. He was about to remark on the editorial about whatever the hell it was about when she tented her book in her lap and reached up to unwind the towel on her head. After that, he couldn't remember much of anything, because her dark hair came tumbling out and spilled around her shoulders in ropes of damp silk.

He watched as she scrubbed her scalp with the towel, something that shouldn't have been sexy but which was unbelievably sexy. Then she draped the towel over the arm of the chair and began to comb her fingers through her hair. Okay, that was something that normally would be sexy—if the woman doing it wasn't wrapped in little cartoon golf carts—but with Renata, it was seriously sexy. Even in little cartoon golf carts. Maybe because of the way the top of the pajama shirt was opening and closing in time with her movements. Or maybe because of the way strands of her hair were clinging to her neck and chest the way Tate wanted to be clinging himself. Or maybe because it was nighttime, and the two of them were stranded here alone, and neither of them was wearing underwear.

Ah, dammit. He'd hoped he wouldn't think about that again.

Did that even matter, though? What Renata was doing was sexy, period. And it was sexy because she was sexy. Hell, at this point, the cartoon golf carts were even sexy. And if Renata gave him the smallest indication that she was thinking about the same things he was thinking about at the moment, then there was nothing that could stop them from—

"Um, Tate?" she asked suddenly. Softly. In a *very* intimate voice.

He did his best to sound noncommittal. "Yes, Renata?"

"Could you… Would you…I mean, I was wondering if you would mind if…I was wondering if you would, um…"

Whatever her very intimate question was, she couldn't seem to finish it. Which naturally made Tate think it was something really, *really* intimate. Something that obviously involved him, too. In a way she wasn't able to put into words, so she was relying on that very intimate tone of voice to convey her very intimate thoughts.

Her very intimate desires?

In an effort to help her along, he assured her, "Whatever you want to do, Renata…whatever you want *me* to do…I promise that I not only could do it, I would do it. I wouldn't mind at all, and I definitely would."

She smiled at his thorough answer to her very intimate question. At least one of them could make clear what was going on in his head. Women were just so damned circuitous.

Slowly, she stood, pushing her mass of dark hair over her shoulder. Then she took a step forward, toward Tate. He tossed aside the magazine, set his beer on the table and sat up for whatever she planned to do. He was about to lift his arms to pull her into his lap when she spun around and, without a word, headed back to the bedroom.

Well, okay, then. He hadn't pegged her as the sort of woman who would want to skip foreplay and get right to the main event, but hey, whatever. He aimed to please. Even if he did actually enjoy foreplay. Maybe next time. Or the time after that. Or the time after that. As she'd said, they could be here a few days.

He followed her to the bedroom only to discover she'd gone into the bathroom and closed the door. Maybe she was shy about undressing in front of him. Not that a woman who had just blurted out that she wanted to have sex should have been shy about anything, but...whatever.

He turned down the bed and switched on the lamp beside it, unleashing a veritable desert sun onto the bed. Well, hell. That wouldn't do. He liked to see what he was doing when he was with a woman, but he didn't want to be blinded while he was doing it. He flicked the switch again, but the lamp in the living room was as dim as the one in here was bright and barely reached the bed.

He remembered finding candles and matches in the kitchen when he was looking for a can opener. They were the stumpy white emergency kind, but they'd do. As quickly as he could, he collected them and returned to the bedroom, setting two on the dresser and two on the nightstand, then lit them all. Once they were going, he stripped off his shirt and went to work on the buttons of his fly.

He'd reached the last one when the bathroom door

opened and Renata emerged, her attention focused on something in her hand she was drying with her towel.

"I really appreciate this, Tate. My hair is just so unmanageable when it's this wet, and there's no hair dryer in this place. It's always a lot easier if someone else brushes it for me. I couldn't find a brush, but I found this comb, and it has wide enough teeth that it should work okay, but I wanted to wash it first, natch, and—"

She stopped in her tracks—and stopped chattering, too—when she saw him standing shirtless and nearly pantsless with the bed unmade behind him and candles burning beside it. "What the…?" she muttered.

"I thought you wanted to have sex," he said.

She expelled a single, humorless chuckle. "No."

She was so emphatic, the two-letter response actually came out with two syllables as *no-oh*. Then, as if he hadn't already figured out how emphatically she was saying no, she hastily clarified, "I want you to comb my hair."

"But you sounded like you wanted to have sex," he persisted, his testosterone, at least, not willing to give up the fight.

She gazed at him, mystified. "What about anything I said could have possibly sounded like I wanted to have sex?"

He replayed their conversation in his head. "Um, all of it?"

She was silent for a moment, but looked thoughtful enough that he could tell she was replaying the conversation in her head, too. For another hopeful moment, he thought she'd reply, *Oh, yeah. I guess I did sound like*

I wanted to have sex. Okay. Let's have sex! Then her expression went confused again.

"There is no way you could have mistaken any of that for me wanting to have sex."

Fine. Tomatoes, tomahtoes.

He countered, "Well, I sure as hell couldn't tell you wanted me to comb your hair."

She said nothing for another moment, then, very quietly, asked, "Could you please button up your pants?"

Tate didn't think he'd ever had a woman ask him that question before. And, truth be told, it kind of startled him to hear it now. He'd just never had a woman turn him down. Ever. Even before he'd become the success he was now, with all the showy plumage of cars and cash and castle. When he was a college student living in a dump of a loft, he'd still always had girls over, whenever he'd asked. Hell, when he was in high school, driving a beat-up Ford Falcon, his backseat had seen constant action. Women had just always flocked to him, from the time he was old enough to want them to.

Except for Renata Twigg.

His gaze still fixed on hers, he began to rebutton his jeans. And he could barely believe his eyes when she actually turned her head to keep from watching him. How could a woman who inspired such abject wantonness in a man be too shy to watch him put himself back together? Especially when he hadn't even been completely undone?

"Thank you," she said when he'd finished. Still not looking at him, she added, "Now could you put your shirt back on, too?"

He bit back a growl of irritation as he grabbed the T-shirt from the bed and thrust it back over his head.

"Thank you," she said again.

But she still wasn't looking at him. Jeez, was he that unappealing?

Then he remembered she hadn't found him unappealing that afternoon. She'd melted into that kiss with as much appetite as he had. Even when she told him it wasn't a good idea for them to continue, she'd been clinging to his shirt as if she wanted to pull him back again. And the look in her eyes… There was no way a man could mistake a look like that. Since then, more than once, he'd caught her eyeing him in a way that made him think—no, made him *know*—she liked what she saw when she looked at him.

So it wasn't that Renata didn't want him the same way he wanted her. It was that she didn't want to want him the same way he wanted her. Which actually just confused him even more.

Women were weird. Why was sex such a big deal to them?

"So I guess this means you won't help me comb out my hair, huh?" she asked quietly.

He'd forgotten that was what she'd asked him to do. Then he surprised himself by saying, "No, this doesn't mean that."

Because, in spite of her not wanting to want him, Tate still wanted her. He had no idea why. Even if no woman had ever rebuffed him before, he wasn't the kind of guy to keep after one who did, regardless of her reasons. But he still wanted to be close to Renata. He still

wanted to touch her. He still wanted to inhale great intoxicating gulps of her scent. And if combing her hair
would bring him close enough to do those things, he
was content to do it.

He sat on the bed and patted the empty place beside
himself. "Sit down," he said. Then he held out his hand.
"Give me the comb."

She studied him warily, then took a small step forward and handed him the comb. He took it without
hesitation, then patted the seat beside him again. She
took another step, one that brought her close enough
for him to tumble her to the bed if he wanted. Which
he did want. But she didn't. So he only patted the mattress one last time.

Finally, she sat, the bed giving enough beneath her to
send her leaning his way. Her shoulder bumped his, but
she ricocheted off and turned her back. After thrusting
two big handfuls of hair over her shoulders, she mumbled another breathy thank-you and waited for him to
begin. Tate lifted the comb to her long, dark, sexy hair
and, as gently as he could, began to tug it through the
mass.

Eight

Boys were weird.

As Renny sat on the edge of the mattress with her back to Tate, she tried to focus on that thought and not the other one attempting to usurp it about how good it felt to have his fingers running through her hair. That first thought made a lot more sense than the second did, anyway. Boys were weird. Men were even weirder.

All they ever thought about was sex, and everything had some kind of sexual component to it. There was no way Tate should have thought she was talking about sex when she was talking about hair combing. She hadn't said a single word that was suggestive. On the other hand, it did feel kind of sexy the way he was combing her hair…

He was surprisingly gentle, cupping one hand tenderly over the crown of her head as he carefully pulled the comb along with small gestures. When he finished one section of hair, he pushed it forward over her shoulder and moved to another to start again. Her scalp warmed under his touch, a sweet, mellow heat that gradually seeped downward, into her neck and over her shoulders, then lower still, along her arms and down to the middle of her back.

"You're good at this," she said softly, closing her eyes.

He said nothing for a moment, then replied, just as softly, "Let me know if I hurt you."

"No worries," she quickly assured him.

Renny stopped thinking and just let herself feel. With her eyes closed, her other senses leaped to the fore. She heard the steady patter of rain on the window, smelled the clean scent of pine soap enveloping them. But most of all, she savored the warmth of Tate's palm on her head and the brush of his fingers along her neck, down her back and up again, as he untangled one strand of hair and moved it over her shoulder, followed by another. And another. And another. Again and again, his hand stroked her from her head to her waist, until all of her hair was streaming over her left shoulder, and the right side of her neck lay exposed.

By then, she felt like a rag doll, boneless and limp, her entire body evanescing into a state of serenity. Although he'd finished his task, Tate still sat behind her, and Renny said nothing to encourage him to move. On the contrary, she kind of wanted him to stay there forever, because even the slightest shift in their positions might ruin the sense of well-being that had come over her, a feeling that nothing in the world could ever go wrong again.

So lovely was the feeling that it seeped from her inside to her outside, manifesting as the brush of soft kisses along her neck and shoulders. Then she realized it wasn't she who was creating the sensation. It was Tate. He was dragging butterfly-soft openmouthed kisses over her sensitive flesh, pushing aside the fabric of her shirt as he went, stirring her already-incited senses to even greater awareness. On some level, she knew she should tell him to stop. But on another level, that was the last thing she wanted him to do.

"Tate," she murmured, still not sure what she wanted to say.

"Shh," he whispered, the soft sough a warm rush against her skin.

She opened her mouth to object again, but he nipped her shoulder lightly, igniting a blast of heat in her belly that flared into her chest and womb. She cried out softly in response, so he placed a soft kiss on the spot, tasted it with the flat of his tongue and peppered her shoulder with more caresses. Somewhere in the dark recesses of her brain, an alarm bell rang out, but the roar of blood in her ears deafened her to it. Especially when he roped an arm around her waist and pulled her back against himself, nuzzling the sensitive place behind her ear before dropping a kiss to her jaw.

It had been so long since she had enjoyed this kind of closeness with another human being. So long…

Too long.

Unable to help herself, Renny arced one arm backward, to skim her fingers through his hair. It was all the encouragement Tate needed. The hand at her waist rose higher, curling over her breast, thumbing the sensitive peak. She cried out again at the contact, the sound fracturing the stillness, and arched her body forward. Deftly, he unbuttoned her shirt and pushed the garment open, then cupped both hands over her naked breasts, kneading softly, rolling her nipples beneath his fingers. She gasped at the heat that shot through her and tried to turn to face him.

"Not yet," he whispered somewhere close to her ear.

She reached her other hand back to join the first, linking her fingers at the nape of his neck. Tate continued to stroke her breast with one hand as he dipped the other to the waistband of her pajamas. He effortlessly found the knot she'd tied in the side to keep them up, and just as effortlessly untied it. Then he dipped his hand beneath the fabric and between her legs, finding the feminine heart of her.

"Oh, God, you're already so wet," he murmured as he slid a finger inside her.

She gasped again, pushing her hips forward. He met her eagerly, driving his finger deeper, then sliding it out to furrow it between the hot folds of her flesh. Slowly, slowly...oh, so slowly...he caressed her, drawing intimate circles over her before pushing in and out of her again. He fingered her for long minutes, a hot coil inside her winding tighter and tighter as he did, until she feared she would explode from the sensations. Her breathing became more ragged, her pulse rate leaped and just when she thought she would come, he removed his hand and drew it upward again, laying it flat against her naked belly.

"Not yet," he whispered again.

In the candlelight, she felt more than saw him slip her shirt from her shoulders and toss it to the floor. But she couldn't help watching when he stood to remove his, too, reaching behind himself to grab a fistful of white cotton and drag it forward over his head. Beneath it, he was an awesome sight, muscle and sinew corded into a torso that could have been wrought by the hands of a Greek god. His biceps bunched as he undid the buttons of his fly one by one, until his blue jeans hung open on his hips, his member pushing hard against the soft denim. Then he joined her again on the bed, urging her toward the mattress until she was on her back and he was atop her, bare flesh to bare flesh. And then his mouth was on hers, consuming her, and it was all Renny could do not to come apart at the seams.

He touched her everywhere as he kissed her. He skimmed his palm along her rib cage, then into the narrow dip of her waist, then over her hip, down to her thigh and back again. Every time his hand moved over her, her pajama bottoms dipped lower, until he was tugging them out from under her and tossing them to the floor, too. And then Renny lay beneath him naked, feeling wanton, scandalous and aroused.

She explored Tate, too, running her hands over the bumps of muscle in his shoulders and arms, splaying her fingers wide over the silky skin of his back, dipping her hands beneath the loose denim on his hips to cup his taut buttocks. There wasn't an inch of him that wasn't hot and hard, especially when she guided her hand between their bodies and into his jeans to curl her fingers around his heavy shaft. He gasped at the contact, tasting her deeply and moving his hand between her legs again.

For long moments, they petted each other, matching their rhythm in languid strokes that gradually grew more demanding. As Renny drew near the precipice of an orgasm again, Tate suddenly pulled away, standing at the side of the bed.

With a devilish grin, he hooked his fingers in the waistband of his jeans and urged them down, until he was naked, too, gilded in the warm candle glow.

And if Renny had thought him an awesome sight before, now he was spectacular.

He moved back to the bed, sitting on its edge and pulling Renny into his lap to face him, straddling him. She guided her hands to his hair, stroking her palms over the silky tresses, loving the feel of having him so close. When he ducked his head to her breast, sucking her nipple deep into his mouth, she cried out again. And when he tucked his fingers gently into the elegant line bisecting her bottom to gently trace it, she gasped. But when he moved his hard shaft toward the damp, heated center of her, she drew herself backward, covering him again with her hand to halt his entry.

She couldn't quite bring herself to tell him to stop, though. She didn't want him to stop. She wanted him. A lot. It had been so long since she'd enjoyed this kind of release. It felt so good to be with him. And he was the kind of man she would never meet again. Why shouldn't she have one night with him? Where was the harm?

Oh, right. They'd had to leave without even the most basic essentials. Like, for instance, birth control.

"I want you, Renata," Tate said, his voice low and erotic, his hot gaze fixed on hers. "I really, really want you."

"I want you, too," she said. "But this is happening so fast, and I didn't exactly come prepared."

Boy, talk about a double entendre. Especially since she was less concerned about the birth control aftermath of a night like this than she was the emotional aftermath. She was at a place in her cycle where pregnancy was extremely unlikely, and her lady parts worked like clockwork. Would that she could be as confident that other parts of her body—like her heart—were as predictable.

"I didn't come prepared for a party, either," he told her. "But that doesn't mean we can't still have fun."

Before she could say any more, he dragged his fingers against her again, catching the sensitive nub of her clitoris gently between his thumb and middle finger. Renny gasped as he caressed her, heat rocketing through her body, pooling in her womb, driving all coherent thought from her brain. When he drove his finger into her again, she knew it would never be enough. She wanted more of him. She wanted all of him. She needed him inside her. Now. Her body demanded it.

That could be the only explanation for why she told him, "I won't get pregnant, Tate. The timing is completely wrong. And I want you inside me. Please. Make love to me. Now."

It was all the encouragement he needed. He pulled her close again, pressing his mouth to hers. Then he lifted her over himself and pulled her down, entering her slow and long and deep. When she opened her legs to accommodate him, he pushed hard against her, filling her, widening her even more. All she could do was wrap her arms around his neck and hang on for the ride.

And she rode him well, rising and falling on him, his shaft going deeper inside her with each new penetration. He moved his mouth to her breasts, cupping his other hand over her bottom to steady her. Faster and faster, they cantered, until he rolled them onto the bed so that Renny was on her back again beneath him. Then he rose to his knees and, gripping her ankles in both hands, spread her wide. With a few more thrusts, he drove himself as deep as he could, then spilled himself inside her until he had nothing left to give. Renny cried out at their culmination, a rocket of heat spiraling through her. She felt as if she would be fused to him forever, hoped they would never be apart again.

And then they were both on their backs, panting for breath and groping for thought, neither seeming to know what the hell had just happened. She gazed up into the candlelit darkness, afraid to look anywhere else. Part of her was already sorry she had succumbed to Tate so quickly, so easily. But part of her couldn't wait for it to happen again.

And that, she supposed, was where the root of her fear lay. That having had Tate once, she would never have him enough. Or, even worse, she would never have him again.

* * *

Renny woke to the steady rat-a-tat of rain on the window and smiled sleepily. She loved rain. Rain made the pace of a day seem slower somehow. She always let herself sleep in a few extra minutes when it rained, and she always gave herself a little more time to get ready for work, since no one at Tarrant, Fiver & Twigg ever seemed to be on time, anyway, when it rained. Today would be no exception. Why not relish a few more minutes of semiconsciousness before the day became too full? She sighed with much contentment and reached across the mattress to the nightstand to push the snooze button on her alarm clock…

Only to discover her alarm clock wasn't where it was supposed to be. Nor had it gone off in the first place. When she opened her eyes, she realized her alarm clock wasn't the only thing missing. So was her bedroom. So was her bed. So were her clothes. What the hell? Why was she naked?

She bolted upright at the memories that flooded over her, each more erotic than the one preceding it. Tate unbuttoning her pajama buttons one by one. Tate tracing the lower curve of her breast with his tongue. Tate guiding his fingers between her legs to wreak havoc on the feminine heart of her.

Oh, *that* was why she was naked.

What had she done? Renny Twigg was not the kind of woman who succumbed to a pretty face that easily, that quickly or that passionately. Even faces as pretty as Tate's that were attached to millions—perhaps billions—of dollars. Even in situations of extreme emotional upheaval like the one in which she'd found herself. Her behavior last night had been completely out of character for her.

But maybe, since the situation she and Tate were in was also uncharacteristic, she shouldn't beat herself up for that. No, what she should beat herself up for was not protecting herself by taking proper precautions. She'd told Tate the truth when she assured him the timing wasn't right for her to get pregnant, and she was confident she wouldn't. But the world was full of large families who'd tried to time that sort of thing correctly. And there were other things to worry about with regard to protection—or the lack thereof. Sure, most of them could be addressed with a simple dose of antibiotics, but still.

She had behaved irresponsibly last night. And there was no way she would let that happen again.

So…where did she put her clothes? Or, rather, where had Tate put her clothes? She had a vague memory of her pajama top cartwheeling over her head in a blur of tiny golf carts, but after that, all she could remember was—

Never mind. Best not to think about those things again. She located both the pajama top and bottoms and was knotting the latter at her waist when she registered the aroma of…bacon? Where was that coming from?

She did her best to wind her hair into something that wouldn't lead to the kind of trouble it had led to last night, then tried to look like someone who knew what she was doing as she exited the bedroom. She discovered the answer to the bacon question immediately. Tate was standing in front of the stove—barefoot and shirtless with his jeans dipping low on his hips—stirring something in a frying pan. As she drew nearer, she saw a modest pile of bacon on a plate beside him and what appeared to be scrambled eggs in the pan. There was even something steaming in a saucepan that looked—and kind of smelled—like…the magic bean! Coffee!

For a minute, she thought maybe she was dreaming. That maybe she'd dreamed the entire frenetic night the two of them had shared, because she knew for a fact that there had been no eggs or bacon in the refrigerator the day before, never mind the magic bean. Then she thought maybe Inspector Grady had returned from town with groceries, something that would mean a potential escape from this place, but would also be mortifying for a number of reasons, few of which had anything to do with tiny cartoon golf carts on her person and everything to do with her having woken up naked in someone else's bed.

But no, her dreams had never included smells, so everything, including last night, must be real. Even the part about a gorgeous guy making breakfast in his bare feet.

"Good morning," she said, hoping she injected just the right blend of aplomb and nonchalance into her voice, despite the fact that she felt neither of those things.

When Tate spun around to smile at her, though, he looked as if he felt enough for both of them, something that just made Renny feel even worse. How could he be nonchalant and aplomby about something that had been so passionate and precarious?

"Good morning," he greeted her cheerfully. "You were sleeping so soundly when I woke up, I didn't want to disturb you." He grinned devilishly. "I figured you could use the extra sleep after last night."

Wow, he was really going to go there. And so quickly, too. Renny rushed to change the subject. Last night was a place she never intended to visit again. Certainly not while the person she'd experienced it with was standing right there in front of her. So she said the only thing she could.

"Coffee. You created coffee. Out of nothing. You must be a god."

He looked a little disappointed that she didn't take his *about last night* comment and run with it. "I kind of created coffee. Out of boiling water. It's instant, so it's more like a coffee impostor. I guess that just makes me a demigod."

Renny didn't care. As long as he poured her some. Which he did. And she tasted it. And it was good.

"Where did you find eggs?" she asked after she'd ingested a few fortifying sips. "I thought Wisconsin was famous for its dairy products, not its roving bands of wild forest chickens."

For a moment, he looked as if he wasn't going to let her get away with changing the subject from what had happened the night before, because he intended to revisit it over and over again. But when he realized she was serious about steering the topic in a new direction, he turned back around to stir the eggs some more.

"They're powdered eggs," he said. "There was a package of them in the cabinet behind the canned stuff.

There's some powdered milk up there, too, if you're worried about calcium deficiency."

Oh, sure. What were powdered eggs without powdered milk to go with them? From singularly icky to doubly icky. Win-win.

"No, that's okay," she said. "But last time I checked, there was no such thing as powdered bacon. Where did you find that?"

"Freezer," he said, still not looking at her. "One of those foil bricks was what was left of a rasher. No idea how long it's been in there, but it smelled fine."

"It still smells fine," she said. "Thanks for making breakfast."

He finally looked at her again. He smiled again, too, but the look wasn't quite as cheerful this time. "You're welcome. It's the least I can do for you after last—"

He stopped before finishing, obviously remembering her reluctance to talk about what had happened, a surprisingly considerate gesture.

He looked down at the eggs again and repeated softly, "It's the least I can do for you."

So he really was cooking breakfast for her. No guy had ever cooked breakfast for Renny. Even with past boyfriends, when she'd stayed at their place, they always expected her to fix breakfast for them in the morning. It was why she'd always made sure to pick up a bag of doughnuts on her way when she knew she'd be staying over at their places.

"Have a seat," he said. "I'll bring you a plate."

She made her way to the sofa, moving aside the book

and magazine she and Tate had discarded there last night before they—

Gah. Was there no escape from thoughts of their lovemaking? Immediately, she corrected herself. They hadn't made love. They'd had sex. A purely physical reaction to a purely physical attraction. Making love was a whole 'nother animal, one she still wasn't sure she'd ever experienced. To make love, you had to be in love. And love was one of those things Renny figured a person didn't know until she felt it. As far as she could tell, she hadn't. Not yet, anyway.

She had just seated herself on the sofa when Tate brought over two plates with identical servings of bacon and eggs. Then he went back for two glasses of orange juice, the concentrate for which, he informed her, had also been lurking under some of the frosted foil in the freezer. A major lover of OJ, Renny enjoyed a healthy taste of it from her glass…only to realize it tasted like freezer-burned aluminum so she immediately spit it back into the vessel again. Much to her horror. The only thing worse than wearing golf-cart pajamas in front of a gorgeous guy was spitting out food in front of a gorgeous guy. Especially food he'd made. But, really, the stuff in that glass… It was way worse than golf-cart pajamas.

Tate looked dashed by her reaction, as if he'd planted, picked and pressed the fruit in his own backyard, and her rejection of it was tantamount to a rejection of him. "Is there a problem with the juice?" he asked.

"Um, no," Renny lied hastily. Even more hastily, she placed the glass back on the table. "I just remembered, uh…orange juice doesn't agree with me."

Tate didn't look convinced. He picked up his glass, filled his mouth with a hefty quaff...and immediately spit it back out again. "That tastes like the hardware store where my father worked." His gaze flew to hers. "Hey. I remembered something about my father. The store where he worked smelled like metal. Why am I just remembering that?"

Renny smiled back. "I think people's five senses are irrevocably synced with their memory banks. Most of my earliest memories are all of things I could taste or hear or smell."

He nodded, but his thoughts seemed to be a million miles away. Or maybe just a few hundred miles away. In the Indiana town where he'd grown up. Or, rather, where he'd been relocated when he was a toddler.

"Sit. Eat," Renny instructed him gently. "Maybe the bacon will taste like metal, too, and you'll remember even more."

Actually, the bacon tasted like Freon. And the eggs tasted like glue. But Renny managed to consume every bite. Because a gorgeous guy had made breakfast for her and that made everything better.

By the time they finished breakfast, the rain had diminished to a soft patter. So soft that a handful of birds were even singing. Renny went to the window and found that the clouds were less ominous than they'd been the day before. When she opened the window this time, she was greeted by a soft, if still damp, breeze, and that aroma of not-so-far-off water.

She inhaled deeply, relishing the fresh air. She liked living in New York, but some days she needed to be surrounded by green space. As bad as it was to be forcibly separated from civilization, it was kind of nice to be forcibly separated from civilization. And now that the rain was letting up some…

"We should get outside today," she said impulsively.

She turned to find Tate looking at her as if she'd just told him they should fly to Mars.

"What?" he asked.

"We should get out of the cottage for a while," she repeated. "Go exploring."

"Are you nuts? Everything out there is soaking wet."

"Then let's go fishing. If Inspector Grady doesn't make it back today—and considering last night's rain, there's a good chance he won't—then I'll make whatever we catch for dinner tonight. It's the least I can do for the guy who made me breakfast."

She might as well have told him they should drink hemlock for dinner, so repelled did he look by the suggestion.

"Really," she said. "We can't be far from water. It might even be Lake Michigan. Maybe there's a boat or something we could take out."

"You want to fish in Lake Michigan?" he said dubiously. "You want to *eat* the fish you catch in Lake Michigan? Do you know how many industries dump waste into Lake Michigan?"

"We're hundreds of miles away from Chicago. Wisconsin lake water has to be totally different from Chicago lake water."

"Funny thing about water. It does this thing where it moves around a lot. 'Flowing,' I think, is the word they use for it. That means the water—and fish—around Chicago could easily make their way to Wisconsin. Along with all the toxic waste they've consumed beforehand."

"Oh, please. You just ate bacon and eggs that might have been brought here by Donnie Brasco."

"Yeah, but that's a one-off from my usual eating habits. It's not like I eat crap every day."

"At least fish is whole food," she said. "Who knows what goes into powdered eggs? Not eggs, I bet."

He said nothing, but she could tell by his expression that he wasn't going to back down.

"Fine," she relented. "You don't have to eat what we catch. There will just be that much more for me. We're still going fishing. Because if I have to be cooped up in this cottage for another day…"

She let her voice trail off. Not because she figured an unspoken threat was a much more ominous threat, even if that was true. But because she started actually thinking about what would happen if she had to be cooped up in the cottage for another day. And it bore a striking resemblance to what had happened in the cottage last night.

Fishing, she reminded herself. She and Tate would spend the day fishing. Just as soon as she could find something to wear.

Tate had to give Renata credit for one thing. Well, actually, he had to give her credit for a lot of things. But most of those he probably shouldn't mention, since she'd made clear she didn't want to talk about last night.

The one thing he could give her credit for at the moment was that she could take a man's gigantic lavender shirt and turn it into…something else. Something without sleeves, since she'd ripped those off and tied them together to make a belt—or something—and with some kind of complicated tying maneuver at the bottom that turned that part of the shirt into shorts that fell just above her knees. Sort of. The rest of the garment was baggy and unhindered by anything resembling a pattern. To him, it just looked like, well…

"It's a romper," she told him in a voice that indicated he should know exactly what that meant.

"So it's for romping?" he asked. "Women have to have special clothes for that?" Frankly, his idea of romping worked a lot better with no clothes at all.

"No, a romper isn't for romping. It's for…" She expelled an irritated sound. "How the hell do I know what a romper is for? Some fashion designer sewed a shirt and shorts together at some point, called it a romper and it stuck. The fashion world hates women, you know. They make us buy things we don't want or need. Hence—" she swept her hands from her shoulders to her knees "—the romper." Now she settled her hands on her hips. "Hey, it beats golf-cart pajamas. Especially for fishing."

Tate battled the urge to shake his head. She really was the strangest woman he'd ever met. Not that he meant that in a disparaging way. Which was weird because, until now, he'd always considered strange people in a disparaging way. Renata brought a certain flair to strangeness. Even her romper had a certain, uh, je ne sais quoi. For lack of a proper industry term. Which probably didn't exist for an outfit like that.

They'd been cleaning up breakfast when Inspector Grady called again to tell them the roads were still out, he was still stuck in Pattypan and it could be another twenty-four hours before he could get to them. But, on the upside, the tech guys were making some headway into the computer breach that had exposed Tate's identity, and with any luck, they'd soon know exactly who John Smith on Craigslist was and just how far his crimes went.

The news that Tate and Renata were going to be stuck here for another day should have been calamitous. Instead, neither of them had been that broken up by it. In fact, it had cemented her conviction that they should spend the day fishing, and she'd gone in search of gear. A closet near the kitchen held a number of discoveries, not the least of which was a stack of board games—something she'd been so excited about she might have stumbled upon the Hope Diamond. Mixed in with them was a quartet of fishing rods and all their accessories.

Satisfied they had all the necessary accoutrements, she'd headed to the bedroom to see what she could do with the remaining clothing. Forty-five minutes later, she emerged in her current getup. He supposed it could sort of qualify for resort wear. In some parts of the world. Where people didn't have any taste.

"What about shoes?" he asked, noting her bare feet. Of course, he was still barefoot, too, but he at least had his polo boots to wear. She only had heels.

"Barefoot is fine," she said. "I love going barefoot.

I never wore shoes when I was a kid. Unless my mom caught me."

Her last statement was short, but she'd delivered it in a tone of voice that spoke volumes. Tate could relate. As much as he'd tried to please his mother and stepfather, he'd never felt he succeeded. Even before that, his mother had always given off a vibe that he was somehow disappointing her. Knowing what he did now, maybe that had had more to do with the fact that his father's family was a little unsavory. Back then, though, he had felt like it was his fault. With his stepfather, he'd always felt like maybe the guy saw him as a reminder that his mother had been involved with another man before him. Or maybe, he, too, thought Tate's origins weren't up to snuff.

Oh, hell, what did it matter? Neither of them was around anymore, and Tate had more than made a success of himself. If parts of his family tree were blighted, that wasn't his fault, was it? You couldn't blame a child for the gene pool that spawned it. Well, you could—and a lot of people did—but it wasn't fair. It wasn't right, either. Lots of people rose above humble, or even lurid, beginnings to make good.

Having obviously given up on his approval of her wardrobe, Renata collected the fishing poles and tackle she'd set aside earlier. "Come on. There's finally a break in the rain. The fish will be looking for food."

"We don't have any bait," he said, making one last-ditch effort to get out of fishing and spend the day in the great indoors instead. Now that the heat had broken— some—it might even be tolerable.

"Fish love freezer-burned bacon. Trust me."

As if he had any choice. He'd never been fishing in his life. She could tell him fish spent their days dancing the merengue in funny hats, and he'd have no way to disprove it.

"Fine," he relented. "But if we haven't caught anything after an hour, we're coming back here."

"Two hours," she bargained.

"Ninety minutes."

She stuck out her hand and smiled. "Deal."

Nine

An hour after slinging their fishing lines into the lake, they'd actually caught three fish, and Tate was itching to catch more. It wasn't Lake Michigan they'd discovered, after all, but Lake Something Else that was small enough to be ensconced by wilderness all around its perimeter. A pier extended a good thirty or forty feet from the shoreline, so they'd made their way to the end of it, sat on its edge and plunked their lines into deep water.

Renata caught the first fish within fifteen minutes of their arrival, a six-inch trout whose breed she'd recognized immediately, and which she'd thrown back in, saying it wasn't big enough. She'd handled it with a confidence he'd envied, then deftly baited the hook again, cast out the line with an easy whir and, after another ten minutes, caught a second, larger trout. Deeming it worthy of dinner, she'd stashed it in the cooler she'd also salvaged from the closet.

It had taken Tate nearly an hour to catch his fish, and it hadn't been much bigger than the first one Renata had caught. She'd been about to throw it back, too, but he rebelled, feeling pretty damned proud of his prize. So she'd smiled like an indulgent scoutmaster and stowed it in the cooler with the first. Then she'd caught the next one. She was two up on him, and hers were bigger. He was competitive enough to find that unacceptable. The next catch would be his, and it would be twice the size of her first one, or his name wasn't Tate Hawthorne. Then again, in reality, his name wasn't Tate Hawthorne, but that was beside the point.

"What's that smile for?"

He looked over to find Renata watching him with laughing eyes. "What smile?" he asked.

"You're grinning like an eight-year-old boy who just caught his first fish," she said.

"That's because I'm a thirty-two-year-old man who just caught my first fish."

She chuckled. "So there's still an eight-year-old boy in there somewhere."

Before today, Tate would have denied that. Hell, he didn't think he'd been an eight-year-old boy even when he was eight. He couldn't remember ever feeling like a child. Whenever he looked back at that time, there seemed to be such a pall over everything. His mother's fear and unhappiness, their struggle just to get through any given day, his small circle of friends that seemed to grow smaller with every passing year.

But he almost felt like a child today, sitting at the edge of a lake pier with his jeans rolled up and his legs dangling above the water. Although the sun was still stuck behind a broad slab of gray, the rain had finally stopped. Birds barnstormed the trees, warbling their happiness at being active again. The wind whispered over their heads, dragging along the scent of pine. Dragonflies darted along the water, leaving trails of what could have been pixie dust in their wakes.

And he'd caught a fish! All in all, not a bad way to spend an afternoon. He wished he'd known a few days like this when he was a kid. Or even one day like this when he was a kid.

He looked at Renata again. She sat on his left, her bare feet hovering within inches of his, her hair half in and half out of a lopsided topknot. Maybe if he'd met a girl like her when he was a boy, he would have had a few days like this one. She looked far more suited to this life—even in her ridiculous romper, which, he had to admit, was less ridiculous than it had seemed a little while ago—than she did to the one that demanded the crisp suit and hairstyle she'd worn when she'd shown up at his front door... Was that only yesterday morning? It felt like a lifetime had passed since then.

"Were you like this when you were a kid?" he asked impulsively.

He had meant for the question to be playful. He had thought it would make her smile. Instead, she sobered.

"Like what?" she asked.

He struggled to find the right words. He'd never been at a loss to describe something, but Renata defied description. "Adventurous," he finally said. Then a few more adjectives popped into his head. "Spontaneous. Unpredictable. Resourceful."

She looked more uncomfortable with every word he spoke. "I don't think I'm any of those things now."

He was about to call her on that—she was all those things and more—but he didn't want to see her withdraw further. Hoping to pull her back from wherever she was retreating, he asked, "Then what were you like as a kid?"

At first he thought she wouldn't answer that question, either. She seemed as determined to ignore it as she was what happened last night. She just reeled in her line until the hook came out of the water empty of even the bacon she had threaded onto it. She looked at the evidence of the one that got away, sighed dispiritedly, then reached into the tackle box for more bait.

And as she went about fixing it on the hook, she said, "As a child, I was…out of place."

He remembered their conversation of the day before, about how she'd attended one of those tony private schools with marble floors and mahogany paneling. He hadn't been surprised by the revelation then. Yesterday, that background had suited her. But looking at her now, he would never peg her as a product of that environment. In his line of work, he knew a lot of people who had grown up that way, clients and colleagues both, and none of them was like Renata. Then again, he wasn't sure if anyone was like Renata. He liked all those other people fine—some he even called friends. But he didn't feel he had a lot in common with them, even living in that world now himself.

He felt he had something in common with Renata, though, despite their disparate beginnings. He wasn't sure what, but they seemed to be kindred spirits. Maybe that was why they'd responded to each other so quickly. He'd been thinking last night was a result of the situation, not the woman. She really wasn't his type. Small, dark and chipper had never turned him on. But Renata did. And now that she did—

Now that she did, she didn't seem inclined to act on the attraction again. Which should have been fine with him. When it came to sex, Tate was pragmatic. Women came and went. He had fun with the ones who wanted to have fun until one or both of them grew tired of it, and then he moved on. Sometimes that happened after months, sometimes it happened after hours. It was looking like Renata was going to be one of those one-timers. So he should be in moving-on mode himself.

Strange thing was, he wasn't ready to move on. He was just starting to get to know her. And he wanted to know more. Those were both new developments. He was never the one who was finished with an encounter last. And he never wanted to know more about a woman than what was on the surface. It wasn't that he was shallow. It was just the way he was. At least, that was what he'd always thought.

It was a big day for firsts. All because of a woman who, twenty-four hours ago, he was wishing had never entered his life.

And he still didn't know what she'd been like when she was a kid. Except for thinking she was out of place.

But instead of asking her to elaborate on what she'd said, he said softly, "Me, too."

Maybe he'd been right about her being adventurous, spontaneous, unpredictable and resourceful as a kid. He could see how all those things would make her feel out of place in a world that valued tradition, orderliness and direction. Funny how he'd yearned for all those things in his childhood, without finding any of them.

They continued to fish in silence for a while, but it wasn't an uncomfortable silence. Nor was it exactly silent silence. The birds and bugs and beasts made sure of that, as did the wind and woods and water. It was almost as if time had dropped them here and stopped, freezing the moment for them because it was so damned near perfect. The only thing that would have made it better was a promise that it would go on forever.

And of all the firsts he'd experienced that day, that one was a monster. He was divorced from every single thing that gave his life meaning—his work, his home, his society, his technology—and there was a not-so-little part of him hoping to stay that way forever. How was that even possible?

He looked at Renata again. She had cast her line back into the water, but she didn't seem to be paying much attention to it. Her gaze was on the opposite shoreline—not that she seemed to be focused on that, either—and her expression was far too somber for someone who should be having fun.

Not sure where the impulse came from, Tate stretched one leg far enough to dip it into the lake, then kicked hard enough to send a small arc of water splashing over her. She squealed in indignant outrage, looking at him as if she couldn't believe he'd done what he did. He couldn't believe he'd done it, either. He was never this spontaneous or unpredictable. Then she smiled devilishly and dipped her own foot into the water. Or, at least, tried to. Unfortunately, her legs were too short to make it.

So Tate took advantage of her disadvantage and splashed her with his foot again.

"Hey! No fair!" she cried.

He was about to retort that all was fair in love and war, but since this was neither, he supposed she was right. But that didn't mean he had to play by the rules. Even though he'd lived his entire life playing by the rules.

He splashed her again.

She gaped even more incredulously. Then she put down her fishing pole and scooted closer to the edge of the pier, stretching her leg as far as it would go. She managed to get a couple of toes submerged, but when she tried to splash him back, all she achieved was a tiny blip of water that barely broke the surface. Tate laughed and splashed her again.

"Why, you little…" she muttered.

She tried to submerge her foot farther but nearly fell off the pier, righting herself at the last minute. Tate laughed some more, then watched with much amusement as she maneuvered herself onto her stomach, her arms dangling over the pier.

"Nice try," he said. "Your arms aren't any longer than your legs, small fry."

"Don't you dare call me 'small fry.' Sean Malone used to call me that, and he lived to regret it."

"Who's Sean Malone? Ex-boyfriend?"

Tate was surprised when a thread of jealousy wound through him. What did he care if Sean Malone was one of her ex-boyfriends? What did he care if he was a current boyfriend? He and Renata would never see each other again once this disaster was sorted out. Which felt less like a disaster today than it had yesterday. They'd still never see each other again after it ended. So whoever Sean Malone was, Tate didn't care. Except that he did, kind of.

"Sean Malone was the scourge of fifth grade," Renata said as she wormed her way closer to the edge of the pier again. "He had a nickname for everyone. Mine was 'small fry.' Until the day his locker started reeking with the massive stench of seafood gone bad, and he was sent to the head of school's office, where they put a mark on his permanent record. The entire east wing of Suffolk Academy had to be fumigated."

"And how exactly did the massive stench of seafood gone bad make its way to the entire east wing of Suffolk Academy?"

She grinned with much satisfaction. "It's amazing how bad a ten-piece deep-fried shrimp meal can smell if it's not refrigerated. Especially if you douse it with blue cheese dressing before you stash it in the locker of someone who's a complete slob and would never notice it until it started to reek. It took three days for it to really start stinking up the place, but once it did… Woo. And once Sean realized who was responsible, he never called me 'small fry' again. You, too, will live to regret it."

She stretched her arm as far as she could toward the water, but was still an inch or two shy of reaching it.

"Oh, yeah," Tate said. "I'm shaking in my boots."

He was about to splash her again when, with a final heroic effort, she pushed herself forward, thrust her hand into the lake and hit him with a palm-sized arc of water right in the face. Fortunately, she had small palms. Unfortunately, she also had bad leverage. He opened his eyes just in time to see her go tumbling into the lake headfirst.

She broke the surface immediately, sputtering indignantly, but quickly began to laugh. She pushed a few strands of hair out of her eyes, treaded water and said, "It was worth it to see the look on your face. I guess not too many people try to get even with you for stuff."

Tate grinned as he wiped the last of the water from his face. "I'm sure a lot of them would like to. They're just too busy."

She paddled back to the pier, and he extended a hand to help her up. She accepted it gratefully…then yanked him into the water alongside her. He had just enough time to suck in a breath before he went under, but when he broke the surface, it was to exhale in a burst of laughter. Renata was cute when she was trying to be vengeful and smug.

They paddled around each other for a moment, each trying to figure out if the other planned further retribution. Then she rolled onto her back to float and closed her eyes. She looked like someone who had all the time in the world to just drift around a Wisconsin lake without a care in the world. So Tate turned his body until he was floating, too. A curious dragonfly buzzed over him for a moment, then darted off. He watched until it disappeared into the trees, then looked up at the clouds. He couldn't remember the last time he'd gone swimming for more than laps at the gym. Hell, he couldn't remember the last time he'd looked up at the clouds. He wondered why not. Then he closed his eyes, too.

"You know," he heard Renata say from what sounded like a very great distance, "Grady could have done a lot worse by us when it came to choosing a safe house."

Her mention of the marshal brought Tate up short. He had momentarily forgotten why the two of them were here. He'd been having such a good time it felt like they'd planned this excursion months ago and finally found the time to sneak away from their jobs to enjoy it. He'd almost forgotten that, this time yesterday, they were practically strangers.

"On TV," she continued, "the cops always stash protected witnesses in some crappy no-tell motel and make them eat Taco Taberna carryout."

"Yeah, Beefaroni and powdered eggs are so much better," he said wryly.

"Don't be dissing my Beefaroni again, mister."

Tate smiled. "Sorry. My bad."

"I just meant that if we have to be held prisoner somewhere, there are worse places than a Wisconsin wilderness."

Until today, Tate would have said having to live any place whose population fell below two million would be hell. What was life without having everything you wanted at your fingertips? The Big Cheese Motor-Inn didn't even have basic cable. Talk about no-frills living. But he had to admit Renata might be right. Grady could have done worse than lakefronts and dragonflies.

"How much longer do you think we'll be here?"

He was surprised it was Renata asking the question. Then again, she didn't sound like someone who was anxious to leave. She sounded like someone who wanted to stay as long as possible.

"I don't know," he said. Funny, but he kind of sounded like someone who wanted to stay, too. "I guess until the feds locate the person who found me for you and make sure my information didn't go any farther than you."

He heard a splash in the water and opened his eyes. They'd drifted away from the pier, and Renata was swimming back to it. He watched as she gripped the edge with both hands and tried to hoist herself up, but it quickly became clear that she wouldn't be able to manage it on her own. Maybe she didn't like being called a small fry, but...she was a small fry. No shame in that. But there was no way she was getting out of the water on her own, either.

Tate swam to join her and did his best not to make it look effortless when he grabbed the edge of the pier and lifted himself up onto it. She tried valiantly to mirror his actions, but it finally became as clear to her that there was no way she was going to make it. Silently, he dropped to his knees and extended a hand to her again.

Even more effortlessly than he had pulled himself out of the water, he tugged her to the pier with him.

And instantly regretted it.

Soaked to the skin as she was, her so-called romper was clinging to every inch of her as if it was skin. And since she had forgone her still-damp underwear—as he had himself, something he really didn't need to be thinking about right now—it left absolutely nothing to the imagination. Her breasts pushed against the wet fabric, her quarter-sized areolae pink and perfect, her nipples stiff and tight. He remembered the feel of them in his mouth, so soft and hot, and it was all he could do not to duck his head to them again. Lower, the indentation of her navel beckoned, drawing his eye lower still, to the shadowy triangle at the apex of her legs. Unable to help himself, he roped an arm around her waist and covered her mouth with his, at the same time scooting his other hand down her torso to dip it between her thighs. She uttered a single small sound of protest, then melted into him and kissed him back.

Everything around him dissolved into nothing after that. All Tate registered was the feel of her mouth under his and the fabric of her shirt beneath his fingers. Hastily, he unbuttoned that part of the garment so he could tuck his hand inside. Then he furrowed his fingers into her damp flesh, catching the button of her clitoris between his knuckles before penetrating her with his middle finger. When she gasped at the invasion, he widened their mouths, tasting her more deeply. He felt her hand at his waist, unfastening his jeans, and then she was touching him just as intimately. Within seconds, he was hard as a rock and ready to rumble.

Where had this come from? This uncontrollable urge to touch her? To have her? He was never like this with other women. He was a disciplined, thorough lover. He liked to take his time. He could keep himself and his partner on a slow simmer until they were both ready to notch it higher. Hell, seduction was half the fun, even when it wasn't necessary because both parties knew they'd be in bed before the night was over.

But with Renata, there was no discipline. There was no simmer. There was just an explosion of wanting and heat and demand. One minute, he was laughing and playful, and the next, he was consumed by a need for her that was so powerful it superseded everything else. They weren't even inside the cabin. They were standing out in the middle of the world where anything could happen, where anyone could see them, even if they were, for the moment, alone. And he didn't even care. Hell, that just made it more exciting.

He withdrew his hand from her shirt long enough to unfasten the rest of the buttons. Then he peeled the wet garment from her body until she stood before him naked. He broke the kiss long enough to strip off his shirt and lower his jeans, and then...

They gazed at each other, silent save for their panting, her hands on his chest, his on her waist. No way could they make love on the pier—too many splinters. But making love in the water with the fish didn't hold much appeal, either. And there was no way he'd make it back to the motel without going off like a rocket.

He tightened his grip on her waist and lifted her into his arms. Her eyes widened when she realized his intention, but she roped her legs around his waist and her arms around his neck, then held on tight as he lowered her over his raging shaft. He slid into her so easily he might have been a missing part of her. Or maybe she was a missing part of him. He only knew they fitted together perfectly.

He bucked his hips upward as he pushed hers down, then repeated the action in reverse, relishing the hot friction. Something about the angle of their vertical bodies brought a new dimension to the sensation, and he knew he wouldn't last long. Not wanting her to be cheated, he braced one arm tightly around her waist and let the other go exploring, down over the curves of her ass, into the delicate crease that bisected it, pushing the tip of one finger into the dimple he found there.

She cried out again at this new intrusion, so he gave her a moment to adjust. She buried her head in the curve of his neck and shoulder and murmured her approval. So he jerked his hips up again, burying himself completely inside her, and gripped her bottom tighter as he deftly fingered her there.

He held off coming as long as he could, but within minutes, he was surging inside her. She tightened around him and cried out her own completion, bucking against him one final time before going limp in his arms. Carefully, he withdrew from her and lowered her back to the ground. But he didn't—couldn't—let her go. For long moments, they clung to each other, their bodies slick from their swim and the aftermath of their passion.

In the distance, thunder rumbled, silencing the chatter of the birds. The water rippled below them, and the wind whispered above them, but Tate was pretty sure its cool caress wasn't why they were both shivering.

Nothing like this had ever happened to him before. And somewhere deep inside, he knew nothing like this would ever happen again. Not the lovemaking in the great outdoors so much, but...something else. Something he wasn't sure he could identify. Something he wasn't sure he *should* identify. Because somehow he knew it had nothing to do with a Wisconsin lakefront.

And everything to do with Renata Twigg.

Ten

By the time Renny and Tate made their way back to the cottage, the sun was beginning its dip toward the trees. In the hours since leaving the motel, they'd put a half-dozen fish in the cooler, filled a T-shirt with wild blackberries, discovered a waterfall, explored a small cave and collected enough pinecones and interesting-looking rocks to fill a pinecone-and-interesting-looking-rocks room in the Smithsonian.

Oh, yeah. And they'd made love in a way Renny would have sworn wasn't possible. Not just the position, but the way it shattered her entire being, too.

She had been totally unprepared for Tate this afternoon…and yet totally ready for him, too. As quickly and feverishly as things had escalated, as wild and wanton as he'd made her feel, as far as she'd allowed things to go after swearing she would never let them go that far again…somehow it all seemed perfectly in keeping with the way of the world. With the way of Renny. At least the way the world and Renny had been since coming here. Being wild and wanton with Tate just felt right somehow. Being with Tate period felt right. It felt normal. With him, here in this place, she felt more like herself than she ever had with anyone anywhere before. And she felt as if she had been with him, here in this place, forever. It was weird. But nice.

Maybe too nice. She was starting to kind of wish the two of them could stay here like this forever.

Probably best not to think about it. She had dinner to make—she'd promised, since Tate made breakfast. Good thing, too, because he'd told her he'd never cleaned a fish in his life and made clear he had no plans to do it that didn't involve a zombie apocalypse—and even then the whole fish-cleaning thing was iffy, since there would be plenty of grocery stores ripe for the pillaging of peanut butter and jelly.

By the time dinner was on the coffee table—panfried trout with a blackberry reduction—the strange heat that had arced between them that afternoon was nearly forgotten. For the most part. Just to be on the safe side, Renny had changed back into her ugly pajamas after her shower when they got back to the cottage—not that those had been much of a deterrent the night before—and Tate was back in his polo jodhpurs and a different white T-shirt. Their clothes from earlier were drying in the bathroom. Not that Renny was in any hurry to put

on the alleged romper again. Not without proper underwear next time, anyway. Ahem.

In spite of that, she couldn't quite keep herself from
lighting a couple of the emergency candles and setting
them on the coffee table with their dinner. Not because
it was romantic, but because, um, they provided some
nice ambience. Yeah, that was it. The only thing that
could have made the setting more romantic…uh, she
meant ambient…was if they'd had a bottle of wine to go
with their meal. Then again, if previous occupants to
the place and their golf-cart pajamas were any indication, it would probably have been a bottle of Wiseguy
Vineyards Lambrusco, vintage last week. So maybe it
was just as well.

If Tate noticed the romantic…uh, ambient…candles
when he sat down, he didn't mention them. She wondered how he felt about what had happened on the pier
this afternoon. About what had happened last night.
About everything that had happened since the two of
them arrived here. Was he as surprised and dazed as
she was about their responses to each other? Did he
feel the same sense of timelessness and otherworldli-
ness about the last two days that she did? Or was all of
this just an inconvenience and ordeal for him to have
to get through, and he was just doing whatever he had
to do to stay sane? He had told her sex would be a nice
way to pass the time. Was that really all it was to him?
Why couldn't that be all it was to her?

And what the hell was she supposed to do about the
whole hacking thing? She could end their forced confinement here by admitting to Inspector Grady that she

knew perfectly well who had hacked the system and located Tate for her and reveal Phoebe's identity. But that would open Phoebe up to federal charges. And probably Renny, too, for being a part of it. What was weird, though, was that Renny was worried less about federal charges and time in the state pen than about Tate's reaction to her admission that she could have prevented this entire episode—or could end it at any time—by just telling the truth. She didn't want to admit anything, and she didn't want to end it right away. And deep down, that had nothing to do with her fear of federal charges and time in the state pen.

In spite of the jumble of thoughts and questions plaguing her, Renny enjoyed her dinner with Tate. They were so comfortable together at this point that they could have been any normal couple eating in their own dining room, the way they would every night—even though they weren't a couple. Then they cleaned up afterward in the same comfortable way. Once that was done, however, they both seemed to be at loose ends. Neither seemed interested in reading, the way they had done the night before, but neither seemed willing to broach the subject of other pursuits. Probably because the pursuit the two of them had enjoyed together the most since their arrival was sex. So it only made sense for Renny to suggest—

"Scrabble," she said, once the last of the dishes were put away. "We should play Scrabble. Everybody loves Scrabble, right?"

Judging by Tate's expression, he didn't love Scrabble. Even so, she hurried to the closet and pulled the game out from the middle of a stack of other board games. When she turned back around, Tate was still standing in the kitchenette, looking like he didn't love Scrabble.

"Or there's Trivial Pursuit," she said, thinking maybe he was more of a trivia buff. "Or Monopoly." Which actually might have been the best choice, because that game went on forever and had the most potential to keep them out of trouble.

He shook his head. "Scrabble is fine."

Before he could change his mind, she scrambled to the sofa and opened the board, putting one wooden rack on her side, and the other on his. As she turned the letter tiles upside down in the box lid—the letter bag was missing, as were a number of tiles, she couldn't help noticing—Tate strode to the chair and moved it closer to the table. By the time he sat down, she had mixed up the letter tiles and chosen her seven. All but one were consonants, but the vowel was at least an *A*. Even so, it would probably be best to let Tate go first, so she could play off whatever he spelled.

"You go first," she said magnanimously.

He weighed his options for a moment, sorting his letters into different combinations. Then he used every single letter he had to spell out *P-H-A-R-Y-N-X*, with the *Y* on the double letter square. Not to mention the extra fifty points for using all his letters.

"What?" she cried. "That's one hundred and fifty-two points, right off the bat!" And of course he had positioned the word so that it was impossible for her to make it plural, even if she did manage to pick an *E* and an *S* at some point.

Tate grinned as he collected seven more tiles. "You're the one who wanted to play Scrabble. Everybody loves Scrabble, right?"

Oh, hardy-har-har-har. Fine. She'd show him. At some point. Once she picked an *E* and a *U* to go with her *C, F, K* and *R.* In the meantime, she used her *A* and *W* with his *P* to spell *P-A-W.* At least that last letter was on a triple letter square. Sixteen points. Not too horribly embarrassing. Except for it being a measly three letters.

"So obviously, you're great at Scrabble," she said. "You must play it a lot."

"Actually, no," he said as he arranged his new tiles. "I like words. I was a huge reader when I was a kid."

She remembered his description of his solitary childhood. Of course he'd been a big reader, if he was alone a lot. But Renny's youthful society had been packed with other kids and tons of activities, and she'd been a big reader, too. All the better to escape that society and those activities, inevitably the kind that had dictated specific roles for male and female alike, and the latter had too often included things like, well, pink tutus.

"What was your favorite book when you were a kid?" she asked.

"Anything with knights and castles. You?"

"Anything with pioneer girls."

He smiled. "Renata Ingalls Wilder."

She smiled back. "Pretty much. Is that why you bought your house? Because it looks like a castle?"

He'd been about to lay down another word but halted. "Noticed that similarity, did you?"

"Kind of impossible not to."

He nodded, then used the *X* he'd used in *P-H-A-R-Y-N-X* to spell out *X-R-A-Y-S*. Dammit.

"The reason I liked castles," he said as he collected four more tiles from the box lid, "was that they're impenetrable. Nobody can get to you when you're in a castle, you know? No Viking hordes in longboats. No lance-bearing Napoleonic armies. No katana-swinging ninjas. No light-saber-wielding Sith lords. Maybe I was trying to find reasons for why I was always alone myself. If I lived in a castle, of course no one would be able to enter my life."

"But you're not alone anymore," she said. A man like him must have scores of friends. "Why do you live in a castle now?"

Still looking at his letters, he replied, "Same reason."

"But—"

"It's your turn," he interrupted her.

Crap. She didn't have any vowels. Hastily, she used her *C*, *R* and *F* with the *T* she'd just drawn to spell *C-R-A-F-T* with the *A* in his *P-H-A-R-Y-N-X*. Better. But her replacement letters were all consonants again. They were definitely going to run out of vowels, unless Tate had just drawn enough to spell *onomatopoeia*. So when he used the *A* in *X-R-A-Y-S* to spell *B-A-R-N*, she knew they were in trouble.

"There," he said. "That word should appeal to your pioneer girl heart. Why were you a fan of early settlers?"

She much preferred to go back to a discussion of his self-inflicted solitary confinement in his castle—why would a man like him want to keep people at bay?—

but the look on his face made clear he was finished talking about it.

So she replied, "Because they were leaving behind society to literally forge their own path in the world. They were going someplace where the rules of culture and civilization as they knew it were changed. Not to mention they spent a lot of time outdoors doing cool pioneer stuff."

Tate chuckled. "Your pioneer girl and my knight boy probably would have gotten along pretty well."

"Only if she could have gotten past his walls. I don't have any vowels," she said before he could reply to her comment. "And we've used up all the ones that are already on the board. I'm going to have to pass."

"I don't have any vowels, either," he said. "Maybe we should just start spelling things phonetically."

Oh, sure. Now he told her. After she'd used up the letters she needed for profanity. Hmm. Even for phonetic spelling, she was at something of a disadvantage. So she used a *J* and an *F* with the *N* in *P-H-A-R-Y-N-X* to spell—

"Jiffin," she said.

He narrowed his eyes at her. "That's not phonetic for anything. There's no such word as *jiffin*."

"Sure there is. It's what you're doing when you smear a certain brand of peanut butter on your bread. You're jiffin' it."

He didn't look anywhere near convinced. But he plucked a few tiles from his rack to use her *J* to spell out *D-J-L-G*.

"What the hell is that?" she asked.

"Dijlig," he said.

"Dijlig," she echoed. "That's ridiculous. At least *jiffin* sounds like it *might* be a real word. *Dijlig* is…" She couldn't finish the sentence. Because *dijlig* didn't sound like anything. "I can barely get my tongue around that."

"It's an arcane sex act that was used by the Etruscans," he told her. With a straight face. Impressive. "Interestingly, it involves the tongue. An Etruscan man would say it when he had his mouth pressed against an Etruscan woman's—"

She held up a hand to stop him. "I get it."

He grinned. "Well, you might. If you ask nicely."

Renny felt heat creeping into her face. Among other body parts. So she quickly drew more tiles—none of them vowels—and, using the *G* he'd just placed on the board, hastily spelled out *K-M-S-G*. She was going to tell him it was a popular Korean side dish—sort of like kimchi, except with less cabbage—but he filled in the definition before she had the chance.

"Oh, *kimsig*. That's another good one from the Etruscans. Even more fun than *dijlig*, actually, because for that position, it's the woman doing it, and she uses *her* mouth and tongue to—"

"Your turn," Renny interrupted him again. Not that she wanted him to take another turn, now that he was completely fixated on the Etruscan equivalent of the *Kama Sutra*, but anything was better than hearing him finish that sentence, because the images exploding in her brain were making her want to leap across the table for a never-ending session of both *dijlig* and *kimsig*. But when he put a *P* in front of the *S* in *X-R-A-Y-S* and she noted he was holding a *Y* in his other hand, she quickly rehearsed all the possible vowel combinations that might result. Passy? Pessy? Pissy? Possy? Pus—

She snapped the board shut with all the tiles still inside. Then she shoved everything into the box, closed it and stood.

"Scrabble is a stupid game," she proclaimed. "And, wow, I'm exhausted. This has been such a full day. I think I'm just going to hit the hay. I could really use a good night's sleep."

And without awaiting a reply, Renny fled to the bedroom, closed the door and locked it behind her—since, knowing Tate, he'd conjure an Etruscan word that meant *roll in the hay,* too. And he'd be delighted to tell her—and then show her—exactly which body parts for that went where.

Tate grinned when he heard the sound of the bedroom door locking behind Renata. Had she done that because she didn't trust him? Or because she didn't trust herself? He'd noticed the candles at dinner. And he'd seen the way she was looking at him as he described for her the finer points of fabricated ancient sexuality. Or, at least, tried to describe them before she cut him off. Then again, he was pretty sure she'd gotten the gist of it both times before ending the game. Shame, really, since Scrabble was a lot more fun than he remembered.

She was right, though. It had been a hell of a day. Even so, he couldn't remember enjoying one more. Which was weird, because until his predinner shower, he'd spent most of it wet and dirty, doing things that just made him wetter and dirtier. They'd actually found a cave and explored it. And a waterfall. Okay, so the waterfall had been only about four feet tall. It was still his first in-the-flesh waterfall discovery. Thirty-two years old, world traveled and experienced to the point of jadedness, and he'd just seen his first waterfall and explored his first cave.

Two days with Renata Twigg, confined to an area no bigger than a sleep-away camp, and he was learning and feeling things about himself he'd never been aware of before. Between this and his newly discovered family ties, it was going to be tough to go back to Chicago and pick up where he'd left off.

Then again, did he really want to pick up where he'd left off? All he'd been doing before Renata came along was working all day, seven days a week, with a break here and there on the weekends to play polo or enjoy the charms of whoever happened to be the femme du jour.

There was a reason for that, though, he reminded himself. His life was the way it was because he worked hard to make it that way. He'd worked hard for years to make it that way. And he *liked* how his life was. Of course he wanted to go back to Chicago and pick up where he left off. Neither his newly discovered East Coast Bacco relations nor his Midwestern adventures with Renata Twigg would change anything. Not unless he wanted something to change. And he didn't. His life in Chicago was near perfect. Why mess with that? Just because he'd spent a day that felt, well, really perfect?

It wasn't real, he reminded himself. The way he and

Renata had passed today wasn't the way people normally passed a day. Today was… He sighed as he remembered some of the funner things they'd done. Today
was like a snow day from school. One of those happy
accidents that seemed magical because it was an unexpected gift of something incredibly special—time.

He shook his head at his own weird thoughts. When
had he started to think about this sojourn as an unexpected gift or a happy accident? Only yesterday, it had
been the worst possible thing that could have happened.
Only yesterday, he'd been blaming Renata for ruining
his life. Now today he felt grateful to her for showing
him how much fun a break in his routine could be.

Clearly, he needed sleep, too. Maybe Renata had
done the right thing, putting a closed and locked door
between them for the night. They could both recharge
after what had been a tumultuous thirty-six hours and
start fresh tomorrow. For all he knew, the spell would
be broken by then. There was every chance the two
of them would wake up fully reverted to the Manhat-
tan attorney and the Chicago businessman. With any
luck, Grady would make it back to the motel with good
news and give the all clear so Tate and Renata could return to their normal lives. Maybe the dragonflies and
blackberry brambles would retreat to the backs of their
brains, where the two of them could visit from time to
time when they had a free moment.

Yeah. That was what they both needed. As much fun
as today had been, it was just a little break from reality.
If every day was like today, then today wouldn't have
been so special.

Tomorrow could be completely different. Everything could go back to normal tomorrow.

Even if nothing was ever the same.

Tate woke on the sofa the next morning to the sound of low thunder. He should have been angered by the sound. More rain meant the road to the motel would be at least another day away from being clear enough for Grady to return.

But hearing thunder and knowing it would rain again today didn't make Tate angry. Instead, all he could think was *There's no school today!* Or if not the actual words, then certainly the childlike feeling of delight that accompanied them. Not just because there was no school—or, rather, no work—today, but because he had another day to play, or something, with his new friend, or something, Renata.

He looked at the bedroom door she had closed and locked the night before. It was still closed. Was it locked? He rolled off the sofa and padded to it, curling his fingers over the knob. It turned easily, and he pushed the door open.

Just for a peek, he told himself. Just to make sure she was okay. Or, you know, actually there and not some fey spirit he'd conjured in a feverish dream. But no, there she was, sound asleep on her side, one hand curled loosely in front of her face, the other stuffed under her pillow. Her coffee-colored hair billowed across the rest of the pillow behind her, save for a single silky strand that streamed down her cheek.

Okay, maybe not just a peek, Tate thought. That

strand of hair was bound to become an annoyance that woke her up before she was ready. He'd just move that back to join the rest of the heavy mass so it wouldn't be a nuisance.

As quietly as he could, he tiptoed to the bed and, as deftly as he could, tucked a finger under the wayward tress. He was able to brush it back over the crown of her head without waking her, but wasn't as successful when he drew his hand away. Probably because he also couldn't resist skimming his fingertip along her cheek. He couldn't help it. He wanted to see if her skin was as soft and warm as it looked. And it was. Which was why he skimmed the backs of his knuckles across her cheek, too.

Her eyes fluttered open, looking as soft and warm as the rest of her, and she smiled. "Good morning," she said in the dreamy sort of voice women used when—

Actually, Tate wasn't sure when women used a voice like that, all quiet and husky and full of affection. He'd never been with a woman who responded to him that way—as if there weren't any face she'd rather see first thing in the morning than his. Maybe because he so seldom spent the entire night with a woman, so he rarely saw one wake up. Or maybe because the women with whom he did spend the night didn't want anything more out of it than great sex, so they didn't care whose face they saw first thing, either.

And, hell, he and Renata hadn't even spent the night together this time.

"Good morning," he greeted her back, wondering how his voice could have the same affectionate timbre as hers. He cleared his throat and tried again. "It's raining. Again. Doesn't look like Grady will be making it back today, either."

Instead of looking disappointed, she smiled. "Oh, well. Maybe today we can explore the other side of the lake."

The suggestion should have been as off-putting as fishing had been the day before. Instead, he smiled. "Then we're going to need our strength. I'll start breakfast."

Renata smiled back. "Give me a minute to wake up, and I'll help you make breakfast."

Tate leaned closer and murmured, "Give me more than a minute, and I'll help you wake up."

In response, she curled her arm around his neck and pulled him the rest of the way down to kiss him. Their lovemaking this time was slower and more thorough, as if each felt they had all the time in the world to give it. This morning, it did feel like they had all the time in the world. It was a feeling Tate had never experienced—as if he had no obligations, no responsibilities, no plans. He had only Renata. She had only him. At least for today. And tomorrow...

He'd think about tomorrow tomorrow. Today just had too much going for it, jam-packed as it was with dragonflies and waterfalls and Renata.

Eleven

It was a pattern Renny and Tate repeated for the nearly three days that followed. Wake up together, make love together, fix breakfast together. Get a call from Inspector Grady telling them the same thing—that the road to the hotel was still impassable, and the tech guys were still working on the breach. Then go exploring in the rain together, eat dinner together and play Erotic Scrabble together—or Porno Pictionary or Lascivious Pursuit—then shower together, go to bed together, make love together, sleep together and start all over again.

They were insatiable. Not just for each other, but for everything around them. Over the course of those days, the Wisconsin wilderness became less wild and more welcoming, and adversity became adventure. In a lot of ways, Renny felt more at home here with Tate than she'd ever felt back home with people she'd known her entire life. She'd always loved the great outdoors. As a girl, she'd never seen a tree she didn't climb, never met a bug she didn't befriend, never encountered a puddle she didn't jump in, never passed a rock she didn't pocket. This place was Utopia for a girl like that, and being here brought the girl right back to the surface. Except that here, that girl was allowed to run free.

And, as a woman, she'd never known a man like Tate. One who saw her and knew her the way she really was—the way she really wanted to be—and seemed to like her anyway.

No. Not seemed to. He did like her. There was no way he could respond to her the way he did if he didn't. They talked constantly, about anything and everything. They had fun. They laughed. A lot. And the night the rain clouds finally cleared, they skinny-dipped in the lake, then lay on a blanket on the pier and gazed at millions—perhaps billions—of stars, talking about nothing and everything and being the way they wanted and needed to be. Renny never wanted it to end.

But it did the morning she awoke to the crunch of gravel outside the bedroom window. Inspector Grady had finally managed to make it back up to the motel.

"Dammit, Tate, wake up," she said urgently as she rolled out of bed. "Grady is back."

Tate mumbled something incoherent as she grabbed her discarded pajamas from the floor. Then he rolled to his side and fell back asleep. She hopped on one foot, then the other, as she yanked on her pajamas and called out to him again, louder this time.

"Tate! Wake up! You have to move to the sofa! Grady is outside!"

As she thrust her arms through the shirtsleeves, she heard the bang of a car door slamming. Tate slept blissfully on.

"Tate!" she tried one last time. He didn't budge.

Fine. Let him look like a jerk, taking the bed and leaving Renny to sleep on the sofa. No way was she going to let Grady know they'd been sharing a bed—and a lake pier and a shower and a sofa and the rug in front of the fireplace—while he was gone. No way was she going to let the marshal find out what had happened during the time she and Tate were here. Not that she was sure herself what had happened. There would be time to think about that later, when she and Tate were home.

Hundreds of miles away from each other.

She let that sink in for a second—how could she and Tate live hundreds of miles away from each other when it felt as if they'd been sharing the same piece of air for a lifetime? Then she grabbed a sheet from the bed, fled the room and closed the door behind her. She had just enough time to lie down on the sofa when the front door opened and Grady announced his arrival. She used it as an excuse to pretend the noise had woken her up, rolling over to greet him in what she hoped was a convincingly slumberous fashion, even though adrenaline was pumping through her body at a rate that would have won her Olympic gold.

"Oh, hi," she said, hopefully in a slumberous manner.

She tried to rouse a yawn, couldn't find one, so opened her mouth and covered it with her hand for a few seconds. In spite of her Olympic prospects at the moment, judging by Grady's expression, she wasn't in the running for an Oscar.

"Sorry to wake you, Ms. Twigg," he said blandly—though, she had to admit, he wasn't exactly in the running for an Oscar, either, since it was clear he wasn't fooled by her sudden wakefulness. "Guess I should have called to let you know I was coming, but I still wasn't sure I'd make it up the hill and didn't want to get your hopes up. Plus, I figured you and Mr. Hawthorne could use the extra sleep."

Gee, why would he assume she and Tate needed the extra sleep?

Probably best not to think about it.

"Well, thank you for your consideration," she said. There was no reason she couldn't be just as vague as Grady.

The bedroom door flew open suddenly, and Tate appeared in the doorway wearing nothing but his borrowed blue jeans, holding his T-shirt in his hand. He looked gorgeous and virile and—there was no way to get around it—recently tumbled, and he did nothing to promote the fallacy Renny was trying so hard to cling to.

"I smell coffee," he said.

Well, good morning to you, too, she wanted to tell him. Of course, her own greeting of *Dammit, Tate* a few minutes ago hadn't exactly been romantic, either, had it? Besides, she didn't want him to be romantic. She didn't. She wanted Grady to think nothing between her and Tate had changed since the last time the marshal had been here. Even though everything had.

"Real coffee," Tate elaborated. Still not being in any way romantic. So, yay, Tate. "Good coffee. Not the powdered horror in a jar we've been having to drink every morning."

Only then did Renny notice that Grady was holding a cardboard drink carrier that housed four cups of covered coffee. When Tate noted the number of cups, his expression turned sublime. "And you brought |automatic refills." He jerked on his T-shirt, strode across the room, took the carrier from Grady and marched it to the coffee table, then uncapped one and moved it under his nose for a healthy inhalation. "Oh, baby, baby, come to Daddy."

Renny battled a twinge of jealousy that he was more in love with coffee at the moment than he was with her. Not that she expected him to be in love with her. But he could at least seem happier to see her this morning than he was caffeine.

On the upside, Grady looked a lot more convinced that her having woken up on the sofa was a credible prospect. He looked even more convinced when it became clear Tate had no intention of opening a cup of coffee for Renny. Yay again. Dammit. So she reached for one herself. There was even real cream and sugar to go with it. She couldn't remember the last time she'd had real coffee with real cream and sugar.

Oh, wait. Yes, she could. It had been less than a week ago. Saturday morning, at O'Hare. Why did it keep feeling like years had passed since her arrival in this part of the country?

Tate continued to sip his coffee in silence, so Renny

did, too. Grady set a bag on the table decorated with a logo from a place called Debbie Does Donuts, and informed them that the lemon chiffon crullers were particularly good, but not to rule out the maple bacon, because he couldn't believe how well that combination worked in a doughnut. Renny peeked into the bag and snagged a basic glazed. She wasn't feeling especially adventurous this morning.

"I've got good news and bad news," Grady said, when it became clear that neither she nor Tate would be especially talkative. "Which do you want first?"

Still looking at his coffee instead of at Renny, Tate said, "Good."

"Okay. I've been given the official all clear that there's no threat to you, Mr. Hawthorne, and you're free to go."

Tate snapped his head up to meet Grady's gaze. "Just like that?"

The marshal nodded. "You'll be home in a matter of hours. I'll drive you myself."

"Then what's the bad news?"

Grady looked at Renny. "The bad news is for Ms. Twigg."

Something cold and unpleasant settled in her midsection. All she could manage by way of a response was "Oh?"

Grady smiled, but there wasn't an ounce of happiness in the look. "Yeah, oh. Do you want to tell Mr. Hawthorne, Ms. Twigg, or should I?"

That, finally, made Tate look at her. He was clearly confused. For a moment, she could almost convince herself there was no way Grady's techs could have discovered what they had obviously discovered, since she and Tate were being given the all clear. For a moment, she could almost convince herself that the fantasy life they had been enjoying for the last five days really would go on forever.

Even though it was pretty clear Grady had discovered where the security breach originated, Renny told herself to keep her mouth shut. She was an attorney, for God's sake. Maybe she only practiced probate law, but she knew better than to say anything to a law enforcement officer that could be used against her in court. She had Phoebe to think about, too.

When Grady realized Renny wasn't going to be more forthcoming, he said, "Does the name Phoebe Resnick ring a bell, Ms. Twigg?"

Okay, it was *very* clear Grady had discovered where the security breach originated. Even so, Renny still said nothing.

"Who's Phoebe Resnick?" Tate asked, sounding even more confused.

"Also known as the Tandem Menace," Grady told him.

Yep, they knew all about Phoebe. She'd been using that nickname since sixth grade. That was when she discovered a way to get into the school's computer so it looked like the hack was coming from two places at once, only she was really coming in from a third place that didn't show up at all. No one in the administration ever figured out who was doing it or how, and Phoebe went to MIT on full scholarship.

These days, she owned a digital security company that was making her a boatload of money. She still hacked on her days off, but she used her powers only for good. She did things like move money from the accounts of despots into the accounts of human rights organizations. Or she took money from human traffickers and donated it to women's shelters and scholarship funds. Or she transferred money from the accounts of corporations that tested on animals and gave it to the ASPCA. And when a friend needed her, she did things like locate a little boy who'd been buried in a federal database.

"What the hell is a tandem menace?" Tate asked.

Grady continued to look at Renny, offering her the opportunity to clear the air with her own explanation instead of clouding it with an indictment of his own. But if the marshals had IDed Phoebe, they must know Renny was involved, too. Although she and Phoebe had only talked about Tate in person—Phoebe never left a digital trail...um, except this time, evidently—the two of them had been friends since preschool. There was no way Renny could credibly deny her involvement with the hack. And now Tate was going to—

She really didn't want to think about what Tate was going to do once he learned the whole truth. Which was another reason she didn't say a word.

Grady, however, still had plenty to say. "Phoebe Resnick is a world-class hacker who goes by the moniker the Tandem Menace on the dark web. She's the one who ransacked the WITSEC databases until she located you, Mr. Hawthorne. And, oh, yeah, she's been a friend of Ms. Twigg's since they were kids."

Renny braved a glance at Tate. He still looked confused.

"But you said it was a guy you found on Craigslist named John Smith."

Renny wanted to tell him she never would have trusted his identity to a guy on Craigslist named John Smith and at least be honest about that. But she couldn't even tell him that much. Not with Grady standing there, listening. She felt horrible now for what she had kept hidden from Tate. If she had just been honest that morning in his office when Grady first arrived...

But if she'd done that, she never would have had the last five days with Tate. And the thought of that was even more horrible. Even if she never had another day with him again—and it was more than likely that, after this, she wouldn't—there was a part of Renny that would never be able to regret her transgression.

As the truth finally sank in, Tate gazed at her incredulously. "Your *friend* was the security breach at the Justice Department?"

Renny still said nothing. She couldn't. Although this time it had nothing to do with incriminating herself or Phoebe. This time, it was because Tate was looking at her as if she were the most heinous villain in the world.

"You've known all along there was no threat to my safety?" he asked.

His anger was almost palpable. Renny remained silent.

But Tate wasn't. "This whole fiasco could have been

avoided if you'd told Grady on Saturday that you knew who was behind the breach?"

He thought this had been a whole fiasco? Had there been nothing about this week he could think of that made it only a partial fiasco? Like maybe how much fun the two of them had had before all hell broke loose? Like maybe how they'd learned about each other and themselves? Or how they'd come to feel about each other? Or how happy they'd been, if only for a little while?

Tate stood and moved to the other side of the room, though whether that was because he suddenly felt restless, or because he wanted to put as much distance between himself and Renny as possible, she couldn't have said. That became clearer, however, as he spoke further.

"Five days," he said. "Five days we've been stuck here. Five days I've been away from work. Do you know how much I missed being away from work for five days? Do you know how much it cost me to be away from work for five days?"

Renny figured she could answer that, at least, without incriminating herself. Even so, all she could do was shake her head.

"Millions, Renata. It's cost me millions. Worse than that, it's cost my clients millions. It's hurt my business. It's compromised my reputation. It's—"

He stopped pacing, hooked his hands on his hips and glared at her. Then he shook his head and began to pace again. When it became clear that the rest of his tirade would be taking place in his head—which was somehow worse than having him sling it at Renny, because she had no way to defend herself even if her actions were indefensible—she looked at Grady again.

She wanted to ask him what was going to happen to Phoebe, wanted to tell him her friend shouldn't be held responsible for any of it, since Renny was the one who put it all in motion. But she knew the law didn't work like that. The law dealt with actions, not intentions. Phoebe had broken the law. Renny was an accessory. Even if neither of them had meant any harm, they could both be looking at some hefty repercussions. And Phoebe, unfortunately, would bear the brunt of it.

Grady crossed his arms over his chest and studied Renny in silence long enough for her to mentally fit herself and Phoebe for orange jumpsuits and realize that no, orange wasn't actually the new black.

He must have realized what she was thinking, though, because he told her, "Relax, Ms. Twigg. Phoebe made a deal with us. She's going to do some favors for Uncle Sam. In exchange, Uncle Sam is going to look the other way with regard to this one…episode…and pretend it never happened. And since this…episode… never happened," Grady added, "then you couldn't be part of it, could you?"

Renny nodded. "Thanks," she said wearily.

"For what?" Grady asked.

No sense pushing it. Especially since she had a lot more to worry about where Tate was concerned. He was still glaring at her with clear disbelief and even clearer fury. She rose from the sofa to approach him, but he held up a hand to stop her.

"Don't say anything," he told her.

"I can explain," she said halfheartedly.

"I don't want to hear it."

"Tate—" she tried again.

But he turned to Grady and said, "When can we leave?"

"As soon as you're ready," the marshal said. Almost as an afterthought, he looked at Renny. "You, too, Ms. Twigg. I've arranged for a flight for you out of Green Bay, so we'll make a brief stop there on the way to Chicago. I have the belongings you left at Mr. Hawthorne's house in the SUV." He turned back to Tate. "Mr. Hawthorne, please accept my apology on behalf of the United States government for your inconvenience and discomfort this week. We only wanted to ensure that you were protected, as we promised you would be when you entered the program thirty years ago."

"Apology accepted," Tate replied automatically.

Oh, sure. He'd accept an apology from Grady, but he wouldn't even let Renny voice one. Then again, Grady hadn't actually been the person who'd caused Tate inconvenience and discomfort this week, had he? No, all of that fell to Renny. She didn't blame him for being angry at her. She was angry at herself. But she wished he would at least give her a chance to explain.

And she hoped that, someday, on some level, Tate would be able to think about the last five days as having been more than inconvenience and discomfort. She hoped that, someday, he remembered too the blackberry brambles and the pine cones and the star-studded night sky and her.

"I should shower and change," she said quietly. "I'll be as fast as I can."

Before either man could reply, she retreated to the bedroom. As she grabbed her wrinkled suit and blouse from the closet, she tried not to notice Tate's polo uniform hanging beside it and how different the two outfits were from each other. How they didn't belong together at all. How, in normal circumstances, they would never have shared the same space.

And how, now that Renny had ruined everything, they would never share the same space again.

Home, sweet castle.

After almost a week away from it, Tate opened the portcullis, strode through the barbican and surveyed his realm. It seemed a lot smaller than he remembered. And it was so empty. Even Madison wasn't around. Tate had instructed Grady to call the butler and tell him to take time off with pay until Tate returned home. Home to his castle-slash-house that he'd bought because he would be living in a fortress where no one would be able to get to him. For years, no one had.

Not until Renata Twigg.

She changed his life when she showed up with her files and photos. Not just because of what he learned about himself from those files but what he learned about himself in the days that followed, too.

He reminded himself that she hadn't just changed his life—she'd messed it up in a way that would take a long time to fix. Then again, was it really *his* life she'd messed up? Just who was Tate Hawthorne, anyway?

The grandson of a reputed New York mobster? A successful Chicago businessman? A babe in the Wisconsin woods? All of the above? None of the above? This week had left his head so full of weirdness he wasn't sure he'd ever know himself again. Not that he'd really known himself before Renata.

Just what the hell had happened to him this week?

He took the stairs two at a time, trying not to notice how the echo of his boots made the house sound—and feel—even emptier. Once in his bedroom, he stripped off the fetid polo uniform and headed for the shower. The massive marble shower with its three jets and bench for two that would have given him and Renata a lot more room to move around than the tiny stall at the motel. In a shower like this, he and Renata could—

Nothing, he told himself. He'd never see her again. She'd lied to him. She'd completely disrupted his life. She'd cost him and his clients a massive amount of money. The last five days had been a total disaster.

Okay, maybe not a total disaster, he backpedaled as he stepped under the jets. But he was happy to be home. He couldn't wait to get back to his normal life. Really. He couldn't. His normal life that would be completely lacking in discomfort and inconvenience and Renata Twigg.

Work, he told himself. He'd been too long away from the thing that gave his life meaning. No wonder he felt so weird. Working grounded him and reminded him what was really important. He needed to work.

He made his way back down the stairs—damn, the house really was way too quiet, even though this must have been the way it always sounded and felt—and made his way to his office. He had a mountain of email waiting, and at least half of them were decorated with the little red exclamation mark that deemed them Important.

But none of the Important emails he read seemed all that important.

Oh, well. He still needed to get back to work. The thing he knew best. The thing he did best. People would come and go in his life. Events would begin and end. But work… That was a constant.

Thankfully, he had enough of it to keep him from thinking about Renata and the damage she'd caused. Enough to keep him from remembering dragonflies and fireflies and picking blackberries with Renata. Enough to forget about counting stars and catching fish and playing Strip Monopoly with Renata. Oh, yeah. He was very, very thankful for all this work.

He went back to the first Important email he'd opened—even if it wasn't all that important—and hit Reply.

It was raining in New York City. Possibly the same rain that had fallen in Wisconsin earlier in the week. Renny—freshly showered and wearing silk pj's that were blissfully devoid of golf carts—gazed out her living room window at the snaking traffic of Tribeca and told herself again how happy she was to be home.

No more freezer-burned food or homemade rompers. She could binge-watch all the BBC mysteries she wanted and soak in her tub for hours. She could be with people who appreciated her for more than her ability to give them an orgasm and didn't hate her guts. She was elated to be here and not in Wisconsin. She was. Even if there was a part of her that would be in Wisconsin forever.

It was just too bad that part would be there alone.

Tate had been silent on the drive from the motel, and he'd ignored her when she climbed out of the SUV at the airport in Green Bay. Not that she blamed him. But she wished he would have at least said goodbye.

In the days that followed, Renny went about her job robotically, telling herself the reason she was so unenthusiastic about her cases was because she was just having trouble getting back in the groove.

But as the days became weeks, and her groove never materialized, she began to think a little differently. Like how maybe the reason she was the only person at Tarrant, Fiver & Twigg who hadn't always found the heir she was looking for, and the reason she'd screwed up her assignment with Tate, and the reason even the cases she didn't screw up never went as smoothly for her as they did for everyone else, the reason for all those things was because, well, Renny wasn't very good at her job. And the reason she wasn't very good at her job was because she didn't actually like her job. Not the way she should like it. Not the way everyone else at Tarrant, Fiver & Twigg liked theirs.

But after a few weeks back at work, Renny did start to think about that. Not just because of her epiphany that she might not be suited to be a suit at Tarrant, Fiver & Twigg, but because, for the first time since she was twelve years old, she was late. Not late for work. Not late for Zumba. Not late for lunch with friends. Renny was late as in *holy-crap-I-have-to-buy-a-home-preg-nancy-test-my-God-how-did-this-happen* late.

Not that she couldn't guess how it happened. Although she'd been confident she was right when she told Tate that first time that the timing was wrong for her to get pregnant, after five days together, the timing might have been just right. So she shouldn't have been surprised one evening to find herself popping into a Duane Reade that was a few—or seventeen—blocks from her condo for some toothpaste, a bottle of biotin, a pack of AAA batteries, the latest issue of *Vanity Fair*, a six pack of Kit Kats and, oh, what the hey, a pregnancy test.

Twenty minutes after she got home, Renny was thinking she might have been better served to pick up a copy of *Parenting* instead of the *Vanity Fair*. But thank God for the Kit Kats. And once that realization set in, another quickly followed it.

HolycrapmyGodhowdidthishappen?

But she already knew how it had happened. So, really, the question she needed to be asking herself was what she was going to do. There was another human being growing inside her that was half Renny and half Tate. Knowing what she did of him, she was sure he would offer financial support. But personal support? That was a tough call. Not only was there the whole hating-her-guts thing to consider, but by now he was back to his usual routine with a work life that included weekend hours and a home office, and a social life that included leggy redheads and evenings out. Would he want any of that interrupted by the patter of little feet and a woman he didn't like? Doubtful.

More to the point, did Renny want her life interrupted? Then again, was her life what and where she wanted it to be in the first place? Not really.

She looked at the little plastic wand in her hand, with its little pink plus sign. And she wondered again what the hell she was going to do.

Twelve

A month after returning from Wisconsin, Tate's life had totally returned to normal. He was back to his normal seven-day workweek, his normal Saturday polo game, his normal Tuesday drinks with friends-slash-colleagues, who, okay, now felt a bit less like friends than they did colleagues. He was also back to his normal nights out with normal leggy redheads—though, admittedly, those nights were slightly less normal, because they always ended early for some reason and never reached their obvious conclusion. Still, except for those small factors, a month after returning from Wisconsin, his life had returned to normal. Totally, totally normal.

Except for how he had never felt less normal in his life. Almost nothing about his daily existence had changed after that brief hiccup that was five days in Wisconsin. Yet somehow everything about his daily existence felt changed.

He told himself it was because part of his life was still unsettled, since he hadn't been in contact with any of his newly discovered relatives on the East Coast. Tate's attorneys had worked with Tarrant, Fiver & Twigg to complete the paperwork necessary for him to decline his inheritance from Joseph Bacco without revealing his new identity to the rest of the family. He'd been surprised when his attorneys had informed him that his aunts and uncles and cousins wanted to meet him if he was amenable. To the Baccos, family was family, and Joey the Knife had spent thirty years wanting to bring his little grandson back into the fold. Even if Tate didn't want to join the family business, they said, they hoped he would someday see clear to join the family. When he was ready to make himself known to them, they were ready to embrace him with a big ol' Bacco hug. Tate just didn't know yet how he felt about all that.

Deep down, though, he knew it wasn't his uncertainty about his East Coast relations that was the source of his current unrest. Mostly because, deep down, he kind of knew what was the source of that. The same thing that had been the source of it a month ago. Renata Twigg.

He hadn't heard a word from her since Grady dropped her at the curb—literally—in Green Bay. Once, about a week ago, when he was up late and after a couple of bourbons, he'd Google-imaged "Renata Twigg." But when a dozen photos of her appeared on his computer screen, he spared barely a minute to look at them. Because he was suddenly sleepy enough to go back to bed, not because one of the photos was of her at some society function, looking breathtaking in a black strapless dress, with some upright, forthright, do-right kind of guy on her arm. Even if the photo had been two years old, it was just a reminder that things between them hadn't ended well. More to the point, things between them had ended. She had a life of her own half a continent away that she'd gone back to, and it doubtless had returned to normal, as well. Anyway, there was no reason for him to be Google-imaging her late at night with a couple of bourbons in him.

The next day, he'd called an event planner he knew and hired her to organize an obscenely gigantic party for him, and money was no object if she could get the damned thing put together by the following weekend, because, man, it had just been too long since he'd had an obscenely gigantic party. Which was how Tate came to be hosting a bash for a hundred of his closest friends, right this very minute, in the house-slash-castle he'd bought to keep people out, and which had been way too empty, and way too quiet for, oh, about a month now.

So why wasn't he downstairs having a blast with his hundred closest friends? Why was he, instead, standing on the balcony off his bedroom gazing down at the ones who were prowling around the grounds? Sure, he'd been a good host at first. He'd dressed the part in his best charcoal trousers and a gray linen shirt. He'd greeted everyone at the door and directed them to the three different bars and let them know the DJ would be starting his first set at eight. And he'd made one per-functory circuit of the goings-on to be sure the noise level was loud enough to indicate everyone was having a good time—it was, and they were. Then he'd fetched a drink from the nearest bar to wait for the spirit of the gathering to overtake him, too.

He was still waiting.

He was about to return to his bedroom when a single guest caught his attention in the garden below. She was standing alone at its very edge, as far removed from the crowd as she could be without actually disappearing. She wore a plain sleeveless dress the color of a Wisconsin wilderness, and her dark hair was shorter than the last time he saw her, just barely brushing her shoulders. He couldn't imagine what had brought Renata to his house—unless it was his thinking about her—but she didn't look happy to be here. In fact, after a sweeping glance at the crowd, she turned around as if she was going to leave.

The music was too loud for her to hear him if he called out to her, so he ran from the bedroom, nearly stumbled down the stairs, raced through the front door and rounded the house on the side where he'd seen her. Thankfully, she'd gotten only as far as the garden boundary nearest him, so he hurried forward to stop her before she could get away. She was looking at the ground, though, so she didn't see him coming, and when she suddenly began to jog away from the goings-on and toward him, he didn't have a chance to move out of her way, and she jogged right into him.

He was able to catch her by the upper arms before

she would have bounced backward, but the minute he touched her, all he wanted to do was pull her forward. How had he gone a month without touching her, when he'd touched her every day for—

Five days. Had they really only spent five days together? How was that possible? It felt as if Renata had been a part of him forever. And why, suddenly, was he thinking about all the moments of those days instead of the end of them when he accused her of messing up his life irrevocably? She hadn't messed up his life, he thought now. He'd only thought she messed up his life because she messed up his work, and back then— a whole month ago—work had been his life. But after those five days in Wisconsin with Renata...

Hell, she hadn't messed up his life. She'd saved it.

"Hey," he said softly as he pulled her up, "slow down. Where's the fire?" Other than in his chest, he meant. Because there was a warmth kindling there that was fast spreading.

He thought she would smile at the question, but when she looked up, her mouth was flat, and her eyebrows were knit downward.

"What, you came all this way just to glare at me?" he asked, injecting a lightness into his voice he wasn't close to feeling.

She shook her head. "No. Why I came isn't important now." She hesitated, then stepped backward, out of his grasp. "I have to go."

Before he could object—hell, before he even knew what he was talking about—she hurried past him, heading toward the front of the house. She was doing more than jogging now. She was running. Why had she come all the way to Chicago if she was just going to run away from him? Why hadn't she told him she was coming in the first place? What the hell was going on?

"Renata, wait!" he called after her. But she only ran faster.

So Tate ran after her.

He caught up with her as she was key-fobbing a sedan that was nondescript enough to indicate it was a rental. She had opened the driver's-side door and tossed her purse into the passenger seat when he caught her by the upper arm again. Only this time he did pull her toward him. Before she could stop him—and because he couldn't help himself—he lowered his head to hers and kissed her.

She kissed him back immediately, her body fairly melting into his. Just like that, a month faded away, and the world dissolved around them. All Tate knew was that he had Renata back, and for the first time in weeks, he didn't feel as if he were in the wrong place and time. For the first time in weeks, he felt as if he were exactly where he belonged.

Reluctantly, he ended the kiss. But he didn't go far. He looped his arms around her waist and bent to touch his forehead to hers. He'd forgotten how small she was. Funny how he'd always avoided small women because he thought he wouldn't know what to do with one. He and this one fitted together perfectly. Then again, that didn't have anything to do with their sizes.

"You don't hate me?" she said by way of a greeting.

"I never hated you," he assured her.

She hesitated, gazing into his eyes as if trying to see

the thoughts inside his head. Finally, she said, "That makes one of us. I hate myself for not telling you the truth right away, Tate. I'm sorry for what happened. I'm sorry I wasn't honest with you. I couldn't be. If I'd said anything in front of Grady, it could have put Phoebe in jail for a long time. But I am so sorry I—"

"I'm not sorry for any of it," he said.

For the first time, he realized that was true. Yes, Renata had lied to him. Yes, for five days, his life had been completely disrupted. If she had been honest the first day, none of that would have been the case. But those five days had ended up being the best five days Tate had ever known. In those five days, he had learned more about himself than he had in the thirty-plus years that preceded them. He'd been able to be himself in Wisconsin. He'd discovered himself there. Even more important, he'd discovered Renata. And he'd realized just how much he needed someone like her in his life to make him happy. Really, honestly, genuinely *happy*, something he had never been before.

No, he didn't need someone like Renata for that. He needed Renata.

She looked confused. "But that last day in Wisconsin—"

"That last day in Wisconsin, I didn't realize a lot of things I should have realized that first day in Wisconsin. Like how much I needed five days in Wisconsin. Especially with someone like you. Let's try this again," he said softly. "Hi."

She still looked confused. But she replied, even more softly, "Hi."

"It's good to see you."

"It's good to see you, too."

"I've missed you," he said, surprised not only to realize the feeling, but to reveal it. Not just because he'd never told a woman—or anyone—that he'd missed her before. But because he'd never actually missed a woman—or anyone—before. He'd missed Renata, though. He'd missed her a lot.

"I've missed you, too," she said.

By now her voice had softened so much he barely heard what she said. He felt it, though. He felt it in the way she'd curled the fingers of one hand into his shirt and cupped the other around his neck. And he felt it in the way she nestled her head against his chest. Mostly, though, he felt it in the air around them. As if whatever it was that made them who they were somehow mingled and joined the same way their bodies had so many times before, and now it was finding its missing pieces, too.

For a moment, they only stood entwined, refamiliarizing themselves with all the nuances of each other's bodies and spirits, remembering how it had felt to be so close, enjoying that nearness again. Tate figured he should wait for Renata to say something first, since she was the one who had traveled across half the country to get here. But she didn't say anything. She just leaned into him as if she never wanted to let him go.

So Tate started instead. "Not that I'm complaining or anything, but what are you doing here?"

She stayed silent for another moment, and he began to think she wouldn't say another word. He even tightened his hold on her a little because he feared she might try to bolt again. But she didn't do that, either. The night closed in around them, the lights of the house and grounds not quite reaching this far, the music of the party a faint burr against the darkness. There was a part of him that would have been perfectly content to stay this way forever. Finally, though, Renata lifted her head from his chest and looked up at him. She still didn't look happy. But she didn't look quite as hurt as she had at first, either.

"I need to tell you something," she said.

He couldn't imagine what. And, truth be told, he wasn't sure he cared. All he knew was that he was with Renata, and the life that had felt so abnormal for the past month suddenly felt right again.

"Okay," he said. "What?"

She freed her fingers from his shirt and dropped her hand from his neck to her side. Then she took a small step backward. But she stopped when he wove his fingers together at the small of her back to keep her from retreating farther. Her reaction wasn't exactly what he had expected. Why had she come this far only to pull away from him? Especially after he'd made clear he wanted her here.

"We need to talk," she said, not telling him what she needed to tell him.

The heat in his midsection took on a new dimension. "I thought that was what we were doing," he said, forcing a smile.

She didn't smile back. She turned to look over her shoulder at his house and the party in full swing inside and behind it. When she looked at him again, the hurt in her expression had returned.

"I should come back tomorrow," she said. "You're entertaining. It's obviously not a good time."

Was she crazy? Not a good time? Didn't she realize the minute he saw her, it was the first good time he'd had in a month?

"Renata, what's going on?" He didn't bother trying to mask his worry now.

"Seriously, it's late," she said. "I don't know what I was thinking to come here this time of night. Well, except maybe that it took me all day to gather my courage. Tomorrow would be better. I'll come back then. What time is good for you?"

She'd been here all day and was just now showing up at his door? She'd had to gather her courage to do that?

"It's barely ten thirty," he said. "That's not late. Especially on a Saturday night."

Her expression changed again, and he could tell she was weighing something very important in her head. He couldn't imagine what would be warring in there to cause her so much turmoil when, as far as he was concerned, having her here made everything fall perfectly into place. Finally, one faction must have won, because her expression changed again. But it was to something he couldn't quite identify. Resignation, maybe. Or acceptance. Of what, though, he had no idea.

"Actually," she said, "ten thirty is pretty late, even on a Saturday, for women like me. I've been turning in a lot earlier than I used to."

Okay. He'd been turning in a little earlier himself since coming home from Wisconsin. Mostly because there hadn't been that much reason to stay up. Except for insomnia. But a couple of bourbons usually fixed that. Then her wording finally struck him.

"Women like you," he repeated. "I don't know what that means. There are no other women like you."

She managed a small smile for that. The alarm bells in his head quieted some. Not a lot. But some.

"I hope you still think that when I tell you why I've been going to bed so early."

"Unless you've been doing that so you can be with someone else, I don't think it's going to make any difference in the way I feel about you."

She bit her lip in a way he remembered her doing in Wisconsin. Mostly when she was fretting over something. "Funny you should say that," she said.

His stomach dropped. No, it wasn't. It wasn't funny at all. Not if she really was going to bed with someone else.

"I have sort of been with someone else at night. Every night."

She'd been smiling when she made the comment, but something in Tate's expression must have told her just how badly he was taking the news. Because she quickly added, "Not like that! I haven't been with anyone since…I mean, there's no one who could ever… You're the only guy who ever…"

When she realized she wasn't finishing any of her thoughts—not that they needed finishing, since Tate was getting the gist of it, and the gist of it was making him feel better, if not less confused—she expelled a restless sound, took a deep breath, then released it slowly.

Finally, she said, "I've been going to bed with someone else every night because…because I'm…" She sighed heavily, and in a rush of words, she finished, "Because I'm pregnant, Tate."

Even though she uttered the comment in a hurry, it took a minute for him to hear it. And even though he heard it, he wasn't sure he heard it correctly. Maybe he'd misinterpreted. Did Renata just say she was—

"You're what?" he asked, just to be certain.

"I'm going to have a baby, Tate. Our baby. Yours and mine."

There wasn't any way to misinterpret that. Renata did indeed say she was pregnant. She was going to have a baby. Their baby. His and hers. Okay then. He waited for his reaction. Surely, it would be one of dread and panic. Any minute now, he would be overcome with both. Dread and panic descending in three, two, one…

But it wasn't dread or panic that overcame him. Instead, what he felt most was wonder.

He was going to have a baby? Well, not him, obviously, but half of it would be his. Would be him. Which was kind of unexpected. And kind of weird. And kind of… Wow. Kind of awesome. But it was also nowhere in his life plan. He'd never considered the prospect of becoming a father. He didn't even want the responsibility that came with having a pet. How was he supposed to accommodate a child in his life? Then again, no one said he had to. He could just mail a monthly check to

Renata and skip the poopy diapers and prepubescent angst and cross-country college exploratory visits. Not to mention the birthday parties and soccer games and piano lessons that ate into a successful venture capitalist's time. A lot of men just mailed checks.

Men who were complete pricks.

"A baby?" he asked.

It was a stupid question, already answered, but he honestly didn't know what else to say. The news was still winding through his brain—and, okay, his heart. But both seemed to be greeting the new development pretty welcomingly.

When Tate said nothing in response to her clarification, Renata continued, "I know that first time we… I mean…I know that first time, I told you the timing wasn't right—and it wasn't," she hastened to add. "Not that time, anyway. But after five days of…you know… And after reading that a man's, ah, swimmers can, well, swim for anywhere from three to five days after, um, jumping into the pool, something I never really thought about but clearly should have, I guess the timing kind of got right."

When he still didn't reply—because he was still processing—she roused a cheerfulness that was clearly feigned and said, "I guess I should give you some time to think about this. I'm staying at the Knickerbocker. Room 315. Call me tomorrow, and we can meet somewhere to talk some more."

She tried to pull out of the circle of his arms, but Tate pulled her close again. "Why would you want to stay at a hotel when you can stay here with me?"

She said nothing in response to that, as if she were the one having trouble processing now.

"I mean, yeah, the Knickerbocker is great," he continued, "but it's not like home."

Not that his home had felt like home, either, for the past month. Tonight, though, it was starting to feel closer to home than it ever had before.

Renata still looked conflicted. Which was fine. Tate still felt conflicted. About some things. But none of it was about her.

She opened her mouth, hesitated, then finally said, "I just thought you might want—"

"You," he finished for her. "Renata, all I want is you. In a way, I think you're all I've ever wanted. I just didn't know it until I met you."

"But the baby will—"

"Look, I won't lie. I don't know what the baby will or won't do. And you're right. I'm going to need some time to process it. One thing I don't need to process, though, is—" He pulled her closer, kissed her again, then let her go. "You being here. With me. Nothing has been clearer in my life than how much better things are when you're around."

"But—"

He let go of her, only to place an index finger gently against her lips to halt any further objections she might make. "But nothing," he said. "The days you and I spent together in Wisconsin were the best days of my life." He grinned. "At least until this one."

It occurred to him then that he didn't know how *she* felt about the pregnancy. She'd had more time for the realization to settle in than he had, but had it settled well? Or had it settled badly? And how did she feel about *him*? He hadn't exactly been kind to her that last day in Wisconsin. Sure, she'd traveled halfway across the country to see him tonight, but that was because the news she had to tell him wasn't the kind of thing you wanted to tell someone in a text. If she hadn't gotten pregnant, would she still be standing here right now?

"I mean, you can stay here at the house if you want to," he started to backpedal. "If you'd rather stay at the hotel…"

He actually held his breath as he waited to see how she would respond. For a moment, she didn't. Then she smiled. "I'd like that," she said. "If it isn't an imposition."

Yeah, right. What was an imposition was a hundred of his closest friends invading his house and yard, not to mention three full bars and a DJ who still had two sets to go.

"You know what?" he said impulsively. "I actually think a night at the Knickerbocker would be better." Before she had a chance to misconstrue, he added, "Just give me ten minutes to pack a bag."

She still looked like she was going to misconstrue. Then she smiled again. Damn, he loved her smile.

"But what about your party?"

"Madison is here. So is the event planner. They can manage without me. Hell, I've spent most of the night in my room, anyway."

"Then why are you having a huge party?"

"I'll explain at the hotel. No, on the way to the hotel,"

he said. "Once we're at the hotel, I have something else in mind."

Her smile shone brighter. "Thank goodness I packed something other than golf-cart pajamas."

It was raining in Wisconsin. Again. But as Renny gazed through the window of her and Tate's stucco cheese wedge, she smiled. The rain this time was different, a light winter drizzle the forecasters had promised would turn to snow after dark—scarcely an hour away. Which was perfect, as tomorrow was Christmas Eve. The cottage hadn't changed much since summer, save for a good cleaning and *much* better food in the kitchen cabinets and fridge, along with a fire in the fireplace that now crackled merrily against the freezing temperatures outside.

Oh, and also the ownership. She and Tate were now co-owners of the Big Cheese Motor Inn and were planning to begin renovation on it in the spring—mid-May probably, to give them both a couple of months to cope with the addition of a baby in their lives, however that addition ended up being organized. They had plans to reopen it in a couple of summers as a family-friendly vacation destination, a throwback to another, simpler time, complete with fishing, hiking, stargazing and cave exploring…and absolutely no technology to speak of.

They had been inseparable since that night at Tate's house in July. He had returned to New York with Renny long enough for her to give her two weeks' notice at Tarrant, Fiver & Twigg and to meet her parents so they could announce together the elder Twiggs' impending grandparenthood. Her mother and father had handled the news the same way Renny and Tate had, first with surprise, then with confusion, then with delight. Since then, delight had pretty much been Renny's constant companion. She'd come back to Chicago with Tate, had rented a condo in the Gold Coast and the two had begun a courtship—for lack of a more contemporary word— that was more conducive to getting to know each other in a normal environment.

Well, except for the fact that they were already expecting a baby, something that didn't normally happen in a courtship until much later.

For Tate and Renny, though, it had worked. In spite of her condition, they'd focused on each other first and foremost those first few months. And by the time she started to show, they were ready to start talking about and be excited by the baby. Neither of them had had a childhood they'd particularly enjoyed, and both were kind of giddy about the prospect of a do-over with their own offspring. They'd each furnished a room in their homes with a nursery. Tate was gradually cutting back on his hours at work—weekends in his home office had been the first thing to go. And Renny had launched a web-based business from home targeted at getting girls into the wilderness to discover the joys of fishing, hiking, stargazing and cave exploring. Among other things. She already had two full-time employees, and when the baby came, she'd hire a third and go down to part-time herself.

The motel would be the centerpiece for that business once it was up and running. For now, though, she and Tate were content to keep it all to themselves.

The front door opened, blowing in both the winter wind and Tate, bundled up in his spanking-new purchases from the North Face and L.L. Bean and carrying two armfuls of wood for the fire.

"Baby, it's cold outside," he said with a grin.

"Gonna get colder," she told him.

"Bring it. We're ready."

As he made his way to the fireplace to stack the wood beside it, Renny went to the kitchen to ladle out the hot chocolate that was warming on the stove. They'd been here for a week already, long enough to hang Christmas lights, decorate a small tree and tuck a dozen presents beneath it, and they were planning to stay through New Year's. But if the weather took a turn for the worse—which she was pretty sure they were both secretly hoping would happen—they had enough supplies to last them for a month.

They couldn't stay much longer than that, though. Tate's cousin Angie the Flamethrower was getting married on Valentine's Day, and no way would they miss that. The Baccos, once Tate had decided to approach them last fall, had been nothing but warm and welcoming to him and Renny both. Apparently, Joey the Knife had been right about family being more important than anything. The Baccos couldn't wait to include Tate—and, by extension, Renny and their baby—in their lives, and Angie's wedding had seemed like the perfect place to start. As Tate's aunt Denise told him the first time they spoke, *"Chi si volta, e chi si gira, sempre a casa va finire."* Translation: "No matter where you go, you'll always end up at home." Renny figured the saying was apt in more ways than one—and for more people than the Baccos.

She returned to the living room with hot chocolate, setting Tate's mug on the coffee table and seating herself on the sofa. By now he had shed his outerwear and was down to jeans and a brown flannel shirt. His attire mirrored Renny's—especially since the striped flannel shirt she was wearing belonged to him. In one fluid move, he picked up his hot chocolate with one hand and, as had become his habit at times like this, splayed his other open over her belly.

"So, how's it been in there today?" he asked.

"Busy," she said. "Your daughter must be learning to do the mambo before she comes out."

"She's just getting ready for all the tree climbing and log rolling you have in store for her."

"Hey, you're going to learn to do those things, too, remember. This parenting thing is going to be an equal partnership. We both decided."

He started to say something else, but Baby Girl Hawthorne-Twigg—yes, after groaning at the realization of what the hyphenated last name would be, they'd decided it was too irresistible to not use it—switched from the mambo to the tarantella, turning circles in Renny's womb in a way that had become familiar to them both. As always, they laughed. Then they entwined their fingers together. Then they kissed. For a really long time.

"Only one more trimester," Renny said when they pulled apart.

He shook his head. "It's gone so fast. Hard to believe we only have three more months left of…"

When he didn't finish, she finished for him. "Of whatever this has been between us. Whatever this *is* between us."

He set his mug on the table and turned to face her but left his fingers entwined with hers on her belly. "Yeah," he said, "we should probably start trying to pin that down."

Over the past five months, they'd talked a lot about the past and even more about the future. At least, the baby's future. What they hadn't talked about much was the present. About what, exactly, the two of them were doing right now. Probably for the very reason Tate had just described—neither really seemed to know what the present was. They'd made a million plans for the baby. But they hadn't made any for themselves.

"I'm okay with the status quo," she said. Even if she kind of wasn't.

"I'm okay with it, too," he replied. Even if he didn't sound like he was. In spite of that, he added, "The status quo is pretty great."

"It is. And no one says we have to go the traditional route, right?" she said. "Lots of people who live separate lives share responsibility for their kids and do just fine."

"Right," he agreed. "They do. But we're not exactly living separate lives, are we?"

"Well, no, but…"

"But…?" he prompted.

Actually, Renny couldn't find a reason to finish her objection. Probably because she didn't have any objection to the two of them *not* living separate lives. They'd just never talked about joining their lives, that was all. Unless that was what they were doing now...

"But..." she said again. Still not sure why. Maybe in case that wasn't what they were talking about. Wondering what she would do if it wasn't, because she suddenly liked the idea a lot and wanted to talk about it.

"So, then," Tate interjected, "maybe we should talk about that aspect of whatever this—" he gestured quickly between the two of them "—is between us."

Renny's stomach lurched at his remark, and she was pretty sure it had nothing to do with the baby. Before she could say anything else, he jumped up from the sofa, went to the Christmas tree and from beneath it withdrew a small box she was positive hadn't been there before tonight. He returned to the sofa and held it up in his open palm.

"When you were a kid," he said, "did you have that tradition where you got to open one present on Christmas Eve?"

She shook her head. "My parents never let us. Even though every other kid in the neighborhood got to do it."

"Me, neither. So I think we're both entitled to open a present the night before Christmas Eve to make up for lost time."

"Then I need to get one for you to open," she said. She started to get up—and with her growing girth, she couldn't move nearly as quickly as he did—but he placed a hand gently on her shoulder and stayed her.

"In a minute," he said. "You first. Open this one."

She would have been an idiot to not entertain the possibility that it might be a ring. The box was perfectly

shaped for it. It was Christmastime. They'd been inseparable for months. They were expecting a baby. But they
kept separate residences. They each had a room for the
baby in those residences. They hadn't once talked about
taking their relationship to another level. It could just as
easily be a Groupon for mommy-and-daddy-and-baby
music classes or something.

She looked at the gift. Then she looked at Tate. He
was smiling in a way that was at once hopeful and anxious. Probably, it wasn't a Groupon. Meaning probably,
it was a...

Carefully, she accepted the present from him. It was
wrapped in forest green foil and had a bow as silver as
a crystal lake. As she gingerly unwrapped it, the baby
began to move inside her again, probably in response to
her quickening pulse and the way the blood was rushing through her body. The crackle of the fire and patter of the rain dulled to faint whispers, and the air in
the room seemed to come alive. Tate watched her intently until she had her fingers poised to open the box
beneath the paper, but he didn't say a word. So Renny
slowly pushed the top upward.

Not a Groupon. Definitely a ring. In fact, it was the
most beautiful ring she'd ever seen.

"The stone is from one of the interesting rocks we
found that day on our hike," he told her. "The quartz
one. It was the same color as the blackberries we picked.
And I had the jeweler set it in silver because the stars
that last night were like silver. And the pattern around
the band is like the pinecones we found. I hope you
don't think it's too corny."

He sounded as excited as…well, a kid on Christmas as he told her the reasons he'd had the ring fashioned the way he had. As if she'd needed him to explain any of that. The moment Renny saw it, all those things flooded into her head—and then her heart. And now, every time she looked at the ring on her finger, she would remember and feel them again.

"It's not corny," she said softly. "It's beautiful."

He expelled a relieved sound. "Then it's yes?"

Whatever he was asking, her answer was yes. Just to be sure he was asking the same question she wanted him to be asking, though, she replied, "Is what yes?"

He looked confused for a moment, then thoughtful. "I never said it out loud, did I? I thought it like ten times while you were unwrapping the ring, but I never actually asked the question, did I?"

Not to be coy, but… "What question?" she asked.

"The one about us…you and me…getting married."

Oh, *that* question. "Depends," she said.

He looked slightly less relieved, slightly less hopeful, slightly more anxious. "On what?"

"On why you're asking. Is it because of the baby?"

He shook his head. "No. It's because of you. Because the last five months have been the best time of my life, rivaled only by five days in June that I never thought could be topped." He took the box from her hand and plucked the ring from its nest. "I love you, Renata Twigg. I think I fell in love with you the minute I saw you standing in the rain outside a giant wedge of cheese." He smiled again, and this time there was only contentment in his expression. "And I will love you until we're both food for the fishies."

Oh. Well. In that case…

"Will you marry me?" he finally asked.

"Of course I'll marry you," she was finally able to say. "I mean, I have to, don't I?"

His contentment slipped a bit. "Why? Because of the baby?"

She shook her head. "No. Because I love you, Tate Hawthorne. I think I fell in love with you the minute I saw you in those zip-up leather polo boots. That I immediately wanted to *unzip*. With my teeth."

He looked mildly shocked, then not-so-mildly turned on. "Unfortunately, I left them at home. But you know…" He arched an eyebrow suggestively. "These hiking boots aren't going to remove themselves. And neither are any of these other things."

Renny arched an eyebrow right back. "Well, in that case, what are we waiting for?"

"Nothing," he said. "We have all the time in the world."

Indeed, they did. Even better, it was a world that exceeded their wildest dreams. A world they had created together. A world where they both belonged.

* * * * *

MILLS & BOON

THE HEART OF ROMANCE

A ROMANCE FOR EVERY KIND OF READER

MODERN

Prepare to be swept off your feet by sophisticated, sexy and seductive heroes, in some of the world's most glamourous and romantic locations, where power and passion collide.
8 stories per month.

HISTORICAL

Escape with historical heroes from time gone by. Whether your passion is for wicked Regency Rakes, muscled Vikings or rugged Highlanders, awaken the romance of the past.
6 stories per month.

MEDICAL

Set your pulse racing with dedicated, delectable doctors in the high-pressure world of medicine, where emotions run high and passion, comfort and love are the best medicine.
6 stories per month.

True Love

Celebrate true love with tender stories of heartfelt romance, from the rush of falling in love to the joy a new baby can bring, and a focus on the emotional heart of a relationship.
8 stories per month.

Desire

Indulge in secrets and scandal, intense drama and plenty of sizzling hot action with powerful and passionate heroes who have it all: wealth, status, good looks…everything but the right woman.
6 stories per month.

HEROES

Experience all the excitement of a gripping thriller, with an intense romance at its heart. Resourceful, true-to-life women and strong, fearless men face danger and desire - a killer combination!
8 stories per month.

DARE

Sensual love stories featuring smart, sassy heroines you'd want as a best friend, and compelling intense heroes who are worthy of them.
4 stories per month.

To see which titles are coming soon, please visit

millsandboon.co.uk/nextmonth

JOIN US ON SOCIAL MEDIA!

Stay up to date with our latest releases, author news and gossip, special offers and discounts, and all the behind-the-scenes action from Mills & Boon...

 millsandboon

 millsandboonuk

 millsandboon

It might just be true love...

MILLS & BOON

MODERN

Power and Passion

Prepare to be swept off your feet by
sophisticated, sexy and seductive heroes, in
some of the world's most glamourous and
romantic locations, where power and
passion collide.